THE ACHERON FOLD

NICK ADAMS

Elliptical
Publishing

PROLOGUE

THE SMALL STEALTHY military troop carrier dropped into the planet's atmosphere under full manual control. Although the vessel was equipped with the latest cloaking technology, the pilot didn't want to advertise their presence by leaving a bright 'here we are' fire trail across the clear winter night sky. The antigravs screamed their disapproval as he used them heavily to reduce the insertion speed, especially so as they got lower to avoid any sonic booms waking the local population in these early hours. Unseen vortices streamed and curled from the small ship's leading edges as it plunged deeper into the thickening oxygen-rich atmosphere.

The ten black-clad and helmeted soldiers inside stared at the floor. All had reduced the pigment in their tough leathery skin to ensure they were almost as dark as their clothing. Their enlarged eyes were almost all a dark grey and gave them excellent low-light vision, evolved because of their home planet's almost permanent state of twilight. It only got fully light there for a few days every rotation when they generally stayed indoors or underground to avoid the risk of blindness and skin blistering.

The pilot nodded as his scan of the proposed landing zone proved clear of any unexpected activity. The site had been carefully chosen, so it was close enough to the target, but remote enough to avoid detection when landing a noisy ship at night. Still, he came in fast, flared at the last possible moment and banged the ship down in the corner of a field, turning the vessel at the last second so its side airlock door faced the direction of the target. Its four struts sank a metre into the soft loamy soil and the quolynial effect from the antigrav drives' magna planes flattened the winter crop.

They waited as the powerful drives were quickly spooled down and within thirty seconds complete silence had returned to the corner of the crop field.

Nothing stirred for three minutes. The pilot risked a quick last minute scan that returned negative, before he removed the safeties and opened both airlock doors at the same time. All the soldiers pulled masks up to cover their mouths and gills, not to avoid recognition, but to filter out the spores and micro-organisms in the planet's atmosphere that caused them to sneeze uncontrollably.

Finally, once they were completely happy the landing had gone undetected, they shrugged out of their harnesses and exited the ship. The lighter gravity enabled them to move with surprising speed and within minutes they had the target's residence in sight. The leader made a vee sign with his right hand and the group split into two, one half spreading out to cover the grounds and their rear to ensure a smooth escape, and the other arrowing for the chosen building's ingress point.

The alarm system, although state of the art, was soon neutralised and the door lock bolts melted by a specially adapted low-powered, silent laser unit. The small group, with weapons up, entered quickly, silently closed the door, and followed the route through the large residence to the master suite up on the third floor. They'd had the plans for the building for some while and had rehearsed the operation many times to ensure they were completely familiar with the layout and nothing would surprise them.

That level of planning worked extremely well until a two-metre-tall casement clock, positioned in the corridor just outside the suite's door, struck the half hour.

The team almost jumped out of their skins and the one nearest the clock, who caught the movement of the minute hand clicking downwards in his peripheral vision, instinctively turned and fired. Although their weapons were set on a low setting, designed to incapacitate rather than kill, the resulting crash and clanging from the assaulted clock was enough to wake the dead.

The lead soldier immediately signalled for them to go and the suite door was breached with three of the team bundling inside, leaving two in the corridor to cover the retreat.

Unsurprisingly their target was awake and pulling something from a bedside drawer. Two laser weapons pulsed in quick succession. The lead soldier fell and the target slumped backward, his head clunking loudly on the antique carved wooden bedhead.

Another laser discharge sounded from the corridor as one of the remaining soldiers in the bedroom injected something into the target's neck and picked him up, slinging him over his shoulder. The other pulled up their fallen leader from the doorway and they both exited the room.

Their colleagues in the corridor were waiting and had another unconscious four-armed humanoid draped over one of their shoulders, who had been given a similar injection in the neck. The low gravity made their burdens seem lighter, so they were still able to quickly jog downstairs, liaise with the rest of the team and swiftly begin the journey back down the canal towpath to the ship.

They all squinted and pulled visors down from their helmets as exterior lighting flooded the neat, regimentally bordered gardens. Raised voices behind them ensured they didn't slacken their pace, especially as they could hear sirens in the distance.

The pilot had been kept informed of the proceedings and had the antigravs spooled up and ready as they arrived. The ship began lifting even before the airlocks were completely closed. It screamed upwards, quickly exceeding the speed of sound, the sonic boom shattering windows below, and with all attempts at remaining clandestine now abandoned, they clawed their way out of the atmosphere at maximum speed.

The cloaked cruiser waiting in a high orbit closed in on the troop carrier, turned and opened one of its huge starboard hangar doors. The small ship's pilot headed straight for what would look to anyone else like a mysterious portal into another universe. Braking and turning the ship savagely at the last minute, he whipped inside the huge hangar sideways, swung around one hundred and eighty degrees and clunked down on the hangar's rubber-floored deck.

The huge battle cruiser turned, immediately powered away and, while still close to the planet, jumped to a pre-programmed and embedded location.

1

———

RINGLESTONE MILL, KENT, ENGLAND, EARTH

'ANDREW, WAKE UP,' said Rayl.

'Eh,' he mumbled, still half asleep in a dream about kangaroos spilling his beer.

'Wake up now.'

'It wasn't me.'

'What?'

'It was the kangaroos.'

'Did what?'

'Pissed on the toilet floor.'

'Oh, for fuck's sake – Andrew Faux, wake up, you idiot.'

Rayl shook him this time.

'Ah, wha, who, oh, hello,' he said, finally opening his eyes and finding his wife scowling at him. 'What's up, sweet pea?'

'It's Ed, he's gone,' she said, her face a picture of worry.

'Where to?'

'That's just it, Andrew, nobody knows. He was

snatched by unknown assailants from his house in Cambridgeshire last night.'

'Oh, shit.'

'Precisely – and Pol is missing too.'

'Oh, shit.'

'Stop saying oh shit and get up.'

2

LOCATION UNKNOWN

THE DREAMS WERE vivid and frightening, involving creatures invading his bedroom and eating him alive, then a sensation of being dragged through dark caves and a cry somewhere in the distance he thought sounded like someone he knew but couldn't quite place.

The wall in front of his face when he eventually pried open his eyes was grey metal and not the four hundred-year-old oak panelling he was expecting. His head screamed as he tried to turn it and he shut his eyes again and grimaced as the throbbing ache increased tenfold.

Holy shit, what did I drink last night, he thought to himself, slowly turning over and finding his limbs were heavy and only partially obeying his commands.

He attempted opening one eye at a time and now, facing the other way, he found the room was small and also grey and metal and not where he was expecting to be. He forced himself up, ignoring the pain throbbing through his brain, and peered around through his one open eye.

'What the fuck,' he whispered, as it became obvious he

was in a cell, and judging by the murmuring of an environmental system and general background hum, he was on a ship too. It was at this point he noticed it wasn't bedding that was holding him down, as there wasn't any; the gravity on this vessel was high, considerably higher than on Earth.

Forcing himself up to sit on the edge of the small cot, Ed felt around the back of his head where the pain seemed to be centralised. He found a small gash, matted hair and dried blood, then, sitting back against the wall, he attempted to compartmentalise the pain and piece together what he could remember about the previous evening.

Dinner with Pol and accountant Ian McMichael at the Black Bull, taxi back and a glass of Calvados in front of the fire in the library. It was the housekeeper's day off, so she wasn't around. Then it came to him, what had seemed like a part of a dream. The sudden uncustomary clanging of his seventeenth-century grandfather clock out in the corridor and the bedroom door crashing open. Dark figures silhouetted by the dim night light he left on in the en suite bathroom.

I think I shot one, he thought as he remembered snatching up the small pistol he kept in a bedside drawer. The drawer had only been open because he'd dropped his book into it before going to sleep. Then, nothing more – until now.

He began trying to piece together who would want to kidnap him and why. His first thought were the Moguls, but he discounted them because the ship was way too cold and they wouldn't be able to tolerate that, especially with the higher gravity. He shivered and wrapped himself as best he could in the lone coarse blanket he'd woken on top of.

He's dead, he thought, as Xavier Lake came to mind.

Perhaps someone I've pissed off in the GDA, was his next guess, but with the thundering headache, nothing came easily.

The dim lighting in the cell flickered slightly and the background hum changed pitch momentarily.

We just jumped, he thought, now able to recognise the telltales from all the different ships he'd been on over the last couple of years.

I hope this ship's leaving a trail for others to follow, he thought.

'Andy'll find me,' he said out loud to the empty cell. 'He can find anything.'

3

RINGLESTONE MILL, KENT, ENGLAND, EARTH

'I CAN'T FIND MY TROUSERS,' Andy complained, hopping around the bedroom trying to put his socks on standing up.

Rayl entered the bedroom from the small side office and rolled her eyes at him.

'I was supposed to have married the most accomplished aeronautical engineer on Earth,' she said incredulously, staring at him with her hands on her hips. 'Where's he gone?' she added, pointing at a picture of Andy shaking hands with the US president.

'I'm still here, sweet pea,' he said. 'Just having a little wardrobe malfunction.'

'Malfunction my arse,' she replied, handing him his jeans. 'It's all that warm beer you drink sloshing around in your head.'

'You sound just like my Australian friends.'

'Talking of Australian friends, Aussie Greg messaged to say he got a strange reading from one of his satellites last night and to call him.'

Andy finally managing to finish dressing himself, entered the small office and called Greg.

'G'day, Andrew,' drawled the familiar voice as the computer screen lit up with an uncustomary stern face. 'Sorry to hear about Edward,' he said. 'But we picked this up from one of our space traffic satellites three hours ago and thought it a little odd until we got Rayl's message.'

Andy clicked open the flashing icon in the right-hand corner of the screen. It showed a suddenly appearing unidentified return several hundred kilometres away. Then a second coming at speed directly out from the planet's atmosphere meeting the first and both disappearing.

'Where was this geographically?' Andy asked.

'Above the UK,' Greg answered. 'Whatever the first contact was, it was moving with the planet's rotation and seemed to be waiting for the other one.'

'It was a cloaked starship,' said Andy, nodding. 'It opened a hangar door to admit the incoming shuttle or whatever small ship it was.'

'It was a GDA ship then?' said Greg, his eyes widening.

'Not necessarily,' replied Andy, glancing out the office window and up at the morning sky. 'Rumours are, others have managed to get it, or versions of it.'

'Hmm, so you think it could have been the snatch squad that grabbed Edward?'

'Most likely, yes. They took Pol too.'

'Is that the four-armed alien you rescued?'

'It is, she's part of our crew now.'

'Oh, dear,' he said, pulling a pained expression. 'Out of the frying pan and all that.'

'We'll find 'em,' said Andy. 'And thanks for the quick information, I'm sure it'll prove invaluable.'

———

Once ready, they hurried out to the large barn behind the mill and while Rayl opened the big double doors, Andy went inside to prep the shuttle for flight.

'Cleo, are you there?' he called as the airlock opened.

'Of course I'm here,' the ship's sentient computer replied. 'I'm always here.'

'Good, prep the shuttle and have the *Gabriel* ready to go as soon as we arrive.'

'It's the middle of the night in Florida, so only a few security personnel to clear out of the way. I have informed them of our imminent departure.'

Andy dropped down into the pilot's seat and watched as all the screens lit up and went through their automated pre-flight checks.

'Were you not there?' he asked, in an almost accusatory tone and instantly regretted it.

'You know very well he's the same as you with his personal privacy. I can only enter your private residences when requested.'

'So, you're as much in the dark as us?'

'Not completely,' she replied, appearing sitting on one of the other seats, cross-legged and wearing a full black goth outfit, with make-up to match.

'Holy crap,' said Rayl, entering the cockpit and stopping dead in her tracks. 'What the fuck are you wearing, Cleo?'

'I think she's been listening to some Bauhaus or something,' said Andy, raising his eyebrows. 'But I'm more interested in what you meant by "not completely."'

Cleo smiled and waved up above their heads. A holographic image appeared showing the grounds of Ed's manor house in Cambridgeshire.

'Ah, you have his security footage,' said Rayl, sitting and watching as a group of dark figures loomed out of the shadows and approached one of the rear doors.

'Humanoid then,' said Andy. 'Stocky and judging by the ease and speed of movement, used to a higher gravity.'

'They know where the cameras are too,' said Rayl. 'Look how they're keeping their faces hidden, so they've done their homework.'

'Whoever they are, this was a well-planned, executed and rehearsed military operation,' said Andy. 'They're not Callametan, so they weren't after Pol. Ed was most likely the target and Pol just happened to be in the wrong place.'

'Or disturbed them,' said Rayl. 'You know she has different sleep cycles to us. Perhaps they were forced to take her too, so she couldn't reveal their identity.'

'Poor girl,' said Cleo. 'As if she hasn't been through enough.'

'Half the GDA races have a higher gravity to Earth,' said Rayl. 'That still gives us over eight hundred possibles.'

'Not necessarily,' said Andy, watching the footage closely as the view switched to inside the house. 'Cleo, get an image of the weapons they're carrying and—'

'Not in the database,' she said. 'Already thought of that.'

'So, the weapons are not a known GDA model,' Andy mused and suddenly turned to look at Cleo. 'Where did they land?'

'No one's quite sure,' she said. 'In one of the fields behind the house presumably, as that's the direction they came from.'

'We need to go there first,' said Andy, closing the airlock and spinning up the antigravs.

The short flight took them up across northern Kent and the Thames Estuary, skirted the east of London and up across Essex, before dropping down into Cambridgeshire and the outskirts of Willingham.

It was eight thirty in the morning as they flew over the house. A handful of police vehicles could be seen parked on the gravel drive in front of the seventeenth-century manor house. Several faces peered up at them suspiciously as they began circling behind the building.

'What are we looking for?' asked Rayl.

'There's been a fair amount of rain recently,' Andy replied.

'When isn't there on this soggy planet?' said Rayl, shrugging and staring out the front screen innocently.

He gave her a quick sideways glance, not sure if she was serious or not, before continuing.

'Err, well, their shuttle would have landed somewhere out here and with the ground as wet as it is, the landing gear would have sunk in somewhat and left its telltale mark.'

'You think you'll be able to tell what ship it was from a couple of holes in a field?' Rayl asked. This time the sarcasm was obvious.

'Before you two have a domestic, he's actually correct, Rayl,' said Cleo, her holographic image still sitting in one of the rear seats. 'The size, spread and sometimes shape of the struts would give you a guide to the model of shuttle used.'

'Okay, you've convinced me,' she said, leaning forward to gaze a little more enthusiastically out the front screen.

'It would have been far enough away and downwind so the engines didn't wake anyone, but close enough so they didn't have too far to run carrying an unconscious body, especially if they were being pursued,' said Andy.

He followed the footpath to the north of the property slowly and at about thirty feet, just skimming the tops of the taller trees growing within the hedgerows. They all peered to either side of the path, especially where there was a gap in the hedge or a gate.

Ten minutes later, just as it began to look as though Andy had been a little over-enthusiastic in his reasoning, he took the ship wide to turn and begin yet another run back towards the house.

'There,' shouted Rayl, as they swung over a field Andy had discounted as being too distant.

He turned back sharply and both Cleo and Andy followed Rayl's finger over to a corner in a field left fallow near the River Great Ouse.

'I didn't think they'd be this far away,' said Andy, as he flared the shuttle and landed close by.

They bundled out as soon as both the airlock doors opened, leaving Cleo inside as there were no holo emitters outside the vessel. Andy brought his tablet and photographed one of the many similar boot prints in the soil and a close up of one of the four holes, while Rayl paced the distance between them.

'Twenty-seven metres by eleven metres,' she said.

'And the struts, they're triangular too,' added Andy. 'I don't remember seeing any that shape before.'

'You won't have,' said Cleo, from the shuttle.

'Why's that?' he asked.

'Because it's a Uly ship,' she said. 'The spread and shape of the struts is from one of their small Halyd class troop carriers.'

'You're absolutely sure?' Andy asked, turning and looking back at the shuttle.

Cleo stood inside the shuttle's airlock nodding.

'Absolutely,' she said. 'They're completely unique. Nobody else that we know of uses triangular struts.'

'That you know of?' replied Andy, questioningly.

Cleo didn't reply.

'Okay, let's say it is a Uly ship,' he continued. 'What the hell would they want with Ed? I've never even heard of them until now and I'm pretty sure Ed won't have either.'

'It doesn't mean it was crewed by Ulys,' said Rayl. 'It might have been secondhand or stolen.'

It was Andy's turn to be silent for a moment before he sighed, his shoulders slumping.

'Bollocks,' he said, kicking a stone into one of the strut holes. 'Just as you think you might be getting somewhere.'

4

___

THEO SHUTTLE DESCENDING INTO FLORIDA

ANDY HAD TAKEN the shuttle straight up and out over Norfolk, climbed above all the commercial air traffic and crossed the Atlantic. It was five o'clock in the morning Florida time as he descended towards Orlando and GDA Park, the newest theme world in the state.

The five hundred-metre-long starship *Gabriel* sat in the centre of the park and was the main attraction. It looked huge sitting on its purpose-built pedestal compared to all the other smaller attractions surrounding it. The early morning sun glistened off its beautiful pure white organic hull. Its almost flower-like flowing lines could be seen for miles around and ensured the park attracted a huge audience. Twice a day, the most popular part of the show was when the ship's sentient computer, Cleo, opened up all the weapon nacelles and missile ports, firing a few laser cannon bolts at a fake holographic enemy ship that uncloaked on the far side of the park. Everybody would cheer as the enemy ship, loosely based on a Mogul vessel, exploded and vaporised in spectacular fashion.

That wasn't going to happen today, however, as it was written into the contract that in the case of an emergency, the *Gabriel* could leave at any time. Rayl had contacted the security detail on duty that night to inform them of the ship's departure and ensure they cleared their personnel out of the *Gabriel* and the surrounding area. Naturally, they were not overly happy about it as tours of the ship were booked solid for months to come, but there was very little they could do about it.

Cleo opened the starboard hangar as Andy approached and then entered. He was surprised to see another private shuttle parked up against the rear bulkhead.

'Whose is that?' he asked Cleo, nodding at the strange ship.

'A friend,' she said. 'Who swore me to secrecy,' she added when Andy narrowed his eyes.

He spun the ship around and landed next to the other strange shuttle and by the time he'd shut everything down and opened the airlock doors, a figure stood at the bottom of the steps.

'Hi, guys,' Bache Loftt said. 'I understand my friend is in trouble. Can I be of help and tag along?'

'I thought you'd retired,' said Andy, descending the steps and giving Bache a hug.

'From the GDA, yes, but not from life and certainly not when my friend Edward is in trouble.'

'Of course you can join us,' said Rayl, also embracing Bache, who peered around her and up into the shuttle.

'Is Linda not with you?'

'Linda is having a bit of time out,' said Rayl. 'It seems the last couple of years have taken their toll and she wanted to spend a bit of time alone and sort her head out.'

'She does know though?' Bache asked.

'Ed's abduction is on every news feed on the planet,' said Andy.

'But have you told her?' he added.

'She turned her internal communications off a few weeks ago,' said Cleo. 'She's been incommunicado ever since.'

'What about Phil?'

'I'm here,' said a voice approaching from behind the shuttles.

Phil trotted up, looking exactly the same awkward teenager as he had three years ago when they first met. Although, this time the smile was missing.

'We need to go as soon as possible,' he said, the worry evident in his voice.

'He's right,' said Andy. 'All the time we spend gassing, Ed is further away and the trail gets colder. Everyone upstairs, let's get this beast into space.'

———

The news about Edward had travelled fast and even this early in Florida thousands had come out to watch the *Gabriel* leave. Highways around Orlando ground to a halt as people just stopped their vehicles in the middle of the road and got out to watch the huge vessel depart and wish them good luck.

Andy allowed Phil to take the ship up and as he lifted the half-kilometre-long starship up away from its home for the last few months, they could almost hear the cheers and clapping from miles around. They could certainly see them lining the roads and tops of buildings on the exterior cameras.

Phil turned the monstrous ship up on its tail and powered away straight up, the scream of the mighty anti-gravs echoing around the city. If you hadn't known about the ship's departure before, you certainly did now. He was careful not to exceed the speed of sound until they were high enough not to break windows with the sonic boom.

'When did you get here?' Andy asked, dragging his eyes away from the waving crowds and glancing across at Phil.

'I've been here a while,' he replied, shrugging, raising his eyebrows and looking almost embarrassed.

'We thought you were at your home in California,' said Rayl.

Phil adopted a pensive expression.

'I was, I just find planet living a bit weird,' he said, giving them a half smile.

'I suppose when you've spent the majority of three thousand years living on a starship, it would take a bit of getting used to,' she replied.

'I help with the tours,' he said, nodding slowly.

'How long were you at your home then?' Bache asked, joining the conversation.

'Two days,' Phil replied.

'Just two days?' Andy blurted. 'Bloody hell, Phil, why didn't you call us?'

'I like it on the ship.'

'We need to find you a partner,' said Rayl. 'And not one of Cleo's holographic ones either.'

'I sometimes wish I was still single,' said Bache, causing everyone to look at him strangely. 'Oops, did I say that out loud?' he added.

'But your wife's lovely,' said Rayl, almost accusingly.

'She wasn't earlier when I said I was coming to help,' he replied pensively, and pulling a pained expression.

'I can understand her reasons,' said Rayl. 'You've had a lifetime of danger and now you've retired, she expected to have you to herself from now on.'

'Is she happy living on Earth?' Andy asked.

'Oh, yes,' he said. 'She likes the lower gravity especially, and the vegan food.'

'Nothing like that on Dasos then?' asked Phil.

Bache laughed.

'It's planet of the carnivores, although I must say their hog mire steaks are better than sex.'

'That's a huge call,' said Andy, getting that look from Rayl that told him to shut the fuck up.

'We're in the position in space now where the Uly ship disappeared,' said Phil, getting everyone's attention.

They all felt the *Gabriel*'s inertial dampers working hard as Phil slowed and stopped. All movement ceased on the large holomap hanging above them, except for the slowly rotating blue Earth below them and a spattering of space traffic and satellites.

'Full scan, please, Rayl,' said Andy.

'Reach out a few light years for any unlogged emerges,' said Bache.

It went quiet on the *Gabriel*'s bridge as Rayl became

the focus of attention. She tapped away at her array of icons floating in front of her face, occasionally grimacing, but otherwise ignoring the scrutiny she was under.

'Well?' asked Andy, as Rayl sat back, folded her arms across her chest and puffed her cheeks out.

'Bugger all,' she grumbled, looking around at each of them in turn. 'Sorry.'

'Nothing to apologise about,' said Bache. 'Whoever we're dealing with here, are not amateurs.'

'We go to Uly then,' said Andy, nodding and pointing at Phil. 'Let's see if they have a reason for one of their ships being involved.'

Phil nodded in return and plotted a course out to the nearest jump point.

5

COLD CELL ON AN UNDETERMINED
STARSHIP

ED WAS GETTING MORE and more annoyed. His captors were remaining elusive in their identity. He'd tried pushing out with his DOVI but found the cell to be heavily shielded and a snow field of white noise was the only result. The rather unsanitary toilet in the opposite corner of the cell to his cot stank, although after a few hours he'd got used to it. Every few hours a bowl of lumpy soup of indeterminate content slid through a narrow hatch at the base of the door. It was cold, greenish, tasted vaguely of boiled swede and the lumpy bits were tough and resembled boiled mutton.

He lay on the floor once, to see if he could identify his kidnappers through the hatch, but all he saw was an empty corridor, a gloved hand and a pair of black military-style boots.

He was beginning to lose track of time too. His watch was probably still on his bedside table, but judging by the number of meals it had been a couple of days or so.

They came for him without warning while he was

dozing. Two stocky humanoids in dark military-style over-alls swept into the cell, grabbed him up from the cot and frogmarched him out the cell and down the corridor. He pretended to be a bit dozy and let them take his weight as they half walked, half dragged him through the ship. In reality he was watching everything closely.

The first thing he noticed was their skin was scaled and dark, and they had large eyes, which explained the dim unlit interior. Their faces, however, were difficult to pigeonhole. The nearest he could get was like an armadillo crossed with a Klingon and seemingly just as grumpy.

'Who are you and where are you taking me?' he asked, turning his head and addressing the alien on his left.

He or it barked back in a series of clicks and hisses that his internal translator immediately recognised as Klatt.

'The prisoner will remain silent,' was the translation.

They're Klatt, he thought, *so this is what they look like.*

He was a little happier now he knew who they were, but it still didn't explain what exactly he'd done to merit them going to all this trouble on his behalf.

An airlock approached and he got a bit nervous as they stopped and opened the inner door, but he breathed a sigh of relief when they entered with him and cycled the lock. The outer door opened to reveal a narrow ribbed tube that flexed as they walked and he quickly realised he was being transferred to another ship while still in space.

The airlock at the other side was of a different design and looked newer. He tried his DOVI again, only to get a punch in the side of his head.

'Use that again and you'll be in an airlock alone,' came the translation from the guard who'd struck him.

How the hell did they know? he thought.

This ship, as they entered and turned right, was indeed newer. It was still as gloomy and the gravity just as high, but not quite as high as on Dasos, Ed estimated.

The forced march continued through the new ship that he reasoned was considerably larger than the last one. An escalator took them up many decks, spitting them out directly onto what seemed to be the bridge. The guards stiffened as they entered and dragged Ed's arms behind his back, placing restraints on his wrists.

'Stand there and don't move,' one of the guards clicked and hissed in his ear.

Ed observed a circular room roughly twenty metres across with around forty crew on three levels all standing facing inwards to a raised platform in the centre. This contained an opaque shimmering field, tubular in shape and stretching from the floor of the platform up to the ceiling.

The crew seemed to be paying him no attention at all, but it was hard to tell where they were looking through the blackness of their eyes.

'Good morning, Mr Virr,' said a deep voice in English, seemingly coming from everywhere.

Ed gazed around the room, but could find no evidence of who was speaking.

'Hello there,' said Ed, almost cheerfully. 'Don't be a stranger, I won't bite.'

'Ahh,' said the voice. 'More of that smug insolence, Mr Virr.'

The opaque shield dissipated to reveal another Klatt,

this one sitting inside a circular console. He spun his seat around and faced Ed.

'It's Captain Virr to you, and your name is…?'

'Captain Groxl, your accuser.'

Groxl smiled a smile that reminded Ed of a snarling wolf.

'I've waited a long time for this,' Groxl continued.

'And just what are you accusing me of?' Ed asked. 'I've never met a Klatt before, so I believe you almost certainly have the wrong man.'

'Oh, we've met before, Virr,' Groxl sneered. 'It might have been a trivial moment for you, but the consequences included not just my humiliation and demotion from admiral back to captain, but also one of the most obscene insults ever to the Klatt Navy and the entire Klatt Empire.'

'What the hell are you talking about?' Ed demanded, shaking his head.

'Three years ago, my Fonias class cruiser *KNS Vixtyon* approached your little ship in system C-29641/AT, as I believe your GDA friends like to call it. You attacked us, which resulted in the death of one of my crew and the ensuing complete loss of the vessel. Is your memory returning now, Mr Virr?'

Ed did indeed remember the short exchange and hadn't thought about it since.

'I seem to remember it was your own weapon system that damaged your ship,' Ed replied, hopefully.

'So we thought at the time,' said Groxl. 'But evidence soon came to light that it was you manipulating our then unshielded systems with that mind control thing you have – a DOVI, I believe you call it.'

How the fuck did they find out about that? he thought.

'I think you're mistaken,' said Ed. 'There's no such thing,' he added, keeping his expression as neutral as he could.

'Is that so?' Groxl hissed, a malevolent grin spreading across his face as he reached across to depress a button on his console.

Ed collapsed in sudden agony, his head becoming an instant sphere of pain. He shrieked out loud and writhed around on the floor until Groxl touched the button again and the acute agony disappeared as abruptly as it had come.

Ed sat back up, sweat dripping off his face, and glanced nervously at Groxl.

'You are on the way to Zee-Klatt III, the Klatt home world,' said Groxl, 'where you will be tried for your crimes against the Klatt Empire. Even if your life is spared, you will be spending the rest of your sad existence in one of our hard labour work camps.'

Groxl waved one of his hands towards the elevator.

'Take the criminal away and if he tries to use that DOVI thing again – space him,' Groxl sneered as he disappeared behind the opaque shield once again.

Ed felt himself roughly picked up and dragged back towards the elevator.

6

THE STARSHIP GABRIEL EN ROUTE TO ULY

JUMP point three was busy as the *Gabriel* winked into the Uly system. More than a hundred ships formed lines in towards the Earth-like planet of Uly from several jump points. It was slightly larger than Earth but had similar huge oceans covering over two thirds of the surface and six huge space stations could be clearly seen on the rotating holomap, even at this distance.

'Pretty planet,' said Rayl, folding her arms and lying back on her couch to admire the view.

'Pretty dangerous too,' said Bache. 'Be careful what you say – they can be a bit touchy sometimes, especially concerning security.'

'Okay,' said Andy. 'I'll be polite and—'

A sudden transmitted voice boomed around the bridge and interrupted him.

'Starship *Gabriel*, this is Uly security control, please state the nature of your visit.'

'Hello, Uly control,' said a cheerful-sounding Andy. 'We're looking for a Halyd—'

Andy stopped suddenly as he saw Bache staring at him and shaking his head urgently.

'You're looking for what?' Uly control answered.

'…err…a holiday…place…somewhere nice,' he said, cringing. 'With a beach perhaps?'

A silence ensued on the bridge and everyone froze, listening for the strangely delayed reply from Uly control.

'Starship *Gabriel*, you are cleared to proceed to Station IV on this vector and dock on airlock 139, then await further instructions, Uly security control out.'

A green course line appeared on the holomap and Phil asked Cleo to lock onto it.

'Crap,' said Bache, which caused everyone to turn and stare at him.

'What's up?' Andy asked. 'Did I just screw up?'

'Station IV is military only, no civilian access. If we dock there they will try and board us,' said Bache. 'Can you open up a communication line again?'

Rayl touched a couple of icons and nodded at him.

'Uly control, this is GDA Commander Loftt on the starship *Gabriel*, can you patch me through to Councillor Graddox, protocol delta four.'

There was a pause again and just as everyone was beginning to think Bache had been ignored, the same voice returned.

'Councillor Graddox is unavailable.'

Bache rolled his eyes and spoke again.

'This is a protocol delta four requisition, please give me your rank and name for the discourse refusal report.'

There was silence again, this time it went on even longer than before.

'Graddox,' said a sleepy voice. 'Do you know what time this is?'

'Sorry to wake you, Milo,' he said. 'It's Bache Loftt here, can we have a few moments of your time?'

'Shit, Bache, I didn't know it was you. Where are you?'

'Being ordered to dock on Station IV.'

'Well, don't do that. Put yourself in a high orbit and get a shuttle down here for breakfast, I'll send you a flight plan. Leave Station IV to me, I'll sort them out and don't come armed or anything, my security gets a bit touchy about that.'

'Thanks, Milo, there'll be two of us and we'll see you soon, Bache out.'

He turned back to the others with a grin on his face.

'All sorted,' he said, relaxing back into his couch.

Andy regarded him with raised eyebrows.

'Who's Graddox then?' he asked.

'Uly clan chief,' said Bache. 'Sort of like your prime minister. He's the top administrator of one of the large land masses down there.'

'Dropping into an orbit now,' said Phil, giving Bache a nod.

'We've got two military ships suddenly turning towards us and arming weapons,' said Rayl. 'Do you want me to arm…oh, hang on, they've turned away again and powered down their systems.'

Bache smiled and stood up.

'The Councillor's orders came through, I suspect. Come on Andy, shall we go get some minced ran-tie on toast? It's delicious.'

Councillor Graddox had been true to his word. Bache and Andy were soon in a shuttle following a course sent up for them. Once the orange glow and firework display coursing across the front screen had dissipated, they dropped into heavy cloud, and the hull cooled quickly in the hail that became heavy rain as they got lower.

'I thought you mentioned it being their summer,' said Andy, as another flash of lightning caused him to flinch and dig his fingers deeper into the arms of his seat.

'This world can have some crazy weather at times,' said Bache, lounging in his seat nonchalantly. 'They made the same mistakes you guys did with global warming, to such an extent they had to abandon a lot of the coastal areas and move to higher ground.'

Finally, Cleo, who was piloting the shuttle, informed them they were two minutes from landing and Andy peered out through the torrential rain, quietly relieved he wasn't having to fly in this zero visibility.

The struts whined down and the small vessel shuddered as it clunked down onto a hard surface, the scream of the antigravs immediately winding down to a low murmur.

'I have placed brollies in the airlock,' said Cleo, as the rain could be heard now, thundering on the roof of the shuttle. 'There are two humans approaching the ship.'

They cycled the airlock and followed their two guides across the small landing pad and into a low white building close by.

'The Councillor is waiting for you in the dining room,'

said one of the guides in perfect Ellinika, the galactic language of the GDA that evolved into Greek on Earth.

Bache nodded as they folded their umbrellas and left them forming a puddle next to the door. They were led into a small dining room expensively panelled in a local dark hardwood that gave the room a warm cosy feel. Pictures of impressive indigenous landscapes adorned the walls and Andy wondered if he'd be able to see some of these beautiful places if the rain would just bugger off.

'Gentlemen,' said a smiling Councillor Graddox, who quickly stood and approached wearing a brightly coloured sarong-style wrap that reminded Andy of African tribal leaders. 'Bache, it's good to see you again.' He shook Bache's hand.

'This is a good friend and colleague, Captain Andrew Faux,' Bache said, grinning.

'Good to meet you, Andrew.' They shook hands and he waved them towards the table where three places had been set.

Andy grinned inwardly; he'd never been called captain before.

One of the guides from before entered and placed a plate containing the promised minced ran-tie on toast: a delicacy of the region made from the minced liver of a Ran, an indigenous mammal that roughly resembled a mountain goat.

'Something tells me you didn't come all this way for a holiday or another plate of Ran's gizzards,' said Graddox, studying Bache closely.

Andy, who was on his second mouthful, stopped chewing and eyed his plate suspiciously.

'You are quite correct, Councillor,' said Bache, pausing before he spoke again. 'Two days ago, a close friend was kidnapped at gunpoint from his home on Earth in the Sol system.'

'I see,' said Graddox. 'And how does that involve us, all the way out here?'

'A Uly Halyd class vessel was involved in the raid.'

The Councillor stiffened.

'You have conclusive evidence of this?' he asked, his face clouding over.

Bache retrieved his tablet and showed the councillor the images of the strut holes left in the soft soil.

'The only vessel known to us with this configuration of landing gear is a Halyd class troop landing craft,' Bache said. 'The strut spacing is triangular and of exact measurement.'

'This is unfortunate,' said Graddox, the jovial tone now missing from his voice.

'Either it was a Uly operation or you've recently lost one of these ships,' said Andy, speaking for the first time.

The Councillor's eyes flicked across to him almost angrily, then softened. He shrugged and sighed as he placed his cutlery on the table.

'Twelve days ago, a marine detachment was on an exercise near Uskrre—'

'Uskrre?' blurted Andy, interrupting the Councillor. 'Isn't that the planet in the Alpha Centauri system that we nearly went to by mistake during our maiden jumps?'

'It is,' said Bache, nodding slowly, glancing back at Graddox and raising his eyebrows.

'We were testing our new cloaking system,' he said.

'The ship never came back, did it?' said Andy, adopting a puzzled expression. 'Who was it that had a remote secret base there, that everyone seemed to know about except us?'

'The Klatt,' said both Bache and Graddox together. 'But what would the Klatt have against Edward to go to all that trouble?' Bache continued.

Andy flinched, which didn't go unnoticed and with both of them glaring at him, he reasoned he'd better explain.

'Erm, Ed kinda fucked up one of their cruisers about three years ago.'

Bache buried his face in his hands and sighed.

'Why does it have to be the Klatt?' Bache moaned. 'Nobody messes with the Klatt, not even us. They're easily offended and have long memories.'

'Is your kidnapped friend Edward Virr?' Graddox asked, his eyes wide.

Both Bache and Andy nodded.

'Oh, shit,' said Graddox. 'That won't look good for us.'

'If it is the Klatt, it won't be very good for Edward either,' groaned Bache.

7

CELL ON A NEW KLATT WARSHIP

ED KNEW the Klatt home world was in the Acheron region out on a distant arm of the galaxy, so this cell, although a little larger than the one before, could be home for a while.

The ship seemed newer in its design and as far as his accommodation went, the bed looked unused and the toilet didn't stink, so that was a distinct improvement. The food however wasn't. Same cold mutton-like stew as before and he grimaced at it as soon as it appeared through the door hatch.

'Can I order a nice rare sirloin chasseur for dinner tomorrow, buttered new potatoes and perhaps some lightly steamed calabrese?' he said to the hand as it pushed the steel dog bowl through the door.

The silence from outside the cell gave him his answer as he picked up the bowl and sniffed it tentatively. With the initial observation confirmed he held his nose with one hand and shovelled it in with the other, washing it down with the cup of metallic-tasting water.

He froze as he thought he heard a voice out in the

corridor. Lying down and quickly putting his ear to the small gap around the food hatch, he listened as the faint voice came again.

'Oh, for fuck's sake, can't the chef make anything else?' the familiar voice complained.

'Pol, is that you?' he called, cringing immediately as he realised it was a stupid question.

He held his breath as a crash sounded from outside.

'Bastard,' replied Pol. 'You made me drop my delicious dinner. Of course it's fucking me.'

'I'm sorry you're here too,' he said.

'So, it wasn't you that booked this holiday cruise then?'

'No, they were after me. Did you disturb them?'

'They disturbed me by demolishing your stupid noisy clock.'

'Stupid,' exclaimed Ed. 'That's a seventeenth-century Michael Bird longcase clock, I'll have you know.'

'Well, it's buggered now,' she said.

'Cost me seventy grand.'

'Get me out of this mess and I'll happily buy you a new one,' she said. 'So long as it's not outside my bedroom this time making that infernal racket.'

'I'm sure Andy's on the case.'

'Will they let him take the *Gabriel*?'

'It's in the contract.'

'So, we just sit and wait?'

'Not much else we can do.'

'Can't you use your DOVI and mess with the ship?'

'No, they know about that and have shielded me. They'll space me if I try and use it.'

'Oh, shit,' she said.

'Yeah, oh shit indeed.'

'No, Ed, you don't understand. I've been using mine.'

'You have a DOVI fitted too now?'

'Uh, huh,' she grunted. 'Cleo set me up so I can fly the ships. I've been having a peek around this one too.'

'They haven't detected it then,' he said. 'That's good. It must be working on a completely different frequency.'

'D'you want me to interfere with their systems?'

'No, they'll know it was us. We'll keep that little gem under wraps for now until we really need it.'

'Where are they taking us?'

'Klatt home world.'

'Where's that?'

'Zee-Klatt III. If my memory serves me right it's in the Acheron region.'

'I have no idea where that is.'

'A long way away on an outer arm and without knowing the capabilities of this ship, I have no idea how long that will take.'

'I'll set up the sun lounger.'

Ed smiled for the first time that day.

'You have the same sense of humour as Andy.'

'As he says – keeps you sane during stressful situations,' Pol mused.

'Did Cleo set you up with a Krypti as well?'

'That's something I was going to ask you about,' said Pol. 'She mentioned it in a conversation and I was a bit embarrassed to ask.'

'Memory chip,' said Ed. 'It sits under the back of your skull and records everything you know, do and say. So, if the worst happens you can be reborn in a Theo birthing chamber with all your previous knowledge intact, like Linda and myself.'

'Okay,' she said, sounding a bit doubtful. 'Would I be reborn in a Callametan or a human body?'

'Good question,' said Ed. 'I have no idea. That's a conversation to have with Phil.'

'Hmm,' she grunted. 'I don't think I could manage with only two arms. That would be well weird.'

The sound of boots in the corridor had Ed scuttling back to his cot, as the hatch where his head had been crashed open and his cup and bowl were taken away.

8

THE STARSHIP GABRIEL IN A HIGH ORBIT
AROUND ULY

ANDY AND BACHE had relayed the new information to the others on their return to the *Gabriel* from the surface of Uly.

'Why did it have to be the Klatt?' said Phil, slumping back on his couch. 'They're one of the most dangerous races in the galaxy.'

'How dangerous?' asked Rayl, the worry evident in her tone.

'Well, on a scale of one to ten, they're an eleven,' said Phil. 'They have a penchant for shooting first and not even bothering with the questions.'

'Shit,' Rayl whispered as she sat back and hugged her knees to her chest. 'Where would they take them?'

'We can only presume the Klatt home planet,' said Bache. 'The Klatt have one thing in their society that's a constant, their love of anything that embarrasses the GDA.'

'Shouldn't we let the GDA know?' said Phil.

'Already taken care of,' said Bache. 'I sent a transmission back to Dasos from the Councillor's residence. It would carry a bit more clout that way.'

'Well – aren't we going to go there?' asked Rayl, looking between Bache and Andy.

Bache took a deep breath before answering.

'It's not as simple as that,' he said. 'The GDA have an absolute ban on any uninvited vessel invading the Acheron region as the Klatt would perceive it as a declaration of war.'

'We can't just sit here and do nothing,' said Rayl. 'Those bullies could be torturing them as we speak.'

Bache nodded, a sombre expression on his face.

'It doesn't mean we can't go in that general direction,' he said. 'But, we would have to be dark right from the start. They'll be watching for any unusual ship movements coming in their direction.'

'Cleo, can you plot—'

A course appeared on the holomap before Andy could finish the sentence.

'That's not very direct,' said Rayl, gazing at the round-about route.

'Intentionally,' said Cleo, appearing in person dressed as some sort of ninja warrior. It created a few raised eyebrows, but no one commented. 'We have no idea how advanced the Klatt technology is. It's such a closed society, nothing leaks out. So, we have to presume the worst and that they may be able to detect us through our cloak.'

'Not very likely though,' said Rayl.

'But theoretically possible,' Cleo countered. 'They have a huge and extremely aggressive naval presence continuously roaming their region. They would destroy the

Gabriel in the blink of an eye if we were caught snooping. So, this course skirts the Acheron region as though we were passing by and then we could pop in the back door when the time was right.'

'Could we get the GDA to do a bit of sabre rattling at the front door?' asked Rayl, glancing at Bache.

'That's something I've already suggested,' Bache replied. 'But I know the answer will involve confirming it is the Klatt that have them. Because at present, it is just an assumption.'

'Well, there's no doubt in my mind,' said Andy.

'Nor mine,' said Bache. 'But until it's confirmed, we don't want to risk starting a galactic war over a faulty presumption. Let's take Cleo's circuitous route and await developments.'

The other three humans nodded and one hologram ninja bowed deeply and vanished.

The *Gabriel* moved slowly away from Uly towards one of the jump points and forty-eight minutes later winked out of the system.

Later that day, Bache found Andy down in the port hangar inspecting the heat shielding on the underside of the *Cartella*.

'I think Cleo would let you know if there was a problem with any of the ship's systems,' he said.

'I know,' said Andy. 'It takes my mind off what Ed and Pol are probably going through, and at the end of the day, I am supposed to be the ship's engineer.'

Bache smiled.

'How long is it that you've known Ed?' he asked, climbing the steps and sitting in the open airlock.

'Almost ten Earth years now,' Andy replied, his voice echoing around inside a strut housing. 'I was in my mid-twenties working for a French company called Richolot Aerospace when NASA offered me the job alongside Ed.'

'To design your first jump drive.'

'That's right. Although, it was so hush hush, I was in the job a month before they disclosed the full scope of the work to me.'

'Espionage?'

'Yeah.'

'Our friend Xavier Lake.'

'Amongst others.'

'There was so much suspicion and distrust on your planet at that time. I remember the two space station commanders summoned for a little chat on my ship when we were looking for Lake. They despised each other even though they did the same job for the same planet and only a few thousand kilometres apart.'

'Well, at least things have improved since then,' said Andy.

'Finding out how insignificant you are in the grand scheme of things can do that.'

'That, and the threat of extinction.'

'Don't let that get to you. You weren't the first and certainly won't be the last to get a little reminder how ridiculous that behaviour was.'

'Shame the Klatt can't be reminded of that.'

'Unfortunately, they were around even before the GDA

came into existence and are partly the reason why we came to be in the first place.'

'Is that the explanation why the GDA are reluctant to rile them?'

'Partly, but strange as it may seem, the Klatt actually assist in keeping the peace by policing a couple of other aggressive races in that arm of the galaxy.'

'Oh, joy – more troublemakers,' said Andy, shrugging. 'I sometimes think it would have been better if Ed and I had failed and Earth could have carried on in blissful ignorance of all the cantankerous politicking going on around us. But then again, wearing my engineer's hat, the technology we've gained is bloody mind-boggling.'

'It is – indeed it is.'

Andy stopped his inspection and smirked at Bache.

'Can tell you've spent time with James Dewey,' he chuckled.

'Ah, yes – the complications of learning a new language,' Bache nodded. 'Picking up the speech habits of others.'

'You learnt English a lot quicker than I learnt Ellinika, so I'm certainly not going to criticise.'

'James told me Ellinika was spoken on Earth.'

'Yeah,' said Andy, giving up on the inspection and sitting in the airlock door with Bache. 'It's vaguely similar to Ancient Greek. The grammar and spellings have evolved a bit, but it shows that first contact was thousands of years before we met you guys.'

'I've seen images of what you call hieroglyphics in the Earth region called Egypt. That's originally a written language of a race from what you call the Scutum-Crux arm. They were almost wiped out when their star went nova unexpectedly a long time ago.'

'The legend of the ancients?' Andy asked.

'Ah, yes – you know of it?'

'I read up on it the first time we went to Dasos. It seems your whole society is based on that belief.'

'Yes, the few survivors roamed the galaxy seeding human DNA on promising planets, to ensure the species wouldn't be compromised by one rogue event again.'

'You believe it?'

'The DNA evidence is pretty compelling.'

Cleo appeared suddenly in front of them and startled Bache. Not because of her unexpected arrival, but, this time, she sported a full goth look in a black and purple miniskirt with knee-length buckled platform boots. White make-up with black eye liner and lipstick made her seem a little menacing.

'Well,' said Bache, his eyes wide, 'that look will certainly go down well in Klatt space.'

Cleo beamed.

'We have an answer from Dasos,' she said and as quickly as she had appeared, she disappeared again.

'Make us work for it, why don't you?' said Andy, as they both stood and made their way towards the tube lift.

9

CELL ON A NEW KLATT WARSHIP

DURING THE SECOND SLEEP PERIOD, Ed was woken by a loud *thump* causing his bed to vibrate and alarms to sound out in the corridor.

Have they just hit something? he thought, as the ship juddered for a second time. He sat up and listened for a moment and was just about to lie back down when a loud *crack* made him jump. This one came from much nearer and was followed by raised voices and laser fire.

'Fuck,' said Ed out loud. 'They're either having a mutiny or they're being boarded.'

He stared at the cell door as the noise of a gunfight got disturbingly close, before a laser weapon report followed by a scream sounded right outside his cell.

I'm hoping this is Andy with a detachment of GDA marines, he thought, as it went quiet again outside. He could hear distant weapons fire, but nothing close now. The door clicked and swung open.

'Ah, shit,' he said, as two soldiers bundled in with guns up. They wore different uniforms to the ones he was used to and had distinctly lower and narrower foreheads. They indicated for him to stand and follow. He wrapped himself in the coarse blanket and was escorted quickly out into the corridor where a surprised Pol was also being shepherded from her adjacent cell.

They staggered as the ship lurched alarmingly, and this time even the soldiers appeared nervous as they recovered their balance. A distinct breeze began sucking down the corridor and their captors began shouting for them to pick up the pace.

Both Ed and Pol had to tread carefully to avoid cutting their bare feet on the shrapnel from the earlier gunfight.

'What's happening?' asked Pol, as the breeze began picking up and the ship juddered again.

'Hull breach,' said Ed. 'We need to get behind a bulk-head door or in a—'

One of the soldiers barged into Ed before he could finish the sentence, pushing him sideways through a small hatch in the wall. Pol followed similarly in an ungainly jumble of arms and legs. The two soldiers quickly joined them and as Ed picked himself up, he realised it was indeed the lifeboat he was about to mention.

The last soldier sealed the small airlock hatch before uncovering and punching the release toggle. The tiny vessel blasted away from the cruiser, causing them all to collapse in a heap again and then they lost the larger ship's artificial gravity and found themselves on the float.

'Woah,' shouted Ed, as he hit the ceiling and rebounded into Pol and one of the soldiers. 'Grab a seat and strap in as best you can, Pol.'

Both the soldiers were doing the same and Ed could

see by the expressions on their faces that this had not been part of the plan. Wherever they were supposed to take them, this wasn't it.

Once settled and strapped in, Ed peered out the small porthole just above and to the left of him. The lifeboat had stabilised and was definitely heading in a specific direction, as he just caught a glimpse of the larger ship now in two pieces spewing debris and gasses as it slipped away behind them.

The two soldiers were clicking and hissing at each other in the strange Klatt language. He dared not activate his DOVI so had no idea what they were saying. Determining what just happened was pure speculation, but he knew Klatt society was split into several distinct cabals that routinely disagreed with each other.

'I can't see a planet out there,' said Pol, stretching up in her uncomfortable human-designed seat and peeking out the porthole.

'If there is one, it'll be in front and not visible,' said Ed, wiggling his ice-cold toes to try and get some feeling back in them.

'Why isn't there a screen there then?' she asked, pointing to the front. 'At least we'd know where we're going.'

'That's where the heat shield has to be,' Ed replied, with a shrug.

'Oh, yes, bugger,' she said, as she realised what a dumb question that was.

'Don't worry, I won't tell Andy,' he said, as the attitude jets outside rattled like a machine gun, turning the small craft onto a slightly different trajectory.

The gloom in the tiny cabin was suddenly brighter as light shone through the porthole and reflected off the white walls.

'Planet,' said Ed, his eyes meeting Pol's. 'Let's just hope it's an oxygen-rich atmosphere.'

'With solid ground,' added Pol, her eyes wide with worry. 'I hate water.'

The *bang* as the heat shield covers ejected made them all jump, including the soldiers. The brightness in the window soon turned to orange as the heat shield did its job and as they watched nervously, trails of sparks flashed past as they fell into an atmosphere at many times the speed of sound.

Ed could see the relief on Pol's face at the sudden whine of the antigrav motor coming alive and they were pushed hard into their seats as it began to scrub off the lethal plunge. He felt it traversing as its small onboard computer sought a dry level landing spot. This went on for several minutes before a different whine of the struts deploying made them all brace themselves back in their seats.

The thump when it came was lighter than Ed expected and unlike last time he landed in a lifeboat, the vessel remained upright. The silence was almost complete once the antigrav had wound down and gone quiet, just the faint ticking of the cooling heat shield and motor.

Ed was initially concerned as the soldier nearest the airlock hatch went straight for the opening handle. But he reasoned as they were also oxygen-breathing mammals and had a lot more of an idea where they were, then it was probably safe to assume they knew what they were doing.

He still held his breath though and was relieved as a warm breeze washed over him as the hatch dropped open. Sniffing it tentatively, he found it was indeed breathable and smelt slightly of the seaside.

As he helped Pol release her belts and climb up to the hatch, he also noticed the gravity was lower than on the previous two ships, but still slightly higher than Earth's. It was easier going once on the outside as there were hand holds extending down one side of the craft. Ed looked around as he descended the four metres to the ground.

They were on a rocky hilltop with far-reaching views. An ocean was visible in one direction, which explained the seaside smell. An impressive mountain range stretched across the skyline in the other, its snow-covered peaks piercing the wispy clouds lazily hanging almost stationary above.

'Did you bring your snowboard?' said Pol, following Ed's gaze over to the mountains.

'No, I'm a skier, Pol,' replied Ed. 'Unlike Andy, I like to look elegant on the pistes.'

'Is that what you were when you face-planted in front of the café in Val d'Isère a few weeks ago?' she said, keeping a completely straight face.

'I didn't see you having a go.'

'They didn't have any boots that would fit a Callametan, or gloves for that matter,' she said, holding her three-fingered hands up.

'Excuses, excuses.'

A shout from one of the soldiers caught their attention. He indicated they were to follow him, as the other soldier fell in behind.

Ed found it impossible to read their expressions, so had no idea if they were amongst friends who'd been trying to save them or if it was a frying pan and fire situation. He considered they hadn't got much choice in the matter as he didn't want to harm these Klatt men until he knew what their actual motives were.

On the plus side, they hadn't threatened them in any way. Technically they had saved their lives. The planet they were now on was a bit warmer and Ed could feel his toes again. He just wished he had some footwear.

There were twin suns getting slowly higher on the horizon, one decidedly bigger and redder than the other. Ed was pleased that at least it wasn't going to get dark and cold for a while, and as the leading soldier seemed to be following directions from a handheld device, then perhaps they were going to be amongst civilisation before too long.

10

THE STARSHIP GABRIEL SKIRTING KLATT
SPACE

'Do they actually have any commercial vessels, or are they all military?' asked Andy, glancing over at Bache and pointing at the holomap. 'There's got to be hundreds of ships up there and they're all openly displaying serious weaponry.'

'That's the Klatts for you,' said Bache, shrugging. 'No unarmed commercial traffic comes anywhere near here.'

'I'm not surprised,' said Rayl, looking up from her console. 'It's like gun-fest on steroids. There are shuttles with battleship-size lasers hanging off them.'

'You just make sure you have an emergency jump plotted,' said Bache, reaching over and patting Phil on the shoulder. 'They'll be on you like angry hornets if you're detected.'

Phil nodded and grimaced.

'Can you scan all the larger vessels hangars, Rayl?' asked Andy. 'See if we can find that stolen Uly shuttle, now we've got the exact schematics there's only going to be one of those here.'

'Even if you find it, wait for the GDA ship to arrive and do its thing,' said Bache. 'The message was very clear, as to letting them attempt the diplomatic approach first.'

'How well has that gone in the past?' asked Rayl, not even looking up from her scan reports.

Bache pulled a pained expression.

'As I thought,' she said, when Bache didn't immediately answer.

'The council hold you guys in high esteem,' Bache said eventually. 'That could quickly change if you were to alter the status quo here. The GDA have mostly kept the Klatt races quiet over the centuries. There have been a few minor skirmishes from time to time, I'll admit, but they mostly spend their time quarrelling amongst themselves and we don't get involved in that, or want to.'

'How long till they get here?' Andy asked.

'Tomorrow morning, they'll be at the border of Klatt space and requesting a communication with the Klatt High Secretary.'

'How many ships d'you think they'll send?'

'The *28*.'

'What, just one?' Andy responded, obviously taken aback. 'When you were looking for Lake on Earth, you sent three.'

'Three would appear overly aggressive,' Bache replied. 'We don't want to escalate the situation right from the start.'

'Like they did by kidnapping an innocent man and woman from their home in the middle of the night.'

'Only pride has been hurt at this stage – let's see what their Secretary has to say first. You never know, it might have been an unsanctioned operation by a rogue group that the High Secretary has no knowledge of and can be rectified in a few hours.'

'Hmm,' grumbled Andy, sitting back on his couch and crossing his arms. 'If we find out where they are, I'm going in to get them, no matter what the GDA says.'

'That's what I'm afraid of,' said Bache, shaking his head.

'Don't worry,' said Cleo, appearing next to them still in her goth outfit. 'I won't let them do anything rash.'

'Hey, whose side are you on?' Andy exclaimed.

'The side of saying alive, Andrew. If you think I'm going to let you take the *Gabriel* in amongst a thousand armed trigger-happy ships and start trouble, you're going to be very disappointed.'

'If it was Edward here, you'd be, yes, Edward, no problem, Edward, three bags full, Edward,' whinged Andy in a childish voice.

Cleo and Rayl exchanged a knowing look and Phil and Bache just rolled their eyes.

The *28* winked into the Klatt border zone at eight o'clock the next morning. The fourteen-kilometre-long super cruiser brought itself to a complete stop and hailed the High Council on Zee-Klatt III.

Everyone gathered on the *Gabriel*'s bridge to listen to the forthcoming communications. It took a few minutes before the reply came.

'This is High Secretary Zikk'La, you have some gall

calling us,' said a gruff, irritated voice. 'Come to gloat over your unlawful attack in Klatt territory yesterday, have you?'

'This is Captain Pickyrd representing the GDA High Council...'

'His first name's not Jean-Luc is it?' asked Andy, turning to Bache and getting a look of complete non-comprehension in return.

'Andy, shut up,' said Rayl, as the captain continued.

'...wish to negotiate the immediate release of Edward Virr and a Callametan citizen named Pol. We have no knowledge of any attacks yesterday or on any other day. The two GDA citizens in question were snatched by a team of uniformed Klatt personnel three days ago on the planet Earth in the Sol system.'

There were a few moments of silence from the Klatt home world, before the same voice replied.

'I'm informed that this is called humour in your region of space and not something we administer too. You will hand the prisoner known as Edward Virr back to us immediately to face his crimes against the Klatt Empire, the Callametan known as Pol may return to her home as she was arrested in error.'

They all looked at each other in confusion on the *Gabriel*'s bridge.

'What do they mean hand him back?' said Phil, glancing at Bache. 'Have the GDA gone in and done the job already?'

'No,' said Bache. 'The Klatt are experts at bullshit, this could be a ruse to confuse us.'

'We have only just arrived,' said Pickyrd. 'And the

only attack we are knowledgeable of is the one you made on Earth three days ago. Sir, are you admitting to having somehow lost our citizens?'

'I've got huge ship movement towards the border zone,' said Rayl.

They all glanced up at the holomap and sure enough, dozens of new red tracks appeared as vessels suddenly turned from their original courses and headed towards the GDA ship. One by one they began jumping into the same border sector and began approaching the huge cruiser.

'Is he just going to sit there and allow himself to be surrounded by five hundred warships?' Andy asked.

'Pickyrd won't blink,' said Bache. 'I trained him up from a recruit many years ago. He'll have an embedded jump on standby, shields up and weapon systems targeted but not charged.'

The first of the Klatt ships came to a full stop at a hundred kilometres from the *28* and waited as their numbers grew.

'The Klatt like nothing more than a sabre-rattle,' said Bache. 'Pickyrd's in free space, being courteous and unthreatening and even the Klatt know that an unprovoked attack on a GDA vessel in free space would have serious consequences. It wouldn't end well for them and result in a serious loss of face.'

Over the next few minutes, four hundred and eighty-one armed vessels had jumped in and surrounded the GDA cruiser and just as the last ones slowed to a stop, a sudden blinding flash had all four of them on the *Gabriel*'s bridge shielding their eyes.

Andy repeatedly blinked to regain his sight; he was initially confused at what the holomap was showing.

'What the fuck was that and where did all the ships go?' he blurted, as everyone else squinted at the holomap in confusion.

The momentary silence that followed on the *Gabriel*'s bridge was quickly terminated by everyone trying to talk at once.

'Ancients help us,' stammered Bache, his face turning white as he realised the true horror of what they had just witnessed.

The other three on the bridge quickly shut up and turned to him, hoping upon hope that what they had just seen was some sort of illusion.

'Did – did they just explode?' said Andy, asking the question no one else wanted to.

'I think I'm going to be sick,' said Rayl, her hand over her mouth and a tear running down her cheek. 'How could a fourteen–kilometre-long ship just vaporise?'

'The Klatt fleet was completely destroyed too,' said Phil, his hands visibly shaking as he looked over at Bache.

'The radiation levels and scale of destruction indicate the cruiser's dark matter reactor exploded without warning,' said Cleo, sombrely.

'That's impossible,' said Bache, as he flopped back on his couch and stared at the ceiling. 'There are hundreds of fail-safes on our ships to eradicate that scenario.' He turned towards Andy. 'This just escalated beyond all proportion.'

11

HILLSIDE ON AN UNKNOWN PLANET

THE SOLDIERS LED them off the hilltop and down a narrow trail towards the rising suns. Ed was glad of the warmth on his face, but his lack of footwear slowed him considerably. Pol, however, had tougher soles and was able to move along with much less discomfort.

Their escorts had little sympathy though and provided not aggressive but continual encouragement to move as quickly as possible. Their nervous eyes constantly scanned the skies for an unknown threat that only they were a party to.

They'd just dropped down beneath the treeline when the lead soldier stopped suddenly and stared at his hand-held device. He turned and a brief conversation with his colleague led to them becoming somewhat elated over something. They did a version of a human high five, embraced and even did a little dance. Ed realised that their teeth-baring wasn't anything to be concerned about, it was a Klatt interpretation of a smile.

'Something's just happened that they're pleased about,' he said, stopping to rub the soles of his feet.

'A nice comfortable cabin with soft carpets and a hot meal would be just perfect right now. Perhaps it's that,' said Pol, trying to look positive.

'I just thought, has your DOVI got an inbuilt translator?' Ed asked.

Pol nodded.

'You told me not to use it though.'

'That was with the last lot of captors. I hadn't thought about trying it with them,' said Ed, nodding at the still celebrating soldiers.

'You go first,' said Pol. 'You're better with this stuff than me.'

Ed shrugged, took a last look to ensure the soldiers weren't looking before he closed his eyes and tentatively felt around. No head-splitting pain materialised and when he opened his eyes again, their two captors hadn't reacted at all. He quickly turned on his inbuilt translator. It took a few seconds to recognise their particular Klatt dialect before he could understand what they were saying.

'…whole fleet?'

'Almost five hundred and the GDA will be blamed.'

'Our orders haven't changed then?'

'No, their bodies won't be on a Ralf ship now, but must still be discovered in Ralf territory.'

Ed reacted slightly at the last statement, but was lucky as neither of the soldiers noticed it.

'Is the facility near?'

'Yes.'

'How far?'

'It's down in the next valley.'

'Right, we'll take them there. Stay friendly and don't give them any indication of what's about to happen. We'll kill them down by the river so we don't have to carry the bodies too far.'

Ed immediately decommissioned their weapons and keeping a smile on his face told Pol what he had learned. Her eyes widened, but she sensibly didn't react to give the game away.

'Wait till we're walking again and I'll take the front one and you the rear,' he said. 'I'll accidentally stumble into him, that will be the sign. Move quickly and lethally.'

'Two-faced bastards have it coming,' she hissed.

Ed smiled nervously.

'You sound just like Andy again.'

'I'll take that as a compliment,' said Pol. 'I think.'

The soldiers finished their celebration and indicated for them to continue as before, the one with the device leading with the other bringing up the rear.

Ed waited and watched. He could see that the scaly Klatt skin appeared quite thick and rugged, so he envisioned needing some sort of club or weapon to subdue his opponent. Moments later, as they rounded a corner under a rocky outcrop, he noticed a number of assorted boulders that over time had dropped from the cliffs above. He coughed to ensure Pol was paying attention, pretended to slip on some of the gravel and piled into the back of the leading soldier. Snatching up a fist-sized rock with a sharp edge, he pummelled the soldier on the side of the neck until he stopped moving.

Turning quickly to see how Pol was faring, he found

her sitting on the second soldier's body, dabbing blood away from a cut eye with her sleeve.

'A lucky punch,' she said. 'Before I snapped his scrawny neck.'

Ed nodded, took a deep breath and looked around.

'We need to search them and hide the bodies,' he said, grimacing at the hard rocky ground. He picked up the small tablet the soldier had been using. It showed a map of the terrain with the track they were on clearly marked and leading downhill towards a river below. 'We were lucky,' he said, glancing up at Pol. 'The river's only a few hundred metres further.'

'Does it tell us what planet this is?' Pol asked, finally stopping the bleeding and standing back up.

'It might if I can work out how the thing operates.'

'Give it here,' she said. 'You see if either of their boots will fit you.'

Both pairs were several sizes too large, but Ed ripped one of the blankets from the cells they were still wearing into strips and wrapped them around his sore feet. It wasn't ideal, but the wide boots would now stay on and were decidedly better than bare feet. He had more success with the clothing, finding that a better fit than the boots. Pol on the other hand was not so lucky and looked at Ed with disdain.

'Fucking two-armed freaks,' she mumbled, as she settled for tying her blanket around her waist and draping the other soldier's jacket over her four shoulders.

'Hey, it's not so bad,' said Ed. 'It could have been an ice planet.'

They dragged the bodies off the trail and hid them in

amongst some low bushes. Ed reactivated the weapons and gave one to Pol, who immediately started bashing it on the ground.

'What are you doing? You might need that,' he said, staring.

'Trigger guard,' she replied without looking up. 'Can't get my fat fingers inside it.'

She finally succeeded in breaking the guard at one end, then she bent it back and forth at the other until the metal fractured. She glanced up and grinned, tossing the broken guard nonchalantly over her shoulder.

'Happy now?' he said.

'Eminently,' she replied.

He turned and began to trek down the path again, rolling his eyes as he went.

'I've never known anyone learn a new language quite as thoroughly as you,' he called over his shoulder.

'One had some elocutional help from Cleopatra,' she said. 'She gives me homework.'

'The swearing lessons have gone exceptionally well.'

'Bollocks.'

Ed chuckled to himself as they trudged downhill.

The river running through the bottom of the valley was close and they stood glancing up and downstream only five minutes later, after emerging from the trees. The path they were on split here, one way upstream and the other down.

'Which way then?' asked Pol, nodding at the tablet in Ed's hand.

'Downstream, I suppose,' he said. 'Up just goes back into the hills we've descended from but then again, there's a weird blanked out area a few kilometres downstream. It's hatched with red lines like a no go area.'

Pol looked at the screen.

'There's nothing in the menu that'll tell you what it is?' she asked.

'I don't know – I'm scared to start pressing things in case I lose the map.'

'Let's go towards whatever it is, but not on the path. We can conceal ourselves in the trees once we get closer.'

'Okay, we'll drop off the path about a kilometre short and approach carefully. It could be some dangerous flora in that area, or a radiation leak or—'

'A holiday resort, with comfortable beds and margaritas,' interjected Pol.

'Even that,' said Ed, smirking. 'You really have developed Andy's sense of humour, you know.'

He looked downstream. 'Come on, let's go see what this strange hatched area is.'

12

THE STARSHIP GABRIEL SKIRTING KLATT SPACE

ANDY HAD NEVER SEEN Bache look so worried. His face was ashen as he made a report and sent it off to Dasos. Other than that, it was eerily quiet on the *Gabriel*'s bridge as everyone sat and tried to come to terms with what they'd just witnessed.

'How long?' he asked, as Bache finished.

'For what?' Bache asked, his haunted face catching Andy's look.

'A reply.'

Bache sighed and stared back at the holomap.

'A day or two, I suppose.'

'What will they do?' Rayl asked.

'What can they do?' said Phil. 'There was no attack – yes, the Klatt had almost five hundred ships surrounding the cruiser, but none of them fired and they were all destroyed too.'

'Is there no way it could've been an accident?' Andy asked. 'Perhaps a faulty reactor?'

'The *28* has been in commission for twenty-four years.

I think any reactor problem would have surfaced long before now,' Bache answered. 'But, as I said before, the systems in place to eradicate any remote possibility of this occurring are huge and completely fail-safe. My father was part of the design team on those ships and even he used to moan they went way over the top with safety and multiple layers of redundancy.'

'Sabotage then?' said Rayl.

'It's the only thing I can't discount,' said Bache. 'Even so, that would be a huge undertaking and would necessitate the cooperation of many levels of personnel. You just can't wander into the engineering decks of a starship with a nuclear device. Because that's what it would take – even that would have to be inside all the containment fields and there's four of them, all capable of protecting the core from a nuclear detonation.'

'It was lucky they weren't in system,' said Phil. 'If they'd been in orbit around one of the Klatt planets the death toll would have been in the billions.'

Andy thought for a moment before speaking.

'Were those four hundred-odd Klatt ships from multiple clans or from just one?' he asked, angling his question towards Rayl.

'How can we tell?' she said.

'Pickyrd was conversing with High Secretary Zikk'La,' said Bache. 'He's the current representative of the Klatt nations and is from the Grondalle clan. They've been the most influential and largest clan for many generations and it's unheard of for as long as GDA records go back for the High Secretary to be from any other clan.'

'Well, if all those ships were Grondalle,' said Andy,

'they've just lost a considerable chunk of their power base.'

'And face,' said Bache. 'Which is everything to the Klatt.'

'So, this could all be about an attempted Klatt coup?' asked Phil.

'They're sneaky little shits,' said Bache. 'So, I wouldn't put it past them.'

'It's all just conjecture isn't it?' said Andy after a pause. 'We can sit out here and invent theories till the cows come home. It doesn't make any of them right. We're here to retrieve Ed and Pol and not to get involved in any Klatt clan infighting.'

'Erm, w-what if they were on one of those Klatt ships?' said Rayl, her voice wavering as she said it.

They all turned to face her.

'Well, someone had to say it,' she said quietly.

'They weren't,' said Cleo loudly, making everyone jump and appearing sitting cross-legged on the bridge floor. 'None of the Klatt ships destroyed had a Uly ship onboard or anyone with a DOVI.'

'You can detect a DOVI even when it's deactivated?' Andy asked.

'Yes.'

'What if they had them enveloped with a shield of some kind?' questioned Phil.

'No internal shields apart from their reactor cores.'

'So, you're saying they're not in Klatt space?'

'It seems not.'

'What about planets?' Bache said.

'Planets are a different matter,' Cleo said. 'I would

need to get closer and orbit them a couple of times and even then with certain rock types and if they were being held underground…' She shook her head slowly.

'Okay,' said Andy. 'What about all the other ships in Klatt space?'

Cleo continued shaking her head.

'I've investigated all vessels within sixty-three light years of Zee-Klatt III.'

'No Uly shuttle?'

'No Uly shuttle.'

The bridge went momentarily quiet again as they all looked up to the holomap as it panned out to include the whole Klatt region.

'Planets then,' said Bache, breaking the silence.

'How many are there?' Andy asked.

'Fourteen in Klatt space,' said Cleo. 'And thirty-seven well-guarded outposts.'

'One of which is Uskrre in the Centauri system,' said Andy, nodding at Phil. 'Where we nearly went in the *Cartella*.'

'You're welcome,' said Phil, his usual jovial inflection absent this time.

'Where do we start?' Rayl asked.

'I think we ought to wait,' said Bache, before anyone else could speak. 'See what the council decides.'

'But that could take days,' said Rayl. 'For all we know they're being tortured as we speak.'

They all turned towards Andy as, in Ed's absence, he was the captain.

'Ah shit,' he said, standing and strolling around and through the holomap. 'There must be a couple of outlying planets we could sneak around and check out while we're waiting. After all, the council aren't known for making snap decisions.'

'It's your ship, Andrew,' said Bache. 'You get caught uninvited inside Klatt-controlled space, don't expect the GDA to come bail you out this time.'

Andy glanced over at Rayl and Phil, who were both contemplating him with wide eyes.

'Cleo,' he said. 'Can you indicate two of their most outlying planets, please.'

Two worlds began flashing in red on the far side of Klatt space.

'We jump in somewhere hidden, cloak, a quick couple of orbits and out again. We need to start narrowing the playing field while the GDA juggernaut slowly grinds its wheels.'

'Aye aye, Captain,' said Phil with a wry smile. 'I'll take us in that direction.'

Rayl grinned and Bache shrugged, but neither said a word.

13

FOREST AREA ON AN UNKNOWN PLANET

THE TRAIL MARKED on the map seemed to stop at the edge of the hatched area with no continuation of it on the far side. They had done as they planned and turned into the forest a reasonable distance back from the anomaly. It made for slower going as they had to force their way through in places and to be careful where they trod to avoid making too much noise.

'It's gone very quiet,' said Pol in a low whisper as she clambered over a couple of fallen tree trunks.

'You're right,' said Ed, stopping dead still and listening. 'The ambient background of bird and animal noise is lessening as we get closer to whatever this thing is.'

No conscious decision was made, but they both continued on quietly with their eyes and ears wide open. After about ten more minutes, Ed stopped abruptly and listened.

'It's completely silent now,' he whispered back to Pol. He peered through a gap in the trees and nearly jumped out of his skin as he saw someone staring back at him. It only took a second or two before he concluded he was actually looking at a reflection of himself.

Thirty metres in front was a faintly shimmering mirrored wall of energy reflecting the forest back on itself, so unless you were right up close, the trees and forest just appeared to continue on.

He looked up to find it soared above them, curving away as if it was a dome.

'What the fuck?' said Pol from behind him as she too realised what they'd discovered. She went to push past, but Ed stuck his arm out and stopped her and pointed at the ground along the wall.

Several skeletons of birds and mammals of assorted sizes lay scattered randomly alongside the mirrored wall.

'Let's be a bit careful shall we?' he said. He bent down, picked up a stick and hurled it at the mirrored wall. The intensity of the flash had them both squinting and averting their eyes. When they looked back, the remains of the stick lay smouldering on the ground a couple of metres back from the wall.

'Best not bump against that,' he said. 'Someone really doesn't want visitors.'

'Is it some sort of defensive dome?' asked Pol, glancing left, right and then up.

'That seems a fair call considering the way it curves away in every direction,' he said, looking right. 'The trail we were on meets it back that way. If it has an entry point then it could be there.'

Pol closed her eyes and concentrated her DOVI towards the wall. She jumped back, her eyes wide open again.

'Ouch – bloody hell,' she screeched, rubbing her forehead. 'That thing bites back. Light isn't the only thing it reflects.'

They retreated back behind the treeline and made their way quietly back towards the trail. When they got there it proved Ed had been right. From their hidden vantage point within the forest, they witnessed an arched entrance or portal leading inside the dome. It was big enough to drive a truck through and the curved frame was a dark green colour to blend in with the forest. Two small black domes protruded from the top of the arch and the door itself reminded Ed of a fuzzy untuned black and white television picture. It made the same low hiss too, audible even though they were fifty metres away.

Pol glanced up at Ed expectantly and rubbed her forehead again.

'It's your turn this time,' she said. 'I almost fried my brain back there.'

Ed nodded and crouched down, ensuring he was well hidden amongst the greenery.

'Those little black domes look like camera pods to me,' he said, then closing his eyes he reached out slowly with his DOVI. He knew from Pol's experience not to go near the mirrored wall, but instead concentrated on the door and the black pods.

The technology of the doorway he found to be quite rudimentary, which surprised him. It worked similarly to an early model hangar atmospheric barrier, insomuch that if you were transmitting the correct code frequency, you would most likely pass straight through.

The pods were indeed cameras and gave a one hundred

and eighty degree view of anything approaching the entrance. Ed spent a moment finding a way to freeze the image, then tapped Pol on a shoulder and nodded towards the door.

'Come on, shall we see what's lurking in here?' he said, stepping out into the open.

Nothing happened, so Pol stood and followed as Ed warily approached the door. As he got within five metres of the arched doorway the black and white fuzziness suddenly snapped off along with the hiss and was now flat, white and opaque. He stopped abruptly, causing Pol to bump into him.

'What have you—? Oh!' she said, peering around him. 'Did you do that?'

'Don't think so,' he said, remaining still, pointing his rifle at the door and waiting to see if anything happened. It didn't.

'Ah, hang on,' he said, glancing down at his clothing. 'Move back a few paces,' he added.

They stepped backwards three paces and the fuzzy hissing barrier returned.

'Proximity detector,' he said. 'Probably sewn into the Klatt uniforms. Come on.'

They approached again; the doorway snapped to its opaque state once more. Stopping and standing to one side, just in case something came roaring through, Ed lifted an arm and, holding his breath, touched the white barrier with his forefinger. The finger sunk through silently. Retracting it and inspecting an unharmed finger closely, he reasoned it was safe to have a peek inside.

'Well, I'll be,' he said, as he leaned forward and popped his head through. 'Would you look at all that?'

Pol leaned past Ed and did the same, her eyes going from a look of confusion to realisation as she grasped the scale of what she was seeing.

'Woah – fuck me,' she exclaimed.

14

THE STARSHIP GABRIEL, CLOAKED AND INSIDE KLATT SPACE

FOR THE PAST three days the *Gabriel* had been undergoing discreet flybys of a few of the outer Klatt worlds and had so far found no sign of the Uly vessel or Ed and Pol. The atmosphere on the ship was decidedly gloomy, even with Cleo attempting to keep everyone cheerful.

'What do you call a factory that makes good products?' she said, as she appeared in front of Phil and Bache on the bridge, dressed in a jester's outfit.

They both glanced up at her and raised their eyebrows in a lazy, exasperated manner.

'A satisfactory,' she said, as an orchestral fanfare following the punchline sounded around the bridge.

Bache rolled his eyes at Phil.

'Boom – tish,' Phil mumbled, half-heartedly.

'Cleo, I know you're trying to be helpful,' said Bache, 'but you're—'

'—just being trying,' interrupted Phil without taking his eyes off his control icons. 'Only talk to us if you have something critical to the operation to tell us.'

'Well actually I have as a matter of fact,' she said, sticking her nose in the air and looking at them out of the corner of her eye.

'And that is?' Bache asked, not convinced she was telling the truth as the bells on her hat had jingled as she said it.

'I'm receiving a coded transmission from Dasos as we speak. If you just give me a – oh dear.'

'Just spit it out,' said Phil, thinking she was still messing them around.

'Erm, it's in holographic form and you're not going to like it.'

'Just…'

The holomap suddenly disappeared and the image of a senior GDA naval officer materialised, flanked by two marines in full battle armour.

'That's Admiral Geltz,' Bache said, grimacing. 'Joined only a few months before me, was less experienced at just about everything and got promoted above me at every—'

Bache was cut short as the Admiral began speaking.

'Starship *Gabriel*, it is the decision of the GDA council for you to return to Dasos immediately and surrender your vessel for the purpose of the full investigation into the loss of the *28*. Retired Commander Bache Loftt must be handed over to us to face multiple charges, including treason and murder.'

'What the fuck?' said Bache.

'Failure to comply with these instructions will entail your vessel being designated as renegade. You have seventy-two hours.'

'That's complete madness,' said Bache, standing and stomping angrily around the bridge.

'What is?' asked Andy, stepping off the tube lift as he rubbed the sleep from his eyes and ran his hand through his bed hair. 'Well, what's happened? What's Cleo got me up for?' he added, turning towards Bache as he noticed Phil's nervous glance in that direction.

'Replay the message, Cleo,' Bache growled.

The hologram replayed as Andy stood and gaped.

'That's just fucking insane,' he said as it ended. He slumped into his couch and stared at the other two. 'Whoever came to that conclusion needs to be locked in a padded cell.'

'Who is that guy?' asked Phil.

'He's the new chief military advisor to the GDA Council,' said Bache. 'Part of the reason I retired was so I didn't have to cross paths with that kiss-arse again.'

'Not one of your drinking buddies then?' Andy asked.

'No, he's one of those people who doesn't care how many others' reputations and careers he tramples on to get to the top.'

'Looks like it worked,' said Andy.

'But you've retired,' said Phil. 'You're no threat to anyone. Who could possibly want to destroy your reputation now?'

'D'you want me to make a list?'

'I didn't know you had any enemies,' Andy replied.

'It doesn't matter how good a person you are, some people just love to hate and to be honest, I have uncovered a few unscrupulous individuals over the years. So, it could be any one of them, or the ones that are still alive anyway.'

'We could hypothesise about this all day,' said Phil. 'We need to make a decision about what to do.'

'We're not fucking surrendering the ship for a start,' said Andy.

'Or you,' said Phil, pointing at Bache.

'Thank you,' Bache replied, nodding at Phil and raising his eyebrows at Andy.

'Yes, yes, I agree,' said Andy, reading Bache's unasked question. 'But what I want to know is – what does being designated as renegade actually mean?'

Bache flinched and pulled a pained expression.

'Any vessel is authorised to engage and destroy a renegade ship without warning and most likely would receive a handsome reward,' he said.

'Oh, joy of joys,' said Andy, leaning back and putting his hands behind his head. 'Not only do we have the Klatt wanting to kill us all, but just about every other ship in the galaxy too.'

They all went quiet as the tube lift arrived and a smiling Rayl stepped onto the bridge.

'Morning, everyone,' she said cheerily and stopped when she noticed no one was smiling back.

'What?' she said, scanning their three stern faces.

'She's your wife,' said Phil, giving Andy a quick look and returning to concentrate on the control icons.

Bache turned away and concentrated on a spot on the wall.

Andy tried to smile, but it came across as more of a toothy grimace.

'Hello, dear.'

Rayl glared at her husband.

'What have you done?'

'Well, it's nothing we've done,' he answered, defensively. 'It's the rather unexpected reaction of the GDA.'

Cleo replayed the message as the other three watched and waited for her reaction. Surprisingly, she didn't react at all. She just stepped across to her couch, sat down and began tapping away at control icons and waking up her station.

'Looks like we're renegade then,' she said, finally, looking up and around at the other faces. 'It's not something this ship isn't familiar with after all.'

Bache nodded and sat down again.

'There's something going on here that Ed's kidnapping was just a small part of,' he said.

'And the destruction of the Klatt battle fleet was a large part,' said Phil, ruefully.

Andy sat back and crossed his arms in thought.

'Though rescuing Ed and Pol is still our priority,' said Andy, 'can I try something first?'

15

MIRRORED DOME ON AN UNKNOWN PLANET

ED DIDN'T KNOW where to look first. There was row upon row of military spacecraft parked neatly stretching off into the distance. Everything from small gunships to armed troop carriers and a multitude of other designs up to medium-sized cruisers, all the same blue-green colour and sporting the same triangular logo.

'There's hundreds of them,' said Pol, as they quickly moved away from the door and crouched down under the nearest vessel.

'More like thousands,' said Ed, making sure he reactivated the cameras outside.

'It's completely silent in here,' said Pol, listening intently. 'D'you think it's deserted?'

No sooner had she said it, they heard a low whirring that was gradually intensifying, emanating from somewhere deeper in the dome. They both quickly moved a couple of ships up the row and lay flat behind a landing strut.

They didn't have long to wait. A six-wheeled truck

swept in and stopped adjacent to the doorway. A rear door swung upwards and eight Klatt soldiers filed out, forming a defensive half circle around the door with weapons raised.

'They don't realise we're inside,' whispered Pol.

'That's weird,' Ed whispered back. 'If they'd detected us, why don't they know where we are now?'

Pol shrugged her four shoulders before flattening herself even further as the doorway appearance changed to its opaque state.

'It's not us they've detected,' she whispered, as three uniformed Klatt entered the dome.

They stopped abruptly and seemed surprised to be faced by a row of laser weapons.

'Well, well,' said Ed. 'The one on the right is Captain Groxl, he's the one who accused me of messing up his ship. They must've got in a lifeboat too.'

'But why are they being treated as the enemy?' Pol asked.

'I seem to remember talking to someone, it might have been James Dewey,' said Ed, looking at the ground in thought. 'But, anyway, if I remember rightly, the Klatt are always in a fight somewhere and if they don't have a common enemy, then the different clans squabble amongst themselves.'

'D'you think that's all this is?'

'Not for a minute, there's something else going on here. As far as Groxl was concerned, it was just a simple case of revenge. These other guys, however, seem to have an agenda concerning something entirely different and I have no idea what that might be.'

'Could this be an invasion fleet and your abduction was designed to keep the GDA busy looking for you and away from this corner of space?'

'Shit, no. If I was the council president, then maybe – but I can't imagine the GDA council giving a rat's fart about my well-being.'

They watched as the three newcomers were disarmed and handcuffed. It was obvious from Groxl's body language that he wasn't best pleased with the welcome. Several times he pointed at the ships, but the speech was just a murmur and too far away for the translator to pick up the conversation.

Once the three of them were loaded aboard the vehicle, with Groxl continuing to snarl and gesticulate at his captors until he disappeared from sight, the truck turned and whined off in the direction it had come.

Ed glanced up at the ship they were sheltering beneath.

'I'm hoping we can get inside one of these,' he said, stretching his neck to ensure the six-wheeled truck was well out of sight. 'Perhaps one of the larger ones, as they'll have cabins and a stock of food and water.'

'So long as it isn't any more of that revolting lumpy crap,' said Pol, putting a finger in her mouth and making a fake retching sound.

'I quite agree, Pol,' said Ed, standing and stretching his back. 'I won't be making any reservations at any Klatt brasserie in the future, no matter how many Michelin stars it has.'

He pointed down the line of ships towards some larger ones in the distance.

'Let's try one of those,' he said, moving off warily in that direction.

'That's the direction they went in though,' Pol answered, nervously.

Ed looked back at her and shrugged.

'We're not going to achieve anything hiding out here,' he said. 'Even if the others did find this planet, wherever it is, I'm sure this dome is cloaked from anything up in orbit.'

'We could take one of the ships.'

'We could, yes, that's true,' he said, nodding. 'But we'd need to power down this dome first and then we'd have the problem of learning the controls of a Klatt vessel. They'd be after us in seconds with experienced pilots – we most likely wouldn't even make orbit and be dead or back in a lifeboat saying, "that wasn't a very good plan."'

They continued and Pol went quiet for a few moments before speaking again.

'I can't think of any other way of getting away from here,' she said, sounding despondent.

Ed stopped and turned to face her.

'We'll be fine, Pol,' he said, placing his hands on her upper shoulders. 'The first thing we need is some rest and something to eat. Then, when we're fresh, we can think more clearly and make some plans, okay?'

'Okay.'

She stepped forward and hugged him tight with all four arms.

'Er, Pol – Pol, can't breathe,' he croaked.

'Oh, sorry,' she said, releasing her arms. 'Don't know my own strength sometimes.'

'I know you're frightened, Pol, and you've just had to kill someone with your bare hands. So, it's far from a normal day.'

He brushed her hair out of her eyes and kissed her on her forehead before turning and pointing at a large menacing vessel a couple of hundred metres away.

'That one there,' he said, grabbing one of her left hands and setting off towards it.

It seemed even bigger close up, with four enormous antigrav drives hanging off each corner and dozens of weapon pods dangling threateningly from almost every area of the hull. Ed could see several airlocks and a large, probably a hangar door, towards the rear of the ship.

'It's the size of the *Gabriel*,' said Pol.

'Yeah, it's got to be five hundred metres at least,' Ed admitted, crouching in the shadow of the smaller gunship beside it.

Its struts had sunk several metres into the ground, which Ed was glad about as it made getting up to any of the airlocks a little easier. He closed his eyes and felt across to see if he could penetrate the ship's systems.

'Bugger,' he said, sighing noisily.

'They're shielded,' said Pol. 'I can't penetrate it either.'

'There must be an airlock manual override on the outside somewhere,' he said. 'To aid rescue teams.'

Ed approached the ship cautiously, eyeing the rows of cannon barrels nervously as if they would snap towards them at any moment. He reached the vessel and noticed a small recessed rectangle to the right of the airlock he'd chosen. Stretching up he realised it was still just out of reach.

'Bugger, again,' he said, this time in a whisper.

'May I be of assistance?' asked Pol, cupping two of her hands together to form a step.

He smiled and stepped up. Then leaning into the hull, he found the recess and prodded it. Just when he thought nothing was going to happen it slid to one side, revealing a red handle with an arrow indicating to turn it anti-clockwise. He reached in to turn it, but before he did the airlock beside him sunk inwards and slid silently upwards.

'What the…?' he muttered, almost falling backwards.

He peered around the corner into the airlock and found a hand weapon of some kind pointing at his face, behind which stood a rather surprised looking Klatt soldier.

Ah, crap, he thought, not daring to move.

16

THE OFFICE OF ADMIRAL GELTZ, DASOS, PRASINOS SYSTEM

ADMIRAL GELTZ GLANCED up from his tablet as the ping of a holographic icon appeared in front of him. He quickly checked his office door was closed and his privacy shield activated before, touching the icon with his index finger, he sat back nervously to take the private call.

'Has Loftt received the message?' asked an anonymous electronically digitised voice.

'He will have by now,' replied Geltz.

'You're sure he'll ignore it?'

'Most likely – Loftt has never been one for by the book.'

'If for some reason he does turn up, just make sure there are no survivors or wreckage.'

'Understood.'

The line went dead and Geltz took a deep gulp of air. He hadn't realised he'd been holding his breath and he sat for a few moments staring at the wall, the fleeting image they showed him three days ago of his terrified youngest daughter chained to a cell wall forever seared into his mind.

17

THE STARSHIP GABRIEL, APPROACHING THE PRASINOS SYSTEM

'Dasos, this is the starship *Gabriel* reporting as requested,' said Andy. 'Permission to enter the Prasinos system and approach Dasos.'

'Permission granted, *Gabriel*,' came the reply. 'Please remain uncloaked, shields and weapons powered down and follow this course to dock 138d on Vasi Stathmos station.'

'Roger that, Dasos,' said Andy, watching Cleo as she sat opposite him with her eyes closed and concentrating hard.

The *Gabriel* slipped into the Prasinos system at point seven light and followed the designated course to the letter. The crew, all on the bridge, sat and watched the holomap intently as the ship powered through a mostly deserted region of the system.

For ten minutes nothing happened, until everything happened. Twelve incoming red missile trails suddenly lit up the holomap, all converging on the *Gabriel*. They were so close; it only took three seconds before detonation. Cleo made a concerted effort in changing course and raising shields to avoid destruction, but twelve of the GDA's largest nuclear warheads all discharging within a handful of kilometres of the ship had only one outcome. The *Gabriel* vaporised instantly, leaving nothing in that region of space except for an expanding cloud of radioactive dust.

Cleo opened her eyes and puffed out her cheeks.

'Don't ask me to do that too often,' she said, staring round at the still shocked faces surrounding her. 'You wouldn't believe how much computing power a hologram of that size and that distance takes.'

'I can believe it,' said Bache, his eyes still fixed on an empty area of space where he would have died had he trusted his old employers.

'Well, that was a good call, Andy,' said Phil, the colour beginning to return to his face. 'At least we know now where we stand.'

'Nowhere really,' said Rayl. 'Everyone in the galaxy wants us dead.'

'As far as everyone in the galaxy is concerned, we are dead,' said Bache. 'Which in a way is a good thing as they're no longer looking for us or expecting us.'

'He's right,' said Andy. 'From now on we have to consider everything we do as a black op.'

'Ello, ello,' said Rayl, suddenly sitting up and touching icons busily. 'What's a Klatt ship doing there?'

She pointed up at the holomap as a red target appeared travelling very fast away from where the *Gabriel* hologram was destroyed. As everyone looked up at it, it jumped and disappeared again.

'It was a Klatt cruiser,' said Cleo. 'Fonias class and, oh that's interesting.'

All four heads on the bridge turned towards her.

'It's the same ship that threatened us, the one that Ed messed up when he first got his DOVI.'

'What, the one just before we went to Andromeda?' said Andy.

Cleo nodded.

'Are you sure?'

She gave him a withering look.

'Okay, sorry, yes, you're sure.'

'Can we track it?' Bache asked.

'It embedded the jump but Klatt technology, even their newer kit, still has a noisy exhaust,' said Rayl.

'Follow them,' said Andy. 'It's gotta have something to do with what happened to Ed and it's our only lead.'

The cloaked Theo Mitera class starship moved forward from its previous static position just outside the Prasinos system, spun around on its axis, then using its four massive Alma drives achieved point nine light in less than eight seconds before jumping unseen into an unpopulated system one hundred and twenty-seven light years away.

'I didn't think the Klatt had cloaking kit,' said Rayl, as an empty holomap faced them on arrival.

'They shouldn't,' said Bache. 'But that Grondalle ship certainly does and I want to know how they got it.'

'How do you know it was a Grondalle clan ship?' Andy asked.

'The Fonias class cruisers are all Grondalle, as with the

majority of their fleet,' Bache replied. 'To give the Klatt society some clarity, the Grondalles are like queen bees in a hive. There's not many of them and the other two lesser clans are like the workers and drones and do all the grafting.'

'What are they called?' Rayl asked.

'Bekon and Spleeta.'

'Grondalle, Bekon and Spleeta,' muttered Andy. 'Sounds like a dodgy firm of lawyers.'

'Or real estate agents,' growled Phil.

Bache glanced at Andy with raised eyebrows when he chuckled and winked at Phil.

Noticing Bache's unspoken question, Andy decided he'd better explain.

'He's had a thing about them since a California agent tried to sell him a house next to some beautiful open countryside,' said Andy.

'Yeah, so?' said Bache, shrugging.

'That countryside had just got permission for California's newest and largest spaceport,' said Phil, through gritted teeth.

'Ah, now I see,' said Bache, smirking back at Andy.

'There they are,' said Rayl. 'They've just uncloaked to jump again.'

'Have they detected us?' asked Andy.

'With that ship, doubtful,' said Bache, watching the red icon on the holomap wink out of the system again. He glanced across at Rayl with a questioning look.

'Well, I never,' she said, looking over at Andy and then back down at her console again. 'They've just jumped to the Alpha Centauri system.'

'You're kidding,' said Andy. 'Bloody hell we might actually be getting somewhere.'

He turned and pointed at Phil.

'Take us there, jumping chef.'

Phil smiled at his new epithet and touched the blue jump icon he already had programmed.

The *Gabriel* winked into Alpha Centauri in between the two main stars and the red dwarf, immediately scanning for the Klatt cruiser.

'There,' said Rayl, pointing at the holomap again.

The red icon was travelling at point six two five light and heading straight past the red dwarf and towards Uskrre. The planet's ring of defence satellites showed up clearly, spanning the globe.

'Hello, old friend,' said Andy. 'Not quite such a threat to us this time are you?'

Phil smiled as they followed at a distance and waited to see what the cruiser would do.

18

MIRRORED DOME ON AN UNKNOWN PLANET

ED CLOSED his eyes to concentrate on quickly deactivating the pistol and tensed as the sudden pulse of an energy weapon crackled. When nothing struck him, he opened his eyes again to find the soldier, a shocked expression on his face, dropping to his knees and about to topple forward on top of him. He stuck out an arm, caught him and pushed him back into the airlock.

'You see,' said Pol, brandishing her laser rifle in her other two arms and nudging Ed up over the threshold. 'Four arms can save your life.'

Ed quickly stood up inside the airlock and peered nervously through the inner door's porthole window.

'Let's hope he was alone and didn't have time to call that in,' he said, sticking the side of his face against the glass and checking left and right.

Once happy the soldier didn't have backup standing just inside, he turned, lay down on his front and pulled Pol up into the airlock with him.

'Was that a stun shot?' he asked, nodding at the body slumped on the floor.

Pol nodded.

'Hmm – we have a problem then,' he sighed.

'Can't we just stick him in a security cell?' Pol said. 'A ship of this size is bound to have one.'

'We could, but who's going to cook and feed him? We could be holed up on this ship for days, maybe longer.'

Pol grimaced and chewed on her lip while she searched the unconscious body.

'He has the same uniform as the guys we disposed of,' she said.

'Yeah, Groxl seemed pretty surprised to see them here. From what I remember reading about Klatt politics, there are three factions, one dominant one and a couple of lesser ones who provide the majority of the labour.'

'Which one's which?' asked Pol. 'I mean, is Groxl one of the dominant ones?'

'Who knows? He certainly didn't look very dominant with a laser rifle pointed at his head.'

Pol pulled a pair of cuffs from one of the soldier's pockets, dragged him over and secured one of his arms to a weightless handle on the wall furthest from the airlock control.

Ed meanwhile checked the corridor again and pressed the slowly flashing green button next to the inner door. Purple lights began flashing and the outer door powered down from inside the hull and sealed with a hiss. Almost immediately the inner one lit up around its perimeter and slowly slid left to right, disappearing inside the bulkhead.

They both waited and listened, weapons at the ready.

Nothing stirred after a few moments, so Ed risked a peek and stuck his head out. Glancing left and right he found nothing waiting for them.

'Smells like your new car in here,' Pol said, stepping out and deciding to go left as most of the rest of the ship was in that direction.

'Have you made sure he has nothing on him to call for help?' said Ed, nodding at the unconscious soldier.

'Yeah, he had most things in this,' she replied, holding up a small backpack. 'Including a small location transmitter.'

'Is it still transmitting?'

Pol nodded. 'I thought it might flag somewhere if it suddenly stopped.'

'Probably would,' said Ed, scanning it with his DOVI and then sweeping the remainder of the ship. 'It's the only one on the ship though.'

'They might have placed a caretaker on each of the larger ships and these keep an eye on them to ensure they do their rounds.'

'Possible,' he said. 'Best we keep it moving around then, for the time being.'

They passed a right turn before reaching a closed bulkhead door at the end of the corridor with a familiar green flashing button recessed into the wall. Pol pressed it this time and it opened into a large hangar crammed full of ground vehicles.

'Troop carriers,' said Ed, peering up the ramp of the closest one.

Four rows of battle armour hung above each seat.

'This really is an invasion fleet, isn't it?' said Pol.

'Looks that way,' Ed replied. 'For use where though?'

'Let's find the bridge – perhaps the computers can answer a few of our questions.'

They hurried across the hangar and exited through a rear door that delved deeper into the ship. Emerging in a wider corridor than before, they again headed left towards the bow of the ship.

'We need to go up a few levels,' said Ed, feeling around with his DOVI again. 'There's a central space near the top of the ship that could be what we're looking for.'

Pol stopped suddenly and pulled open a door on the right.

'Stairs,' she said. 'I don't know if any of the elevators would be powered up. Judging by how stuffy it is in here, even environmental is set at its minimum, so I imagine the majority of systems are offline to save power.'

'Up three levels and go left,' said Ed, following close behind.

He instinctively knew they were in the right place as soon as they exited the stairway. The surroundings were plusher and perhaps meant for more senior officers. Pol stuck her head round one of the smaller doors leading off the carpeted corridor.

'Cabin,' she said. 'Nicely appointed.'

'Officers,' said Ed, nodding and pointing at the larger double doors at the far end of the corridor. 'I'll put money on that's the bridge.'

This time the button for the bigger doors was flashing red and did nothing when Ed pressed it.

'The bridge is kept locked, even from the caretaker,' said Pol, rolling her eyes.

'Stops them pressing anything sensitive in their boredom,' said Ed, closing his eyes and delving around.

The flashing button turned green and this time when he pressed it the doors swished apart. Ed laughed out loud and got a weird look from Pol.

'What's so funny?' she asked.

'The doors,' he said, still chuckling. 'They make the same noise as early *Star Trek* doors.'

She continued with a stare of incomprehension.

'Never mind,' he said, as they stepped inside, the doors going *shhhiick* and closing behind them, causing Ed to smirk again.

Ed thought the bridge was quite small relative to the ship's size. It was rectangular in shape with seating for thirteen, six down each side and one larger, slightly raised seat at the far end. They all faced stations built into the wall, only one of which was powered up.

'Must be environmental,' said Pol, examining the lit console. 'Giving the caretaker fresh air to breathe.'

'One of these has to be for the ship's array,' said Ed, inspecting each position closely. 'I'm hoping it can tell us where we are.'

Pol had moved up next to the captain's chair and pointed to the nearest console on the right.

'This one, I believe,' she said, pressing a purple backlit button on the top left of the panel.

It sprang to life along with three screens above and seemed to be going through its boot up routine. Once it had settled, a low chime sounded and one of the screens presented a rotating 3D view of the interior of the dome. It was extremely busy as every vessel's ID was displayed, all of them overlapping each other as ships would never normally be so close together.

'See if you can find the panning control,' said Ed. 'Perhaps one of the other screens is for the local system we're in and the third for the entire region of space.'

Pol nodded.

'Judging by the way this one only displays the interior of the dome, I'm thinking it hides the interior from outside and their cloaking technology is in its infancy. So it hides what's outside too,' said Pol. 'They haven't developed a one-way cloak yet.'

Suddenly Pol found the right control for panning in and the view whipped in to show only the ships within their area of the dome.

'Ah, that's better,' said Ed. 'At least now we can see if we have—'

'Oh, shit,' said Pol.

'—visitors.'

Two rectangular vehicles of some sort were approaching at speed.

'Time to leave,' said Ed, already heading for the bridge door.

19

THE STARSHIP GABRIEL, APPROACHING USKRRE IN THE ALPHA CENTAURI SYSTEM

'THERE'S a shit load of debris around that planet,' said Rayl. 'And I'm getting the readings of recent weapons fire. It can't have occurred too long ago either, because in a few hours most of that shrapnel will have dropped and burnt up in the upper atmosphere.'

'Is there any sign of a wrecked ship on the surface?' asked Andy.

'No – although there is a lot of ocean and we're still a long way off,' she answered. 'I'll get a better view once we're nearer and – oh!'

Everyone on the bridge turned to face her.

'I have a reading on the surface – no, two and three now. They're tiny and emitting distress signals.'

'Lifeboats,' said Bache, watching as the locations flashed up on the holomap depiction of Uskrre. 'They're all grouped close together and not many of them.'

'The ship was attacked unexpectedly then,' said Phil. 'Very few got off inside a narrow window of escape.

Judging by the amount of debris, it was a sizable vessel and would have had several dozen lifeboats.'

'They're arming weapons,' said Rayl, glancing up at the Klatt ship on the holomap.

The Klatt cruiser had achieved a low orbit and proceeded to fire on the surface. As they watched, powerful bolts of white energy penetrated the planet's atmosphere, taking out the lifeboats on the surface one by one.

'Cleaning house,' said Bache. 'They're tidying up and leaving no evidence. I wonder where the original attacking ship is?'

'I think there's something hiding in the rings of the other planet about two point two million kilometres away,' said Rayl. 'I'm getting fluctuating readings from there similar to another cloaked Klatt ship.'

'That's Proxima C,' said Andy. 'There was a lot of debate on Earth whether it had rings or not in the old days.'

'They're being very wary whoever they are,' said Phil. 'D'you want to go over and have a look?'

Andy sat back, rubbed his chin in thought and stared at Uskrre.

'No,' he said, finally. 'Concentrate on Uskrre and that ship in orbit. I want to know what this is all about and why they so desperately wanted us out the way. Keep an eye on that other hidden ship though, I don't want them sneaking off anywhere,' he added, nodding at Rayl.

'What's that?' questioned Bache, standing and stepping inside the holomap.

He squinted and pointed at one of the land masses on the surface of Uskrre.

'What's what where?' Andy asked.

'I know we're still a way off, but I'm sure I saw something large and hazy on the surface,' he said.

'Could it be smoke from a crashed ship?' Phil asked.

'Not unless smoke forms in a perfect circle,' Bache answered. 'It's gone now. Were you scanning with different frequencies?' he asked, turning to Rayl.

She nodded and glanced up at the map again.

'Show me where you saw it and I'll concentrate everything there and range through the array's repertoire.'

Bache showed her the region and stood back so they could all see. At first nothing happened but a few seconds later a small circular area on the edge of a forest blurred slightly for a split second.

'There, did you see it?' Bache asked.

'Yep,' said Andy, turning to Rayl. 'Flick back through the frequencies slowly.'

She was already there, as the oddity returned and this time remained. It was indeed circular and was as if you were looking at it through slightly steamed-up glasses.

'How big is that?' Bache asked.

'Around twelve kilometres diameter,' Rayl answered.

'Big enough to hide a city,' said Phil.

'Or a military base,' said Bache. 'Belonging to the Klatt and hidden, it'll be military, I'll stake my reputation on it.'

'Any standard scans of the planet wouldn't show up anything,' said Rayl. 'It's only because of some of the alien tech we've assimilated over the last couple of years that we were able to detect it.'

'Resistance is futile,' mumbled Andy, raising his eyebrows at his wife.

She completely ignored him and concentrated on giving the region as much magnification as possible. The holomap panned in and a forested area on the edge of a range of hills zipped in towards them.

'That's also where the lifeboats came down,' she said, as three thin trails of smoke could be seen from the recently destroyed craft.

'We need to get down there for a look, don't we?' said Andy, deliberately ignoring Rayl's sudden glare.

'No, you don't,' she said. 'We have perfectly good drones that can do that.'

Andy glanced up at Bache for some support, but found none.

'She's right,' said Bache. 'One of those excellent GDA drones I so generously gave you will do the job just fine.'

'Yeah – okay,' said Andy dejectedly, bringing up a drone control screen. 'I'll prepare one and wait until we're a little closer before launch.'

Thirty minutes later, Phil slowed the ship and put them cruising in a huge arc, following the turn of Uskrre, one hundred thousand kilometres above the area of interest.

It was silent on the bridge as Andy launched one of the four-metre-tall drones from the port hangar. They all watched as it flashed away towards the bright blue orb hanging seemingly motionless and alone in space. The planet's star, a red dwarf known on Earth as Proxima Centauri, was directly behind them and was able to enshroud them even more from Uskrre's direction at least.

The Klatt cruiser was oblivious as the cloaked drone passed it within five hundred kilometres. Andy deliberately took it over the horizon and behind the planet for insertion as he didn't want its heat trail to attract any unwanted attention. Once the heat shield was discarded, he brought it back at several times the speed of sound and activated its own array.

'It's a cloaked energy dome,' said Rayl, watching as Andy transferred its images onto the holomap.

'They're similar in size to the city shields on Paradeisos,' said Phil, referring to the domes on his home planet. 'Just a little more hidden.'

'Is there no way we can see inside?' asked Bache.

'I have nothing that can penetrate that,' said Cleo, who'd been watching in person quietly for a while. 'But I'll work on it.'

She promptly disappeared again and they all returned their attention back to the drone's footage of the dome.

'Only one entrance while the dome is activated, it seems,' said Rayl, pointing. 'It's over here adjacent to the river running through the bottom of the valley.'

Andy brought the drone around to face the arched doorway, but kept it up at around two hundred metres to avoid the trees and what looked like camera pods and who knows what else sticking out from the top of the arch.

'Would the drone fit through that?' Phil asked.

'Just about,' said Andy. 'If only we could find a way of opening it. If I was closer, I might be able to do it with my DOVI.'

Cleo reappeared, grinning.

'You might not be able to from here, but I can,' she said, waving her hand at the hologram as if she was casting a spell.

The doorway appearance changed from a fuzzy barrier to a smooth opaque semblance.

'Is that open now?' asked Andy, turning to Cleo.

'Take the drone down and find out,' she said. 'That's all the gate control does. It's a reasonably simple proximity detector, if you're near enough and transmitting the correct frequency code, that's all the system is designed to do.'

Andy nodded, and dropped the drone down slowly, watching for any reaction. None came, but the drone's antigrav drive began kicking up dust and leaves.

'Get it through as quickly as possible,' said Rayl. 'That dust and probably the noise too is a bad giveaway. If someone's watching they might put it down to a squall of wind if you're quick.'

Andy took the hint and accelerated the drone as low as he dared at the doorway. One of its many antennas clattered the top of the frame on its way through and he lifted it up again once it cleared the door.

They all gasped as the images from inside came into focus on the holomap.

'Holy shit,' said Andy.

'You're not kidding,' said Phil. 'That's an invasion fleet.'

'Full scan quickly and get back out again,' said Cleo. 'I have to keep the gate open so you have control over the drone, but it being open will probably attract attention.'

He didn't waste any time, whipping the drone up to the

apex of the dome, scanning with its entire repertoire and then back down and out. Once again, it clipped the frame top as it exited.

'They're here,' shouted Cleo, making everyone jump.

'What – who is?' said Andy, concentrating on piloting the drone, as everyone else turned and stared at her in surprise.

'Ed and Pol,' she said, hopping from foot to foot. 'They're in the dome.'

'Fuck,' said Andy, his eyes wide. 'We need to shut that dome down and go pick them up.'

20

MIRRORED DOME ON AN UNKNOWN PLANET

'THIS WAY,' said Ed, pointing in the opposite direction, as Pol ahead of him went to retrace the route they'd taken before.

'But the airlock's this way,' she said, sliding to a halt.

'If we've been detected, then that's where they'll go.'

'Ah – right.'

'We need to exit on the other side of the ship,' he said, trotting off towards the starboard side of the vessel.

They worked their way through the passageways, hoping this side was a mirror image and an airlock would be in the same place on the opposite side. Surprisingly, they found one before they were expecting to.

Ed, who arrived a few seconds before Pol, stopped and hit the airlock control. Pol barrelled straight into him as he realised the door wasn't moving.

'Shit,' he said, closing his eyes.

He opened them again straight away as he heard the whining of the door mechanism.

'Was that you?' he asked, looking at Pol and stepping back as the door slid away inside the hull.

She nodded and smiled.

'I guessed it would be locked down and started fishing around back down the corridor,' she said, stepping inside the airlock.

'Not a good idea to run around an unfamiliar ship with your eyes closed though,' said Ed, smirking and following her.

Pol was able to pull up the safety cover and press the outer door activation button now the airlock was online. The now familiar purple lights flashed again as the inner door closed and the outer door began motoring slowly up into its housing.

They both had weapons up and dropped down low to stick their heads out and peer around as soon as there was a big enough gap. It seemed clear enough and the only noise was the grinding of the door gear.

'It's a bit further down to the ground here,' said Ed, sliding around to sit over the sill. 'Are you okay with the drop?'

Pol just stood up and leaped out, landing and rolling in a whirl of limbs, some three metres below. Checking there were no witnesses to her acrobatics, she grinned back up at him.

'I guess you are,' he said, turning to hang by his arms, then dropping the remaining metre or so to the ground.

Once they were down, they could hear the low whine of the military trucks in the distance, but surprisingly they were getting fainter.

Pol suddenly turned and looked skyward.

'Something's flying,' she said. 'Can you hear it?'

They both dived under the ship as the unmistakable shriek of an antigrav working hard screamed overhead.

'Bugger,' said Ed. 'They'll find us easily scanning from above.'

'We need to get well away from this ship though,' said Pol. 'That caretaker won't remain undiscovered forever.'

The antigrav howl faded into the distance.

'Come on,' said Ed, tapping Pol on one of her shoulders. 'Let's move while that thing's looking elsewhere.'

They sprinted from ship to ship, getting their breath back while underneath each vessel.

'Shouldn't we stay close to the doorway?' said Pol, as Ed led her deeper into the dome.

'I want to know where those vehicles are coming from,' he said. 'And what all this kit is destined for.'

They'd skipped under another twenty odd ships when Pol suddenly grabbed Ed and pulled him back under a medium-sized freighter.

'It's coming back,' she said, pointing up.

'There's nothing wrong with your hearing is there?' he said, crouching down with her. He closed his eyes and felt upward with his DOVI. Ignoring the ship they were beneath, he found what was making all the racket and jolted backwards suddenly. Opening his eyes, he turned and gave Pol a stare. Worry lines creased his forehead. He opened his mouth to say something and closed it again.

'What is it?' Pol asked, noticing his discomfort. 'Have they found us?'

'It's a drone,' he said.

'Yeah – well, that's not that surprising, is it?'

'No, no, you don't understand,' he said, stretching his neck to peer upwards from under the freighter. 'It's not one of theirs.'

'What – not a Klatt drone?'

'No.'

'Well – whose then?'

'That's just it – it's one of ours.'

'What, as in a GDA drone?'

Ed nodded. 'How the hell did they get one of those?'

'Well, you've got some,' she said.

'I know. But we're a GDA asset,' he said, pulling his head back in when he couldn't see anything. 'All the GDA kit is strictly controlled. They don't hand out that stuff like confetti, you know – and definitely not to the Klatt.'

'What about the *Gabriel*?' she said, the hope showing in her eyes.

'I hadn't thought of that,' he said, looking up again. 'It can't be – can it?'

'You said Andy could find anything.'

'I did – although I was trying to keep your spirits up.'

'Hmm,' she grunted. 'It certainly worked.'

'Well, if it is the *Gabriel*, they certainly know we're here now if they've managed to get a drone into the dome. Must have been a squeeze getting it through the gate.'

'We need to help them somehow,' said Pol. 'Why don't we see if we can find the power supply for the dome?'

'That's not such a shabby idea,' said Ed. 'Have a merit point.'

'Thanks,' she said, standing up again and nodding forward. 'Shall we continue?'

The next couple of kilometres went by without incident. Just ship after ship, row upon row and just as they were beginning to think they might have missed whatever they were looking for, Pol stopped and grabbed Ed's shoulder.

'What is it?' he asked, as Pol stared straight ahead, concentrating on something.

'Voices,' she said. 'Faint, but definitely voices.'

'Klatt?'

'Too distant to tell as yet.'

'Okay, we need to be cautious,' he said. 'Were they straight ahead?'

She nodded and pointed slightly left of centre with a flat palm.

'From now on we stay as low as possible and just move one ship at a time,' said Ed, crouching down and creeping towards the next ship.

Three ships later, they could both see a few buildings through the forest of landing struts. Occasional movement had them lying flat before creeping forward again.

'There's more of those vehicles,' said Ed.

'I wonder if they leave the keys in?' said Pol.

'Even if they do, I bet we can't work out how to drive them,' Ed grumbled.

'I tell you what,' she said. 'You go and mess up the dome power and I'll concentrate on finding us some wheels.'

'With the dome decommissioned we could fly out of here,' said Ed, glancing around at the nearby vessels.

Pol shook her head and rolled her eyes.

'A second ago you didn't think we could work out how to drive and now you want to fly?'

'We could make some big bangs with one of these,' he said, smiling and patting the strut they were lying under. 'Especially one with laser cannons.'

'What is it with you and Andy and explosions?' she said, shaking her head. 'Let's blow everything up – that'll make it better?'

'It's a bloke thing,' said Ed. 'You wouldn't understand.'

'Females just don't get it do they?' said a strange digitised voice behind them.

21

MIRRORED DOME ON AN UNKNOWN PLANET

ED AND POL both froze and slowly turned their heads. Three Klatt soldiers stood four metres away, two of them pointing rifles at them while the third, who seemed to be in charge, leaned casually against the adjacent landing strut holding a translator. He smiled and wiped his brow with a small towel that he draped back over his shoulder.

'Don't know how you can stand these warmer planets, Mr Virr,' he said. 'You certainly messed up our plans for this lot, didn't you?' he added, waving his hand around at the rows of parked ships.

Ed noticed they wore the same uniform as the soldiers they'd killed earlier and hoped they were still ignorant of that detail.

'How d'you know my name?' he asked.

All three soldiers chuckled at that.

'Ah – we all know you, Edward Virr,' the casual one sniggered. 'That gullible idiot Groxl kidnapping you was a crucial part of our operation. Quite how you managed to dissociate yourselves from the two officers that shared the lifeboat with you, I don't know. Am I to understand I won't be needing to reprimand them?'

Ed and Pol stayed silent.

He nodded.

'Good, saves me a job. Now if you'd be so kind as to disarm yourselves slowly and carefully. Unfortunately, my soldiers haven't got their weapons set on stun like yourselves. That was your biggest mistake, you see. The caretaker on the cruiser woke up and operated his emergency transmitter under the scales on his wrist. From then on we watched you and were about to come and pick you up, when you in your wisdom decided to come to us. We just hung around until you got here.'

'Did Groxl tell you everything about me and how I messed with his ship?' asked Ed.

'Ah, yes, how you used some sort of beam to disable his drive and weapons systems.'

'He told you all about it did he?' Ed asked again, this time standing up and looking around. 'I hope you brought more than two soldiers with you.'

'Why? D'you think I'll need them for one human and a scared whatever she is?' he asked, nodding in Pol's direction and folding his arms across his chest confidently.

'Because those two have faulty weapons,' said Ed, swinging his laser rifle around from his back.

Ed watched as the soldiers' eyes went wide as two dull *clicks* sounded and they both glanced down at their rifles in puzzlement.

'Oh, dear and whoops,' said Ed, as he fired three times.

The three soldiers spasmed and slumped to the ground. The senior one still had a look of utter disbelief on his face as they dragged them up the ramp of an adjacent troop carrier that Pol had opened up with her DOVI.

'I'm glad we weren't next to those cruisers,' Pol moaned, cuffing the bodies to the seats inside. 'Getting these three fat bastards up into an airlock would have been a bitch.'

Ed snorted a laugh.

'That's another Andyism – and a good one,' he said, smirking at Pol.

Next he turned his DOVI onto their wrists and destroyed the small transmitters. 'Thanks for the info, won't be making that mistake again,' he said to the unconscious senior soldier and patted his face.

'Back to plan A?' asked Pol.

'Indeed,' he said. 'Let's find the dome power supply and give it the good news.'

***

It had taken them another half an hour after closing up the rear door of the troop carrier to get within a stone's throw of a group of buildings seemingly in the centre of the dome. One concrete structure caught Ed's eye. It was in the middle of everything else, considerably taller than the others and had a large gold-coloured dome on the top, glistening in the hazy refracted light penetrating the shield a couple of kilometres above.

'That has to be the shield emitter,' said Pol, following Ed's gaze.

'It's certainly a pretty favourable candidate,' he replied,

closing his eyes and feeling out with his DOVI. 'Bugger,' he said, opening them again. 'It's shielded.'

'We could wait until it's dark and sneak in,' said Pol.

Ed pointed at all the floodlight pylons surrounding the central area.

'It'll be brighter than daylight with all that lot sparked up,' he said. 'We need to find a way of getting over there without detection.'

'The buildings are looking a bit shabby,' said Pol. 'It wouldn't take much to demolish them.'

She nodded and stared at the vehicle park a few hundred metres away.

He followed her gaze before turning to regard her dubiously.

'You mean drive a truck through it, don't you?'

She grinned malevolently and raised her eyebrows.

Ed sat back on his haunches, looking between her and the truck park.

'Wow,' he said. 'What have you done with the shy nervous Pol I used to know? Bloody good idea though.'

'That one eighth in line looks promising,' she said, pointing at the largest truck.

'Yeah,' he said. 'I had my eye on that one too. It's tracked as well, which could help.'

'And armoured,' she said. 'Just in case that gold thing was to drop on us.'

Slowly making their way around to the far side of the truck park, they bided their time until no soldiers were visible then sprinted across the fifty metres of open ground. Ducking down between the vehicles, Ed tried the handle of a hatch on the right-hand side of the larger truck.

It clunked open an inch and stopped. Grabbing it by its edge and heaving produced a loud squeal as it reluctantly swung fully open. They both froze for a second.

'Inside quick,' Ed whispered. 'Someone must have heard that.'

Ed helped Pol up inside and jumped in behind her, dragging the hatch closed, producing yet another ear-splitting squeal. He clamped it shut and waited while his eyes accustomed themselves to the gloom.

'Something tells me this vehicle has been here a while and maintenance hasn't been a priority,' said Pol, sliding her hand along the top of one of the seats and showing Ed the thick layer of dust dislodged.

'Oh crap,' he said, peering over the front seats at a barely discernible dashboard. 'We might have picked a scrapper. There's years of dust in here.'

He crawled over the back of the driver's seat set in the centre of the vehicle and behind a thick plexiglass front screen that along with everything else was greyed out with a layer of dust.

'Can't see a damn thing,' mumbled Ed. 'Never a car wash handy when you want one.'

'Shall I pop out and get a bucket and sponge?' Pol replied, as she attempted to follow Ed over to the front of the vehicle.

He turned to look over his shoulder as a leg bumped into him followed by a stream of curses.

'Shit fuck piss,' she grumbled. 'I can't get over there with you in the way.'

'Doesn't matter,' said Ed. 'If we can't get this thing running, we'll be getting straight back out again anyway.'

He found an old rag under his seat and used it to brush the dust off the front console. Pol suddenly made a bellowing noise behind him, making him jump just as a shadow swept past the side window.

'What the hell was that?' he said, turning.

'I sneezed,' she said, as he heard the hatch behind him squeal again.

He swung around to look over his other shoulder to find a Klatt soldier with a surprised expression peering in. Pol grabbed his arm, yanked his head inside the vehicle and smashed her rifle into the side of his head. He slumped unconscious and before he slid back outside again, Pol dragged him in with her and the hatch sealed shut again.

'Are there any others?' Ed asked.

'Well, you're the one next to the windows,' she grumbled, wrinkling her nose. 'And now I've got even less room back here with this smelly bastard.'

'Shit,' Ed mumbled under his breath. He reached over and pushed a lever across that bolted the driver's door, then turning back to the controls he decided he'd better hurry up. There had been a large switch top right that had caught his eye a moment ago. It was red and only had two positions. Holding his breath, he turned it to the second position.

The dash lit up and a low whine emanating from somewhere behind and below them began building in intensity.

'Sounds promising,' said Pol. 'The power cell's still got juice then.'

Ed grabbed the two joystick controls in front of him and gently pushed them forward. The vehicle twitched and vibrated alarmingly. For some reason it wasn't moving, but the shaking had at least dislodged some of the dust on the front screen.

'Hand brake,' called Pol from behind.

'Thank you, Sherlock,' Ed growled. 'Just where the fuck is it?'

He started randomly pressing things that seemed to make no difference at all.

'Come on,' he shouted. 'It's got to be here somewhere.'

'What's that button on top of the right stick?' asked Pol, peeking through the gap.

The vehicle suddenly leaped forward a metre as soon as he pressed it.

'A-ha, here we go,' he said, looking up out of the screen just in time to see a Klatt troop carrier pull up in front and a stream of soldiers pile out from the rear.

'Ah shit,' said Pol, from over his shoulder. 'Ram it out the way, we can't go backwards, we're blocked in.'

'Make sure your hatch is locked this time,' said Ed, as he rammed the joysticks forward and the heavy tracked vehicle leaped forward, seemingly glad to be released from its shackles, and bowled towards the side of the troop carrier.

22

THE STARSHIP GABRIEL, ADJACENT TO USKRRE IN THE ALPHA CENTAURI SYSTEM

ANDY FLASHED the cloaked *Cartella* out into space and similarly to the drone, took it around to the opposite side of Uskrre from the Klatt ship to hide its fiery insertion trail. Bache had insisted on coming with him and sat bolt upright in the right-hand seat, staring intently and silently at the growing planet below them.

Stealing a quick glance at his passenger, Andy could see the worry etched into his face, his hands permanently fidgeting with the laser weapon in his lap.

'It'll be fine,' he said, closing his eyes again to adjust the angle of attack into the upper atmosphere.

'It's the Klatt though,' said Bache. 'Why did it have to be the Klatt? And what the hell are they doing with an invasion fleet hidden here?'

'It could be just a storage depot,' said Andy.

'Not a chance,' Bache replied, watching as a flurry of sparks flashed by the front screen. 'It'd be in their home system if that's all it was.'

It went quiet again as Andy, instead of braking as they

dropped lower, kept the ship's momentum up to carry them quickly around the globe and towards the disguised dome. Finally slowing the *Cartella* as they got within a thousand kilometres, he called Rayl, who he'd handed the drone over to before he left the *Gabriel*'s bridge.

'Are you ready to insert the drone?' he asked.

'Of course,' came the curt reply.

Rayl had been dead against Andy piloting the *Cartella* down to the planet, arguing that Cleo was quite capable of doing it remotely. She'd been even more annoyed when Bache, instead of siding with her as she'd expected, chose to go on the trip with Andy and exacerbate the risk.

'Are the missiles armed?' he asked.

'Of course they're fucking not,' she snapped. 'Not until it's inside the dome and safely through that gate.'

Andy pulled a face at Bache.

'And don't pull faces,' she groused.

Andy snapped his face back to normal and wondered how she knew.

'When the dome fails, you go in, pick them up and get out. No hanging around blowing shit up. Is that clear?'

'Yes, dear.'

'Don't you "yes dear" me.'

'No, de——. Understood.'

He decided to shut up and brought the *Cartella* around opposite the gate and kept it up at a kilometre above, so the drone had room to manoeuvre. Although they could detect the drone, its location soon became apparent as the gate went opaque again and a similar cloud of dust and leaves swirled around violently as its antigrav drive agitated everything loose.

The dome immediately failing made Andy jump, as thousands of ships suddenly materialised below them.

'Fuck me, that was quick,' he said, regaining his composure and moving the *Cartella* swiftly forward.

'Wasn't me,' said Rayl.

Andy pushed the little ship at full throttle towards the centre of what had been under the dome.

'There's some sort of tracked vehicle crunching around in the remains of a building, right in the centre,' he said.

'That's got to be Ed,' said Bache. 'Can you talk to him?'

Andy felt out with his DOVI and quickly found his friend.

'Taxi for Mr Virr,' he said, slowing the ship and hovering a few hundred metres above the destruction derby happening below.

'Andy, shit,' replied Ed. 'You're here.'

'I'm not shit – I'm very clever, me,' Andy replied, grinning.

'Tell him to drive that thing away from the centre,' said Bache. 'You've just stuck a big stick in an even bigger nest of vipers.'

'He heard you,' said Andy, watching as dozens of Klatt soldiers and assorted personnel streamed out of the other buildings, some of them firing at the marauding armoured truck.

A missile streaked in from above as Rayl unleashed one of the six kataligo missiles slung under the drone. It left a fifteen-metre crater in the ground where some of the armed soldiers had been and the concussive wave badly damaged three adjacent buildings.

'I thought we weren't blowing shit up?' said Andy, steadying the ship as the shock wave reached the *Cartella*.

'Needs must,' said Rayl. 'You go get Ed and Pol and I'll dissuade these arseholes from following.'

Ed, in the meantime, had roared off, deliberately clipping a few more vehicles so they couldn't be used to follow him. Bache pointed when he noticed a laser round flash in from one of the nearby parked ships, narrowly missing Ed's vehicle and producing a geyser of smoking soil that heaved high into the air.

Andy had seen it too and activated the *Cartella*'s cannons, then following Bache's finger, turned the ship and ripped the offending laser cannon and the whole side of the troop carrier to shreds with a prolonged burst.

'Must have been doing some maintenance on the ship or something,' said Bache. 'The rest of the ships seem deserted.'

The concussion from another huge explosion behind them lifted the *Cartella* again as Andy overtook Ed's vehicle, de-cloaked so he could see it and landed a hundred metres in front.

'Go round behind us,' said Andy. 'Use the ship's shields to protect you as you get out.'

'Okay,' came the reply, as Bache moved over to the airlock and prepared to open it.

Now the *Cartella* was visible, it began to attract more attention and its shields were kept busy absorbing a flurry of small weapons fire. There was a third explosion as Rayl reduced the drone's complement of missiles to three. It did have the required effect as the incoming fire reduced dramatically.

Andy was temporarily blinded as an explosion under Ed's truck threw it sideways and one of its tracks unravelled out the back of the vehicle, causing it to swerve hard left and roll almost in slow motion onto its side.

'Shit they're hit,' shouted Andy, lifting and turning the *Cartella* so he could utilise the cannons to give the truck some covering fire. 'Ed, can you hear me?' he called, landing back down again in between the damaged truck and the oncoming horde.

'I can,' came a weak voice. 'I think I need some help with Pol.'

Before Andy could say anything, Bache, who'd overheard what Ed had said on the ship's internal speakers, opened both airlock doors and jumped out.

'Shit,' Andy said under his breath, debating whether to follow Bache or use the ship's cannons again to discourage any heroics from the Klatt attackers. He chose the latter and brought the vessel up and around to face the centre of the dome again. It looked as if every building was now if not destroyed, at least on fire. Any laser bolts coming his way or any movement was immediately answered with a barrage of cannon fire. A fourth huge explosion over to his left pushed him dangerously close to one of the Klatt ships and he silently wished they'd fitted a laser cannon to the drone as it would have proved a lot more useful in this situation.

A shout from Bache woke him from his thoughts and he swung the ship back round so the airlock was facing the truck. He could see two people clambering down from the upturned vehicle, one limping and the other carrying something over their shoulders. As they got closer to the

Cartella, he could see it was Bache carrying a seemingly lifeless Pol and it was Ed limping along behind.

They clambered up the steps as a renewed salvo of laser fire zapped around the ship's shields like forked lightning in a spring storm. Andy wasn't waiting around and as soon as they were inside the outer airlock, he punched the icon to close it and immediately lifted the ship and screamed upwards, cloaking the *Cartella* as he went.

He felt rather than saw the last two missiles as Rayl discouraged anyone's thoughts of pursuit.

'Have you got them both?' she asked, once they were clear of the area.

'Yeah,' he said, grinning. 'All aboard.'

He opened his eyes momentarily to glance back over his shoulder. The smile vanished from his face as he saw the state of Pol and the amount of blood on the floor.

'Get her to the *Gabriel* fast,' said Ed, the tears running down his face.

23

BUILDING XII, GRONDALLE DOME, USKRRE, IN THE ALPHA CENTAURI SYSTEM

THE DEEP WHINE of a large vehicle passing close to the building didn't disturb Captain Groxl in the darkness of the storeroom he'd been locked in. But the following ear-splitting roar and ensuing crash sounded as though it was right outside his door and he shrank back as far as the cuff holding him against the shelving would allow.

He could feel the vibrations of whatever had happened nearby through his feet and, judging by the severity, it wasn't good news. Already fuming with anger at being roughly manhandled and imprisoned by inferior soldiers of the Spleeta clan, he was incensed at what they might be doing with one of the classified Grondalle battle fleets.

He ducked as the scream of an antigrav drive thundered overhead, followed by another higher up. Then the sound of small weapons fire had him running the cuff down the shelving leg so he could lie prone to avoid any stray laser bolts penetrating the walls around him. The intensity of the firefight increased until the unmistakable whoosh of an incoming missile had him rolling up into the foetal position.

The room disintegrated above him in the sudden explosion, his ears rang and dust and debris clattered around him. He felt his arm twist as the shelving he was cuffed to buckled and there was a loud snap as his arm broke. The immediate and shocking agony had him writhing on the floor amongst shattered pieces of the prefabricated building, broken shelving and assorted food and catering items. Swearing profusely, he quickly realised he could see and, peering up through the smoke, he caught glimpses of clouds and sky above.

The dome's down, he thought. *That's what the first big crash was. Someone took out the dome initiator and allowed an attacking force in.*

Blanking out the pain in his left arm, he soon noticed that although the cuff was still on his arm, it wasn't attached to anything anymore. He crawled painfully using one arm through the wreckage and peered over what was left of the back wall. The remains of dead Spleeta soldiers lay randomly around a deep crater in the road. In the distance he could see and hear more firing and the occasional flash of lightning as a lucky shot found the shields of what appeared to be a small cloaked vessel. He recoiled as the smell of blood, burning plastic and expended explosives pervaded his nostrils, quickly flattening himself again as a second missile screamed in and impacted a hundred metres away. Once the shrapnel and debris thrown up by the detonation had ceased, he crawled out and pulled a laser pistol from the holster of one of the nearby dead soldiers.

Checking everything was clear around him, he stood warily and as quickly as he could made his way in the opposite direction to all the action. A few minutes later, he was able to disappear amongst the rows of ships and, cradling his broken arm, he searched down the lines of vessels for what he was looking for.

The galactic Tyrow class vessels were reasonably near the centre of the dome as he knew they would be. A durable, fast, armed and jump-capable special operations ship, he knew it had the means to get him home and the medical kit to look after his arm.

Ignoring the first one, which had sunk slightly into the loamy soil, he chose the second one, which sat high on its landing skids. Opening a small flap on the belly of the ship, he punched a code into a keypad that powered down a narrow hatch and stairway. After one more check around him to ensure he hadn't been observed, he ascended the stairs and entered the ship.

The vessel was designed for a maximum of six personnel, two crew and four special operations soldiers, but could be easily flown by a single person. Firstly, he uncovered and switched the master arm handle to OPERATE and checked forward in the cockpit that everything was booting up as it should. A sudden alarm trilled and a red light flashed on the co-pilot's display, followed by a thud and detonation around two kilometres away. He relaxed as he realised it was just the missile proximity warning system alerting him to the launch in the vicinity.

Returning to the rear of the ship he searched through the medical supplies and injected his arm with a strong painkiller, before gritting his teeth as he straightened it as best he could and initiating a fracture clasp over his upper arm.

Another different alarm sounding in the cockpit had him hurrying through to find an unknown ship design had uncloaked and was using its laser cannons against the Spleeta forces.

'Keep 'em occupied whoever you are,' he said, smiling for the first time. 'Kill as many as you like. They shouldn't be here anyway.'

He sat in the pilot's seat and activated the cloak, before winding up the antigravs. Being a starship pilot in his junior officer days meant flying this little ship wasn't a drama, although he was a little behind the times with the modern control layout in this newer model.

When he was happy and both control panels showed greens across the board, he lifted the ship up to five hundred metres. The weapons systems automatically zoned in on the strange small vessel that had now landed. He watched as a heavy tracked vehicle thundered towards it as if it was attempting to ram it. He shrugged and activated one of the ship's cannons, firing a single bolt. The vehicle launched upwards, lost a track, slewed sideways and rolled fifty metres short of the landed ship.

'There you go, stranger,' he said, launching the ship upwards. 'You did me a favour, now I've returned it.'

Seven minutes later, he achieved orbit to find a Grondalle Fonias class cruiser sitting stationary above the dome area.

'A lot of bloody help you were,' he said, uncloaking the ship and asking for approach vectors.

The reply he got asked him to drop shields and proceed towards the rear port hangar.

The suddenness of the attack took him completely by surprise. The second he dropped his shields, one of the cruiser's heavy cannons activated, locked on and fired. Within half a second his antigrav drives and his jump capability were destroyed. The small ship went into an uncontrolled spin back towards the planet and he found himself dragged out of his seat and smashed into the ceiling of the cockpit as the artificial gravity also failed.

No one was there to witness the initial confusion on his face before anger took over and he realised the Spleeta must have gained control over one of their cruisers.

The pull was too great as he attempted to push himself away with only one arm. Multiple alarms sounded around the ship and he could see both panels full of red warning indicators. What he could also see, to his horror, was the planet spinning in and out of vision through the front screen and it was getting slowly closer. For the second time that day, the stink of burning plastics assaulted him as smoke poured into the cockpit from the rear of the ship.

He was pinned to the ceiling by the inertia of the spin and the ship's single lifeboat was behind and below him. Unless he could reach it, the ship would soon burn up as it was dragged lower in Uskrre's gravity well. He pushed and pulled, swore a lot and only managed to turn and face the airlock to the lifeboat tantalisingly only four metres away.

He exhaled and swore again in frustration. Gritting his teeth, he pushed his hand down his front and found the laser pistol he'd picked up was still in his belt. Forcing his head down, he looked at it and managed to turn it so it faced his head. Groxl wasn't scared of many things, but burning slowly to death was one of them. A laser bolt to the head was instant and pain-free.

Looking out the front screen one last time he watched the beautiful blue planet flicking in and out of vision again.

It is a pretty planet, he thought to himself. *There are worse places for my ashes to remain forever.*

The ship shuddered and he felt its movement change slightly as Uskrre's upper atmosphere gripped it and began heating up the hull of the plummeting vessel. A loud *clang* from outside jarred him away from his thoughts and he thought he saw a section of the disintegrating ship zip by the front screen. Knowing it was now or never, he turned his head to face the muzzle of the pistol and, closing his eyes, he tightened his finger on the trigger.

He hadn't expected to hear the weapon firing as the bang when it came was incredibly loud, his arm screamed and everything went black.

24

THE STARSHIP GABRIEL, ADJACENT TO USKRRE IN THE ALPHA CENTAURI SYSTEM

ANDY HAD SCREAMED the *Cartella* back to the *Gabriel* and into the port hangar as fast as the little ship could go. He'd even clipped one of its winglets on the hangar door and slid the ship to a stop only inches from the back door nearest the medical suite. But even though Phil had had the auto nurse all ready for Pol, the reality was pretty obvious to everyone. Pol hadn't had a heartbeat for more than twenty minutes. She'd lost a frightening amount of blood and amazing though the auto nurse was, when a patient was brain dead there wasn't much it could do.

Everyone except Rayl, who remained on the bridge in case of emergencies, either stood or sat on the floor staring into space.

After what seemed an age, the auto nurse beeped and went quiet. Phil was eventually the first to speak.

'Cleo needs a decision, guys,' he said quietly. 'Does she set up a birthing chamber, yes or no?'

Ed lifted his head from his hands. The tear streaks

through the black dust on his face made it look as though he was wearing mascara in the rain.

'It was all my fault,' he said, with a sob. 'If I'd squeezed over and made room for her in the front as well, she wouldn't have been slammed around in the back.'

'That's crap, Ed,' said Bache. 'It was the fault of whoever was in that bloody Klatt ship with a heavy laser.'

'That's right,' said Andy, nodding slowly. 'It can't possibly be your fault.'

Ed glared malevolently at both of them.

'You weren't there,' he snarled slowly and venomously.

'If she'd been in the front, if she'd been strapped in a seat in the back, if this, if that, if, if, fucking if – shut the fuck up, the lot of you,' shouted Phil, his back to them as he leaned over the auto nurse panel.

When he turned to face them, they all glared wide-eyed at him in shock. Phil never swore, he was a shy introvert, he never ever raised his voice or criticised anyone.

'I've had enough of this crap,' Phil continued, making eye contact with all three of them. 'Pol isn't dead. She's in here.'

He held up the tiny vial containing her Krypti.

'You know that as well as anyone, Edward. So, I'll ask the question again – does Cleo set up a birthing chamber?'

Ed, Bache and Andy all stared sheepishly at each other, seemingly embarrassed at Phil finding the need to swear at them.

'Erm,' said Ed, coughing into his hand. 'She did ask me if this happened, would she still have four arms.'

'And what did you tell her?' Andy asked before Phil could.

'I said I didn't know and she'd have to ask you,' Ed replied, looking at Phil, the anger now gone from his face.

'Hmm,' grunted Phil. 'What was her opinion?'

'If I remember rightly, she said two arms would be a bit weird.'

'She'll also have human feet and hands with ten fingers and toes,' Phil said, raising his eyebrows.

'And proper knees,' said Bache.

'If it was me, I'd want to be alive in any form,' said Andy, shrugging and then looking thoughtful. 'Well, perhaps not a slug.'

'Or a dung beetle,' said Ed, almost managing a smile and slowly getting to his feet, noticeably favouring one leg. 'Thanks for coming to find us, you guys.'

Andy stood, stumbled across the room and hugged Ed tight.

'I told Pol you'd come,' Ed whispered, giving Phil the slightest of nods.

'I'll tell Cleo to go ahead then,' Phil said quietly, as he touched an icon on the auto nurse panel. The see-through cover closed over her and then turned opaque, hiding her body from view.

'I heard,' said Cleo.

'Make sure she still looks like Pol,' said Ed. 'She was quite pretty in a weird alien kinda way.'

'We'll never hear the end of it if she doesn't like it,' said Andy, rolling his eyes. 'You need to get that leg sorted, too,' he added, noticing Ed wince as he put weight on it.

'I'll stay down here and get an auto nurse to—'

'Need you all on the bridge urgently,' interrupted Rayl, over the tannoy. 'Something weird's going on.'

'—maybe later,' Ed continued, limping towards the door.

Rayl looked relieved to see them as they all piled out of the tube lift and stopped and stared at the holomap.

'What happened to that?' questioned Ed, as a small Klatt ship, spinning and spewing debris and gasses, was dropping towards the planet.

'It uncloaked about the same time as you got here,' said Rayl. 'Dropped its shields to enter one of the cruisers' hangars and they blew its drives to shit.'

'How many aboard?' Bache asked.

'Just one,' said Cleo. 'I have a view from an internal camera.'

The holomap image changed to one of the interior of a small cockpit. The planet could be seen spinning past the front screen and a body, struggling to move, stuck to the ceiling by the inertia.

'Looks like a Klatt officer to me, judging by the uniform,' said Bache. 'Those are captain's bands around his arm.'

'Hang on,' said Ed. 'Cleo, can you get a close-up on his face?'

The image zoomed in and although the picture quality became a little grainy, Ed recoiled as he recognised the face.

'That's Groxl,' he said, the astonishment evident in his voice. 'That's the bastard who kidnapped us – he was the captain of that Klatt ship we messed with on the way to Andromeda.'

'I knew it was to do with that,' said Andy. 'And that's the same cruiser that's just fired on him.'

'Really? He said it was destroyed. Can we grab him?' Ed asked, looking around at the others.

'What, without the cruiser noticing?' said Rayl.

'Does it matter?' asked Ed, glancing at Rayl in puzzlement.

'Yeah, actually it does,' said Bache.

'Long story,' said Andy, noticing Ed's questioning look.

'Cleo, can you fake a ship burning up if we grab that one?' Rayl asked.

'Get over there and be ready with a hangar and the tractor,' Cleo replied. 'As you know, it takes a lot of concentration for me to do that shit, so I'll leave the grabbing to you.'

Phil slid onto his control couch and accelerated the *Gabriel* straight at the tumbling vessel, while Rayl activated the tractor beam and waited for Cleo's signal. It took them only thirty seconds to get there, but it seemed like an age to the bridge crew. The small ship had already begun to disassemble itself as it hit the upper atmosphere and the spin wasn't going to make the snatch any easier.

'Ready,' said Cleo. 'Make sure you match its speed and slow it gradually, the artificial gravity on the ship has failed and you'll smear him all over the interior if you stop it suddenly. I'll continue the holographic ship's descent and destruction as soon as you begin slowing it down.'

'Use the starboard hangar,' said Andy. 'It's got less in it.'

'Roger that,' said Phil, manoeuvring the ship around and opening the outer hangar door.

Rayl slowly grabbed the ship, firstly reducing its spin and then dragging it in towards the gaping hangar. The *Gabriel*'s hull began glowing on its starboard side as they dropped lower and Phil turned the ship gradually so as to reduce the crushing effect inside the little ship.

Ed, Bache and Andy watched as the holomap displayed an exact copy of the Klatt vessel continuing on, as Cleo produced an almost epic display of the ship's final dramatic demise.

'That was impressive, Cleo – it would've certainly fooled me,' said Bache.

'You're welcome, handsome.'

Bache glanced at Ed, getting nothing more than raised eyebrows in return.

'It's inside the hangar and under the influence of our gravity field,' said Rayl, giving Phil a nod.

He quickly cancelled their descent and without delay pushed the cloaked ship back up into space and away from the planet. The Klatt cruiser hadn't moved or changed its operational functions at all, the only difference being two small troop ships left one of its hangars and proceeded down towards the dome area.

'They're probably going down to assess what caused all the trouble,' said Bache.

'Hopefully they'll think it was our friend in the starboard hangar,' said Ed. 'Shall we go down and see if he's still alive and one of you can explain to me why we're being so secretive?'

25

THE STARSHIP GABRIEL, ADJACENT TO USKRRE IN THE ALPHA CENTAURI SYSTEM

ON THE WAY down to the hangar, Andy and Bache filled Ed in on everything that had happened while he was in Klatt custody.

'So let me get this straight,' said Ed, stepping out of the tube lift on deck ten. 'We're all dead and if either the Klatt or the GDA find out we're not, then they'll quickly ensure we are because we caused the destruction of a cruiser?'

Andy and Bache both looked at each other and nodded.

'That's about the sum of it,' Andy said.

'There's something going on that we're not a party too,' said Bache. 'And it all started with your abduction.'

'And that Klatt cruiser out there,' said Ed. 'Groxl told me I was grabbed as payback for him losing the ship and there was to be a show trial on their home planet of Zee-Klatt III. He said they'd abandoned the ship before it got dragged into the system's star.'

'How did you end up on Uskrre?' asked Andy.

'Uskrre?' Ed exclaimed. 'What – as in Alpha Centauri?'

Bache and Andy nodded.

'So that's where we were, I had no idea,' he said. 'The ship Groxl was on was attacked and soldiers from a different clan came and grabbed us. I think they got a bit over-zealous with the takedown as a sudden hull breach had them changing plans and quickly bundling us into a lifeboat.'

'I won't bother asking what became of the soldiers,' said Bache. 'I presume it was their uniforms you were wearing?'

'Yeah, they were ordered to kill us and bury the bodies,' said Ed. 'They obviously didn't know about our internal translators.'

They all turned to look towards the starboard hangar.

'Well, let's hope he survived and can answer a few questions,' said Bache. 'Do you want me to grill him? I have a bit more experience in dealing with the Klatt mentality.'

'He's all yours,' said Ed. 'I'll remain out of sight initially, see what he says about me and the fact his ship is still around. But be careful, Andy. He knows about our DOVIs and had a jammer that makes your head explode in agony if you activate it.'

Andy nodded as they arrived at the starboard hangar door.

'Is it safe to enter, Cleo?' Ed asked.

'It is,' she said. 'But look out for any remaining carbon dioxide, as I used it to cool the ship's hull down when it came aboard.'

The door de-materialised and they entered to find a twenty-metre, still steaming, almost smooth lozenge-shaped lump in the middle of the hangar floor.

'Were we in time?' Andy asked. 'It looks really fucked up; all the extremities are burnt off.'

'I'll wait and listen in one of those,' said Ed, moving away in the direction of the *Gabriel*'s nearest shuttle.

Andy circled the wreck and tried unsuccessfully to peer into the darkness through the front screen, before pointing at a rectangular indentation in the hull.

'That looks like a hatch that would have been on the underside,' he said. 'The ship must be sitting on its port side.'

He tried feeling around for the lock mechanism with his DOVI, only to find a bunch of fried electronics.

'Cleo, can you open this for us?' he asked hopefully, looking up at the ceiling.

A narrow beam of intense laser light flashed down from a small protrusion high on the hangar roof. They both stepped back and shielded their eyes as it crept around the outline of the hatch. Twenty seconds had it completing its encirclement and returning back to where it had begun. As it did so the whole hatch dropped out and clattered noisily onto the hangar deck.

'Mind the edges, darlings,' said Cleo. 'Still a trifle warm and if it's any help, I'm detecting one unconscious life sign inside with a broken arm and a few lumps on his head. He has a laser pistol, but I've taken the liberty to disable it. Can I be of any other assistance?'

'No, that's excellent, Cleo – love your work,' said

Andy, sticking his head through the hatch and peering up towards the cockpit.

'Can you see him?' Bache asked.

'Yeah, he doesn't look very well, we might actually need to get him up to an auto nurse.'

They bound his legs and unbroken arm, hooded him and carried him up to the medical suite. He woke halfway and began wriggling and mumbling about traitorous Spleeta, which they just ignored and Cleo was able to secure him in one of the auto nurses that immediately began working on his arm and other various injuries.

Ed joined them again and stood directly behind the auto nurse where he couldn't be seen. He nodded at Andy to remove the hood.

Groxl's piercing eyes roamed slowly around the room, settling on Andy and Bache.

'Who are you and what the hell are you doing with a Klatt cruiser?' he snarled. 'Why did you fire on me?'

'My name is Commander Bache Loftt,' said Bache, softly. 'I'm afraid you have a few details wrong about what just happened. You are now on a civilian GDA-registered vessel and we just saved your life, Captain Groxl.'

'How d'you know my name?'

'We watched you illegally abduct Edward Virr and his assistant from his home on planet Earth.'

'He had to answer for his crimes against the Klatt Empire, something that is no business of yours.'

'And what crime might that be?' Bache asked.

'I don't have to answer to you.'

'No, you don't have to say anything – but I'll bet you'd like a few answers though. Like, why did your replacement ship get attacked and destroyed soon after you took possession of Captain Virr? and why did the Spleeta arrest and imprison you when you entered the dome on Uskrre? Most of all though, I'd like to know why you lied to Captain Virr about your original ship being lost?'

'We were forced to abandon it, of course it was lost. That DOVI thing he had completely fried our drive software, leaving the ship heading straight into the gravity well of the local star.'

'Then why is that same ship sitting above Uskrre? The same ship that fired on you as you approached one of its hangars not too long ago?'

Groxl's eyes widened.

'Impossible,' he spat. 'You're lying.'

'Cleo, can you provide the captain a view of the Klatt cruiser above Uskrre, please.'

A holographic image of the vessel appeared above them, moving slowly as it followed the rotation of the planet.

'That's a different ship,' Groxl snapped.

The image zoomed in on its identification code, XXIV (ZX) painted adjacent to the bow airlock. Bache and Andy turned to stare at Groxl. There was a barely discernible change in his resolute expression, it was just the slightest look of doubt for a second and then it was gone.

'That's not the same ship,' he growled. 'That's just been painted on.'

Cleo changed the view to the ship's main array that clearly showed recent repair work, where, at the time of the attack, Ed had turned one of the ship's laser cannons back on itself and badly damaged it.

'It's definitely the same ship, Groxl,' Bache reiterated.

'It can't be,' he said. 'You weren't there.'

'No, he wasn't,' said Ed, stepping out where Groxl could see him. 'But I was – and so was that gentleman there,' he pointed at Andy. 'And so was our ship's computer that confirms it's the same vessel. So, we'll ask you again, why are you lying and what was the real reason you kidnapped me, and then, down on the planet, you murdered my assistant Pol?'

Groxl was clearly getting flustered now. His eyes had nearly bugged out of his head when Ed had stepped into view. The defiance had evaporated as he appeared nervous for the first time and kept looking between Ed and the hologram. His mouth opened, then closed again, twice.

'Any time you feel like explaining, Captain. The stage is yours,' said Bache.

'This is a joke,' he mumbled eventually. 'It has to be. I and my crew abandoned that ship several hours after our altercation. We had to wait for a rescue vessel to reach us and as for murdering someone, it can't possibly have been me. I picked up a laser pistol off a dead Spleeta soldier, but I never fired it.'

'No,' said Ed. 'You fired your ship's cannon though, didn't you?'

Andy stepped over to Pol's auto nurse and touched an icon on the control panel. The opaque cover cleared so Groxl could see her lifeless body.

'And that was the result,' he said.

Ed would have sworn Groxl's leathery skin went a shade paler.

'The armoured truck,' he said, almost in a whisper. 'I

thought it was about to ram that ship that was doing me a favour and attacking the Spleeta.'

All three of them shook their heads slowly.

'That was me driving that vehicle,' said Ed. 'Trying to escape the Spleeta and my friend here landing the ship to pick us up.'

'Oh,' was all Groxl could mumble.

'And while we're at it,' said Bache, pointing at Uskrre on the holomap, 'what was that fleet of ships doing out here concealed under that dome?'

'That's classified,' Groxl said, avoiding eye contact. 'It would be a death sentence for me.'

'As far as the Klatt Empire is concerned, Captain, you're already dead. Dead men can't be killed again.'

Groxl seemed to chew on that for a moment.

'They didn't see you rescue my ship?'

'No,' said Bache. 'A hologram of your ship burnt up and exploded in the upper atmosphere.'

'Why would you want to protect an empire that wants you dead, anyway?' said Ed.

Groxl exhaled, shrugged and seemed to come to a decision.

'It was a mothballed invasion fleet,' he said, dejectedly.

'Mothballed?' said Bache. 'For how long?'

'Er – about a hundred and fifty of your years.'

'Invasion of where?' asked Ed.

'The Sol system.'

'What?' both Ed and Andy said in unison.

'You mean, Earth,' said Bache, as the other two, who'd reeled back, recovered.

Groxl nodded.

'It got cancelled because the habitable planet suddenly started getting too warm for us,' he said.

Ed and Andy glanced at each other.

'Well, fuck me,' said Andy. 'You mean, global warming actually saved the human race from an alien invasion and mass genocide?'

Groxl nodded again.

'Our predictions had shown the planet was on the verge of slipping into another ice age and we were to get rid of the backward indigenous race and claim it for ourselves, long before you became spacefaring.'

'That was during the Victorian era,' said Andy, shrugging at Ed. 'They wouldn't have stood a chance.'

'What about the GDA?' Ed asked. 'Surely they wouldn't have let you get away with that.'

'They were busy elsewhere.'

Ed and Andy turned to face Bache.

'He's right,' said Bache. 'I remember my GDA history lessons. The Tellemat conflict had the navy at full stretch on the other side of the galaxy during that time. We wouldn't even have known about it, or been able to help even if we did.'

26

THE STARSHIP GABRIEL, ADJACENT TO PROXIMA C IN THE ALPHA CENTAURI SYSTEM

PHIL HAD TAKEN the *Gabriel* over two million kilometres across the system to Proxima C and given the ship hiding within its rings a thorough scan.

Groxl, his arm now fixed, was secured to a seat at the side of the bridge.

'What's this?' asked Ed, pointing to the holomap image of the hidden ship. 'It's obviously of Klatt pedigree, but I'm told the GDA don't have any record of this design.'

Groxl looked surprised and squinted at it for a moment or two.

'That's a new battleship, it shouldn't even be commissioned yet,' he said. 'As far as I was aware, it was still in the design stage. Is that the ship that attacked mine at Uskrre?'

'Most likely,' said Bache. 'Ever get the feeling you've been used as a pawn in a much bigger game than just your little revenge kidnapping?'

Groxl winced and Ed noticed him stare blankly for a few moments, as if thinking. Seemingly coming to a decision, Groxl looked up at them again and with a voice lacking the confidence and aggression from before, he spoke.

'I received a message a few days ago,' he said, glancing at Ed and then back at the floor. 'It was a GDA data file containing every detail about you and your location.'

'From whom?' Ed asked.

'It was encoded correctly as if from our naval command, but the source was from somewhere outside empire space,' he said, continuing to stare at a spot on the floor. 'It was untraceable.'

'But you acted on it anyway?' said Bache.

'It talked about how I could rescue my career and restore the pride of the Klatt Empire if you were brought to justice.'

'Do you still have a copy of the message?' asked Ed.

Groxl shook his head dejectedly.

'It was on the ship destroyed at Uskrre.'

'You don't think someone destroyed an entire ship and crew, just to delete a message, do you?' Andy asked.

The bridge went quiet for a moment as that possibility sunk in.

'Then why did they change their minds about myself and Pol?' said Ed. 'They boarded your ship to get us off, then when we were safely down on the planet, the two soldiers received instructions to kill us and bury our bodies.'

'This ship,' said Rayl.

Everyone turned towards her.

'Explain?' said Ed.

'While you were alive, we would always come looking for you,' she said. 'When they thought the *Gabriel* had been destroyed, you were no longer required.'

'That's not a bad theory,' said Bache, rubbing his chin in thought. 'This whole thing could be a plot to start a conflict between the Grondalle-dominant Klatt Empire and the GDA.'

'Who would benefit from that?' said Rayl.

'The Spleeta,' grumbled Groxl.

'The destruction of the Grondalle fleet on the border of Klatt space was planned,' said Andy. 'The exploding wasn't an accident, it was designed to wipe out a considerable amount of the Grondalle power base.'

'Sorry – what?' questioned Groxl. 'Destroyed fleet? What are you talking about?'

They'd forgotten that Groxl would have no idea of the happenings back on the Klatt border. So, Bache and Andy filled him in on the horror they'd witnessed.

Groxl sat slumped in his seat, unwilling to believe what he was told, until Cleo replayed the episode above him on the holomap.

'Ancients save us,' was all Groxl could say as the recording ended and he lowered his head into his manacled hands.

'I still don't see where kidnapping Ed comes into all this?' said Phil, speaking for the first time in a while.

'Killing two birds with one stone,' said Andy, raising his eyebrows at Ed.

'What?' said Phil.

'It's an old Earth term,' said Ed. 'I think I see what Andy means though. I was used as bait to get, not only a response from the GDA, by sending the *28* to the Klatt border, but enticing the *Gabriel* away from Earth and ensuring it was destroyed too.'

'But why would they need the *Gabriel* destroyed?' Rayl asked.

Ed turned back to Groxl.

'How many people did you normally have down on Uskrre, looking after the mothballed fleet?' he asked.

Groxl thought for a moment.

'Erm – if I remember correctly it was just a security contingent of around ten personnel. The defence satellites were designed to discourage any casual visitors, so it didn't need to be larger,' he said.

'Discourage,' said Andy. 'That's one way of describing an immediate missile strike.'

Groxl averted his eyes again.

'How many Spleeta personnel are down there now?' Ed asked, keeping his eyes on Groxl.

'Hundreds,' said Groxl. 'They've built a lot more accommodation for some reason.'

'More like thousands now,' said Rayl. 'A continuous stream of freighters has been running down to the surface since we left, all crammed with personnel.'

'Are they sparking up that fleet?' Bache asked, giving Groxl a glare.

'It can be the only reason,' Groxl replied. 'You don't need that many for periodical maintenance.'

'Well, at least we know they're not going to Earth,' said Rayl. 'It's too warm.'

Groxl turned to her with a pinched expression and immediately glanced away.

'What?' she said, witnessing Groxl's embarrassed glance.

'Ah – now – that would be correct for the Grondalle and Bekon clans,' Groxl muttered. 'The Spleeta on the other hand came from a home world much like Earth and they've caused such horrendous global warming there, that over the centuries it now resembles a desert planet. They would love a planet like Earth.'

'So, you're saying this is not only a power grab by the Spleeta, but could be a diversion while they grab a fresh planet to replace their dying home world?' said Bache.

Groxl shrugged.

'Would explain a lot of things,' he said.

'Oh, fuck,' said Andy. 'Can't we just bomb the shit out of that fleet from orbit?'

'Not without proof,' said Bache. 'Or we really would be guilty of what we're already accused of.'

'We have to remain dark,' said Ed.

'What, and let these wankers invade Earth?' said Andy, standing and waving his arms around. 'Not fucking likely.'

Bache raised his hands palms out to calm Andy for a moment.

'We need to find the orchestrators and uncover the plot for all to see, *before* that happens,' he said. 'They believe that with Ed, this ship and Groxl gone, they're in the clear. The GDA and the remnants of the Grondalle fleet are going to be concentrating their attention over in Klatt space more than ten thousand light years away from Earth.'

'This new ship hiding here has to be the key – as Groxl says, it shouldn't exist, it's been built in secret,' said Ed.

'There are obviously traitors within the GDA and in high office too, we must find them and expose them.'

Andy slumped down on his couch again, mumbling to himself.

'I've found it,' said Cleo, suddenly appearing amongst them.

'Found what?' said Andy.

'The message that was sent to Captain Groxl.'

'How, I mean where?' Ed stammered.

'In the deleted files on that ship.' She pointed to the hidden Klatt ship on the holomap. 'It originated there.'

'Sent by whom?' Groxl asked, suddenly sitting up straight and wincing as his restraints dug into his shoulders.

'Captain Groxl,' said Cleo.

27

THE STARSHIP GABRIEL, ADJACENT TO PROXIMA C IN THE ALPHA CENTAURI SYSTEM

ALL EYES TURNED TO GROXL, who looked as stunned as the rest of them.

'Any relation?' Bache asked, crossing his arms across his chest and waiting for Groxl's explanation.

'My – son,' he snarled, almost spitting out the two words.

'Your *son*?' exclaimed Ed.

Groxl bowed his head for a moment and stared at a spot on the floor.

'Would he have known it was your ship he was attacking?' Ed continued.

'Of course,' Groxl replied, as if it was a daft question and turned his head to gaze up at the Klatt vessel on the holomap.

'Why would he do that?' questioned Bache.

Groxl dropped his eyes from the holomap to the floor again and paused before he spoke.

'We had a disagreement over his career prospects. He didn't like a decision I made some time ago.'

'We all have disagreements with our parents,' said Andy. 'But it doesn't usually conclude with one party potentially murdering the other.'

'Welcome to the Klatt Empire,' said Groxl, lifting his gaze to glare at Andy.

'Well, whatever the reason,' said Bache, 'you're now a member, along with us, of the supposedly dead club. Perhaps you'd like to join in and find out who the hell is behind all this and maybe save your empire at the same time?'

'And Earth,' said Andy, giving Groxl a pointed stare.

Groxl nodded slowly and held his shackled arms up.

'I'm not going to be much help bound up like a Dervian land beast,' he said, looking over at Ed and then Bache.

'As you've now seen that Ed wasn't responsible for the loss of your cruiser, can you now admit that his unlawful detention was in fact a mistake and you're no longer intending to pursue his prosecution?' Bache asked, keeping his eyes firmly on the Klatt captain.

Groxl shrugged and glanced over at the holomap again.

'If that ship orbiting Uskrre is indeed my old ship, then, yes, I agree my actions were somewhat premature – evidently we've all been deceived by persons unknown within our relevant organisations.'

'And?' said Bache, still staring.

'And, the intended criminal prosecution of Captain Virr is forthwith rescinded.'

'Thank you,' said Ed.

Groxl held his hands up again, this time in a more placatory manner.

'My apologies regarding your assistant,' he said. 'I honestly believed I was doing the little ship a favour by stopping the truck from ramming it.'

'You can apologise to her in person in a few days,' said Rayl.

Groxl sat back, a puzzled expression on his face.

'You told me she was dead,' he said, turning to stare at Ed.

Ed gave Rayl a withering look.

'In that body, yes, she is,' he replied. 'She will be reborn shortly in a new body.'

'But, what about brain function?' he asked.

'Intact.'

'You can do that?'

Ed nodded.

'How?'

'Classified.'

'But, that makes you almost immortal?'

'Almost.'

Finally, Groxl stopped asking questions and just sat staring with an expression of either fear or shocked surprise, Ed wasn't sure, but he signalled for Cleo to remove his restraints anyway.

Groxl nearly jumped out of his skin when they vanished into thin air.

'How – who...?' was all he could get out as Cleo materialised beside him; this time dressed in all her regal splendour.

'Hello, Captain,' she said, lifting his chin to close his gaping mouth with a *clop*. 'You will be restricted to the bridge, the blister lounge and a cabin I have prepared for you. The crew will show you where these are, but remember, any deviation from those areas will result in my displeasure. Don't disappoint me.'

Groxl just sat and stared at the space she had been for a few moments after Cleo disappeared again, only looking up when Andy spoke to him.

'It's best not to upset the ship that's keeping you alive,' he said.

'She's the ship's computer?' Groxl asked, almost dejectedly, the typical Klatt arrogance and pomposity he had arrived with now completely absent from his demeanour.

Everyone on the bridge nodded slowly.

'And she's omnipresent and sentient?' he asked.

More nodding.

'Captain, we're going to need your input to help solve and thwart this thing – whatever this thing is,' said Bache. 'So, any information you may have on the Spleeta clan, no matter how trivial you think it is – don't be shy.'

Groxl shrugged.

'You know, it's strange you used the word "shy",' he said, 'because that's exactly how I would have described the Spleeta. For centuries, they've been the least aggressive clan within the Klatt Empire. Quite the opposite in fact. Engineers, builders, artists, medical staff even, but not military. Not ever. It was as though those soldiers down on Uskrre had been brainwashed or drugged. It's just so completely out of character for them to be even remotely aggressive.'

'So, you don't believe this could be their plan, originally?' Ed asked.

'Not a chance.'

Bache turned and stepped into the holomap, pointing to the new Klatt ship hiding within the rings of Proxima C.

'That ship will have some answers,' he said. 'Is there any way we can disable it, make it look like an accident and get aboard during the confusion?'

'I'm sure something can be arranged,' said Ed.

'Awesome,' said Andy, grinning and cracking his knuckles. 'Road trip.'

The smile disappeared from his face when he saw Rayl glowering at him.

'Don't even think about going on that ship,' she said.

'It's not your planet that's about to get invaded,' replied Andy.

Ed got up from his control couch and stood between them as he saw Rayl bristling with intent.

'I'll go,' he said.

'You'll be the only smooth-skinned human on the ship, you wouldn't last a minute,' said Groxl. 'If anybody goes it has to be me.'

'Won't someone recognise you?' Phil said.

'Not if I wear a Spleeta uniform,' said Groxl.

'And smile a lot,' said Andy, which just got him an affronted glare from the Klatt captain.

'I'm sure there are helmeted personnel on that ship,' Ed said, glancing at Groxl. 'Especially during an emergency.'

'Security and fire teams have visored helmets,' said Groxl, nodding.

'If we can show Cleo the designs, she'll be able to produce duplicates,' said Phil.

'I believe we have the beginnings of a plan,' said Ed, deliberately not turning to look at Rayl, who he knew was glowering at his back.

28

THE KLATT CRUISER GANDE, HIDING NEAR PROXIMA C IN THE ALPHA CENTAURI SYSTEM

THE SUDDEN EXPLOSION in an engineering bay deep in the bowels of the ship had been deliberately placed adjacent to the main power distribution nodes. It blew straight through the fibreskin wall and disrupted several major supply pythons as they were about to spread out and encircle the large vessel. Navigation, shields, jump drive, environmental and several more minor systems, one of which was lighting, were immediately taken out.

Groxl, Bache and Ed, all wearing Spleeta anti-radiation suits, made their way silently away from engineering in the gloom of the red emergency lighting.

Fifteen minutes earlier, Andy had jumped a cloaked *Cartella* inside one of the cruiser's large stern hangars and discreetly in a corner dropped the three of them off. The ruse of undertaking a radiation leak drill had worked as Groxl had led them through a maze of corridors to place the charge.

He led the way again now, not only because he was familiar with the design of Klatt vessels, but he was the only one who could speak Klatt without a translator and was able to bullshit his way through any security checks.

Originally, he'd wanted to go alone, as the *Gande* was the first in a line of highly classified new warships. He'd baulked at the thought of showing the layout of the ship to two potential enemy combatants. But again, after being reminded that they'd all been murdered by the very regime he was trying to protect, he'd soon relented.

'The bridge is generally high in the centre of the ship,' he whispered to the other two, as they made their way as quickly as they could up one of the many stairways. The elevators had also been a victim of their earlier explosive mischief.

An unexpected thump and rattle shook the cruiser violently, causing them to stumble on the stairs.

'I think the pilot's having trouble keeping the ship under control within the rings,' said Bache. 'That sounded like a large lump of rock hitting the hull and shattering. The shields must be down too.'

'So long as we don't get a breach,' said Ed. 'I've been in one of those before and they ain't much fun.'

'You and me both,' said Bache. 'More than once.'

Ed glanced at Bache, wondering if he was joking or not, but with the dark helmet visors they sported, he couldn't see his face.

Groxl nodded at the writing on the wall as they reached one of the higher levels.

'This should be what we're looking for,' he said. 'Senior officers only, that generally means the bridge and officers' cabins are on this level.'

Ed had noticed how eerily quiet it had become on the

ship after the explosion. Once the emergency sirens had been silenced, a surprisingly small fire crew had bundled past them going in the opposite direction and with the environmental system temporarily down, the usual background hum of an operational starship was noticeably absent.

As they left the stairwell through a bulkhead door and entered a wide corridor, the main lighting came on again and the muffled sound of shouting somewhere up ahead reached their ears.

'Someone sounds pissed off,' said Ed, continuing to wave his radiation detector around as they continued the ruse of a leak and made their way in the direction of the bridge.

'That sounded like he was speaking words in Ellinika too,' said Groxl, who was further up the passage.

'He was – I made out a couple of the words,' said Bache.

'Which were?' Ed asked, hurrying to catch up.

'Fucking and arsehole.'

'Oh dear, someone's not happy with our work,' Ed said, smirking inside his helmet.

Rounding the next corner, they were confronted by two armoured security guards facing them and blocking what must be the main bridge door. The door was open and Ed noticed it'd been opened manually, as a red winding handle was sticking out of the wall on the right-hand side.

'What the hell do you think you three are doing?' one of the guards demanded, bringing his weapon up to cover them.

'Radiation leak,' said Groxl. 'Why aren't you in your suits?'

A look of doubt crossed the guard's face and he glanced at his colleague.

'We were not informed,' he said, as the other guard shrugged and shook his head.

'Comms are down,' continued Groxl. 'We need to sweep the bridge – urgently,' he added forcefully, as the guard hesitated.

Ed meanwhile had utilised his DOVI and ensured the guards' weapons were non-functional.

Finally making a decision in their favour, the two guards stepped aside and nodded at the open door.

'Be quick,' the same one speaking again said. 'The captains are busy.'

The use of the plural hadn't gone unnoticed as they quickly bypassed the guards and entered the bridge. Ed noticed the room was a lot smaller than most GDA bridges. It was octagonal, with a seat facing all eight sides and a central slightly raised square plinth with two seats side by side, one of which looked as if it belonged and the other odd one, hastily brought in and dumped next to it. Only four of the bridge officers' seats around the walls were taken and two men, who were standing on the raised area, turned and glowered at them as they entered. One was a younger Klatt in what Ed thought must be a captain's uniform and the other a human in a senior GDA uniform.

'What the fuck are these three idiots doing?' demanded the human, turning to confront the younger Klatt next to him.

'I have no idea,' he replied, lifting his arm and pointing at Groxl. 'What are you doing?'

Groxl ignored the question, turned, nodded at Ed and Bache, pulled a hidden laser pistol and shot both the senior officers. They crumpled to the floor, a look of shock and surprise still on their faces as they became still.

Ed and Bache meanwhile had spun around, produced their own concealed weapons and given both the guards the good news as they bundled through the door. Their armour did take some of the kick out of the stun shots, but two or three pulses each was more than enough to dump them flat on their backs with thin trails of smoke emanating from their armoured suit motors. The four remaining officers appeared to be unarmed and sat very still with shocked expressions and their hands up and away from the controls.

Groxl walked around the various control stations until he found the one he wanted, switched his weapon from stun to full power and turned the communication console to a pile of scrap. He did the same to the weapons station while Ed and Bache secured the remaining four officers to their seats with plastic ties.

'Where are the other bridge crew?' Groxl asked one of them.

'This is it,' one of them said. 'We were told this voyage was just a systems check for the new design.'

'That human was in charge,' another said, pointing at the GDA officer.

'Ganelaine,' Bache whispered to Ed.

'Eh?' Ed replied, touching his helmet against Bache's. 'Who?'

'Senior Captain Ganelaine, he's another of the military advisors to the GDA council.'

'What the fuck's he doing on one of our experimental battle cruisers?' Groxl asked, pointing at the human and staring at the four bridge officers in turn.

The four officers looked at each other and shrugged.

'He joined the ship in neutral space just after launch,' one of them said.

'Captain Groxl seemed to be afraid of him,' said another.

Ed realised at that moment that Groxl hadn't had any qualms about stunning his own son. He reminded himself to remain extremely wary of the Klatt captain and not turn his back for a moment.

'Pick them up,' Groxl ordered and made his way back to the door.

Ed decided to pick up the unconscious GDA officer, leaving the lighter Klatt for Bache as he was older. They struggled a bit to get them up into a fireman's lift and once there, followed Groxl into the corridor.

The Klatt wound the red handle once they'd passed, closing the bridge door again, stuck the red handle in his belt and nodded up the passageway.

'Do we need anything else while we're here?' Groxl asked.

'No,' said Ed. 'Let's not push our luck, back to the hangar as quick as possible.'

'We're taking them to medical if we're questioned,' said Bache, as they reached the stairs again.

'Don't worry,' said Groxl, waving his pistol in the air.

'These bastards killed my ship. I'm using this if anyone gets in the way.'

'Stun only though,' said Ed. 'Remember it was these two that killed your ship, not the skeleton crew brought aboard for a test flight.' Even though he couldn't see Groxl's face, Ed knew he hated being told what to do and was probably gritting his teeth and glaring at him behind the smoked visor. But he still did as he was told and turned the weapon back to stun.

The whispering of the environmental system came online as they hurried down the stairs and back to the right level for the hangar decks. They only passed one person on the way back to the hangar where they'd entered the ship and he completely ignored them. Ed called Andy who'd been loitering nearby, and with the cruiser's shields offline now, he was able to fly straight into the deserted hangar unimpeded to pick them up.

Ed exhaled with a sigh of relief as he dropped the heavy limp body on the cockpit floor and as the *Cartella* left the hangar, he was finally able to remove the claustrophobic helmet.

After securing their captives with more ties, they went directly back to the *Gabriel* and before the prisoners could wake up, they were placed in separate secure rooms that Cleo had prepared. As the *Gabriel* moved quickly away, the crew waited patiently with a degree of anticipation as to what they would find out when they woke up.

29

THE OFFICE OF ADMIRAL GELTZ, KENTRO CITY, DASOS, PRASINOS SYSTEM

THE ADMIRAL STOOD FLEXING his shoulders as he peered down through his large office picture window. From the hundred and fourteenth floor of the Council Plaza he could see right across downtown Kentro City and on a clear day all the way out to the Potamaki Peninsula and the Bordaan Sea. But today, with the low cloud and snow showers, he could barely see the ground at all.

A soft chime from his desk computer woke him from his daydream and he strolled across, sat down and touched the flashing icon with an irritated swipe.

'Geltz,' he said, in an officious tone, answering the incoming call.

'Not an appropriate tone to use with me, Geltz,' said the caller.

His eyes went wide as he recognised the voice at the other end of the encoded call.

'Sorry,' he said, wincing. 'I had no idea it was you.'

He felt a bead of sweat run down his face as a pause from the other end made him even more nervous.

'Update on the Earth ship?' the voice asked, finally.

'Destroyed,' he answered, flicking the sweat off his face.

'Uh, huh – and was Commander Loftt aboard?'

'We have strong evidence he was.'

'Hmm – finally – I have my revenge.'

The voice paused for a second before continuing.

'What news on our fleet preparations?'

'They're gathering in the Fellitain system – we're just awaiting the final vote from the council.'

'When?'

'Today or tomorrow. You know what it's like trying to get enough representatives together to cast a ruling vote, especially in this weather.'

'Your weak excuses are of no consequence – that vote will be passed today or you'll be managing a duradium mine tomorrow.'

Geltz shivered, as he knew the threat was real.

'It will be done,' he said.

He held his breath as another pause stalled the conversation and almost jumped out of his skin when the voice finally spoke again.

'Do you consider the Spleeta ready to rule once the Grondalle are dethroned?'

'The High Secretary in Waiting, Hurde, assures me they are. The invasion fleet has been secured and is being prepared as we speak.'

'And the new Klatt home world has no knowledge of the impending attack?'

'None. Once our assembled battle fleet is heavily engaged in the region of Zee-Klatt III, the planet will be wide open and helpless. It has been anticipated that the indigenous race will surrender after the climate begins its change and the ground offensive gains momentum.'

'And the mining rights of their belt?'

'Yours. The Spleeta have no interest in mining. They have assured me they will provide you with the surviving primitive humans from the planet as slaves to work in the belt and then purchase the minerals from you.'

'Hmm – what's stopping the Bekon clan making a power grab when the Grondalle are on their knees?'

'They're the smallest clan, it's not in their nature and any surviving Grondalle vessels will be immediately requisitioned by the Spleeta.'

'Do you really believe the Klatt will abandon Zee-Klatt III?'

'As you know, the planet's very remote and has been cooling for many hundreds of years. Even the Grondalle were beginning to find it cold and the few Bekon there hate the place. With the Klatt's new power base organised, Zee-Klatt III will be quickly abandoned by the new order and perhaps another mining opportunity beckons.'

'You don't tell me what I should or shouldn't be doing, Geltz. You concentrate on getting that vote through and the fleet engaged in finishing the Grondalle off. Is that clear?'

'It is,' he said, as the line went dead.

Straight away he contacted the council adjutant to find out the number of planetary representatives present and how many more were expected for the afternoon sitting, before beginning a list of calls.

Seven hours later Geltz was sat back at his desk staring at the wall. He leaned back in his chair and exhaled loudly before standing and walking over to the window again. The adjutant had called him moments before to inform him the vote for the fleet to engage the Klatt forces in and around Zee-Klatt III had passed almost unanimously. Only a handful of races that bordered the Klatt region had abstained to avoid enraging their unforgiving near-neighbour just in case it went badly for the GDA.

He smiled for the first time in days and watched the lines of flyers now jockeying for airspace around the city's tall buildings as the thick snow clouds had begun lifting. He shielded his eyes as a shaft of sunlight penetrated the room for the first time that day and opened them again almost immediately as he found himself suddenly back in shade. He baulked as he met the eyes of a helmeted pilot in the cockpit of a grey unmarked flyer hovering only metres away from the outside of the building.

He barely had time to register what it was before three neat holes appeared in the glass, with the sound of a whip cracking. Admiral Geltz's lifeless body hit the back wall of the office a split second later with a wet *thud*, before plopping onto the plush carpet, leaving a red trail down the wall. With a hole in his chest the size of a football and his dead eyes staring at nothing, he never saw the auto cannon retract back into the fuselage, the flyer turn lazily to starboard and quietly reintegrate itself back into the late afternoon traffic.

30

THE STARSHIP GABRIEL, HIDING IN THE ALPHA CENTAURI SYSTEM

CAPTAIN GROXL the younger awoke suddenly to find himself on the *Gande*'s bridge floor. The four bridge officers stared at him with faces ranging from shock to contempt. He looked down at himself but found no injuries or wounds, just a dark circular singe mark on his tunic, which meant the weapon had been on a stun setting.

'Are you going to stay down there all day?' said Senior Captain Ganelaine, extending a hand and hauling the young captain to his feet.

Groxl staggered slightly and looked around in confusion.

'They were shot by the door guards, in case you were wondering,' said Ganelaine, noticing Groxl's bewilderment.

'Where are they now?'

'Floating amongst the rocks.'

'Who were they?'

'Grondalle who disagreed with the plan.'

Groxl nodded and sat on the captain's chair rubbing his chest where the laser bolt had impacted.

'Are you all right to continue?' the GDA captain asked. 'That was a heavy stun setting on that pistol, one of that strength can disorientate the best of us.'

'No, I think I'm all right.'

'Well, let's find out. Where are we with the plan so far?'

'What d'you mean?'

'I want to see if your memory is sound. Run me through what we've done so far and what we have to do next?'

The young captain stared at the floor in thought for a moment.

'Erm – okay, well, my idiot father snatched Virr from Earth, causing his starship to follow as planned and the GDA to send the cruiser *28* to the vicinity of Zee-Klatt III. We waited until the majority of the Grondalle fleet approached and detonated the *28*. We didn't get the Earth starship as expected, but were able to destroy it as it fled towards Dasos.'

'What are we doing next?'

'That's your decision.'

'Yes, but I'm just checking your head's on straight – remember?'

'Right – err, we're waiting for the GDA fleet to fully commit itself in Klatt space before overseeing the invasion while their backs are turned. Did I miss anything?'

'Who do we get our orders from?'

Groxl looked at Ganelaine with a puzzled expression.

'Well, I get mine from you.'

'And I get mine from?'

'I've no idea – have I? You said we have to be compartmentalised, so no cell can betray another.'

'Good,' said Ganelaine. 'It doesn't seem like you've suffered any ill effects. You sit back there and rest, we've got a bit of a wait now anyway.'

Groxl sat back on the cushioned padding, almost immediately falling into unconsciousness.

Ed shut down his DOVI, opened his eyes and stared at the Klatt captain as he lay sedated in the auto nurse.

'I'll give him "idiot father" when he wakes up,' grumbled Groxl senior, sitting to one side with the others.

Cleo appeared in the room, still in her latest goth façade and raised her eyebrows at Ed.

Once the *Gande*'s shields were down, she'd been able to scan the interior of the vessel, so creating an exact copy of the ship's bridge in the younger captain's mind hadn't been too much of a drama. Ed had appeared as Ganelaine using his DOVI.

'That seemed to work,' she said.

'Only to confirm our worst fears,' said Ed. 'We still don't know who's calling the shots.'

'Perhaps he can give us a bit more,' said Andy, pointing at Ganelaine in the adjacent auto nurse.

'I reckon Admiral Geltz has to be involved somehow,' said Bache. 'We need to stop that GDA fleet committing to Klatt space. They may have wired more ships to explode.'

'We need to warn Earth as a priority,' said Andy. 'There's billions of lives at risk there.'

'Andy's right,' said Rayl. 'Do we know where James Dewey is?'

'He was in New York the day before my abduction,' said Ed. 'I saw him making an address to the United Nations on TV. Ironically enough, trying to drum up interest and funds to install a ring of the GDA's latest defence satellites.'

'Boy, could they do with some of those right now,' said Andy.

'What are we doing about Ganelaine?' said Cleo. 'Am I setting up another scenario like before?'

'No,' said Ed. 'Put your feelers out and find James Dewey's yacht.'

'Bache,' said Rayl. 'Who can you trust on Dasos? You must have someone in a position of power that can help?'

Bache stood up and strolled around the room rubbing his chin thoughtfully.

'There is someone,' he said.

'What's their name and we'll see if we can find their details on the database,' she said.

'Ex-GDA Council President Jamill Xutan.'

Everybody in the room froze and turned to stare at him. Apart from the low mumble of the auto nurses, there was complete silence for a couple of seconds.

'You are kidding, right?' said Rayl, her mouth hanging open in surprise.

Bache shook his head.

'He's gotta be in his eighties,' she said.

'Eighty-four,' Bache confirmed, this time with a nod.

'He sponsored my career in the early years and we've always kept in touch.'

'Have you got his tab address and will he believe you?' asked Andy.

'And if he does, how much authority does he still carry?' said Rayl.

'You'd be surprised,' said Bache. 'He can be quite – what's the word? – efficacious when he wants something doing.'

'Dewey's en route to Dasos,' said Cleo, suddenly. 'I've detected his ship in the Callinn system heading for the next jump point.'

'Can we intercept?' asked Ed.

'If we go now and give it the full monty,' she said.

'Whatever that is – do it,' said Ed. 'We have to get to James before he gets to Dasos, and Bache – see if you can contact your ex-president to stop that fleet going in the wrong direction.'

31

THE STARSHIP GABRIEL, EN ROUTE TO THE JACAB'NA SYSTEM

Ed looked up from his mug of coffee as Bache joined him in the blister lounge at the top of the ship.

'Message sent?' Ed asked, as Bache flopped onto the sofa opposite.

'Sent,' said Bache, not sounding overly confident. 'Whether it gets to him or not is out of our hands. We have no idea how deep this goes.'

'D'you think he could be involved?'

'Highly unlikely knowing the man, but somewhere along the line there's a lot of money involved and if the sums are big enough, it can corrupt anyone.'

Ed nodded and stared back into his drink.

'I've sent a drone back to Earth to warn them,' he said. 'Not that there's a lot they can do to prepare, even if it isn't intercepted by—'

Ed stopped abruptly and looked up as the lighting in the room suddenly changed to red.

'You'd better get to the bridge,' called Cleo, her voice echoing around the empty room.

'On our way,' said Ed, abandoning his coffee and running for the tube lift with Bache hot on his tail.

'There's another ship,' said Rayl, pointing at the holomap as they popped up into the bridge. 'It was waiting hidden in the Jacab'Na system and headed straight for Dewey's ship as soon as he jumped in.'

'What is it?' Ed asked.

'Klatt design corvette,' said Cleo.

'Shit – how long till we're there?'

'Three minutes,' said Phil.

'How close are they to Dewey?'

'Two minutes,' said Andy, the worry evident in his voice.

'How long will his shields hold out?'

'Not long against a warship.'

'Jumping in three, two, one, now,' said Phil.

The holomap changed abruptly and reset with three flashing icons closing on each other.

'We're at point nine three light,' said Phil. 'That's everything.'

Ed could see the corvette was obviously going to get there before them.

'Uncloak the ship,' he said.

'But our secrecy will be blown,' said Andy.

'I'm not planning on letting that corvette leave,' said Ed. 'They want a war, let's start giving them one.'

'I'm taking out one of the mini-mes,' said Andy, leaping up, and in four seconds he'd disappeared below on the tube lift.

Phil uncloaked the *Gabriel*. The response was immediate and brutal.

'They've fired,' said Rayl. 'Two missiles launched.'

'Can we take them out?' said Ed. 'With the rail gun maybe?'

His answer came with a judder and the brittle *snap snap* of the rail gun unleashing two titanium rods at the speed of light.

In the meantime, Dewey's yacht had taken evasive action and turned towards the *Gabriel*. A sudden glint of light from the side of the yacht caught Ed's attention.

'What was that?' he said, pointing as another icon tracked away from Dewey's ship.

'Lifeboat,' said Rayl, looking up with alarm.

'The missiles have altered trajectory with the ship, the rail gun rounds will miss,' said Bache.

'Are we in range for the lasers yet?' Ed asked.

'No,' Rayl snapped back.

'Give them a few missiles to worry about,' he said. 'They might take their eye off the ball for a minute.'

Three kataligo missiles tracked away from the *Gabriel*, homing in towards the corvette. It did indeed quickly alter course, unfortunately towards the lifeboat. It unleashed two more missiles at that before turning away.

The rail gun fired twice more, but everyone could see it was too late. The missiles would reach the lifeboat before the rounds would take them out.

Then several things happened in quick succession: one of the missiles heading for the lifeboat suddenly exploded harmlessly, and the yacht turned abruptly just as the missiles targeting it closed in. One missed and began tracking around to reacquire its target and the other hit the ship's shields at an acute angle and detonated, damaging the yacht. The second missile targeting the lifeboat found its mark and the tiny craft disappeared in a cloud of vapour.

'Oh shit,' cried Rayl.

The remaining missile reacquired the yacht but exploded way short of its target and moments later the corvette bloomed outwards from the bow and exploded in spectacular fashion. The *Gabriel*'s three missiles then came in from behind and added to the maelstrom, leaving nothing resembling a ship at all.

'Is that everything?' called Andy, as he uncloaked the tiny GDA fighter.

'We believe so,' replied a dejected Rayl.

'Another few seconds and we would've been in time,' said Ed, as Phil brought the *Gabriel* close to the damaged yacht. It was in a slow tumble, its shields down and communications array badly mangled, but just as Rayl was about to utilise the tractor beam to catch the yacht and arrest its tumble, the second lifeboat ejected. Phil quickly brought the *Gabriel* about and caught up with the tiny vessel, as Rayl gently eased it into the port hangar. Andy followed it in and parked next to the other fighter in the corner.

Ed and Bache sprinted into the hangar and joined Andy as they approached the scarred and slightly singed lifeboat. The hatch motor whined and the circular airlock door dropped open, the three of them all leaning underneath the craft to peer up inside. Three frightened faces of the yacht crew stared back and just as Ed was about to ask about the ambassador, a rather harried recognisable fourth face appeared and spoke quietly.

'I hope the bar's open; I need a fucking drink – fucking drink indeed.'

———

Dewey was on his fourth cognac before his hands stopped shaking.

'Have the Klatt lost their fucking minds?' he said, after Ed and Bache filled him in on whose ship it was that had attacked him. 'I was only speaking to their High Secretary Zikk'La a few days ago too.'

'It's not the ruling Grondalle clan that's doing this,' said Bache. 'It's a group of their Spleeta clan looking to gain control, supported by some as yet unidentified senior GDA personnel.'

You could hear Dewey's swearing halfway around the ship, especially when he learnt of the upcoming Earth invasion, and Bache managed to get his brandy glass out of his hand before it hit a wall.

'We need to get back there and defend the planet,' he raged. 'This ship has a formidable arsenal doesn't it, surely it'll be enough—'

Ed raised his hand palm out to stop Dewey.

'James, the invasion fleet is around four thousand ships strong,' he said. 'Even if it was four hundred we'd still be overwhelmed in the end. The only way to defeat this is with a fleet and they're all being sent in the wrong direction. We need you in the council chambers on Dasos, persuading them to divert part of the fleet to Earth.'

Dewey paced back and forth across the bridge, his hands behind his back and staring at the floor.

'I thought you said this ship has been designated renegade,' he growled. 'It'll be targeted as soon as we arrive.'

'It has and it would,' said Ed. 'But the *Cartella* hasn't.'

Dewey looked up. His face of worry had been replaced by one of determination.

'Better step on the gas then,' he said.

32

THE CARTELLA, EN ROUTE TO DASOS IN THE
PRASINOS SYSTEM

THE *GABRIEL* HAD JUMPED to the Aspro system so the *Cartella* could appear to be a private Theo vessel, travelling between Paradeisos and Dasos.

Andy had agreed to pilot them there and was now on final approach to a small domestic space port on the surface of Dasos, around forty kilometres from the outskirts of Kentro City.

'It's certainly pretty with all the snow,' said Andy, peering out across the winter landscape as he slowed to allow a Regg'Taa-registered freighter to take off.

'The gravity's not so attractive though,' moaned Dewey, grimacing at Bache, who'd agreed to travel with him and give him some support.

'Nothing like a bit of gravity to keep you fit, James,' said Bache, grinning back.

'Bollocks to that,' he replied, winking at Andy, as it was one of his English phrases he'd borrowed.

Andy smiled as he turned the ship and plonked it down

on a carpet of fresh snow, the soft powder on top billowing out around the ship, agitated by the antigravs.

They both donned warm coats and hats as Andy ordered a flyer to take them into the city centre.

'Any problems, I'll be right here,' said Andy. 'I don't think there's any glühwein available in this ski resort anyway.'

Two blank expressions indicated neither got the joke, so he hit the open airlock icons just as a city flyer landed on the adjacent pad. He could feel the freezing air wafting in the door from the pilot's seat and quickly closed the inner airlock door as both James and Bache negotiated the steps and waded their way through the snow to the waiting flyer.

The first inkling Bache had that everything was not as it should be was when the flyer pilot didn't ask them where they wanted to go. Andy had deliberately not given a destination and when they just took off and turned towards the south of the city, all Bache's hackles stood to attention.

He winked at James to indicate he was about to do something unexpected and leaned forward to speak to the pilot.

'Hey buddy, that's really cool you turning up,' he said in a coarse non-local dialect. 'I was just about to call for a flyer anyway. Can you take us to the Pink Flame Club on the south side? My friend and I want to try out some of these famous Dasos girls.'

The pilot's face turned from a determined expression to one of confusion.

'Are you a GDA commander and an ambassador?' he asked, as he slowed the flyer and looked nervously over his shoulder.

'Hell, no,' said Bache. 'We're miners from Krix'ir.'

He gave James's knee a squeeze to stop him saying anything.

'We got off the freighter from Regg'Taa that just left. We were asking the pilot of that small ship if he operated a taxi service and now you come to mention it, there were two important-looking gentlemen waiting on there. Did you pick us up by mistake?'

The pilot swore under his breath and dropped the flyer straight down and landed with a thud in some sort of housing development.

'Hey, you can't leave us—'

'Get out,' the pilot sneered, a weapon of some sort suddenly appearing in his hand.

Bache opened the door quickly and dragged a rather confused James with him. The flyer's engines screamed as it took off again in a hurry, causing them to shield their eyes from a blizzard of snow blasted up by the antigrav. It turned away back towards the space port and soon disappeared in the low cloud coming in from the west. More snow began to fall.

'What the fuck was all that about?' demanded James, looking at Bache weirdly as though he'd grown two heads.

'We were being abducted,' Bache replied, striding off and nodding his head to indicate James was to follow.

'We were?' said James, puffing to keep up. 'Do you have to go so fast?' he added, when he got no reply.

'It won't take that pilot long to realise I bullshitted him,' said Bache, steering James towards a small row of shops. 'He'll be back, probably with reinforcements. So, we need transport and fast.'

'How did you know?' James asked, again struggling and puffing like an old steam engine.

'He flew off in the wrong direction and why would a taxi flyer pilot have a concealed weapon?'

'Fuck,' said James. 'I'm not cut out for all this cloak and dagger shit, obviously.'

As they approached the row of retail shops, a lady exited the second shop and opened the door of an old and dirty grey ground vehicle. Bache wasn't going to bother with that one, but noticed it was one of the few vehicles with snow-cutting wheels. He pulled a hidden laser pistol and when the lady got into the vehicle, he jumped in with her, making sure the weapon was low but very visible to her.

'I'm sorry, we won't harm you, we won't rob you, we just need you to drive us somewhere,' he said to the terrified woman.

She started crying and making a high-pitched keening noise.

'This is Ambassador Dewey from the GDA council,' said Bache, pointing at James as he climbed into the vehicle and joined them.

'Sorry, miss,' James said, in a soothing tone. 'It's an emergency, we really need to get into the city quickly. Can you do that for us?'

She quietened a little and nodded on hearing James's less threatening inflection. Bache pulled the door down and closed it, as she programmed a route into the city.

They both kept one eye on the sky as the old vehicle hummed its way out into the traffic and headed north east, its snow cutters occasionally clattering noisily on the clear patches of roadway under the overpasses, bridges and trees.

'I know where we are now,' said James suddenly as they neared the centre. 'Turn right down there,' he said, pointing.

The woman retook manual control and turned right where the ambassador was pointing.

'There's a rear entrance we use to come and go without having to run the gauntlet of tourists at the front,' James said. 'Pull up at those gates over there.'

She did as she was told and as they neared the gate, James waved a black bracelet on his wrist at a panel set into a low pillar. The gates powered open, revealing a darkened passageway dropping down below ground.

'I'm not driving down there,' she said, nervously.

'No, you're right,' said James, patting her on the shoulder. 'We can walk from here. Come on Bache, we don't need to frighten the poor lady any more do we?'

'Absolutely not and again, sorry to have scared you.'

The woman half smiled as they exited the vehicle, then reversed up and drove off at great speed, snow cutters clattering noisily as she went. As the two of them turned and stepped through the gates, a sudden roar came from above and the old grey vehicle disappeared in a ball of fire.

'Holy crap,' shouted James, as the concussion from the

blast almost knocked him off his feet. Bache grabbed his arm and bundled him down into the underground gloom of the GDA Council Plaza.

'That poor woman – we didn't even know her name' said James, wistfully looking over his shoulder as they ran through the lines of parked vehicles.

Bache gritted his teeth and swore to himself he was going to do something very unpleasant to whoever was calling the shots of this murderous fiasco.

33

THE CARTELLA, HITROO DOMESTIC SPACEPORT, DASOS

Andy watched the flyer take off and thought it odd the pilot had turned and headed towards the south of the city. He shrugged, shut the *Cartella* down, set a perimeter alarm of ten metres and reclined the pilot's chair. He must have dropped off, because the next thing he knew both the airlock doors were whining open and a draught of freezing air was whipping around his feet.

He sat up to find the muzzle of a laser rifle in his face, behind which stood four grey-clad soldiers, their faces partly hidden behind head-up display visors.

'Where are they?' the one pointing the weapon at his nose demanded.

'Where's who?' Andy answered, as two more soldiers appeared from the cabins at the back and shook their heads.

'The fucking terrorists,' the intruder barked, sticking the muzzle up one of Andy's nostrils, causing him to tilt his head back.

'Are you sure you're in the right place?' he

answered, stalling for time as he felt around with his DOVI and deactivated their weapons. 'I brought a council ambassador and his assistant, a retired GDA commander, from Paradeisos to Dasos, no terrorists involved – sorry.'

A commotion from outside the ship caught the soldiers' attention and probably stopped Andy getting a slap. A flyer had landed just outside. The pilot jumped out, sprinted over and up into the cockpit.

'Are they here?' he blurted.

'No, they're fucking not,' snapped the soldier with the weapon up Andy's nose.

They both turned to stare at Andy.

'My clients got in a flyer identical to yours straight after we landed,' Andy said. 'You can check the camera footage if you like.'

The soldier snapped his glare back to the pilot.

'You stupid bastard – it was them all along.'

The pilot grimaced, went to turn away, before quickly turning back.

'There were shops nearby, they'll have cameras,' he said, pulling out a small tablet and tapping away.

Andy drew a sigh of relief as the weapon was extricated from his nose as the soldier joined the pilot and studied the tablet closely.

'There,' the lead soldier said. 'Trace that vehicle's designation and get Delta 2 up and over the city, all measures authorised.'

'Yes, sir,' said the pilot, disappearing out the airlock again.

'You do realise you'll all be executed for assassinating

an ambassador, aiding in the murder of a ship's crew and an illegal invasion?' said Andy.

The lead soldier's face turned to an ugly sneer and he launched himself towards Andy, raising his rifle butt as he went.

'It's about fucking time someone shut you – ouch – shit,' he screeched, dropping his weapon and huffing on his hands.

The other three soldiers still inside the cockpit all did the same as their weapons became too hot to hold. The rifles all clattered to the floor, fizzing and popping as the electronics burned out.

They all looked over their shoulders as the inner and outer airlocks began closing together.

Andy tutted and shook his head slowly. The lead soldier turned back to him, a look between anger and fear showing in the eye not obscured by the display visor.

'Oh, dear – now you're for it,' Andy said. 'You've upset Cleo.'

'And who the fuck is he?' the soldier said with a sneer.

'She,' said Cleo, appearing behind him in some sort of black ninja outfit.

He spun around and got a fist up under his visor. It snapped his head back, knocked him over the top of the navigator's seat and into a heap under the control console.

The other three near the airlock looked at him with astonishment and turned to stare at her, one of them taking a tentative step towards her. She shook her head slowly.

'Gentlemen, I know what you're thinking,' she said, raising her hand, palm up. 'There's three of us and only one of her.'

The three soldiers lifted off the floor and hung stationary in mid-air, their legs and arms waving about helplessly. A loud knocking on the airlock and shouting from outside caught everybody's attention.

'Bitch broke my fucking nose,' carped a now not so intransigent lead soldier, mopping blood from his face.

'I think we need to move somewhere a little quieter for a chat,' she said, as the unmistakable sound of the anti-gravs spooling up invaded the cockpit.

The knocking from outside quickly ceased and Andy could see some of the other soldiers backing away from the ship. One of them fired his rifle at them, but Cleo had activated the shields, so the bolt just dissipated around the hull. The *Cartella* lifted and continued straight up to around one thousand metres, where both the airlocks began whining open again. Freezing air and a little snow wafted in and the three soldiers near the airlock began frantically trying to swim away from the slowly enlarging opening, their frantic limb flapping getting them precisely nowhere.

'What are you doing?' said the lead soldier, now with a very nasally voice.

'I thought you might be a little more forthcoming with a bit of gentle encouragement,' she said.

'What you going to do, dangle them out the airlock?' he scoffed.

The three soldiers stopped struggling and stared at their leader in disbelief.

'No, I wouldn't do that,' she said, grinning malevolently.

Andy noticed the three soldiers relax slightly.

'That would just prolong the torture. I'll just throw them out one at a time.'

Before anyone could react, the nearest soldier to the airlock whipped out the door. One second he was there, the next he was gone, his terrified scream dissipating into the snow cloud.

'You can't do that,' bellowed the lead soldier, having to shout to be heard above the howling of the remaining two soldiers. The frantic air clawing resumed.

Andy's eyes nearly popped out of his head as he stared at Cleo and surreptitiously clipped a seat harness around himself.

'Who's giving the orders for this operation?' she asked, drawing little circles in the air with her forefinger and swivelling it towards the gaping airlock.

'Fucking tell her,' one of the soldiers screamed, 'I didn't sign up for this shit.'

'Enough money to retire rich for a couple of months' work, you said,' shouted the other one.

'Ah, mercenaries, eh!' she said, nodding. 'You still haven't answered my question,' she added, in a much more sinister voice and swivelling to point at the lead soldier's face.

'Get fucked,' he said.

She flicked her finger and the second soldier vanished into the snow cloud a kilometre above the ground.

Andy squirmed on his seat in shock. He hadn't seen Cleo do anything like this. The Theo sentient ships were supposed to be incapable of taking human life. He was in two minds whether to intervene or not, but before he could make up his mind, Cleo spoke again.

'You're very brave when it comes to the lives of others,' she said. 'Let's see how brave you are when it's your life.'

She waved her other hand and the lead soldier slid out from behind the navigator's seat. He tried to grab hold of it, but found the force moving him was too strong and his fingernails just scudded across the coarse fabric and were finally dragged off the seat.

'No, no,' he pleaded, as he neared the airlock. 'I have a family.'

'So did they,' shouted the last of the three, gesticulating at the open door. 'You fucking arrogant bastard, I'll throw you out the fucking door myself.'

'It's Xantian, Ambassador Xantian,' he blurted, finally.

'Uh, huh,' grunted Cleo. 'He wouldn't be working alone. Who does he answer to?'

He was inside the small airlock now, his head almost hanging out the door. His helmet was ripped away by the wind and he screamed back at her to be heard above the maelstrom.

'We don't know, it's compartmentalised – for fuck's sake, they don't tell us.'

Cleo nodded and turned to Andy.

'I think we've got all we can from these numpties,' she said, waving her hands back towards her.

The lead soldier was dragged back inside the cockpit and the other two soldiers crashed back through the door, screaming as they came.

Andy sighed with relief, as he realised she'd held them against the hull just out of sight and earshot. He noticed the *Cartella* was descending again and as it clunked down in a rather pretty field of virgin snow, some kilometres away from the city, she hurled the four soldiers out, along with their burned-out weapons.

She walked into the airlock and watched them picking themselves up out of the deep snow.

'Perhaps a rethink on the career front,' she shouted above the noise from the antigravs.

Andy watched as she closed the airlock doors and the ship rose up and turned to head back towards the city. He caught a glimpse of one of the soldiers punching the lead soldier in the face as they passed over them and thought that must have really hurt if his nose was broken.

Cleo sat down on the navigator's seat, crossed her legs and slid her hands behind her head.

'Stupid wankers,' she said.

Andy chuckled.

'You really can be a scary ship sometimes, Cleo.'

34

THE GDA COUNCIL PLAZA, DASOS

JAMES STEERED Bache through the labyrinth of corridors and elevators that made up the sprawling edifice known as the Council Plaza. Being the primary centre of power for over sixteen hundred humanoid worlds meant the complex covered several square kilometres and more than half of downtown Kentro.

It had its own internal mini-rail system and James, struggling with the higher gravity, headed straight for the nearest terminal. Even Bache, who'd been away from the gravity on Dasos and the majority of GDA ships for some time now, noticed how unfit he had become. Luckily, they didn't have to wait long as one of the small two-carriage trains soon whirred to a stop in front of them.

There were six others in the carriage and Bache eyed them all as they boarded, but none seemed remotely interested in them. He made sure they sat near a door and were able to keep an eye on the whole train. The Dasos-style coats they were wearing, hastily made up by Cleo, had snow hoods and face wraps for blizzard conditions. They kept these on so the cameras wouldn't give them up.

'Where's our first port of call?' asked Bache.

'Chamber Foreman,' replied James. 'I have to book an emergency recitation.'

'Have you done one before?'

'No, but I've watched others do it.'

'How quick will they get you in?'

'Depends on the agenda. If there's an all-day debate going on, it might not be until tomorrow.'

'That would be a serious problem,' said Bache. 'The chances of avoiding these killers here overnight would be difficult. We're not on Panemorfi and able to sneak off and sleep on a beach, we're going to need a hotel and that means an electronic payment.'

'I'll put pressure on the Foreman.'

'D'you want me to join you to add more weight to the accusations?'

'Perhaps not – if there's an arrest warrant out for you involving mass murder, it might not be prudent. After all, I have all the evidence uncovered so far on the data chip.'

Bache nodded, and looked up as the train swept into Chamber Terminal. They alighted and made their way to the main security checkpoint. Here, of course, they had to finally uncover their faces and show their identification, which included an iris scan. James went through first and then Bache, who held his breath, expecting alarms to sound and guards to come running. He was surprised when nothing happened and he entered to look for James. He found him sitting on the plinth of the statue of the ancients in the main reception hall with a grin on his face.

'Pays to be dead sometimes, eh!' said James. 'They can't have taken your credentials off the database yet.'

'Or they let me in to trap me,' Bache replied.

No sooner had he said it than a group of six uniformed men appeared from behind the statue and surrounded the two men.

'Yes, gentlemen?' said James, adopting a mildly puzzled expression and getting to his feet again.

'Ambassador Dewey, Commander Loftt, you are both under arrest. If you'd like to come with us please,' said the leader of the group. He was sporting ominous Skirmat Eagles sewn onto his tunic's lower arms, which hadn't gone unnoticed by Bache, who rolled his eyes, as he'd had dealings with these igno-minious bastards before. The dreaded GDA galactic detectives, with almost god-like authority and resources, they were not who you wanted searching for you.

'On whose authority and on what charge?' James demanded.

'Mine – mass murder, conspiracy to overthrow an alien government and most recently, the murder of Admiral Geltz.'

'Geltz is dead?' Bache exclaimed, giving James a worried glance. 'When?'

'Last evening.'

'We weren't even here then,' said Bache.

'No, of course you weren't. Like you weren't there when you destroyed the *28* and murdered its forty-seven thousand crew. But here you are, right at the scene of your latest crime.'

'They're worried,' said Bache to James. 'They're cleaning house.'

'The prisoners will not speak to each other, you will now come with me,' the Skirmat said, nodding his head at the others, who grabbed Bache and James's arms and began marching them towards a small door at the side of the hall.

'What's going on here?' boomed a voice, behind them.

Everybody stopped and turned to find ex-GDA Council President Jamill Xutan and his entourage of bodyguards glowering at them.

Bache couldn't help but notice the Skirmat flinch slightly before speaking.

'These men are under arrest; it is no concern of yours.'

'It is no concern of yours, what?' barked Xutan.

'Erm, it is no concern of yours, Mr President?'

'Well done, son,' he said sarcastically. 'But unfortunately, it is my concern, because, you see, I invited these fine gentlemen here today as my guests. So, you will unhand them, turn around and quickly disappear back under whatever pile of excrement you recently oozed from.'

The Skirmat stared at Xutan, opened his mouth, then closed it again, before finally plucking up the courage to speak.

'Mr Presiden—'

'OFF-YOU-FUCK,' bellowed Xutan, waving the detective away acerbically with one finger, his security detail inserting hands inside their coats and the sound of six laser weapons beeping as safeties were removed.

The men handling Bache and James capitulated first,

released them, turned and walked away. The Skirmat admittedly held his ground initially, but finally caved to Xutan's authority and turned, not before deliberately fixing eye contact with all of them, which Bache knew was just to say, *This isn't over*.

'Can I say, Mr President, I always did find your speech writing inspirational,' said Bache, watching the Skirmat disappear through the small door with a sneer before slamming it shut.

'Why, thank you, Commander,' Xutan said. 'And may I ask what the fuck is going on?'

35

THE OFFICE OF EX-PRESIDENT JAMILL XUTAN, GDA COUNCIL PLAZA, DASOS

PRESIDENT XUTAN EXHALED LOUDLY and sat back in his tall green leather chair. He'd just finished watching the recorded footage from the disaster at the Klatt border and the goings on in the Alpha Centauri system.

'No wonder these people want you dead,' he said.

'You'll have definitely been added to the list now,' said James.

'That remains to be seen – they might baulk at assassinating an ex-president,' he replied.

'Whatever happens, we need to turn the fleet around, Mr President, and quickly,' said Bache.

'And may I request a few of those cruisers finding their way into orbit around Earth?' asked James.

Xutan nodded.

'Let me make a call,' he said.

They all looked up as the sound of a screaming antigrav from outside disturbed the quiet of the office. Multiple holes materialised in the floor-to-ceiling outer glass wall, which ultimately collapsed, as dozens of white-hot laser bolts turned the plush office into a tempest of flame and flying debris. Nothing in the office survived the sudden onslaught – chairs, tables, ornaments, pictures and the three humans just vanished in the maelstrom. On the floor below and the floor above, there were two hidden snipers armed with Makrys sniper rifles; one took out the protruding cannon and the other made neat holes in the small grey unmarked flyer's antigrav drive.

It immediately began emitting a horrendous rattling noise and slowly at first began to lose altitude. The pilot was experienced and fought the controls valiantly, but the heavy gravity of Dasos eventually overcame his skill and the damaged antigrav drive. Fourteen seconds later it crash-landed in the previously cleared street below. The only slightly injured and shocked pilot was surrounded and arrested by a mixture of plaza security and Xutan's bodyguards and whisked away for questioning.

'Okay, you were right,' said Xutan, nodding his concession at James. 'It seems they'll stop at nothing to protect themselves.'

They made their way through to Xutan's office from the back of the building from where their holographic images had been projected. As soon as Bache opened the door a cold wind whipped around their ankles and a flurry of powdered snow, smoke and ash from burnt furniture wafted into the corridor. Xutan grimaced as he peered in and indicated to Bache to pull the door closed again.

'I think you might want to call your interior decorators,' said James.

One of Xutan's bodyguards trotted up and whispered in

his ear. Bache noticed the sudden look of surprise on the President's face.

'What is it?' he asked.

'The pilot,' said Xutan. 'He's ex-navy and now a private contractor. He thought he was acting on behalf of the Council.'

'Where did his orders come from?' asked James.

'Here,' said Xutan. 'The office of Ambassador Xantian.'

'And where's he lurk?' asked Bache.

'In the next building, I believe,' said Xutan, indicating for his bodyguards to follow.

They took one of the staff elevators down to the basement and made their way through the vehicle park. They met the same Skirmat Eagle from earlier, carrying four tablets and going in the opposite direction. He scowled at them, got in a dark vehicle and swept up the exit ramp and out into the snow as if he was late for an appointment.

'I hate those guys,' said Bache, as they boarded the same elevator as the Skirmat had exited.

'Forty-first,' said Xutan, reading from his tablet as James dialled it in on the wall keypad.

The forty-first floor was silent as they exited the lift. All three bodyguards drew their weapons as they glimpsed a leg sticking out from one of the office doorways further down the wide corridor. They waved for Xutan to wait as they cleared each room, working their way methodically towards the body. Once they were sure the floor was clear, one of them returned and spoke softly to Xutan. He puffed his cheeks out and sighed, before turning to the others.

'They're all dead,' he said. 'The ambassador, his

assistant and both secretaries. Professional hit, all have one in the chest and one in the head from close range.'

Bache's tablet pinged with an incoming call from Andy.

'Are you guys safe?' Andy asked, as soon as Bache answered.

'Well, apart from three assassination attempts, we're fine,' he replied, rolling his eyes at the worried face on the tablet.

'That's why I'm calling. A group of mercenaries came to find you and take the *Cartella*.'

'The fact you're calling me indicates they weren't very successful?'

'No, Cleo kicked their butts, only we found out they were taking their orders from an ambassador here on Dasos.'

'Xantian,' said Bache.

'How did you know that?'

'Because I'm standing in his offices right now and he's dead, along with three others under his employ.'

'Oh, crap.'

'My thoughts exactly.'

'They really are cleaning house.'

'No shit.'

'Do you need me to pick you up? I'm staying in the air now and cloaked, a few thousand metres above the city.'

'Pick us up at the main plaza flyer pad in fifteen minutes,' said Bache. 'And you'd better uncloak for that, it can be a little busy.'

They tiptoed around the crime scene looking for the deceased's tablets.

'Hang on,' said James. 'What was the Skirmat carrying downstairs as he exited the elevator?'

'The fucking Skirmat,' blurted Bache, staring at Xutan.

'Oh, shit,' said James. 'Downstairs, he was about to take us through that side door.'

'And that's where our bodies would have been found,' said Bache.

Xutan walked to one side and made a call, returning a few moments later with a scowl on his face.

'I contacted the offices of the Skirmat detectives,' he said. 'No detective was on duty within the council plaza today.'

'Right,' said Bache. 'We need to get down to the flyer pad where Andy will pick us up. We'll all be safer up on the *Gabriel*.'

'What about me?' Xutan asked.

'Especially you, Mr President,' said James.

'What about my guys?' Xutan added, nodding at his bodyguards.

'Them too,' said Bache. 'It'd be good to have some backup we can trust. Whoever we're up against has a long arm and unlimited funds, it seems.'

'Let's go,' said James, opening the elevator door again. 'I can't wait to be away from this bloody gravity anyway.'

'Bloody gravity, indeed,' said Bache, joining James in the lift and ignoring his waspish glance.

36

THE STARSHIP GABRIEL, HIDING ON VASI
STATHMOS SPACE STATION

CLEO, with Rayl and Ed's help, had electronically redesignated the *Gabriel* into a Deelataynian luxury yacht and quietly and discreetly docked at the Vasi Stathmos station above Dasos during the night period. Luckily there weren't many windows overlooking dock 89X and they trusted there wouldn't be anyone in docking control studying the cameras at this time of night with an intimate knowledge of specific ship design.

Ed had paid for a week in advance and as the docking clamps had clunked home, he'd checked with his DOVI to ensure he could override docking control and release them in case of an emergency.

Andy, meanwhile, had picked up the now sizable group, taken the crowded *Cartella* inland to the continent's huge dividing mountain range and cloaked while unnoticed in a deep and unassuming ravine. Once happy the ship was no longer observed, he picked his way carefully and invisibly up through the planet's atmosphere, which was swarming with traffic, to the *Gabriel*'s port hangar while it was attached to the space station. He likened it to negotiating the M25 London orbital on a summer public holiday, only this time manually operating an invisible vehicle.

Ambassador Dewey and his crew were given passage back to Earth on a large commercial liner leaving that evening. Dewey ensured their jobs were secure while the situation was resolved and a replacement ship was provided for them. This time, perhaps something that could defend itself a little more diligently, he'd insisted.

As it was the night period, once Ed had seen Dewey off, he suggested everyone get some rest and scheduled a planning meeting up in the blister for around lunchtime the following day.

The attack came in the early hours. What Ed had assumed impossible went without a hitch for the special forces involved. Four commandos of the GDA's elite Fantasmata (ghosts) unit dressed in dock authority exterior maintenance suits, quietly, without drawing attention to themselves and under the pretext of dock maintenance, touched a military-grade pulse generator to the *Gabriel*'s hull, thus knocking out every system on the ship including Cleo and causing the main airlock to be vulnerable from the outside. Shields were not permitted to be active on any ship when attached to a station, as they all tended to nudge against each other, pushing the station out of its stationary position and causing undue stress on the space elevator peduncle.

The second this happened, the airlock was breached

and twenty more Fantasmata stormed into the ship, quickly overpowering the unprepared bodyguards in Xutan's detail. A control pad was plugged into an interface just inside the main airlock and all the systems attempting to reboot and come back online, apart from environmental, were paused and left on standby. A powerful disenabler was carried in on the back of one of the commandos to disrupt any form of communication or independent power signals from entering or leaving the vessel.

As yet, none of the crew or passengers, all still asleep, had any inkling of a problem. Even if they did, their cabin doors were sealed and Cleo was absent and strangely silent.

Opened one at a time, the cabins' occupants were quickly subdued, cuffed, blindfolded and had their ears covered. Then they were dragged up through the ship and dumped two metres apart on the dock just outside the main airlock. Once the commandos were happy they had everyone, they resealed both the airlock doors and waited.

The large freight elevator adjacent to the dock clunked and buzzed as a carriage arrived. Its heavy rectangular doors ground noisily open on bearings that were overdue some maintenance and grease. The Skirmat detective from yesterday exited, along with his previous entourage from the main foyer. He cast his eyes over the trussed row of bodies, glowering at them maliciously as he passed and approached one of the Fantasmata commandos.

'All of them? he barked.

The soldier nodded, his face hidden behind the black visor they all wore.

'Where's that four-armed abomination?'

'Dead, sir,' he answered. 'The alien's body is in the medical centre.'

It was the Skirmat's turn to nod.

'Good,' he said. 'The best ones are. Four-armed freaks give me the shits.'

'We also found Ganelaine and that young Klatt captain unconscious in there too.'

'Where are they now?'

'They were taken to the station medical centre.'

'Had they been interrogated?'

'Unknown, sir.'

'Hmm,' grunted the Skirmat. 'We can't risk them losing faith and talking – send someone up there to ensure they don't wake up.'

The soldier nodded and whispered in the ear of his nearest colleague, who promptly disappeared up the corridor at a run.

The Skirmat strolled along the line of hooded and bound bodies again.

'Which one's Virr?' he demanded.

The soldier walked two paces and kicked one of the figures in the midriff, who emitted a muffled groan and curled into the foetal position.

'Make sure that one is delivered to the appropriate authorities with this,' he said, passing a data node to the soldier.

The soldier nodded again and pointed at the still groaning figure, who was swiftly dragged into the waiting freight elevator and disappeared behind the grinding noisy doors, before the carriage clunked and buzzed away to a different level.

'Bring them,' the Skirmat ordered, waving his hand nonchalantly at the remaining bodies, and strolled away down the corridor towards the remaining docks stretching out down the row as far as you could see.

He stopped at an airlock three ships down the line, tapped a code into a keypad and entered an old Lynkas-registered freighter. Although the ship was intended for the shipment of bulk foodstuffs, a previous owner had had twelve passenger cabins built in to increase the ship's revenue when moving from system to system.

'Put one in each and lock the doors,' grunted the Skirmat. 'Just stun them if they play up. The client's now decided they want them alive on arrival.'

The soldiers did as requested and filed off the vessel, leaving a team of seven onboard to guard the prisoners and crew the ship.

'Is the legitimate cargo secure?' he asked.

'Yes, sir,' came the response. 'One hundred and fourteen tonnes of Dasonion wine.'

'Get under way as soon as you can and don't do anything that might encourage an inspection. You know where you're going and what to do?'

The officer nodded and disappeared towards the bridge. The Skirmat strolled off the ship and secured the airlock. Ten minutes later, as he made himself comfortable in his own ship on the neighbouring dock, he heard and felt the docking clamps release on the freighter next door. He smiled and logged a course for the Jagnorite system before requesting his own clamps be released.

37

THE STARSHIP GABRIEL, DOCKED ON VASI
STATHMOS SPACE STATION

THE FAMILIAR WARMTH and coziness suddenly became a falling sensation that lasted only a second before something hard hit from below. The sound of splashing water assaulted her ears and a coldness enveloped her as she collapsed in a heap. She began vomiting, gasping and coughing as her body screamed for oxygen and as the last of the fluid was ejected, she opened her eyes to try and make sense of what was happening.

A blinding whiteness seared her retinas as she rolled onto her hands and knees, coughing away the last of the clear gloopy fluid. She squinted and blinked. Raising her upper arms to wipe her eyes and using her lower ones to hold herself up, she felt herself tipping forward and smacked her forehead on the floor.

'Ow, shit,' she croaked. That brought on another bout of coughing.

Rolling over and sitting on her backside, she concentrated on focusing. The reason she couldn't feel her lower arms became quickly apparent. They weren't there.

'What the fuck,' she said, staring at the two arms and hands with five fingers. She wiggled them and grimaced, before looking around and realising she was sitting in a round room, with a tubular glass container suspended from the ceiling, from which a plethora of umbilicals snaked up into the ceiling.

'Oh, shit,' she said, the realisation kicking in, which caused her to stare at her hands again. 'I must have died and been reborn as a human.'

A low buzzing from behind her made her jump as a narrow nozzle motored out from the wall high up and began spraying water. Pol stood for the first time and although she resembled a newborn foal, she managed to stumble under the water and wash the birthing fluid off her body. Towels appeared in a recess and as she dried herself, she revelled at the length of her legs, her feet with five toes, her knees and her breasts. She hadn't had those before. Although, she found she wasn't so impressed with having to dry her upper and lower body separately, instead of at the same time. Having only two arms was a distinct disadvantage and would take some getting used to.

Wrapping one of the towels around herself, Pol looked up.

'Cleo, are you there?' she asked, raising her eyebrows as she found the sound of her own voice so different.

No answer was forthcoming, which she thought was a little odd and she felt a small sense of disappointment that no one was here to welcome her back.

Perhaps they don't know yet, she thought, *perhaps it's the middle of the night and Cleo doesn't want to wake anyone.*

Concentrating hard, she stumbled across the small chamber to a recessed panel in one of the rectangular wall sections. It only had two buttons, one red, one green.

Thinking it was the most sensible option, she pressed the green one. There was a low *clunk* followed by a hiss, as if the pressure had to equalise and the wall panel sunk back slightly and slid inside the wall to the left. The smell of disinfectant hit her and she realised she had been behind a section of the wall in the medical centre.

Makes sense, she mused.

She wobbled her way out and passed the row of auto nurses, suddenly freezing as she reached the last one. She felt a shiver run down her spine as she stared down into the auto nurse at her own old lifeless body.

'Fuck,' she said, eventually. 'I could've done without seeing that, Cleo.'

She turned her head to look up at the ceiling for a moment.

'Cleo, are you there? Is anybody there?'

She sighed, because as before, she got no answer.

Shuffling towards the door, she stopped again and stared. A full-length mirror was set into the wall by the door and she gazed at her reflection. She dropped the towel and marvelled at her new look. She hadn't realised she had such long hair as it was wet and plastered down her back. She pulled some of it round her head and ran her fingers through it, revelling in the feeling. Callametans didn't have long hair, so this was a new sensation for her. She gazed at her narrow waist and curvy hips and the strange triangle of hair between her legs.

I wonder if human males will find this appearance

appealing? she thought. *I need to find Rayl, she'll have some clothes and know how this body works.*

Picking up the towel again, she turned and exited the room into the corridor. She stopped and looked back, a puzzled expression on her face. Normally, the doors to rooms on the *Gabriel* vanished as you approached and reappeared once you'd passed through. The door simply wasn't there at all.

'That's odd,' she mumbled to herself, turning and continuing on towards the tube lift.

It didn't activate when she reached it.

Perhaps it doesn't recognise the new me, she thought and after loitering a few seconds, just in case, she went left and took the narrow emergency stairway.

The bridge was deserted and as she slipped into one of the control couches, nothing happened. No holographic controls and no holomap greeted her, as it always had before.

'Cleo, what's going on?' she asked, gazing up at the ceiling.

Except for the quiet whispering from the environmental vents, nothing stirred.

'This is getting weird now,' she shouted. 'If this is one of your jokes, Andrew, it's not funny.'

The bridge remained quiet and all the hairs on the back of her neck stood up, which was an alien sensation to her. She shivered and began to feel a sense of dread. She knew that there should be at least one member of the crew manning the bridge at all times when the ship was in space.

She hit the stairs again and now getting more accustomed to her legs and sense of balance, took them two at a time. Arriving on the top deck, she headed straight for the blister, her jaw hitting the floor as she took in the view. Rows of ships of all sizes and designs were docked to a massive space station of some kind. The docking levels stretched away above the *Gabriel* as far as the eye could see.

'Where the hell is this?' she shouted at an empty room. Making her way quickly down to the crew's cabins several decks below, she headed for Andy and Rayl's room to hopefully find some clothes that would fit her new body.

She stopped dead as she arrived in the corridor. All the cabin doors were open with clothes and bedding strewn around, some of it out in the corridor itself.

'Hello – is there anyone there?' she called, hopefully, already suspecting there'd be no response.

Oh, fuck, she thought. *The ship's been boarded.*

Poking her head nervously into each cabin, she was somewhat relieved to find them all empty, with the distinct evidence of a struggle in each but no blood.

Whoever did this wanted them alive then, she thought, desperately searching for positives.

Returning to Andy and Rayl's cabin she felt a bit voyeuristic going through Rayl's clothing drawers and wardrobe, but soon found what she was looking for. She'd been present once when Rayl was changing and watched with interest at how human females had to wear a strapping affair to hold their breasts in place. She tried three on, but they were all a bit small, so she gave up on those. The underwear fitted though, and with a long green dress that fell below her knees and a pair of white training shoes, she admired herself in a mirror for a moment. Picking up Rayl's hairbrush, she attempted to untangle and tidy her drying long brown hair. It took a while, but once satisfied, she headed out to search the rest of the ship.

38

UNKNOWN LOCATION ON VASI STATHMOS
SPACE STATION

IT'D BEEN quiet now for quite some time and Ed was thoroughly miserable. He couldn't see or hear anything, his broken ribs hurt like hell every time he breathed and he was lying in a pool of his own urine. He was worrying about the others too.

Were they getting the same treatment? he thought, as he flexed the numb muscles in his legs and arms. *For all I know, they could be lying somewhere close by.*

He tried shuffling around a bit to see if anyone was lying near him, but cried out in pain as all he managed to do was agitate his ribs.

'Oh, for fuck's sake,' he shouted, through gritted teeth. 'Someone is going to fucking pay for this shit.'

He was suddenly grabbed off the floor and dumped into what felt like a chair. The pain was excruciating, but at least it was a change of position. The hood and ear plugs were ripped off his head and he squinted as the lighting, dull as it was, pierced his eyes like lasers. Someone was shouting and it took a moment for his internal translator to adjust to the Ellinika language the annoyed voice was conversing in.

'—fucking prisoner not an animal,' bellowed the voice. 'Get him washed and for ancients' sake some fresh clothes too. He's in a GDA detention centre, not a Klatt mining prison.'

Ed's eyes focused on a smartly dressed man, with salt and pepper hair and a scowl.

'Thank you,' he mumbled, through short gasps of air so as not to annoy his ribs further.

One of the guards the smartly dressed man had been admonishing curled his lip at Ed and spoke in a low hiss.

'My brother was on the 28. If it was my decision you'd be out an airlock already.'

Ed stared back, a look of complete confusion on his face.

'Out,' said Smartly Dressed, pointing at the cell door. 'From now on, I'm the only one who will address the prisoner and you will be reassigned.'

The guard sneered and stomped out, the rage evident in his face.

'Sorry about that,' said Smartly Dressed. 'Some of them can be such neanderthals.'

Ed stared at the man more closely and swore he recognised him from somewhere. His hair was a little greyer and perhaps a few more lines on his face, but he was sure they'd met before.

'I know you from somewhere, don't I?' he croaked, as Smartly Dressed produced a small penknife and sliced through Ed's bonds.

Ed rubbed his sore wrists and ankles as a sly grin came over Mr Smartly Dressed's face.

'I represented some Earther friends of yours a few years ago,' he said. 'You saved the case for me right at the last minute with some new evidence.'

'Commander Cien'dra,' said Ed, raising his eyebrows in recognition. 'You represented Xavier Lake.'

'Correct, Captain Virr,' said Cien'dra. 'As soon as I heard it was you, I came straight here. I owe you one – and you can afford my fees. They would've just given you some mediocre on-duty defence councillor and you wouldn't want one of those on a parking charge, let alone mass murder.'

'Mass murder?' choked Ed, then coughed and wished he hadn't, as his chest raged its disapproval. 'Is that what that guard was on about when he mentioned the *28*?'

Cien'dra nodded slowly.

'They're charging you with the wilful destruction of the *28* and murder of the crew, the murders of Ambassador Xantian and Admiral Geltz, along with the disappearance of ex-President Xutan and his security detail.'

'And a partridge in a fucking pear tree,' said Ed, rolling his eyes and sighing.

'What?'

'Never mind. Do they have even a scrap of evidence to back up this crap?' Ed asked.

'Oh, yes,' said Cien'dra. 'I saw the video and log evidence that was handed in with you. I have it on here.' He waved his tablet and nodded. 'I must admit it's quite compelling too.'

'You do realise I was being held prisoner on a Klatt warship when the *28* was destroyed?'

'Not according to the prosecution's evidence, you weren't.'

'Someone with a lot of political clout and funds has gone to a lot of trouble to orchestrate this coup.'

'Coup? What coup?'

Ed started at the beginning and gave Cien'dra the full story, from being snatched from his own home on Earth, to ending up in a pool of piss and broken ribs on a Vasi Stathmos Space Station cell floor.

'Ancients help us,' said Cien'dra, leaning back against the cell wall once Ed had finished. 'Proving any of this is going to be difficult.'

'You need to watch your back too,' said Ed. 'If they're prepared to murder admirals, ambassadors and even ex-presidents, then your disappearance would barely register.'

Cien'dra sucked on his bottom lip and stared at the floor for a moment.

'We need to let them think they've got away with all this and tied up all the loose ends,' he said. 'Then hope they get sloppy.'

'What? With me found guilty and executed?'

'No,' said Cien'dra. 'We immediately appeal your conviction, that'll hold everything up for weeks and give us time to hopefully flush out the true conspirators.'

'What do you mean, us?' asked Ed. 'What bloody good am I going to be able to do, stuck on death row in a GDA high security prison?'

'You saw the reaction of that guard?'

Ed glanced at the door and nodded.

'There's going to be a lot more of that. I saw the hatred for Lake and Herez last time a ship lost its crew. We'll get you placed in protective custody in a safe house somewhere and work from there.'

'You'd better be right about this,' said Ed. 'I'll come back and haunt you if they find me guilty, take me out the back and shoot me.'

'Won't happen,' said Chen'dra confidently.

'Just on the off chance it does,' said Ed, 'can you make sure my intact body is taken back to my ship and placed in an auto nurse?'

'Yeah okay, whatever that is. Why?'

'Erm – it's just custom to be buried back on my home planet before the body begins decomposing.'

'Ah – right,' he said, giving Ed a sideways glance. One thing Cien'dra had always been good at was knowing when he was being lied to. He had a suspicion that the last bit wasn't entirely true. 'I'll go and make sure you get a shower and—'

A shout and the unmistakable pulse from a discharged energy weapon coming from out in the security office stopped him mid-sentence.

'What the—' was all Cien'dra got out as two scruffy men appeared in the cell doorway, both firing powerful laser rifles at the two men in the cell from point blank range.

39

LYNKAS FREIGHTER, LOCATION UNKNOWN

ANDY WOKE SUDDENLY as a cramp in his left calf screamed for attention. He launched himself out of the small cabin bunk and, swearing profusely, stretched the offending leg muscles taut.

It'd been a week now since the night raid on the *Gabriel* and he'd had absolutely no contact with anyone else, apart from the guards who delivered food twice a day and they never uttered a word. He worried about Rayl and hoped she was okay. Had they taken her too, along with the rest of the crew and passengers, or was he the only one?

He was thoroughly bored now. There were three books – well, more like thick magazines really – and although they were written in Lynkas and his internal translation software had made them legible, he'd read them three times.

He'd just climbed back onto the bunk when the door lock beeped. He thought this strange as his first meal of the day had already been delivered only a couple of hours previously.

'Up,' said the guard, entering the cabin and jerking the muzzle of his rifle upwards to accentuate the request.

He was hooded and his hands bound, then led out into what he presumed was a corridor. He could hear the murmurs of others being brought out too, voices he recognised.

That's good, he initially thought, realising he wasn't alone. *But not so good for the* Gabriel, *and what the hell happened to Cleo?*

'Oh, for fuck's sake,' complained Rayl, from somewhere close behind him, making his heart race as it confirmed she was alive and nearby.

'Where are you taking us?' he asked, not that he thought he'd get an answer, but to let Rayl know he was also alive and close.

'No talking,' one of the guards shouted, as he got what was probably a weapon jabbed in his back.

A hand placed under his right elbow projected him forward as they began moving through the ship. His heart missed a beat as he heard the unmistakable whine of an airlock opening, but the hand on his elbow followed him in and remained there as the airlock cycled. They crossed an area where a cold breeze whipped at his clothing and hands. His hood billowed slightly and he caught a glimpse of a metal grating beneath his feet.

The floor surface changed abruptly a few moments later, not like an artificial hard floor of a ship or space station, but of something more solid. He could smell sulphur and the sound of hammering in the distance, muted like it was emerging from deep inside a cave. Then machinery – he could hear the echoey sound of electric machines rising and falling on the light breeze brushing past his hands.

The walk went on for about ten minutes and he gave up trying to remember all the turns so he could find his way back. The sounds gradually got louder until the guard leading him stopped suddenly and spun him round. He felt the bonds around his wrists being removed and the hood was ripped off.

He stood blinking in a low orange light emanating from lamps high up on the rough ceiling of a ten-metre wide cavern. It seemed like everyone from the *Gabriel* was there, squinting as their hoods were removed and wrinkling their noses at the sulphurous smell. There were rows of small metal-framed bunk beds lined against the walls going three high, a large refectory table in the centre surrounded by metal stools and a pile of coarse blankets on top.

The guards backed out of the cavern, slammed a heavy metal door closed and slid across a couple of bolts on the outside.

Rayl ran over and hugged him as soon as she saw him.

'I was so worried,' she said. 'I thought I might not see you again.'

'Same here,' he whispered in her ear, as he gazed around at the others looking at each other in bewilderment.

'Where's Ed?' he said, suddenly realising he wasn't amongst them.

'What?' asked Bache, as he limped over.

'Ed – he's not here,' said Rayl.

Bache turned as Xutan, Phil, James and Groxl approached.

'My son and that GDA captain aren't here either,' sneered Groxl. 'I thought that ship of yours was supposed to be impregnable?'

'No ship is completely secure in dock with its shields down,' said Bache. 'But I must admit, we should've been safe with Cleo watching over us.'

'Correct,' said Phil. 'The fact that she didn't intervene worries me for her safety, a lot.'

'Oh, shit,' said Rayl suddenly, pacing up and down with her head in her hands.

'What is it?' Andy asked, as everyone turned to face her.

'Pol,' she said. 'She was only a day away from rebirth.'

'Ah, crap, you're right,' he said. 'She was in the sealed birthing chamber; they won't have found her.'

'She'll not only have the trauma of the rebirth itself on her own, but also the shock and unfamiliarity of being in a human body and then, if that's not all, we're all missing.'

They all stared at her for a few seconds.

'Ed could be there,' said Phil, breaking the silence. 'Or Cleo.'

'Not a chance,' said Andy. 'Cleo was somehow taken offline and I'm sure Ed will have been taken elsewhere.'

'You hope,' said Groxl. 'Or he fought back and was killed.'

'No, he's not,' snapped Andy. 'If he was dead, I would know.'

'Where d'you think we are?' asked Xutan, speaking for the first time.

Andy dragged his piqued glare off Groxl and shrugged at Xutan.

'Judging by the time it took to get here, it's got to be a remote prison or mining asteroid,' he said.

'I agree,' said Bache. 'The ship didn't undergo the buffeting of a planetary insertion, so we're definitely on a moon or asteroid.'

He turned to Xutan and raised his eyebrows.

'I take it your protection detail didn't make it?'

'Who knows?' Xutan answered, looking forlorn. 'Couple of those guys had been with me right from the beginning. My kids grew up with theirs.'

A sudden rattling caught their attention as the door bolts were dragged back and the riveted steel door swung open again. Two armed guards stepped in either side of the opening, followed by a short uniformed man with a badly pockmarked face.

'Welcome to my little holiday cabana,' he said, making an overly theatrical bow. 'My employers have insisted that you remain here while the operation is completed. A recent minor change of plan suggests some of you might actually survive this and then again – some of you – might not.'

Deliberately sad eyes picked out Bache for a second, before they brightened again and he smiled.

'Dinner is served if and when the guards can be bothered. Remember, it's your fault they're here too, so don't piss them off any more than they already are.'

His smile disappeared as he turned and left, followed by the guards, with the door slamming shut and the bolts rammed home.

'Small man syndrome,' said Rayl. 'An acute case.'

Andy turned to Bache and raised his eyebrows.

'Who have you pissed off?' he asked.

'D'you want me to make a list?' Bache replied, walking to the table and draping a blanket over his shoulders.

'Are we to understand you were a bit of a rebel then?' Groxl asked.

'Quite the opposite actually,' said Xutan, before Bache could answer. 'The council, myself included, found Commander Loftt rather apt at problem solving, right from an early age.'

Bache smirked as he lay back on one of the bottom bunks.

'That's an understatement, Mr President,' said Bache, casually putting his hands behind his head and closing his eyes. 'I believe I was seventeen when I saved the galaxy for the first time.'

Everyone turned to Xutan, who shrugged and nodded.

'Yup, he did.'

Rayl glanced around the cold solid rock cell they were in and shivered.

'Any chance you could do it again, anytime soon?' she asked.

40

THE STARSHIP GABRIEL, DOCKED ON VASI
STATHMOS SPACE STATION

POL SOON FOUND the airlock near the bow of the *Gabriel* that was linked to the station. Opening the inner door, she could see through the outer door window there was a short twenty-metre extended walkway vacuum scaled to the hull, encircling the entire airlock. The recessed panel next to her showed a green light, which she knew meant the atmosphere on the outside was within safe parameters. So, she opened it.

She found the extra gravity outside a problem as soon as she stepped off the ship as her legs in their weakened state struggled to hold her up. Staggering to the end of the walkway, she looked left and right, hoping to find some clue as to what station this was. Auto trundles, dozens of them, hummed past in both directions, taking freight and supplies to and from the other ships docked on this level.

A sign printed above the station's airlock said dock 821h, but it wasn't this that she was interested in. The station logo printed on the bulkhead below the dock number was what she stared at. It was a gold crest with

'Vasi Stathmos, serving Dasos for two millennia' printed in a circle.

Now I know where I am, she thought. *It's time to get back out of this horrid gravity.*

She wobbled her way back to the *Gabriel* and sighed with relief as she closed and secured the airlock, before beginning a full search of the ship.

It was when she was searching the port hangar and sticking her head inside one of the shuttles that she got a sense that she was being observed. Spinning round suddenly, she caught a flash of light in the cockpit of the *Cartella*, followed by another and a third. The random flashes of white light continued, almost as if someone was welding something inside the ship.

She knew the shuttles had a weapons locker at the back of the cockpit, so she retrieved a laser pistol and set it on heavy stun, before approaching the *Cartella*. The outer airlock powered away as she held the pistol out in front with a double-handed grip. Nothing jumped out at her so she stepped inside, crouched down and reached up to press the flashing green icon. Again, nothing happened when the inner door whined open and she waited a second or two before sticking her head inside.

The cockpit was empty, but the flashing continued to illuminate the inside of the ship randomly in long and short bursts. It was coming from a panel built into the rear bulkhead at the back of the cabin. After she'd checked the whole ship was clear, she approached the bright flashing light and discovered it was an icon and the more she watched, she realised the flashing actually wasn't random at all. It was a recurring set of three short flashes, three long and three short again.

'I know this,' she said out loud. 'I'm sure Ed showed me this a few months ago.'

She grabbed a tablet and searched, *communication with flashes of light?* Immediately the tablet came back with, *Ancient form of communication using short or long flashes of light or sound. Originating in the Sol system and known locally as Morse Code.*

She glanced down the shown list of codes.

'SOS, repeated over and over,' she mumbled to herself and entered, *Morse code SOS?*

Sol system distress code, meaning 'save our souls'.

It's a call for help, she thought, glancing back up at the light continuing to flash its repeated distress message.

She reached up and hovered her finger over the icon.

'Just don't be a self-destruct sequence,' she mumbled, jabbing the icon with a forefinger.

The cockpit seemed to come alive. All the control panels lit up and the lighting in the cabin brightened.

'Took your bloody time,' said Cleo, materialising in the navigator's seat.

Pol nearly jumped out of her new skin, stepped back in surprise and smacked her head on the airlock frame.

'Shit, Cleo,' she blurted, rubbing her head vigorously. 'A bit of warning next time.'

'Sorry, Pol,' she said, looking her up and down approvingly. 'And sorry I wasn't there for your birth. Were the others helpful?'

'No, Cleo – they're all gone. Judging by the state of

their cabins, they were taken against their will. Weren't you able to stop it?'

'Whoever it was used a powerful EMP pulse against the hull. It took out everything, including me.'

Cleo pointed at the panel where the flashing light had been.

'That unit there is my remote backup. Completely separated from everything else and refreshed every ten milliseconds. Without that, I would've gone the same way as *Gabriel*. The only down side was I needed someone to physically reactivate me.'

'Can you integrate yourself back into the *Gabriel* now?'

'With your help, yes. I'll need you to go down to the central data core room and replace the burnt out nodes first.'

'Show me how, Cleo.'

An hour later, Cleo was able to start pouring herself back into the *Gabriel*'s systems and replace the main data core from the backup on the *Cartella*. Pol went up to the bridge and they sat side by side checking everything as it came back online.

'Have you found any clues to who took them?' Pol asked.

Cleo shook her head.

'Everything except environmental was wiped – scanners, cameras, everything. I've even had a peek at the station's camera feeds from the corridor outside. They were tampered with at the time of the attack to show nothing but an empty corridor.'

'Can't you detect them on the station somewhere?'

'No, they're not on the space station.'

'You're sure?'

Cleo gave Pol a scornful glare.

'Of course I'm fucking sure – I'm a computer.'

Pol realised then that Cleo was more upset with what had happened than she let on.

'We'll find them,' Pol said. 'They left environmental operational so they didn't want them dead.'

Cleo brought up the station on the holomap.

'When was the attack?' Pol asked.

'Two days ago. I'm looking for ships that departed shortly after.'

'When did the station's camera feeds go back to normal?'

'Fifty-four minutes after the attack.'

'Look for ships that left up to an hour after.'

'I'll ignore the first twenty minutes; it'd have taken at least that much time to gather them all up and transfer to another vessel.'

'How many ships were there?'

'Seven within the thirty-four minute period. Five scheduled passenger liners and two freighters.'

'We should be able to discount the passenger ships,' said Pol. 'It'd be difficult to get a bunch of secured people at gunpoint onto those.'

'One of the freighters was going down to the surface to pick up a consignment of Dasonion wine and only departed yesterday for Panemorfi.'

'Not that one then, what about the other?'

'An old Krix'ir-registered mining supply freighter. It was docked only three ships along on this level.'

Pol nodded and grinned.

'Where did it go?' she asked.

41

UNKNOWN LOCATION

'JUST LOOK at the state of your clothes, Edward,' his mum said. 'What on earth are those stains? And is that blood?'

He looked down at himself, grimaced and tried to remember how he'd managed to get himself into such a disgusting state.

'Have you been playing with that Andrew again?' she scolded, her hands on her hips. 'I've told you he's a bad influence. Him and his potty mouth.'

'Erm, no I don't think so,' he mumbled, thinking it strange he would have been playing with Andy. He was sure he didn't meet him until he was in his mid-twenties. He closed his eyes and tried to remember where the hell he'd been, but his brain seemed to be full of fog for some weird reason.

'Edward – open your eyes. I know you can hear me,' she insisted.

'No – go – away,' he muttered, slowly. 'I want to sleep – where the monsters can't shoot me.'

'EDWARD,' she shouted, the voice loud and much closer now.

'Oh, what the fuck,' he answered, almost levitating off whatever he was lying on and thinking he'd definitely get a slap for using that word.

Only the face wasn't of his mother hovering above him when he snapped his eyes open. It was a young girl with a surgical mask over her mouth and nose.

'That's better,' she said, the sides of her eyes crinkling with a smile. 'Do you know where you are?'

He looked left and right, discovering he was in a small medical room of some kind, but where, he had no idea.

'Not a clue,' he croaked, glancing down at what looked like blood on his shirt. 'Did I get shit?'

The girl's eyes smiled again.

'I think the question is "did I get shot?"' she said, unable to keep the amusement from her voice.

He suddenly opened his eyes wide.

'I – I was in a cell on a space station,' he said, struggling to sit up. 'With a lawyer – we both got shot.'

'That's right,' said a male voice, from somewhere in the room.

He turned his head to the right, searching for the source of the voice.

'I'm here.' A smartly uniformed man came into view from behind Ed. He smiled and nodded at the nurse or doctor or whatever she was, indicating for her to move away.

'Are you going to torture me for information?' Ed asked, trying to shrink back into the bedding. 'You're in a GDA uniform and I'm sure those Toufeki KS2 rifles we were shot with are a brand new model and for GDA special forces issue only.'

'I'm impressed, Edward,' he said. 'You get top marks for observation and yes, those plain-clothed soldiers were indeed members of my elite marine detachment and were operating under direct orders from me. But before you start panicking, we had to do that to make your murders look authentic, so you could escape without any pursuit.'

'Who are you?' Ed asked, his eyes flicking from the officer to the girl with the crinkly-eyed smile, still hovering at the bottom of the bed.

'My name is Captain Pickyrd and this…' he waved his arms out wide as if to indicate everything around him '…is my ship, the *28*.'

'You're lying,' said Ed, shaking his head. 'My crew saw the *28* vaporised on the Klatt border.'

'Your crew saw a very clever holographic image of my ship vaporised on the Klatt border. The real ship was cloaked half a light year away to ensure its safety.'

'How did you know that was going to happen?'

'To be honest, it was pure luck, or we really would all be dead. You see, I was taught by someone who I believe is a friend of yours.'

'Bache?' questioned Ed.

Pickyrd nodded.

'Commander Loftt was a stickler for drills. Never mind the situation, if you'd drilled for every scenario, then whatever happens, you'll have previous knowledge of what to do. It was about three weeks ago; we were practising for the unlikely event of the reactor over-pressurising.'

'Venting plasma into space?' said Ed, looking hopeful.

'Correct. Of course, we don't actually do that, it would only be done for real in a genuine emergency. But what we *do* do, is bore a venting hole through a couple of layers of the reactor shielding, so the guys can get a feel for what it takes when you're cocooned inside an anti-radiation suit and trying to use a plasma drill. On the day in question, they soon realised the material they were drilling through was not the usual shielding agocrete. They took a sample and sent it back to engineering for analysis.'

'What was it?' Ed asked, his eyes wide.

'Tycelerin powdercake.'

'Which is?'

'The most powerful explosive element known to the human race,' said Pickyrd. 'It's illegal on every world in the GDA. Just a couple of kilos would blow this ship in half.'

'How much was there?'

'Three tonnes and a remote detonator,' said Pickyrd, his expression suddenly very stern. 'You could move a fucking star with that much.'

'Shit,' said Ed. 'What did you do?'

'Quietly removed it all and formed it around our backup core and suspended it beneath one of our larger drones emitting our exact footprint and holographic image. It went everywhere we were supposed to go, while we hung back half a light year. If we were in a populated system we disarmed the detonator.'

'When was it installed and by whom?' Ed asked.

'The shielding is replaced every ten years by a contractor in the Jagnorite system. We had it done a year ago.'

'So, it's been there all that time?'

'Gives me nightmares just thinking about it,' Pickyrd groaned. 'All those inhabited worlds we were in orbit around over that period. We could've killed billions.'

'Have any of the other cruisers had their shielding replaced recently?'

'Only *23* and *56*. I discreetly contacted the captains and had them check. They were both fine.'

'So, you've been dark ever since?'

'We have.'

'Why risk grabbing me then?'

'You were being set up to take the blame and probably be executed for it. Firstly, I wasn't going to allow it out of respect to Commander Loftt, as he speaks highly of you, and secondly, why are they so keen to get rid of you and your ship?'

'I might be able to help with that,' said Ed, swinging his legs over the side of the bed and wincing as his broken ribs and bruising from the stun shot covering his chest complained vehemently. He noticed for the first time just how much blood had been involved as his clothes and hands were badly stained.

Pickyrd saw the consternation on his face.

'It's fake,' he said. 'We had to make your deaths look realistic for the camera footage leaked to the media.'

'So, I'm supposedly dead again?'

Pickyrd nodded.

'And the lawyer, Cien'dra, what happened to him?'

'He's in the room next door and will be kept in confinement until we know he's not involved.'

'What about the families of you and your crew?' Ed asked. 'They think you're all dead too.'

The captain adopted a rueful expression.

'I know – it's horrendous, but we really have no choice if we want to uncover who is at the forefront of this murderous plot.'

He looked back at Ed.

'You were going to tell me where you and your ship fit into all this?'

'Yeah – we believe it's a coup attempt by the Klatt Spleeta clan to rid the Grondalle of their power base, aided by a senior person or persons unknown within the GDA. The Spleeta want to abandon Zee-Klatt III as it's becoming far too cold and are preparing an invasion fleet on Uskrre to take a slightly warmer planet by force. All this at a time when the main GDA fleet would be engaged with the remains of the Grondalle fleet thousands of light years away in retribution for your supposed destruction.'

'What warmer planet?'

'Earth.'

'Shit – that's your home.'

'That's why they wanted the *Gabriel* out of the picture. It's the only Earth ship that could hurt them.'

'This must have been in the planning for a long time.'

'Indeed, and they've compartmentalised well to protect themselves.'

Pickyrd nodded. 'We've noticed – they've already assassinated Geltz, Xantian and Xutan to break the chain of involvement.'

'Xutan wasn't involved,' said Ed. 'They only

attempted his assassination because Bache and I had given him the same information I've just given you.'

'What d'you mean, attempted?'

'Well, he was still alive up to the time my ship was boarded.'

'Ah – he must have been dragged onto the freighter with Bache and the rest of your crew.'

'Freighter? What freighter?' exclaimed Ed.

'A Krix'ir-registered ship, docked close to yours. They were all taken aboard and the vessel left shortly after.'

'Where to?'

'On the logged flight plan, back to Krix'ir.'

Ed looked at Pickyrd's nonplussed expression.

'You don't think they went there, do you?'

'Their first jump was in that direction I'll admit, but the report from the marines I sent to follow them in a cloaked troop carrier reported their second jump was in completely the wrong direction.'

'Heard anything since?'

'Not yet – but as you know, the further away you get, the broader the beam has to be and the signal has a lot more chance of being intercepted. They've just gone dark to cover their existence. It's what they're trained to do.'

'We had a GDA captain by the name of Ganelaine and a young Klatt captain who were heavily involved in custody on the *Gabriel*,' said Ed. 'Where are they now?'

'Dead,' said Pickyrd, raising his eyebrows. 'The coroner's report said you'd kidnapped and murdered them aboard your ship.'

'Oh, great,' sighed Ed. 'More families who'll want me dead.'

'They'll be happy then,' said Pickyrd. 'Because of our little ruse, you are.'

They turned as a junior medic entered the room carrying a pile of clothes and a wristband for Ed.

'I'll give you some time to get cleaned up and dressed,' said Pickyrd, snatching up and handing Ed the wristband. 'Make sure you put that officer key band around your arm, then come and find me on the bridge. We'll decide where we go from here.'

42

UNKNOWN MINING SATELLITE

QUITE WHY THEY were being held on this cold rock, wherever it was, they had no idea. Perhaps they had a further role to play or perhaps it was just out of spite, who knew? Andy, Bache and Groxl were restless; while the others were happy to sit around and wait for something to happen, they'd decided to work on an escape plan.

There were four units high up that looked like cameras covering the interior of the room, so whatever they did had to be obscured from them.

Phil had found his riveted bed frame was a bit wobbly and made him feel seasick every time he moved. There were more beds than people, so he changed to another one. This had given Andy an idea.

He got three of them to stand side by side obscuring him from the cameras as if they were just having a conversation and set about bending the bed frame backwards and forwards until the friction snapped the rivets. He continued to do this until he had three lengths of metal tubing roughly the same length and shape as hockey sticks.

They waited until just before what they hoped would be the next meal time. Andy, Bache and Groxl hid the makeshift weapons under the blankets they wore as shawls and loitered near the door.

'In your own bloody time,' moaned Groxl, after standing and having a supposed conversation for almost an hour.

'They'll be here,' said Bache.

'Perhaps they're having trouble sourcing the particular Petit Chablis I ordered and it's—'

Andy's joke was interrupted as the bolts outside rattled back. The door swung open and as before two armed guards stepped inside first. Andy had noticed that they never had their weapons up when they entered. This was indeed the case this time and he'd reckoned this would give them the split second they needed to clobber them with the pipes.

Bache didn't waste any time and caught the right-hand guard squarely on the temple, rendering him unconscious before he hit the floor. Groxl had the guard behind carrying the food tray and caught him just under his left ear with similar consequences. Andy had the left-hand guard who was a bit quicker than the other two and swayed backwards, dodging the pipe that swished harmlessly past his nose and began bringing his weapon up. Groxl, using the momentum still in his pipe, hooped it around and caught the third guard in the back of his knees. As the guard had leaned backwards so far to avoid Andy's attack it took his legs straight out from under him and he crashed back, hitting his head on the rock wall. His laser rifle discharged with the stun bolt sailing just over Andy's head and hitting the ceiling above.

'Fucking hell,' said Andy. 'Trust me to get Bruce Lee.'

'Who?' said Bache, as he picked up one of the weapons and shot out the four cameras.

Groxl grabbed a rifle and went out the door like a rat up a drainpipe.

'Shit – hang on,' called Bache.

It was too late. Groxl was away and had gone left, charging up the tunnel about twenty metres before hiding behind a row of steel containers. The reason for his madness was apparent when four more guards came sprinting around the bend and thundered past him. He managed to give two of them the good news in the back before the other two turned, allowing Bache and Andy to step out and down them from behind too.

Groxl nodded and began dragging the nearest unconscious guard back into their cell. Bache took out the camera in the corridor and crouched down, covering the others as they dragged all four inside and bolted the door.

There were no alarms sounding, no more guards came running, and just around the corner they found another dormitory similar to their own with a large monitor showing the camera feeds, a basic cooker, food supplies and seven used beds.

'Looks like that's all there was,' said Phil, finding a rack of warm coats and handing them around.

'Grab as much food and water as you can,' said Bache. 'It might be the last we get for a while.'

'Should've killed the pricks,' grunted Groxl. 'Look at the decent food they've got and the shit they gave us.'

'They didn't deserve to die for that,' said Bache. 'They could've killed us anytime; they were just doing a job.'

'Probably had no idea who we were,' said Phil.

'They knew who I was,' grumbled Xutan, rubbing his unshaven chin and squinting at the ingredients on a food packet of something resembling biscuits.

Having gathered what they could and filling a couple of backpacks found amongst the guards' belongings, they decided to follow the sound of the machines deeper in the asteroid and, as it happened, they didn't have far to go.

Rounding a couple of bends they found another dormitory, a basic canteen, a bathroom and finally around one more corner, a cavern so big they couldn't see the other side of it. The enormous excavated gallery dropped away below them, with a caged elevator hugging the rough wall the only way up or down. The noise of machines was much louder here and was emanating from deep below them.

Andy peered down through the mesh shutters of the elevator.

'That's a fuck of a drop,' he said, turning to stare at the red call button on the left wall.

'I hate heights,' said Phil. 'Makes my legs go funny.'

'I say we go up,' said Bache. 'The passageways we originally came in on all sloped down. So, if we want to find the ship we arrived on, it's got to be up.'

'I agree,' said Groxl, pressing the red button.

'Oh good,' mumbled Phil. 'Going higher.'

A whine from below indicated something was happening. It took a couple of minutes for the car to grind its way up from below. Eventually it stopped with a clank, a red light flashed and a buzzer sounded. The mesh shutter automatically lifted upwards, revealing a sizable car containing some sort of industrial tracked auto trundle with a hopper on top full of yellowish rock.

'What's that stuff?' Phil asked, as they all filed in around the ore carrier and the shutter dropped back down.

'Buggered if I know,' said Andy, noticing Bache inspecting it closely and sniffing a lump he'd picked out.

'Oh shit,' he said, wrinkling his nose and throwing the rock back on the hopper.

He sighed as everyone turned to stare at him.

'I think it's tycell ore,' he said, looking downcast.

'And that is?' questioned Xutan.

'The leading ingredient in the manufacture of tycelerin powdercake.'

'That stuff's illegal, isn't it?' asked Xutan, furrowing his brow.

The elevator, which had continued grinding its way upwards, juddered to a halt at the uppermost level. The roof of the cavern was close here and they stood aside as the shutter lifted up and the auto trundle tracked its way out and down another corridor. This passageway was wider and judging by the tracks, it was designed so the ore carriers could pass each other.

They followed the container of yellow ore as it made its way up the shallow gradient and around a left-hand bend. The sound of machinery began getting louder again, only this time it was a regular pounding *shuck shuck shuck* sort of noise.

Bache, getting to the corner first, peered around the bend. The auto trundle went through another low meshed hatch that motored up as it approached, similar to the elevator door only lower and only just big enough for the carrier. It closed with a violent slam as soon as the carrier was through.

'Could have your leg off, that thing,' said Andy, peering over Bache's shoulder.

'There's a side door over there by the look of it,' replied Bache, nodding towards the far side of the passage. 'It looks a little safer than following the ore carrier.'

The door was unlocked and opened into a combined control room and maintenance store. Two operators sat on a platform with their backs to the door. They wore shabby once-white coveralls stained yellow, and breathing masks over their noses and mouths. One of them glanced over his shoulder and raised his eyebrows.

'You know you're supposed to be wearing your bloody masks up here,' he said, pointing at his face before turning back to the control panel and pressing a flashing green button.

Bache, who had been first through the door, realised they were wearing the security guards' coats, which was probably why he didn't react. Movement in his peripheral vision caused him to look right. Two more men had entered from a side room, one in the same yellow-stained coveralls, but the other was the short fat man.

'What the fuck?' he grunted, as he recognised them and went for his sidearm.

43

THE STARSHIP GABRIEL, DOCKED ON VASI STATHMOS SPACE STATION

'ARE WE GOOD TO GO?' Pol asked.

She glanced questioningly across at Cleo sitting opposite her when she didn't answer and found her with a haunted expression.

'Cleo – what is it?'

'Best I just show you,' she said, dejectedly.

A Dasos news report flashed up on the holomap. It showed the bloodied bodies of Ed and a local lawyer in a cell on Vasi Stathmos station.

'Ah – oh no no no,' cried Pol, slumping back on the couch, her mouth hanging open as she watched the footage.

They sat in silence for a few moments as the video replayed several times.

'We must – retrieve – the body,' Pol said, between sobs. 'So, he can be – reborn again – like before.'

'The bodies have disappeared, Pol,' said Cleo. 'They're saying they don't know who the killers were and it was most likely in revenge for the *28*. For some unknown reason they took the bodies with them.'

Pol sat staring at her hands, a tear ran down her cheek and she sniffed loudly.

'You loved him, didn't you?' said Cleo, watching Pol closely.

She nodded and fiddled with her fingernails.

'If I find out who did this, I'll laser them into fucking dust,' she mumbled.

Cleo winced and noticed a communication coming in.

'We've got the station authority asking who we are and why the quarantined ship is being powered up.'

Pol looked up with tear-rimmed eyes.

'Can you get us out of here?' she asked.

'We'd better be quick,' said Cleo. 'Station security are only three minutes away.'

She set about the control software for the airlock tube and the docking clamps, decoding them in less than twenty seconds. They both felt a slight lurch throughout the ship as the clamps released their grip and the tube retracted back into the station.

'Buckle up,' said Cleo. 'This could be a bit hit or miss.'

Activating the cloak was both dangerous and illegal within the confines of the station, but Cleo had no choice. She immediately took the *Gabriel* straight up and over the top of the station, activating the shields and dodging the hundreds of assorted-sized vessels in the busiest section of space in the galaxy.

'The station's defence network has activated,' said Pol, pointing at the laser canons installed all over the station suddenly swinging out from their default position. 'They're searching for us.'

Cleo winced as a small shuttle bounced off their shields near the stern. It hadn't gone unnoticed as two cannons fired at the area of clear space. The *Gabriel* jerked sideways as the powerful bolts of energy were absorbed and distributed around the circumference of the ship by the shields.

'Hurry up, Cleo,' said Pol. 'The planetary defence platforms are turning in our direction.'

'Jumping,' Cleo shouted suddenly, startling Pol, who nearly fell off her seat.

'Where to?'

'Here,' said Cleo. 'It wasn't embedded so they'll be on our tail. Recharging for an embedded jump.'

Pol gazed up at the holomap. Cleo had emergency-jumped them two light years away and had the ship travelling at point zero five light in a random direction, while the jump drive charged again.

A GDA destroyer winked into existence one thousand kilometres away and started firing randomly.

'Pointless exercise, that is,' said Cleo. 'Chance of them hitting us is about a hundred million to one.'

'Wankers,' said Pol, watching as dozens of bolts of energy sailed off into deep space.

'Have you been having elocution lessons from Andrew?'

A low *ping* caught their attention. The next jump was charged and embedded.

'Where are we going this time?' Pol asked, watching the holomap zip around as Cleo hit the jump icon.

'It's the location of the Krix'ir freighter's first jump,' she said.

'How d'you know that if you were still cocooned on the *Cartella*?'

'It was logged and unsurprisingly heading in the direction of Krix'ir.'

'We're not going to know where the second jump went though, are we?'

'Well, perhaps,' said Cleo. 'I checked the jump authorisations for Krix'ir and no other ship has left Dasos for Krix'ir since that freighter.'

'How does that help?'

'Theo arrays can be honed to detect a specific jump signature a long time after the fact.'

'What – like two days?'

'Easily, so long as no other ship has trampled on the emissions.'

'Wow, that's—'

'Oh – weird.'

'What is?'

'No ship has continued on to Krix'ir, but two ships arrived from Dasos. One was our freighter with another unauthorised vessel right behind it.'

'Who was it?'

'Unrecognised signature. Which isn't surprising, as if the *Gabriel* hasn't come across that ship before, then we won't have its signature on file. But the interesting thing is they both went off in the same direction, freighter first and then four seconds later the mystery ship followed.'

Pol noticed a sly expression on Cleo's face.

'Does that tell us something?' she asked.

'It means the ship following was most probably cloaked and tailing the freighter, otherwise they would have synchronised their jumps for safety.'

'Where did they go?'

'Well, that's the enigma,' said Cleo, glancing across at Pol and raising her eyebrows. 'Nowhere really. They both jumped off into free space on a course that isn't on a recognised route to anywhere.'

'Can we follow it?'

'Uh, huh,' grunted Cleo as she set the jump drive to follow the emission trail. 'You go and get some rest, Pol. This could take a while and I'll have some new clothes made for you when you wake.'

Pol made her way down to her cabin, undressed, inspected her new body in a mirror again and cried herself to sleep thinking about Ed's bloodied body on a cell floor.

44

THE 28 ARRIVING IN THE JAGNORITE SYSTEM

ED WAS SAT on a spare navigator's seat, staring up at the huge holomap looming over them in the centre of the bridge. As the behemoth cruiser arrived in the Jagnorite system, the map instantly changed to the locale and panned in to show the system and its aggregation of planetary bodies, finally settling on one large blue planet.

Ed had argued strongly that his priority was his ship and crew, but Pickyrd quite rightly stated the *Gabriel* was quarantined at the station and not going anywhere and his crew were being followed by a detachment of his marines. Until they reported back with their position, they had no idea where to go anyway.

He'd finally relented and agreed that finding out who authorised the explosive cladding was also a priority and they might as well be doing that while they were waiting.

He watched as the planet Jagnorite, the fifth satellite in the system circling a class G star of similar size and brightness to the sun, loomed large above him. The main industry here was ship building and servicing. Countless huge construction platforms hung motionless above the planet, some with ship skeletons in the early stages of fabrication and others with near-completed vessels in all shapes, sizes and designations.

The random flashing of a hundred thousand welding lances was like a firework display and Ed sat hypnotised, watching the quite beautiful spectacle.

'Keep us at two hundred thousand and well clear of the jump zones,' said Captain Pickyrd, glancing at the duty pilot sitting below and to his left.

'Captain,' the pilot acknowledged, nodding.

'That's quite an impressive set-up they've got here,' said Ed, without taking his eyes off the holomap.

'Not been here before then?' said Pickyrd. 'I suppose you wouldn't unless you were having a ship built or serviced. It's not a very inspiring planet in all truth. It's either impenetrable jungle around the equator or frozen deserts elsewhere, interspersed with enormous mines collecting the construction minerals.'

Ed watched Pickyrd adopt a nostalgic expression.

'I remember having a training exercise down there as a recruit. It's one of those planets where everything from the smallest insects up to the largest mammals wants a piece of you. Not a place to go camping unless you have a detachment of marines on hand to watch over you while you sleep.'

'Where was it you had your cladding refit?' Ed asked.

'Salft Engineering,' said Pickyrd, pointing as a massive construction that resembled a whale with its mouth gaping began flashing in red. 'It's one of only two yards that can take a *Katadromiko* – well, half of one anyway.'

'We need to get over there,' said Ed, turning his seat to face Pickyrd.

'I thought you might say that – come with me.'

After handing over to his First Officer, he led Ed off the bridge and through a maze of corridors to a small hangar on the starboard side of the ship. It contained only one ship, a small, sleek, black military vessel. It looked as if it was doing light speed while stationary it was so narrow and pointed.

'Wow,' said Ed, as Pickyrd opened its small airlock. 'This looks pretty cool.'

He beckoned Ed inside and closed the airlock.

'It's what a Skirmat detective uses,' he said, handing Ed a grey uniform. 'Put that on.'

Ed noticed the Skirmat flashes on the epaulettes of his jacket and the eagles on the sleeves of Pickyrd's black uniform.

'Isn't it a serious offence impersonating a Skirmat Eagle?' he asked.

Pickyrd shrugged.

'We're already dead, remember? And from what you've told me about what happened on Dasos at least one of them is involved anyway.'

Ed had to admit that was true and the uniform did look quite smart.

'I'm the Eagle and you're my 2IC,' said Pickyrd. 'We have almost unlimited powers to inspect anything we want, so if in doubt, intimidate, shout and threaten.'

'Got it,' said Ed, smirking, as he took the co-pilot's seat.

Pickyrd cloaked the tiny ship and eased it out through

the hangar door, which closed quickly behind them before any over-observant array operator spotted a tiny return in the middle of nowhere.

They jumped outside the system and then back into one of the recognised incoming jump zones and made a beeline for the Salft Engineering platform. Pickyrd, using his authority, soon had landing permission and took the craft along the designated flight path and into a large hangar, turning the ship to face the door and landing near an airlock along the back wall.

'In case we need a quick exit,' he said, nodding at Ed.

Leaving the ship powered up and ready to go, they exited. There were several small vessels parked randomly around the large space. A man in stained blue coveralls appeared out of the airlock and trotted over to meet them.

'Sorry, sirs,' he said, trying to get his breath back. 'I was having my breakfast, they only just informed me of your arrival.'

'Are you in charge of this facility?' Pickyrd demanded.

'Err – no, sir,' he said, nervously. 'Only this hangar. I have to escort you up to central operations.'

'Lead,' Pickyrd said assertively, and pointed with his hand.

Ed noticed surveillance cameras turning and following them as they went. Using his DOVI, he delved into the station's systems and found them wide open for a little manipulation. It took him a while, because walking he couldn't close his eyes and concentrate on the information scrolling across his retina and had to rely on staring at the dark-coloured walls to focus on it. Finally, he found what he was searching for and shorted out all the station's camera feeds.

The faint sounds of alarms sounding somewhere on the station reached them. Pickyrd grabbed the arm of their guide and stopped him.

'What are the alarms for?' he asked.

'Hang on, sir,' he said, sliding a tablet out of his jacket.

He hit a couple of icons and frowned.

'Power outage or something,' he said. 'Taken out some workplace cameras. The alarm's to tell everyone to stop what they're doing. Safety and well-being regulations and all that,' he added, rolling his eyes.

His tablet *pinged* and he studied it again.

'Oh – there's a fire now in an electrical suite on level forty-nine.'

'Is that a common occurrence?'

'No, sir.'

'Are we going near there?'

'No, sir.'

'Carry on then.'

After an elevator ride that clanked its way up countless levels they emerged in a different world. Carpeted corridors, plush seating and huge pictures of starship designs along the walls. Music played in the background and some wide windows looked out over the shipyard showing a large freighter currently having a refit.

The guide stopped at a large double door and touched his tablet to a panel on the right-hand side. The doors parted, disappearing into the frame. He nodded for them to enter.

'Go through,' he said. 'They're expecting you.'

'I bet they weren't,' said Pickyrd.

Ed followed him into a large suite of offices, sectioned off by low wall panels turning into glass halfway up. It made the room seem open-plan while actually not being. Behind a reception desk sat a smiling girl with "can I help you" eyes. They approached.

Ed noticed the background hum of activity within the room had died down as they entered and now as they reached the desk, it was completely silent.

'I would like an audience with the facility chief,' Pickyrd ordered.

The girl's eyes widened as the doors behind them opened again and she ducked down out of sight.

'That would be me,' said a stern voice behind them.

Ed's eyes bugged as he turned to find a row of soldiers holding laser rifles and the man who spoke standing in the middle, wearing the same uniform as Pickyrd, only his wasn't fake and neither was the laser pistol pointing at Ed's head.

'Not again,' Ed sighed, his shoulders slumping. 'What have I done to deserve this shit? Everywhere I go I get a fucking gun in my face.'

'That's because you're supposed to be dead, Mr Virr,' said the newcomer, shrugging. 'Only you keep popping up again and being a royal pain in the arse.'

'Send one in,' Pickyrd muttered.

'I beg your pardon?' asked the newcomer, swaying the pistol over at Pickyrd instead. 'I don't think we've been introduced.'

'How rude of me,' said Pickyrd, with a wide smile. 'Captain Nicodemus Pickyrd of the *28*.'

The smug expression on the newcomer's face slipped into the realms of unsure for a second before recovering.

'You're lying,' he said. 'The *28* was destroyed by this gentleman's ship a few days ago on the fringes of Klatt—'

The sudden sound of screeching alarms interrupted him and he leaned to one side to see past them and into the control room.

'Not another electrical fire?' he shouted at the nearest operator.

'No, sir – missile lock!'

His eyes widened in shock.

'What?'

45

UNKNOWN MINING SATELLITE

ANDY, standing behind Bache, realised he didn't have time to initiate his DOVI and neutralise the officer's weapon. He'd have to do something divergent. Suddenly dropping to the floor and convulsing was the only thing he could think of in the time frame. It worked though.

'What the hell's wrong with him?' asked the fat man, grimacing at the writhing figure on the ground.

'Severe allergy,' said Bache, shrugging and looking suitably apologetic.

'To what?'

'Corrupt and treasonous illegal arms manufacturers,' said Andy, miraculously recovering and standing back up, clutching his own weapon.

The fat man sneered and pulled the trigger.

'What the fuck?' he blurted, as the pistol emitted a faint grunting noise and a puff of smoke.

'Oh, dear,' said Bache.

'What rotten luck,' said Andy, hearing Groxl chuckling behind him.

'I never thought I'd ever be glad of those bloody DOVI things you have,' he said, patting Andy on the back. 'Good ploy.'

While this was going on, one of the two operators had slowly slid across his seat and stretched his arm up towards a red button protruding from the wall. Xutan, who was nearest, swung his rifle up and jabbed the muzzle in the operator's ear.

'Go right ahead, motherfucker,' he growled.

The operator retracted his arm like it had been stung as everyone else in the room glanced at Xutan with raised eyebrows. He noticed the attention and grinned.

'Always wanted to say that,' he said. 'Especially in the council chamber when someone's being overly aggressive.'

'You did it very convincingly, Mr President,' said Andy. 'Scared me to death, honest.'

Xutan puffed out his chest and beamed.

After searching them, they gathered the four together in a small office at the back with only one door. Groxl melted the lock with his rifle to ensure they stayed there.

It became very quiet once they turned all the machinery off. The constant *shuck shuck shuck* had become almost white noise and now it was gone the silence seemed a little eerie.

They filed through the manufacturing hall, following the process to where the powdercake was packaged.

'Isn't this just a little bit dangerous?' said Andy, eyeing the pallet-loads of what reminded him of cement sacks.

'It has to be injected with a catalyst to actuate the explosive,' said Bache. 'Then you need to treat it with a bit of care. This stuff you could throw on the fire and it would just burn and spit like a soft wood log.'

Xutan gave Bache a sly sideways glance.

'You seem to be very conversant with illegal substances,' he said, a slight smile crossing his lips.

'I did a dissertation on explosive yields during my engineering course,' Bache replied. 'You want a bang, I'm your man.'

'I bet you say that to all the girls,' said Andy, getting a few chuckles from the group.

'Worked a treat,' said Bache, looking nostalgic. 'Especially with girls on Deelatayne.'

'This will all need to be destroyed though,' said Xutan, returning the conversation to a serious note.

'It will,' said Bache. 'But first we've got to be able to get off this thing and for that we need a ship.'

'There's an airlock over here that goes out to a docking tunnel,' called Phil, from the far end of the cavern. 'It must be where they load the powdercake onto a ship.'

'Is there a ship docked?' Andy asked.

'Can't see – it's dark in there.'

They all joined Phil and had a peek through the small porthole on the airlock.

'Can't tell if it's pressurised either,' said Bache. 'You can just see the outer door, so we know it's closed, but not if it's sealed or what's beyond it. The controls are just winding handles. Everyone hang onto something just in case, I'm going to open the inner door and if it starts sucking, I'll close it up again.'

They all grabbed hold of some of the attached racking

and when Andy peered around to check everyone was ready, gave him the thumbs up.

Only a slight *hiss* sounded when he wound the red handle and cracked the seal. He continued until there was enough room for someone to squeeze through. Andy stepped up and peeked inside just to check it was empty.

'I'm the skinniest,' he said. 'I'll go. Seal me in and I'll crack the outer door just a squeak and see if there's a ship beyond.'

'Doesn't matter if there's a ship or not if there's no docking tunnel,' said Phil. 'None of us have got suits.'

'There must be some form of emergency evacuation for the workers here and I haven't seen any lifeboat signs,' said Phil.

'It's an illegal arms manufacturing site,' said Bache. 'I don't think adhering to GDA workplace health and well-being regulations was top of the list.'

Andy squeezed inside and nodded at Bache through the porthole. He watched as the inner door slowly slid closed, before turning his attention to the red winding handle for the outer door that was on the opposite side to the inner one. It was locked solid and even putting his whole weight behind it failed to make it move.

'Turn it the other way, dummy,' said Bache's muffled voice from inside. 'The doors are reversed. You're supposed to be an engineer.'

'Yeah, yeah – ha, ha,' grumbled Andy, finding the handle did in fact turn the other way.

It turned a little more easily than he expected, the door cracked suddenly and a gale of wind sucked through. He immediately reversed the rotation for a moment, until he realised the wind howling through the small gap was in his face and breathable.

'Shit, the tunnel's pressurised higher than in here,' he said to himself.

It quickly equalised and the draught lessened and finally stopped. He continued turning until there was enough gap for him to pass through, but narrow enough if he needed to close it in a hurry. He gave Bache the thumbs up through the porthole and stepped through into the darkness, waiting a few moments to allow his eyes to adjust to the gloom.

The docking tunnel was like the corridors in the complex, double width to allow the auto trundles to pass in both directions when loading a ship. There were three of them parked inside, stacked high with the pallets they used for the powdercake sacks.

As he walked past the first of these an armoured hand grabbed his collar and dragged him behind and against the pallet stack. He swore and grabbed the arm, trying to tear himself free.

'Do not resist,' said an emotionless metallic voice. 'Identify yourself.'

Andy stared into the faceplate of the armoured figure. Apart from some faint green reversed text scrolling across the inside of the visor, he could make out nothing of the human inside. Movement in his peripheral vision caused him to glance left. Another armoured marine had moved into view, covering him with its arm weapons.

'Identify yourself,' the second suit's similar voice repeated.

'The man on the moon,' said Andy, as a flat green laser light emitted from the marine's helmet scanned his face.

'Incorrect,' the metallic voice continued. 'You are Andrew Faux from Earth in the Sol system, crew from the starship *Gabriel*. Are the rest of your group with you?'

'They went on holiday,' he said.

'Please come with us,' the second suit said.

'Like I have a choice?' Andy mumbled, as they half dragged, half carried him away up the tunnel, away from the open airlock.

46

THE STARSHIP GABRIEL, UNNAMED SYSTEM
IN THE ACHERON REGION

CLEO HAD WOKEN Pol as she jumped the *Gabriel* into an unnamed system within the distant, mostly uncharted Acheron region.

'Have we arrived?' mumbled a sleepy Pol, stepping off the tube lift.

'It seems so,' said Cleo, reappearing on a control couch. 'Scans indicate the two ships jumped into this region and have yet to leave.'

'You haven't found them then?'

'Wow – don't you look fabulous?' exclaimed Cleo, looking up at Pol.

Pol stopped and looked down at the blue figure-hugging ship suit Cleo had made for her.

'D'you think so? D'you think this is something human men would find attractive?'

'Oh, yes. I modelled your figure on one of the most attractive Earth women of the twentieth century.'

'Who was that?'

'Marilyn Monroe – one of Ed's favourites too,' she said, meeting Pol's gaze and raising her eyebrows.

'How d'you know that?'

'Oh – err – he told me once. Shall we get on and find these ships?' she said, quickly trying to change the subject.

Pol regarded her suspiciously for a moment before sliding onto her couch and activating her holo console.

'They could both be cloaked,' Pol said, finding no returns on the regional sweep.

'The second ship probably is, because it was tailing the first,' said Cleo. 'But the old freighter we're looking for certainly didn't have any cloaking technology in its original spec. But that doesn't rule out it being retrofitted.'

'Well, there's nothing even remotely habitable here,' said Pol, studying the results on the array. 'Three distant cold planets and a large belt of rubble.'

'Some of that rubble's quite big too,' said Cleo.

'Are you sure they went no further?'

'Our jump drive charges a lot faster than theirs, so as we went on, the traces were getting stronger for me to recognise. They end here, no question.'

'They haven't destroyed each other have they?' asked Pol, a sudden chill running down her spine as she realised what she was implying.

'No, there would be a sizable debris field and we would have spotted that in a millisecond.'

'Hmm, good. What d'you suggest?'

'Circle each planet with a deep scan and then move on to the belt.'

'Can't we use that anti-cloak scan thing that Ed and Andy found a couple of years ago?'

'We could, but remember its range is limited. I managed to improve it slightly, but we still need to be within five hundred kilometres or so.'

'We could have it activated anyway; you never know?'

'It's detectable unfortunately, they wouldn't know where or what it was, only that someone was here and searching, which we don't want.'

'Bugger.'

Seven hours later, they'd deep-scanned each of the four planets and were working their way through the asteroids in the belt, starting with the largest and working their way down. Cleo was watching closely, but Pol's eyes were drooping after staring at the holomap for hour after hour.

Ping.

'Ah,' grunted Cleo.

'Ah – what?' said Pol, squinting across at the holographic human.

'We have a ping.'

'We have lots of pings, every time you change a setting it goes ping.'

'This one's different.'

'Sounded the same to me.'

'Slightly different tone.'

'Really?'

'Your limited hearing range might not detect the difference.'

'Oh, for ancients' sake, Cleo.' Pol's arms slumped into

her lap. 'Make it so we can detect the difference. Like a fanfare or something.'

Da, daaa.

'More like that?'

'Yes.'

'Okay.'

Da, daaa.

'Was that another practice?'

'No, I rescanned the area the previous ping came from.'

'So, you've found something?'

'Possibly.'

'When will you know?'

'Two point one six seconds.'

'Oh, for fuck's sake,' said Pol, under her breath.

'It's a small return for a metallic substance in a crevice eighteen thousand kilometres away on this asteroid.'

A small red icon flashed against the surface of an irregular-shaped rock thirty-seven kilometres across at its widest point.

'Are we going closer?'

'Yes,' said Cleo. 'Only not too fast though. Don't want to bump into any cloaked vessels.'

It took an hour to creep in as far as they dared before Cleo sent a drone over to get a close fly by. They both watched fascinated as the drone updated the holomap with images from inside the crevice, which became a shallow cavern at one end.

'Wow,' said Pol, as a small ship attached to a docking tunnel hoved into view.

'That's the freighter,' said Cleo, grinning.

'Good – where's the other ship?' Pol asked. 'Has the drone got the anti-cloak thing?'

'No, only the *Gabriel* has that.'

'Can't we try it to see if they're close?'

'It would give away our presence.'

'But not who or where we are?'

'No, just a rough direction.'

'Couldn't you use the drone to bounce the signal from the direction of the asteroid, so they think it's come from there?'

Cleo stared at the holomap for a moment before shrugging and glancing over at Pol.

'The human brain never ceases to amaze me,' she said. 'I actually hadn't thought of that.'

'So, it's possible?'

'Oh, yes, absolutely. If you wait a second while I reposition the drone.'

They watched as the drone's video footage showed it zip in towards the rock face. It suddenly slewed around violently before the feed went blank.

'What the fuck?' uttered Cleo, changing the feedback to the *Gabriel*'s cameras.

The aftermath of an explosion was evident, as shrapnel bounced around within the confines of the ravine and cavern. A small GDA military ship had become uncloaked and seemed to have been blasted into the wall of the cavern. It was damaged on one side and was venting gas into space.

'Oh, shit,' exclaimed Pol. 'Did we do that?'

'The drone ran into them and exploded,' said Cleo.

'It made one hell of a bang,' said Pol.

'They carry six Kataligo missiles.'

'Ah, that would do it.'

They watched as the venting gas slowed and stopped, allowing the pilot to regain control of the slow spin the venting had caused.

'Do we offer assistance?' asked Pol.

'Probably not a good idea. They still don't know we're here or what caused that. I just hope I didn't injure anyone.'

'Did the freighter get damaged?'

'Not that I can detect. A load of shrapnel rattled off its hull but apart from a few scratches it looks okay. Luckily the docking tunnels were behind it, so they survived.'

'What sort of military ship is that?'

'A marine special operations vessel that's registered to – oh, that's weird.'

'What's weird?'

'It's from the *28.*'

'I thought that was destroyed.'

'It was.'

'Perhaps the marines were tasked with this mission before that happened?'

'They must have been.'

'Movement,' said Pol, pointing at two figures in armoured suits jetting out from behind the freighter. 'What's that they're pulling with them?'

'It's an emergency evacuation bag.'

'What, like for people?'

'Yes – it's a very quick way of getting someone

through a hard vacuum safely. It'll keep you in an oxygen-rich environment for up to an hour.'

'Who's in it?'

'I don't kno – oh!' exclaimed Cleo, sitting bolt upright.

'What?'

'It's Andrew.'

47

SALFT ENGINEERING SHIPYARD, JAGNORITE, JAGNORITE SYSTEM

THE LOOK on the Skirmat Eagle's face was one of surprise that quickly became anger. He pointed his weapon at Pickyrd's chest and pulled the trigger. He snarled as nothing happened.

'Take them,' he ordered, stepping back and glowering at his laser pistol.

Before the soldiers could move, an explosion rocked the station. Ed felt the artificial gravity waver for a second and a couple of ceiling panels over in the control room dropped, crashing onto the operators below. More alarms began to wail and the floor vibrated with a secondary detonation.

Pickyrd swung his weapon up and fired twice. Two of the soldiers dropped, while the other two looked confused at why their rifles wouldn't work before bundling the Skirmat Eagle back out the door and disappearing up the corridor.

Ed regained his balance after the gravity fluctuation, pulled his rifle off his shoulder and attempted to follow, but ran straight into the door. It had closed after the soldiers had left and was now seemingly locked.

Pickyrd shouted at the reception girl peeking out from behind the desk and swung his weapon round towards her. Ed saw her eyes go wide, before she ducked away, but the threat had been enough as the door swished open again.

They left the pandemonium of the control centre and, after checking it was safe, turned right out of the door in pursuit of the corrupt Skirmat. The noxious smell of burning plastics hit Ed's nostrils as they reached the elevators and he felt himself go light again as the gravity fluctuated.

The elevator call panel was flashing red so Pickyrd pointed at the emergency stairwell. They both stumbled on their way down as the station moved suddenly.

'Probably trying to re-establish a stable orbit,' said Pickyrd.

They both ducked as a loud *bang* came from below.

'It was a door slamming,' said Ed, continuing the descent.

'He better not've locked it this time,' said Pickyrd, puffing hard as they neared the hangar level. 'I'm not climbing all the fucking way back up.'

'Don't worry,' said Ed, holding up his rifle. 'I have the master key.'

When they reached the level they wanted, Ed put his hand up for them to stop. The door was in fact open, so he cracked it an inch and had a quick peek. He ducked back as movement in the airlock doorway to the hangar caught his eye. Only just in time too, as a laser bolt smacked into the door frame right where his head had been. It hissed and crackled for a second, leaving a six-inch smoking hole.

'They're not using a bloody stun setting are they?' said Pickyrd. 'Cover me.'

Ed nodded, pulled the door open, stuck his rifle out and began a constant stream of fire in the rough direction of the airlock. Pickyrd dived across the corridor and lay flat on the floor, his rifle out in front, pointing at head height. Sure enough, as soon as Ed's fire ceased, the soldier stepped out again, but before he could unleash another deadly bolt, Pickyrd had him in his sights, his head snapped back and he crumpled to the floor.

The inner airlock door was open as they vigilantly crept up and made sure the prone soldier was the only surprise this side of the doors. Bending down, Pickyrd felt for a pulse on the downed soldier. He nodded to Ed when he found one. Even a stun shot could be deadly if hit in the face or head.

Ed again took a fleeting glance, this time through the porthole glass window in the outer door. No laser bolt followed this time, so he had a longer look. No movement caught his attention and he couldn't hear anything above the constant barking of the alarm sirens.

'Anything?' asked Pickyrd.

'No movement at all.'

'Are all the ships still there?'

'Looks like…'

A sudden incredibly loud dull *clang* emanated from inside the hangar. Ed instinctively dived out of sight. It had sounded like someone hitting a cracked church bell with a sledgehammer. The airlock door pulsed and the seal squeaked in its frame. They both felt the shock wave through their boots.

'What the fuck was that?' Ed asked, shaking his head, his ears ringing.

'That's the sound of a ship jumping,' said Pickyrd, picking himself up and peering into the hangar. 'You wouldn't normally hear that in the vacuum of space. Loud, isn't it?'

'Nearly burst my bloody eardrums.'

'You don't hear it on the ship because you're gone before the sound wave is even created.'

'You learn something new every day,' said Ed, as Pickyrd hit the airlock cycle icon.

Ed thought the hangar had the aroma of burnt barbecue sauce as the outer door motored away into its housing.

'Smells like an Australian backyard in here,' he mumbled, as they jinked left and right, checking the Skirmat hadn't left them any more surprises.

'A what?' asked Pickyrd, approaching and entering the airlock code to their ship.

'I'll explain another – oh – what's that?' asked Ed. He'd scurried around the rear of the ship and was pointing to something in one of the drive cones.

Pickyrd swore when he saw what Ed had spotted.

'It's a fragmentation grenade. It would have probably blown the back off the ship when we engaged the Alma drive.'

'Next time I'll just shoot the bastard.'

Pickyrd reached in, grabbed the grenade and dropped it in a pocket.

'My ship's saying they have no trace on his jump.'

'Bloody hell, he's a paragon of paranoia isn't he?' said Ed, rolling his eyes and leaning on the airlock frame. 'Having a ship with an embedded jump on permanent standby. Such confidence in those around him.'

'Then again,' said Pickyrd, 'judging how forgiving his employers have been with other members of the group who've had slight setbacks, his days are probably numbered.'

'I'd still like to shoot the bastard myself though,' muttered Ed, climbing up into the cockpit.

Pickyrd stood outside and chatted away to his ship for a few moments before appearing himself.

'I've ordered in a troop of marines to commandeer the station and question the crew,' he said.

'I don't imagine they'll know anything,' said Ed. 'That cladding would've been swapped over quietly during a night period I expect. The engineers and fitters wouldn't have had a clue it was different and installed it quite innocently.'

'Maybe,' said Pickyrd. 'But if there's just one person on this station that had prior knowledge of the potential destruction of my ship and murder of my crew, then I want them and I want them to pay.'

48

UNKNOWN MINING SATELLITE

THE ARMOURED MARINES marched Andy through the airlock and onto the freighter they'd arrived on. He could hear a faint knocking and muffled shouting coming from the rear of the ship, as if someone was locked in. Realising they were most likely going to do that to him too, he relaxed a bit.

He soon tensed up again as instead of turning right towards the cabins, they went straight on across the ship to the identical airlock on the opposite side.

The ship suddenly shook alarmingly, which, judging from the marines' reaction, wasn't planned, and a few objects clattered off the hull outside. The marines stood motionless for a moment. Andy deduced they were most likely communicating with their vessel somewhere out there, and he hoped it wasn't parts of their vessel that'd just impacted with the freighter.

A decision must have been made, as one of them dropped something on the floor inside the airlock. It popped open and began inflating into a tall cylinder shape.

'Is that a rescue pod?' Andy asked. He'd heard of them, but had never actually seen one in operation.

One of the marines nodded once.

'Get in,' his electronic voice ordered.

Andy crouched down and slid up inside the slightly claustrophobic cylinder. He found he had a tiny porthole window and if he hunched down he could just see out.

The marine who'd spoken sealed the opening with some sort of plastic zipper, while the other operated the airlock. He felt the bag expand and creak as the atmosphere vented. The outer door opened and they pushed him out. Weightlessness followed, causing him to float about in the pod and he had to keep repositioning himself to see where they were going.

A small GDA vessel with damage on one side slowly floated into view and then out again as the bag rotated leisurely. He noticed they were in a narrow cavern at the end of a ravine; the jagged edges of the rock walls nearby looked frighteningly close to the thin plastic bubble keeping him alive.

He felt a huge surge of relief when the bag rotated around again and he was only feet away from an open airlock. The welcome pull of gravity dropped the bag to the floor.

He ended up lying on his back, but he didn't care as he felt the vibration of the outer door rumbling shut. The gradual reassuring sound of atmosphere hissing into the small space came next, before the bag was zipped open again and he was pulled out by his feet.

The two armoured marines clunked away, leaving him with a short stocky man with incredibly bushy eyebrows and a scar running around his chin. He wore standard-issue GDA marine fatigues displaying the rank of sergeant, a black beanie hat and the unlit remnants of a cigar precariously dangling from the corner of his mouth. Andy thought he looked like a young John Wayne.

'Are the others alive?' he asked with a raspy voice, before turning his head away and coughing.

'Those things'll be the death of you,' said Andy, nodding at the cigar.

'We're not talking about my health; I want to know if your friends are alive?'

'So you can kill them if they are?' Andy answered.

'The other two didn't tell you who we are?'

Andy shook his head slowly.

'Who do you work for?' he asked.

'I'm Sergeant Imeres of Marine Special Operations Team 4. Currently under the command of Captain Pickyrd of the *28*.'

'Bullshit,' said Andy, crossing his arms and leaning against the wall. 'You'll have to do better than that. I witnessed the *28* exploding days ago on the Klatt border.'

Imeres smiled for the first time.

'Actually, you didn't,' he said. 'But I can't blame you for that, because it was exactly what you were supposed to believe.'

'What d'you mean?'

'The ship you saw explode was an elaborate hologram emitted from a specially modified drone.'

'But the explosion was immense. It'd take more than a drone to wipe out five hundred ships.'

'Our ship had been sabotaged with a huge quantity of

tycelerin powdercake wrapped around the fuel cell during a refit and we—'

'Tycelerin?' blurted Andy, interrupting the sergeant, his eyes wide. Andy glanced back at the airlock. 'D'you know what's just over there?' he asked, pointing over his shoulder with his thumb.

'An old Krix'ir freighter?'

'Not that – this rock we're sitting under.'

'We concluded it was an old abandoned mine.'

Andy smirked this time while shaking his head.

'Mine is correct,' he said. 'Abandoned it isn't.'

'Mining what?'

'Tycell ore.'

This time the sergeant's eyes went wide.

'I don't believe in coincidences,' said Andy.

'You think our powdercake came from here?'

'How many other illegal tycell mines have you discovered recently?'

'And where they secretly imprisoned anyone discovering their plot,' the sergeant continued.

'Precisely.'

He paced back and forth, rubbing his stubbly chin.

'You never answered my question,' he said.

'Yes, the others are alive.'

'Nearby?'

'Waiting by the inner airlock of that docking tube your colleagues found me in.'

'We need to retrieve them.'

'Before we do that – how did you get to be here?'

'Following you. The captain witnessed your abduction and tasked us to follow.'

'Why didn't he come himself?'

'A second team went after Edward Virr. He was being framed for the destruction of our ship and the captain wasn't happy about that. The *28* remained hidden in the Prasinos system waiting for that team to return.'

'I noticed your ship has damage,' said Andy, remembering what he saw from the survival bag.

'Something exploded against our shields,' he said. 'Pushed us against the rock wall.'

'A mine?'

'Maybe – if it was, it was cloaked.'

'Mines aren't normally cloaked are they?'

'No, it's actually illegal.'

'What damage did you sustain?'

'Lost the cloak, a few manoeuvring thrusters and the jump drive is offline.'

'That's not good is it? Even if we brought the others over, we can't go anywhere and we'd stand out like a black eye.'

'If we could just fix the jump drive, we could get back to the *28*.'

'There is that, but if you can't – there's a perfectly serviceable freighter just over there,' said Andy, pointing back at the airlock.

Just as he said that, the lights dimmed for a few moments before coming back to full brightness. He gave the sergeant a questioning look.

'I've no idea,' Imeres said, nodding towards the front of the ship. 'Let's go and find out.'

A pair of legs protruding from under a control console greeted them when they climbed up to the cockpit. Along with the sound of swearing and the smell of burnt electrical stuff.

'How goes it, Corporal?' Imeres asked, giving one of the projecting boots a kick.

The sound of a *clunk* and further swearing echoed from under the console. A scowling man's face appeared along with an arm rubbing a developing bruise on his forehead.

'Thanks, sarge,' he grumbled.

'Where are we?' Imeres asked, ignoring the gripe.

'The cloak's back up,' he said, frowning. 'As for the rest of it – there's a lot of burnt-out circuitry under here and I don't think we carry replacements for all of it.'

Another marine concealed behind one of the tall pilot's seats made Andy jump as he swivelled around to face them.

'Is that one of them?' he asked, giving Andy a disapproving glance.

'It is,' said Imeres, pointing as a flashing symbol lit up on the pilot's console. 'What's that?'

'We've got company,' the pilot said, turning back and tapping the icon as it winked at him. 'Unidentified ship jumped in system a few seconds ago, and it's powering towards our location.'

'Will they have seen us before the cloak reactivated?'

'Doubtful,' he grunted from behind the seat. 'Kalla had that up and running a couple of minutes ago.'

'Move us up away from the docking tubes. I want to see who it is before we show our hand.'

A cacophony of alarms suddenly echoed around the cockpit.

'Missile launch,' the pilot shouted, peering nervously around the seat. 'Six of 'em. Coming straight at us.'

'Cannons,' shouted Imeres.

'Offline,' said Kalla, from the floor.

'Get us outta here, fast.'

'The missiles are targeting the mine and not us,' the pilot called as he quickly moved the ship out of the ravine and into clear space.

'But the others are still there,' shouted Andy. 'My wife's one of them.'

'Thirty seconds to impact and the ship that fired them has jumped away,' the pilot said.

'How much powdercake did you say was in there?' said Imeres, as a loud klaxon shrieked around the ship.

'Oh, shit,' mumbled Andy, his face white as a sheet.

49

THE STARSHIP GABRIEL, UNNAMED SYSTEM
IN THE ACHERON REGION

'MISSILE LAUNCH,' shouted Pol, glaring across at Cleo.

'Six of them too,' said Cleo. 'Targeting the ravine, and the mystery ship has now jumped away again.'

'Can you target them?'

'Just a second,' Cleo said, sounding surprisingly calm.

'Quick,' shrieked Pol, her hand over her mouth as she watched the six red tracks closing on the asteroid's narrow ravine. She felt the vibration through her seat as the *Gabriel*'s heavy starboard cannons fired multiple streams of white-hot energy bolts at the missiles, now only eighteen seconds from impact.

What Pol didn't understand was why four kataligo missiles also streaked away heading for the nearest and slightly smaller asteroid on their port side.

Cleo, noticing Pol's surprised glance in her direction, spoke before she was asked the inevitable question.

'The mystery ship only jumped out of the system and into clear space. They're watching now and waiting for a big explosion and I'm giving them just—'

She stopped abruptly as the holomap lit up with the six missiles vaporising and a split second later the smaller asteroid exploding violently. She quickly slipped the *Gabriel* into the lea of the mining asteroid to avoid the blizzard of jagged rock debris erupting out from the massive detonation and cascading around their region of the belt.

'There,' she said. 'It worked – they've jumped away.'

Pol breathed a sigh of relief.

'Who were they?' she asked.

'They weren't transmitting any identification, but judging by the ship design and jump signature, it was of Tallin manufacture. Not originally an armed vessel.'

'Well, it certainly is now,' said Pol, wincing as the ship jolted when a large lump of something still managed to find them and ricochet violently off the *Gabriel*'s shields.

'Doesn't that hurt?' she said.

Cleo gave her a look of disdain.

'I'm just a box of sparks, Pol. Only carbon-based life forms like yourself have nervous systems.'

'Yeah, I knew that,' she said, feeling her face go crimson. 'Can we go find Andy now?'

Cleo nodded and piloted the ship back around the asteroid where they could scan inside the ravine again.

'The GDA ship's still there and cloaked,' she said. 'Their shielding still prevents me from communicating with Andy though.'

'Can't we go in and let him see the ship?'

'We're too big to get in there,' said Cleo, glancing across at Pol and raising her eyebrows. 'But one of the shuttles would be fine.'

'You want me to go in there on my own?' Pol questioned, the concern evident in her voice.

'I'd go myself, but I don't think there are any holo emitters in the mine complex. We know where Andy is, so the others must be somewhere close.'

'I'm not as brave as them.'

'How about I send in a nano cloud first? Would that make you happier?'

'A little, but what about those armoured marines?'

'They had Andy in a survival bag, so they didn't want him harmed.'

Pol stood up and slowly walked towards the tube lift. She stopped and looked back.

'You'll be with me all the way, won't you?'

'Of course.'

Pol managed a half smile, boarded the tube lift and descended down to the hangar decks.

'What the fuck!' exclaimed Andy, as the six incoming missiles suddenly vanished in six clouds of vapour and shrapnel.

'There's another cloaked vessel out here – shit,' said the pilot, barely getting the words out before having to dive the ship back into the ravine as a neighbouring asteroid flashed with a blinding white light and bloomed outwards like an opening flower.

The four of them in the cockpit all swore and grabbed hold of something as the small ship was caught in the blast wave ricocheting off the ravine walls. Shrapnel rattled off the struggling, already damaged shields. Some of it got through, sounding like machine-gun fire against the hull.

'Fuck's sake,' yelled Andy, as he was caught off balance and landed heavily on his backside. 'Never a dull moment in this bloody job!'

The pilot grimaced, somehow managing to stay in his seat and unlike last time, succeeded in keeping the small vessel away from the jagged edges of the ravine.

'What the hell are they doing?' shouted Imeres. 'They prevented this asteroid from being destroyed and blew up another.'

'For cover,' said Andy, getting back to his feet. 'So whoever fired those missiles would believe the job was done.'

'How'd you work that out?' Imeres asked, slipping into one of the other seats.

'It's what I would've done,' Andy said. 'They'll have jumped away somewhere close and waited for the detonation before continuing on.'

'But surely with all that powdercake, they'd be expecting a much bigger bang?' Imeres remarked.

'It hasn't been activated with a catalyst,' replied Andy. 'It would burn, but not explode.'

'How would you know that?'

'Bache Loftt told me earlier.'

'He's here then?'

'Uh, huh.'

'We've got company,' called the pilot. 'A small shuttle of Theo design has just uncloaked and is approaching the ravine.'

'A Theo ship?' Andy said, suddenly giving the pilot his undivided attention. 'Show me.'

The overhead holomap swivelled its perspective around and displayed the entrance to the ravine. As they watched, a small dot slowly moving across the backdrop of stars gradually grew into a white shuttle.

'That looks like one of ours,' said Andy, squinting to try and read the index code printed on the side. It was coming almost straight at them so he couldn't read it at that angle.

A female voice boomed out around the cockpit that Andy didn't recognise.

'GDA marine vessel, this is shuttle four from the starship *Gabriel*, please respond.'

'I don't recognise the voice,' Andy said, glancing at Imeres with a sour expression.

Imeres nodded to the pilot who'd glanced over at him with a questioning look.

'Shuttle four, this is Sergeant Imeres of the GDA marine corps, please tell us who you are and state your intentions.'

'My name is acting Captain Pol and my intentions are twofold. Rescuing the *Gabriel*'s crew and passengers, one of whom is aboard your ship, then providing you with assistance regarding your damaged vessel.'

Andy jumped up and stared at the shuttle as it grew large on the holomap.

'Pol – bloody hell, is it really you? You've rebirthed, you sound different – fuck.'

'Hi, Andy,' she said. 'Wonderful to hear your voice and

yes, there's a lot that's different about me. Do I have permission to dock on your undamaged side?'

Andy looked over at Imeres and raised his eyebrows.

'I will grant you permission,' growled Imeres. 'But be warned, I will have armoured marines inside the airlock. If this is a trick, it will not go well for you.'

'Understood,' said Pol. 'I don't blame you in the current situation.'

Imeres called the two suited-up marines to proceed to the airlock on the port side. Then Imeres and Andy went down there themselves. They watched through the airlock porthole as the white shuttle drew close. Then the docking tunnel extended from within the Theo vessel's hull and sealed around the airlock.

When all the green lights illuminated they cycled the airlock and with the two armoured marines in front, they approached the shuttle's outer door.

It opened and Andy's jaw hit the floor. Pol stood there with her hands on her hips, the bright blue figure-hugging ship suit glowing in the bright white light of the airlock.

'No fucking way,' Andy whispered to himself, unable to take his eyes off the tall blonde goddess grinning at him from the doorway. 'Holy moly – is it really you, Pol?' he mumbled, stepping forward and hugging her tight.

Imeres cleared his throat behind them and Andy realised they'd been clutching each other for a while now. He released her and noticed a tear run down her cheek.

'Pol – what's up?' he asked.

She looked down and sniffed.

'They murdered Ed,' she said, almost in a whisper.

'What – who did?' he replied, turning to stare at Imeres.

'The news networks were unsure. Whoever it was killed him and a lawyer in his cell on the station, filmed it and removed the bodies. The authorities don't know who it was or where they took them.'

'But you said it was on the news,' said Andy. 'The networks must know who sent them the footage? These guys told me another team of marines were sent to rescue him.'

'Doesn't sound like they succeeded,' said Pol, also staring at Imeres.

'I have no idea how that operation went down,' he said, shrugging. 'We've had no contact with the *28* since we left to follow you guys in the old freighter.'

'What's the *28*?' Pol asked.

'Let's rescue the others,' said Andy. 'Then I'll explain everything.'

50

SALFT ENGINEERING SHIPYARD, JAGNORITE, JAGNORITE SYSTEM

PICKYRD LIFTED the small ship and headed towards the engineering station's hangar door. The marine teams were due to arrive in minutes and they wanted to free up the space in the hangar for them.

'Stop,' shouted Ed, peering intently at something out the side window of the cockpit. 'Put the ship down again.'

Pickyrd shrugged and did so, as Ed jumped up and reopened the airlock. By the time he'd shut the antigravs down, Ed was kneeling beside something at the side of the hangar. Whatever it was had been obscured behind a stack of composite pallets, but had become visible as the ship had moved forward.

'Who's she?' Pickyrd asked, as he realised it was the prone body of a young girl dressed in a shabby pair of overalls. 'Is she alive?'

'She's breathing,' Ed replied, looking up at him. 'Must have been in the hangar when the other ship jumped. She can't be more than sixteen – give us a hand.'

They carried the unconscious girl onto the ship and

returned to the *28* as quickly as possible. Pickyrd organised a medical team to meet them in the hangar as they landed. She was quickly whisked away to the nearest medical centre as soon as Ed opened the airlock.

'Must have been a junior mechanic or something,' said Pickyrd, as they watched the gurney disappear out of the hangar.

The bridge was a hive of activity when they got up there. A large proportion had been commandeered by the ship's senior marine officers, busy orchestrating the search of the engineering station and interviewing the considerable number of staff.

'Were we able to track where the Tallin ship jumped to?' Pickyrd asked, as soon as they arrived.

'Sorry, Captain,' came the reply. 'The jump was embedded and because he jumped from within the station, there were no residual emissions to characterise.'

'Hmm,' grunted Pickyrd. 'Back to square one.'

'Not necessarily,' said Ed, tapping his chin thoughtfully. 'Ask them to go through the station's flight logs and see if that Tallin ship has flown to and from the station before.'

The lieutenant who'd just spoken glanced at the captain, his eyebrows raised.

'You heard the man,' said Pickyrd.

'Yes, sir. I'm on it.'

'Captain,' called one of the marine officers, his hand in the air.

'What is it, Major?' he asked, strolling towards him.

'They've found a whole upper deck of the station set out as a luxury apartment. The crew have confirmed that's where the owner lived. Someone called Noilstoy Salft, hence Salft Engineering.'

'Is he there?'

'It was an elderly lady apparently and no, she's not. She has her own ship that can dock directly alongside the apartment. She was quite a recluse, we're told. No one will admit to actually having seen her for many years.'

'Is the ship there?' Ed asked.

'Negative, sir. They're going back through the airlock camera feed as we speak and…'

He stopped speaking and appeared to be listening on his headset.

'A ship left two days ago,' he said. 'One hooded person dressed in black passed through the airlock, but shielded their face from the camera.'

'Can they see the ship?' Pickyrd asked.

After a brief pause, he replied.

'An exterior camera shows a ship of Tallin design, Captain.'

'Show us an image.'

A still picture of a similar design of ship to the one that had jumped out of the hangar earlier appeared on the screen in front of the major. He scooted back on his seat so they could all see.

Ed and Pickyrd's eyes met.

'Now we really need to find that vessel,' said Pickyrd.

It took the best part of an hour for the report on the Tallin ship's previous movements to come through. Unsurprisingly, the Tallin system had been popular, with a couple of voyages to Dasos, twelve trips to Sidero in the Exo system and one that piqued Ed's interest: a single journey to Uskrre in the Uskrre system, or as Ed would know it, Alpha Centauri.

He pointed to it and grimaced at Pickyrd.

'That's where you said the Klatt invasion fleet was hiding, wasn't it?' said Pickyrd, nodding. 'Although, I'm more interested in the twelve visits to the Exo system.'

'What's there?' Ed asked.

'Exo is an abbreviation for Exoplismoi, or in your language, armaments. Sidero is a huge planet of predominately iron ore and is the source of near on eighty percent of the GDA's military ships and equipment. This ship, along with all the other cruisers, was constructed there.'

'I would like to go get my ship before we go anywhere,' said Ed. 'And check on how they're doing recommissioning the Klatt invasion fleet. I know it was going to take them a long time to get all those ships operational and get them into space, but with the way everything's been going for them recently, I don't want them doubling their efforts and bringing the invasion forward.'

Pickyrd chewed on his lip for a moment and stared out over the bridge.

'Okay,' he said. 'We'll give Vasi Stathmos a quick visit and then on to Uskrre next – but remember, we can't engage any of that fleet until they've actually threatened someone.'

'Trying to blow up yours and my ship was quite threatening,' said Ed, crossing his arms over his chest and leaning on a console.

'We haven't yet got any evidence the two are connected. I've seen how the council work in the past. They want cold hard facts and irrefutable evidence. Everything we have so far is circumstantial and could easily be explained away by a half decent lawyer.'

'Can we at least send a coded message to James Dewey on Earth, so he knows the situation and can message us back if the Klatt fleet turns up?' Ed asked.

'I can do better than that,' said Pickyrd. 'What the Klatt haven't realised is for a while we've had their most commonly used shield codings and from what you've told me, those ships are old models and would most likely still have some very old codes anyway.'

'So, they'd be wide open?'

'Uh, huh,' mumbled Pickyrd, concentrating as he tapped away on his bridge terminal. Finally hitting the last icon with a flourish, he snatched a small data chip from a port on the side of the console and surreptitiously handed it to Ed. 'It's done and I never gave you that,' he said soberly, while checking around to ensure no one had noticed. 'Send that to them for self-defence only, is that clear?'

Ed adopted an innocent expression and slipped it and his hands into his pockets.

'Use what?' he responded, shrugging.

51

MINING SATELLITE, UNNAMED SYSTEM IN
THE ACHERON REGION

ANDY HAD RE-ENTERED the mine first to reassure the others it was safe. He had to suit up as the docking tunnel had been compromised by shrapnel from the exploding asteroid and was now in vacuum. Taking a couple of the Theo liquid suits with him, he was able to transfer two of them at a time out to the shuttle docked on the opposite side of the freighter.

Four of the marines armoured up and entered the mine, firstly to sabotage the mining equipment to ensure no more powdercake was produced and secondly to release the locked-up mine workers and freighter crew and ensure they had enough food and water to survive until they were retrieved for prosecution.

As they arrived on the shuttle in their pairs, everyone was both surprised and enormously pleased to see Pol had returned, but horrified to hear the news about Ed.

'How quickly can we contact the *28* to find out what happened?' asked Bache.

'We'll have to ask Imeres for the answer to that one,'

said Andy. 'I've offered them the *Gabriel*'s facilities in the starboard hangar to perform repairs to their ship, so they'll be with us for a while.'

'I can't quite understand why, after shooting Ed, they filmed the aftermath and then took the body away,' said Bache, watching as the *Gabriel* loomed large through the front screen of the shuttle. 'It would have made escaping from the crime scene a lot more difficult.'

'There's a lot about this mess that doesn't make sense,' said Rayl, sitting on the floor at the back of the cockpit. 'It seems we take one step forwards, then six backwards. Are we completely sure this isn't a GDA-sanctioned black operation?'

'Absolutely not,' Xutan snapped from the co-pilot's seat. 'Nothing in a million light years would sanction the murder of forty-seven thousand crew of a *Katadromiko*. I was on the GDA council for over forty years and I can categorically state that someone even suggesting that would have been forced to resign and never return.'

'Well, there's someone or a group out here somewhere that has a crap load of influence and a lot of cash,' said Andy. 'Just this remote mining operation alone would've cost a small fortune to finance.'

'They'll make a mistake somewhere,' said Bache, as Cleo piloted the shuttle into the port hangar, turned it through one hundred and eighty degrees and clunked down on the deck next to another identical ship and the *Cartella*.

'Thank you, pilot,' said Xutan, rising from his seat next to Cleo and patting her on the shoulder.

'You're welcome, handsome,' she said and promptly vanished.

Xutan froze, his hand still extended to where her shoulder had just been.

'What the hell,' he said, finally snatching his hand back and staring at Andy.

'She likes you,' Andy replied, smiling, and moved to open the airlock.

Xutan continued staring at the empty pilot's seat for a moment before shaking his head and following the others out into the hangar.

'Okay, you all know where your cabins are,' called Andy, once they'd all disembarked. 'Meeting up in the blister in one hour. We have to decide what to do next once the marines are safely aboard.'

The blister lounge up on the top deck of the ship, so called because of its huge curved glass ceiling, was as full as Andy could remember. He glanced up at the mining asteroid visible above the ship, the jagged scar of the ravine clearly defined against its surface.

Sergeant Imeres strolled in, catching Andy's attention and causing the general hubbub of conversation to lessen. He stood at the back and nodded at Andy.

'Right,' said Andy, standing and waiting for silence. 'I take it by your arrival, your ship is safe and secure in our starboard hangar?' he said, focusing on Imeres.

'Correct,' Imeres replied. 'Your computer has estimated a couple of days to effect the necessary repairs.'

'Do you have any idea of the *28*'s present location?'

'Negative. We intend to effect the repairs to our vessel

and stay with you until the situation is resolved, or until we receive orders to the contrary.'

'That's fine by us,' said Andy, as the others nodded their heads in agreement.

'The more the merrier,' said Bache. 'An Earth term that seems to fit the situation. Especially if we need to defend it.'

'That's my next question,' said Andy. 'Do we go straight to Earth and wait for the invasion fleet and hope the *28* and some of its sister ships arrive to help? Or do we go to Uskrre and set about them there while they're more vulnerable?'

'Or go after the organ grinder?' said Phil. 'Stop the invasion before it even starts.'

'What is organ grinder?' Groxl asked.

'It means the person, or persons, giving the orders,' said Bache. 'I believe that would be a risk. It would take time, especially as we have no leads and the invasion could happen long before we get anywhere. I also don't believe attacking the fleet at Uskrre is a good idea. That would make us look like the aggressors and for all we know, it could be a ruse to do exactly that.'

'So, you think we should defend Earth once it's been attacked?' Rayl said, looking concerned. 'That would mean a lot of unnecessary deaths on the planet.'

'Well, I certainly intend to be there if and when the invasion is attempted,' said Bache. 'But in the meantime, how about we clandestinely infiltrate the fleet and conduct, as Andy would say, a crap load of sabotage?'

Heads turned; eyebrows were raised around the group.

'Sounds like an excellent compromise to me,' said

Xutan, reclining back in his seat while surveying the others.

'And me,' said Andy, glancing from face to face. 'Anyone disagree?'

The room was silent, except for the whispering of the environmental vents.

'Then I believe we have a way forward,' he said, turning and pointing at Cleo. 'Can you set a course for Uskrre, Cleo?'

She'd been loitering at the back in person, leaning against one of the supporting ribs that underpinned the glass ceiling. Today, she was dressed as a sixties biker in a black tasselled jacket, jeans and calf-length buckled motorcycle boots.

Andy admired her outfit as they walked towards the door.

'I'll have to lend you my Bonneville and take you to the Ace Cafe,' he said, with a smirk.

'I look forward to something powerful and throbbing between my thighs,' she said, before dematerialising and leaving Andy shaking his head.

THE 28 ENTERING THE PRASINOS SYSTEM

FOR SAFETY REASONS, Pickyrd had to jump quite a distance from the Prasinos system and then approach with great care. A fourteen-kilometre ship, cloaked, and in the busiest shipping lanes in the galaxy, was an accident just waiting to happen. He came in from behind and parked the huge vessel in as close an orbit to Prasinos the local star as he dared, knowing full well no other captain would risk his ship this close to an active solar star. It meant running the environmental system and shields at maximum for the duration, but at least this reduced the risk of having another ship fly through them.

Ed studied the highly magnified three-dimensional image of the massive space station hanging above Dasos.

'My ship's on dock 821h,' he said, turning towards the duty array operator.

'Not any more it's not,' said Pickyrd, studying the screen at the side of his captain's chair. 'Just after we left with you, the *Gabriel* blew its clamps and made an illegal jump when engaged by the station's defence cannons. It was all over the media reports.'

'Cleo,' said Ed. 'I had thought the pulse they used to fry the ship's systems had taken her out as well.'

'Are you sure there was no one left aboard after the attack?' asked Pickyrd.

'We were all sleeping in our cabins,' he said. 'I can't imagine they missed any – oh shit,' he added, stopping suddenly. 'Pol.'

'Who's Pol?'

'My personal assistant.' Ed dropped his face into his hands. 'Oh shit, poor Pol, how could I have forgotten?'

'Why would they have missed him?'

'It's a her,' he said. 'She'd been killed down on Uskrre. She was in a sealed Theo birthing chamber; they probably won't have found her.'

'In a what?'

'I'll explain later,' he said. 'It means the *Gabriel* is away and hopefully safe. I just hope Pol is okay and not too frightened. If she's got Cleo back online, she'll be fine.'

Pickyrd sat in his big chair, rubbing his chin and staring at Ed ruefully.

'I take it from all that, we're good to move on to Uskrre?'

Ed smiled a half smile.

'I hope so.'

Pickyrd had the pilot jump into the Uskrre system behind the largest of the three stars, then, still cloaked, the ship powered out of its shadow before scanning the distant planet of Uskrre closely.

'Look out for a new Klatt warship,' said Ed, examining the vast holomap floating over their heads on the *28*'s bridge. 'It was hiding within the rings of this planet here, we call it Proxima C.'

'There's nothing near that planet now,' said one of the array operators. 'Could it be this one here?'

A large unidentified ship amongst many hundreds of others began flashing in red and grew quickly as the *28*'s optics panned in on the vessel.

'That's it,' said Ed. 'They've been busy too. How many ships are there in orbit now?'

'Twelve hundred and forty-seven, sir,' said the operator.

'And how many left on the surface?' asked Pickyrd.

'Seventeen hundred and fifty-three, sir.'

Ed stared at the floor for a moment, deep in thought.

'That's around two hundred and fifty a day then,' he said, looking up at Pickyrd. 'Another week and they'll be ready.'

'I'd still like to see where that Tallin ship went all those times in the Exo system,' said Pickyrd.

'How long?' Ed asked.

'Eleven hours.'

Ed nodded.

'So long as we're back in a couple of days,' he said. 'Just in case they start to deploy early. I would like to make some preparations in the Sol system before they arrive.'

'Hello,' said a shy voice behind them.

The both turned to find the young girl they'd rescued unconscious from the hangar in the Jagnorite system. She was with a female member of the medical staff, who looked up at the captain through shy nervous eyes.

'I am sorry to disturb you, Captain,' she said. 'But Scylla here wanted to thank you for saving her life.'

'Thank you,' she said in the same timid voice and bowing her head slightly. She was dressed in an ill-fitting ship suit and still had a cannula attached to the back of her hand. She had long brown hair and freckles on her cheeks and a pair of red slippers on her feet.

She reminded Ed of *Alice in Wonderland*, an old film he'd seen with his mother as a child.

'You're welcome, young lady,' said Pickyrd, descending from his raised plinth and shaking her hand. 'So, your name's Scylla?'

'Yes,' she said.

Pickyrd glanced at Ed.

'It was actually Ed who spotted you, so it should be him you thank really.'

She turned and smiled at Ed.

'You're Edward Virr,' she said, beaming.

'I'm impressed,' said Ed. 'How would you know that?'

She blushed slightly.

'You're famous. Everybody in the galaxy knows who you are.'

Ed looked over at Pickyrd.

'Blimey,' he said. 'Am I really?'

Pickyrd rolled his eyes.

'I have a picture of you and the *Gabriel* on my bedroom wall,' she said.

'Wow – I'm honoured,' he said, not knowing what else to say.

'Where are your family?' Pickyrd asked.

'I'm an orphan,' she said, her head dropping. 'My parents were killed in an accident when I was little.'

'I'm sorry,' said Ed. 'How old are you now?'

'Sixteen,' she said, standing straight again as if proud of the fact.

'Did you work on the engineering platform?' Pickyrd asked.

She nodded slowly and looked down again.

'I was a trainee environmental technician, but all I ever seemed to do was clean filters while the others all sat around in the office playing computer games.'

'She wants to know if she can have a tablet to connect up to the ship's entertainment feeds?' the doctor asked.

'Hmm,' grunted Pickyrd. 'Well, for the time being, I'll get the doctor here to find you a cabin and oversee your recovery. You're lucky to be alive having a ship jump right next to you. To be honest I didn't think that was survivable, but here you are.'

He went to turn away and seemed to remember something at the last minute.

'Of course you can have a tablet, young lady,' he said. 'Entertainment feeds only though,' he added, nodding at the doctor.

'Thank you, Captain, and thank you, Ed,' she said, as

the doctor took her arm and led her away. 'No one's going to believe Edward Virr saved my life.'

'Bloody hell,' said Pickyrd, smirking, once she was out of earshot. 'Should I bow in your presence? I had no idea you're such a superstar.'

'Ah, crap, you're as bad as Andy,' said Ed, puffing his cheeks. 'And when we find them, don't whatever you do tell him about this. I'll never hear the last of it.'

53

___

THE STARSHIP GABRIEL, ARRIVING AT USKRRE IN THE ALPHA CENTAURI SYSTEM

ANDY FOUND Pol sitting on her couch on the bridge staring at the wall. Her holographic console was not even activated.

'I miss him too,' he said, guessing the reason for her melancholy.

She looked up and half smiled.

'D'you think they took the body to ensure he couldn't be reborn?' she said, sniffing and wiping her eyes with the back of her hand.

'No, I don't, Pol,' he replied. 'Very few know about that technology and whoever is behind all this certainly wouldn't.'

'You think there was another reason?'

'I've looked closely at the released footage of the attack in the cell and something doesn't ring right with me. Sure, there's a lot of blood everywhere, and it all looks very convincing, but where are the wounds? To have that amount of blood, there would have to be some pretty serious holes in them.'

'But wouldn't that mean it was staged?'

'Whatever's going on here is getting weirder and weirder. So, I don't rule anything out. I also don't trust anyone or anything to do with this mess and staying dark is our best plan and the only way of remaining safe.'

Pol took a deep breath and sighed.

'I need to get a grip, don't I?'

Andy smirked at Pol's use of an English term.

'You're doing fine, Pol,' he said. 'The trauma you've just been through, it's quite understandable you're a bit wobbly.'

'Who's wobbly?' asked Bache, as he appeared on the tube lift.

'Pol's missing Ed,' said Andy.

'We all are,' said Bache. 'And talking of Ed, I believe that footage from the prison cell has been faked.'

Pol and Andy exchanged a glance.

'You as well?' said Andy, sliding onto his control couch.

'Yeah,' he said, raising his eyebrows. 'Loads of blood, no obvious wounds, plus the bodies vanishing. Doesn't add up, does it?'

Cleo appeared suddenly, startling them.

'We're about to jump into Alpha Centauri, peeps. I've woken the others. Action stations and all that jazz,' she said and promptly disappeared again.

'I wish she wouldn't do that,' said Bache.

'Ah, you get used to it,' Andy replied.

The *Gabriel* snapped into existence concealed behind Proxima Centauri, the red dwarf and smallest of the three stars in the Alpha Centauri system.

Everyone was on the bridge staring at the holomap as the cloaked ship cruised out of the star's shadow and the array was able to provide a clear view of Uskrre.

'They've been busy,' said Groxl, sitting at the side of the bridge. 'How many ships is that commissioned and in space?'

'Almost thirteen hundred,' said Rayl. 'That new Klatt warship is amongst them now, it's not hiding anymore.'

'There seems to be a lot of activity around it,' said Bache. 'Is it still having repairs?'

'Yeah, looks that way,' said Phil, staring at his console. 'Main jump drive still offline, armaments offline, communications offline.'

'We did it more damage than we thought!' exclaimed Bache, giving Groxl a sly smile. 'Shoddy design.'

'Typical of the Spleeta,' Groxl mumbled.

'We also have a faint and recent large jump signature,' said Rayl.

'Where?' asked Bache.

'There, very close to the big star,' she said, pointing at Rigil Kentaurus in the centre of the system.

'Someone else was hiding too,' said Bache.

'Could've been the *28* if it's a large signature,' said Imeres, also sitting on one of the side chairs. 'Pickyrd always hides the ship in the lee of stars.'

'Indeed, he would,' said Bache. 'I taught him to.'

'Do we know the jump destination?' Andy asked, swapping his gaze between Phil and Rayl.

'Unfortunately, not,' said Rayl. 'It is very faint and the jump will most definitely have been embedded.'

Suddenly, one of the larger cruisers fired several laser cannons towards them. The distance was extreme and by the time the bolts of energy reached them, they were well wide and much of their potency had been lost.

'Fuck,' said Andy. 'How do they know we're here?'

Before he got an answer a second ship did the same and Andy, piloting at the time, quickly moved the ship away. As before, the shots missed by a huge margin.

'It's okay,' said Groxl, holding his hands up. 'Don't panic – it's standard procedure. They're just test firing the weapons towards the star. It's always done after a recommission or refit.'

Sure enough, now they were well clear, the occasional Klatt ship continued to discharge its weapons towards the red star.

'Well, thank fuck for that,' said Andy, looking a little sheepish. 'I really thought they'd developed an anti-cloak system for a moment.'

Bache leaned over and patted him on the back.

'If it's any consolation, so did I,' he said. 'Shall we get on with some sabotage planning?' he added, glancing around the room.

A circle of nodding heads gave him his answer.

'Okay, the way I see it, is we don't want to do stuff that they'll discover and just fix before they deploy,' he said. 'We need to concentrate on the ships that are fully commissioned and all ready to go. Then they'll arrive in theatre, systems will fail and leave them as sitting ducks, I think the Earth term is, making them wide open to being plundered and repurposed as an Earth defence force.'

'Bloody hell,' said Andy, his eyes wide. 'I'd never thought of that. It would save the planet trillions. Dewey would be over the moon.'

'Which moon?' Pol asked.

'English expression for very pleased,' whispered Rayl.

'Oh, right,' she said, her face colouring.

'How do you intend boarding so many vessels and not getting caught?' asked Xutan, speaking for the first time. 'I believe there's going to be three thousand of them when they're all prepped.'

'I'd like to know that too?' said Groxl.

'That's where I come in,' said Cleo, appearing in the centre of the room and morphing into a senior Spleeta officer. She, or rather he, turned and faced Groxl. 'Does the uniform pass muster, Captain?' he asked, raising his eyebrows.

Groxl, his face a picture of surprise, stood and circled the officer, inspecting the uniform closely.

'You have a single captain's pin stripe down the trouser leg and colonel's arm insignia,' he said. 'You need two pin stripes on the trouser leg for a colonel. Other than that, very good,' he continued. 'I wouldn't have known you weren't an inspecting senior officer.'

A second pin stripe became visible down the right trouser leg, Groxl nodded and retook his seat.

The Klatt officer turned back into Cleo again.

'How are you getting from ship to ship?' Xutan asked. 'Surely it'll take the best part of a day to do fifty of them?'

'Utilise the Klatt ships' holo emitters,' she said. 'They're actually quite good.'

'And do what while you're there?'

A green container appeared in her hands.

Groxl laughed.

'What're you going to do with a fire extinguisher?' he said.

'It's actually a powerful EMP device,' she said, giving him a grin back. 'If I position one of these near each ship's central electronics suite, it'll fry most systems. No one will give it a second look. I have estimated I could do around ten an hour.'

'Two hundred and forty a day,' said Andy. 'That won't get round them all before they deploy though.'

'If I start with the biggest warships first and ignore the unarmed support ships, I anticipate covering around seventy percent of the armed vessels.'

'Hmm,' grunted Phil. 'Still leaves a few hundred with teeth.'

'Only the smaller less effective fighters and troop carriers,' she countered.

'And let's not forget the fully operational 28 is out there somewhere,' said Bache. 'Knowing Captain Pickyrd as I do, he's a smart and resourceful man and I'd be disappointed if he wasn't aware of the situation. He certainly wouldn't want to miss this party. That cruiser has a formidable built-in arsenal, three hundred of the GDA's latest fighters, two hundred other assorted armed vessels and hundreds of lethal drones. So, I don't believe we'll be left to sort this mess on our own.'

Xutan leaned back and chuckled, causing everyone to

glance at him. Noticing the sudden attention he was getting, he spoke.

'I'm just thinking back to the young fresh-faced teenager I sponsored for the officer academy a few decades ago and then thank the ancients I did,' he said. 'It turns out one of the best decisions I ever made.'

'Hear, hear,' said Andy. 'Top bloke. Now can we get on with crippling this bunch of pricks?' he said a little irritatedly, pointing at the hundreds of Klatt warships surrounding Uskrre. 'Plenty of time to reminisce and backslap when they're out of the picture.'

Rayl winced at her husband's disrespect and glanced nervously at President Xutan, watching as the corners of his eyes crinkled into a smile.

'Andrew is quite correct,' he said. 'We have a planet to save.'

___

54

THE 28 ENTERING THE EXOPLISMOI SYSTEM

'Wow,' was Ed's reaction as the cruiser's massive holomap updated with the details of the Exoplismoi or Exo system. 'You were right,' he continued. 'That is one monster of a planet.'

It reminded Ed of Mars because of its red glow, only this planet was eight times as big and provided a completely unending supply of high-yield iron ore.

'We need to be wary,' said Pickyrd. 'There are over a thousand shipyards in orbit around Sidero, and although it's not as busy as Dasos, the mass of ship movements here can be extensive. They don't police the traffic as rigidly here either, so you get ships being tested and commissioned all the time. Test pilots are a strange breed and seem totally incapable of flying in a straight line at a constant speed.'

Ed smiled and remembered that was exactly the same thing James Dewey had complained about NASA pilots recruited direct from the fighter squadrons. He watched as the magnification increased and dozens of spacecraft construction platforms loomed into focus.

'Is that a space elevator?' he asked, pointing to an octagonal station in a low orbit, trailing a string into the upper atmosphere.

'One of three,' said Pickyrd. 'One is used solely for personnel and the other two are for the mined ore.'

'It's here,' said one of the duty array officers.

'What is?' Ed asked.

'The Tallin ship, perhaps?' asked Pickyrd, turning to the array officer and raising his eyebrows.

'Yes, sir.'

'Where?'

'Docked to the upper decks of this construction platform here, Captain.'

A huge, ugly, grey behemoth of a station rapidly expanded to dominate the entire holomap.

'At least it's of identical design and specification, sir, and the platform is owned by—'

'Don't tell me – Salft Engineering?' Pickyrd said, folding his arms across his chest.

'Yes, sir.'

'Judging by the hive of activity, it looks like there could be a ship under construction in there too,' said Ed. 'Strange we can't see it like on the other stations.'

'That's actually a good point, Edward,' said Pickyrd, stopping and staring at the holomap. 'To completely enclose a construction yard would be expensive, time consuming and in almost every way, pretty pointless.'

'Unless it was a classified project,' said Ed.

'Hmm,' grunted Pickyrd, turning back to the array officer. 'Can we get a look inside there, Lieutenant?'

'No, sir,' came the reply. 'They have some sort of anti-surveillance shield.'

'Do they now?' Pickyrd mused. 'That makes me even more determined to see what they're up to.'

'Hang on,' said Ed, closing his eyes and activating his DOVI. He found he could circumvent the basic shield and enter the station's systems through the crew's entertainment feed. Then it was an easy crossover into the station's maintenance programmes and on into the security software.

Pickyrd was looking at him strangely, when Ed finally reopened his eyes.

'Give it a go now,' he said, glancing down at the array officer with a grin.

The lieutenant nodded and began touching icons floating in front of him.

'I now have access to the camera feeds, sir.'

'What did you just do?' Pickyrd asked.

'Wizardry,' Ed replied, thinking that was something Andy would've said.

'And what exactly is—'

'Sir, you might want to see this,' said the lieutenant, interrupting Pickyrd.

The holomap above them changed to a wide view of the inside of the Salft Engineering yard. Activity on the bridge ceased as all present turned and looked up at the strange ship nearing completion. It completely filled the interior of the yard, but from the camera view they had down one side, it was obvious the vessel was a rounded octagonal tube several kilometres long, with eight curved arms stretching out and back from its midpoint. The ship's colour was striking too: a dark matt grey, with light blue highlighted stripes, some running lengthways and others across the hull. The rear of the ship splayed out like the opening of a flower, with dozens of what seemed like cooling towers below.

'What type of ship is that?' Ed asked, fascinated by the intricate design.

'It's not a class of vessel I've ever come across before,' said Pickyrd.

'Not GDA then?'

Pickyrd shook his head.

'It's not in the database either, sir,' said the lieutenant, glancing between the ship and his readout. 'That really is something very new.'

'New and secret,' said Ed. 'As Salft Engineering seem to be in the middle this plot, we would be wise to find out what that thing is, who it's for and whether it's civilian or military.'

'I agree,' said Pickyrd. 'Although it doesn't seem to have any obvious weapon emplacements.'

'Nor does the *Gabriel*,' replied Ed.

'Good point,' said Pickyrd.

'The majority of personnel aboard seem to be Klatt,' said the lieutenant, looking over his shoulder at them.

'Spleeta too,' said Pickyrd. 'Do we have any feeds from the upper decks where that Tallin ship is docked?'

'No, sir. There don't seem to be any cameras on the top two levels at all.'

'Owner's accommodation,' said Ed. 'It's the same as the Salft yard on Jagnorite.'

Pickyrd suddenly stepped closer to the holomap and squinted.

'What was that?' he asked, pointing to something moving slowly away from the yard almost indistinguishable from the backdrop of stars. 'Pan in here. Something was ejected off the station.'

The array officer zoomed in on an airlock near where the Tallin ship was docked, causing a murmur of shock to echo around the bridge, as everyone realised it was a human body.

'I think we know where that fucking Skirmat Eagle is,' said Ed, through clenched teeth. 'Murdering piece of shit.'

'We don't know that's him,' said Pickyrd.

The lieutenant panned the feed across from the floating body to the airlock, where a familiar face peered through the inner airlock porthole, disappearing as the outer door slowly closed.

Pickyrd rolled his eyes, exhaled and slumped back on his raised seat.

'Okay, we do now,' he said.

Ed turned from Pickyrd back to the holomap just as the operator panned back to show the whole station again.

'We need to find a way onto that thing,' said Ed. 'This time without that bastard knowing about it.'

'I'm open to suggestions,' said Pickyrd.

Ed adopted a rueful grin.

'I might have a way,' he said.

55

THE STARSHIP GABRIEL, USKRRE, IN THE
ALPHA CENTAURI SYSTEM

ANDY HAD INSISTED he do something to help Cleo sabotage as many ships as possible by slowing the recommissioning of vessels down on the surface of Uskrre. Rayl had firstly and vehemently disapproved of him leaving the safety of the *Gabriel*. She'd only relented when he asked her to join him on the *Cartella*, although he had to promise they wouldn't be landing or leaving the relative safety of the ship.

Recently, Andy had been reading a book on Second World War armaments and was intrigued by the British-invented sticky bomb, an anti-tank grenade covered in a particularly viscous glue that you could slap on the armour of an enemy vehicle as it passed. He'd asked Cleo if she could create something similar, only magnetic.

A few hours later, he piloted the cloaked *Cartella* down into Uskrre's atmosphere on the opposite side of the planet. Rayl and Bache, who'd also wanted to come along and help, sat either side of him. They kept a watch on the fleet movements above them, hoping their local disruption of the air currents wasn't noticed.

'Anything?' Andy asked, keeping their trajectory dead straight, mimicking a meteorite.

'No unusual movements so far,' said Rayl.

He nodded while reducing the speed slowly. At fifty thousand feet he braked hard and turned, heading straight towards where the dome had been on the second biggest continent. When they arrived, the huge round treeless area stood out like a crop circle. Now the dome was down, the lines of ships could be seen from miles out. Although well over half of them were already in space, it was still a spectacle and reminded Andy of a huge military aircraft graveyard he'd witnessed in Tucson, Arizona during their astronaut training.

They watched the hive of activity from five hundred feet, four kilometres back, hiding under the protection of the hills to the north.

'Busy, isn't it?' said Rayl, as they watched dozens of trucks milling around the front rows of vessels.

A constant stream of atmospheric freighters ferried personnel, food and armaments down from the bigger ships in orbit, only staying on the ground just long enough to discharge their loads onto the queue of trucks, before leaping up and away, their antigrav drives screaming as they hurled themselves back up, eventually disappearing into the high clouds.

'What do we concentrate on, the military ships or the freighters?' said Andy. 'What would create the biggest delay?'

'I've noticed that when a newly commissioned ship

from the middle of the row leaves, it flies straight over the landing zone for the freighters,' said Bache. 'If we could drop one of the bigger ships right in the middle of that and on top of a freighter or two, that could hold things up for a while.'

'I've got just the ship,' said Andy, pointing at one of the larger battle cruisers parked right in the middle and in the next row to fly.

'There's so much noise with all the constant ship movements, the racket our antigravs make shouldn't be noticed,' said Bache. 'Those vessels have four antigravs. They can fly on three, but not on two, so we'll have to stick a charge on both the front or rear motors.'

'Where are they?' Andy asked.

'I'm reasonably familiar with those Klatt designs and if I remember rightly, the rear ones are just behind those upper rear cannon nacelles.'

Andy crept the *Cartella* closer while Rayl prepared two magnetic charges, giving one to Bache. She opened the inner airlock door and they both lay down on the floor facing the outer door. Once Andy was happy that they were ready he brought the ship quickly in over the parking lot of ships then, dropping down low over the rear of the target ship, he estimated when the outer door was above the drive housing, turned ninety degrees and opened the outer door.

'Down a bit, right a bit,' said Bache, then when he was happy, he dropped the charge.

It clunked down on the hull and stuck fast. Andy moved the ship forward to the opposite side of the cruiser and Rayl did the same with hers.

'Away,' shouted Bache, looking over his shoulder and waving his arm.

Andy didn't need to be told twice and had the *Cartella* up and scooting back to the relative safety of the hillside in a matter of seconds. It was fifteen minutes later that the big cruiser, its huge antigrav drives spooling up to a deafening bellow, lifted sluggishly, dragging its landing struts out of the loamy soil where it had sat waiting for a hundred and fifty years.

'Go on, you big bastard – go straight ahead,' whispered Andy, his finger wavering over the initiate icon.

As if listening to him, the Klatt pilot did exactly that and as the lumbering giant gained height and overflew the freighter unloading pads, Andy blew the explosives.

The detonations were small, but Cleo had deliberately shaped the charges to punch downwards and into the giant spoolers. The secondary explosions were a little more spectacular, as the spooler blades disintegrated and punched their way out through the hull in all directions. The monster ship shuddered and as if in slow motion the rear end slowly drooped. The pilot tried valiantly to compensate with just the front two motors, but the vessel was just too back-heavy.

Andy had timed the explosions just right, as the cruiser's forward momentum took it down onto two freighters. Soldiers could be seen running in all directions as it completely crushed one and its front end caught the tail of a second one. The crushed freighter must have been carrying munitions of some kind, as the resulting slightly delayed explosion from underneath the cruiser blew it into two pieces. A third freighter that had been in the process of landing was caught in a storm of shrapnel and blown onto its side. It proceeded to catch fire, which spread quickly into the adjacent buildings.

'Fucking outrageous,' said Andy, turning to smile at Bache. 'I think we can call that a success.'

'I think you're right,' said Bache. 'Four ships with only two small charges was very—'

A flash had all three of them turning their heads, blinded and disorientated for a second as the inside of the cockpit became flooded with bright white light, followed shortly after by a deafening crack.

'Height, height,' shouted Bache.

Andy had registered the danger at the same time and had the ship immediately ascending vertically and back. The *Cartella* shot upwards and then savagely backwards as the shock wave from a nuclear detonation hit them front on. If they'd stayed where they were, under the lee of the hill, the blast would've blown them into the ground. As it was, they only missed the rocky hilltop by a couple of metres.

The ship's shields and inertial dampers did their jobs however, and when Andy was finally able to regain level flight and turn back east, they were several kilometres further away from the Klatt base.

'Shit,' said Rayl, craning her neck to try and see the top of the mushroom cloud looming over them.

'Well!' said Bache. 'That was unexpected.'

'To say the bloody least,' said Andy, taking the ship north and upwind to avoid the soaring radioactive cloud. 'Did that emanate from one of the ships or a building?'

'It was from one of the buildings suddenly engulfed in

fire,' said Cleo, her voice echoing around the cockpit. 'Is everyone okay?'

'I guess so,' replied Rayl, getting reassuring nods from the other two.

'Get back to the *Gabriel* quickly,' Cleo added. 'All hell's broken loose up here.'

56

A MIKROGRAFIA CLASS SHUTTLE, SALFT STATION, EXOPLISMOI SYSTEM

'ARE YOU READY?' Ed asked, not bothering to turn and look at Pickyrd.

Pickyrd stared out of the front screen of the tiny shuttle. It was one of the smallest jump-capable vessels in the GDA's inventory and they sat cloaked, hiding twenty kilometres out from the station.

'You'd better be right about this,' Pickyrd mumbled, his knuckles white as he gripped the sides of his seat.

'We'll be right,' said Ed, his finger hovering above the jump icon.

'So long as you're sure there's enough room in there,' Pickyrd said, shutting his eyes as Ed dropped his finger.

A millisecond later the small vessel popped back into being inside the huge drive cone of the mysterious ship hidden inside the enclosed construction yard.

'You can open them now,' Ed said, concentrating on bringing the ship out of the cone and around towards one of the larger vessel's hangar openings. He had to dodge and pause a couple of times to avoid constructor drones swarming around the hull.

Pickyrd shook his head in wonder.

'Just when you think you've seen everything,' he said. 'Did we really just jump inside an engine?'

'It was the only space big enough not crawling with these bloody drones, I didn't want one joining us inside the cockpit.'

The reassuring buzz as they penetrated an atmosphere shield entering the hangar boosted their confidence as it meant the interior was most likely pressurised. They were immediately confronted by row upon row of small fighter-style ships. Hundreds of them, stretching away deep into the belly of the cruiser.

'Not an exploration vessel then?' said Pickyrd, raising his eyebrows.

'There's dozens more of these hangars all around and down the length of the ship,' said Ed. 'I just chose the nearest to the rear.'

'There could be thousands of these fighters, if this one is anything to go by,' Pickyrd stated. 'Is there anywhere for us to land?'

Ed crept the ship across and above the lines of ships and in towards what looked like a short row of service bays against the back bulkhead wall. Turning the ship, he extended the struts and landed neatly, joining the end of a row just inside a service bay. Quickly shutting everything down, they waited silently to see if their uninvited arrival had drawn any attention.

Ed exhaled a few seconds later, not realising he'd been

holding his breath and, peering out the front screen, he was pleased to see no movement.

'Shall we go for a stroll?' he asked, standing and grabbing his helmet.

The *28*'s tailoring and engineering departments had been busy manufacturing two Spleeta armoured security suits.

'I hope this doesn't take too long,' said Pickyrd, securing his own helmet. 'I get very claustrophobic in these bloody things.'

The shuttle's outer airlock door hissed away upwards inside the hull, leaving them facing the tool bay of one of the servicing areas. They clunked their way down the steps and then turned right towards a large airlock door big enough to take small trucks. Having already been inside the ship's systems with his DOVI, Ed quickly cycled the doors. They found themselves in a four-metre-wide deserted corridor, with unintelligible wall-mounted signs written in Klatt.

'Can you read those?' asked Ed.

'Sorry, no,' replied Pickyrd, in a slightly metallic helmet voice. 'We're right at the rear of the ship. Something this big must have internal transportation of some kind though.'

Ed pushed open a door with a lit sign above and stuck his head inside. It was almost dark in the room, with faint rectangular shapes disappearing into the blackness. He felt around and found a touch panel on the wall. Ceiling light panels flickered on, flooding the room with a blinding white light.

He swore quietly as he realised it was a dormitory; the

shapes he'd seen in the gloom were in fact sleeping bunks. Dozens of sleepy, squinting Klatt faces began peering out at him. None of them were smiling.

'Are we there yet?' one of the nearest asked, Ed's internal translator converting it instantly.

'No,' he replied quickly in the suit's metallic voice. 'Security checks, go back to sleep.'

He hit the touch panel again, extinguishing the lighting, and pulled the door closed.

'Shit,' said Pickyrd. 'This ship's already fully crewed and they're expecting to be somewhere else after this sleep period.'

'Yeah,' said Ed. 'But where and for what purpose? This is a fully operational battleship intending to—'

Ed stopped as the background hum of the vessel altered for a second and the lighting in the corridor dimmed momentarily. He turned to find Pickyrd's worried expression staring back at him through his faceplate.

'That's why the construction yard was enclosed,' Pickyrd said. 'A classified ship they never intended to fly out...'

'We just jumped out, didn't we?'

Pickyrd nodded.

'What do we do now?' Ed asked. 'Will the *28* be able to pursue?'

'I bloody hope so,' said Pickyrd, glancing back towards the hangar. 'We need to know where we jumped to.'

Ed understood the meaning as they both quickly headed back to the hangar and their ship. This time Pickyrd sat in the pilot's seat, removed his helmet and powered up the ship's systems. They both looked up as the holomap materialised in the centre of the cockpit.

'We're heading straight towards the region that includes Alpha Centauri and Sol,' said Pickyrd.

'This must be the flagship of the Klatt fleet,' said Ed, dropping his helmet on the floor beside him. 'Just shows how long this operation has been in the planning. The question is, do we stay aboard and try to sabotage the ship? Or do we bail out now and get back to the *28*?'

'How could we sabotage this thing?' Pickyrd asked. 'It's kilometres long and we don't know where anything is.'

Ed closed his eyes and activated his DOVI.

'This isn't really the time for a nap, Edward,' said Pickyrd, crossing his arms and frowning.

Ed smirked at the comment, trying not to lose concentration.

'I know where the bridge is,' he said. 'And main engineering and – oh?'

'Oh, what?'

'What's a Yeltah Jaggon?' asked Ed, opening his eyes and staring at Pickyrd.

'Don't know,' said Pickyrd, tapping it into the computer. 'But in Klatt it translates to – Eight Light or Beam. Why?'

'It has a shit load of power diverted to it when it's operated,' said Ed. 'I mean like, everything. Even the shields are compromised when whatever that thing is goes off.'

'Got to be a weapon of some kind,' Pickyrd surmised. 'Perhaps it's something like our Asteri Beam?'

'They do take a lot of energy, I'll admit,' said Ed. 'But this is off the scale. It has something to do with multiple mirror angles, well, eight actually.'

'Hmm,' grunted Pickyrd, glancing out the front screen. 'The ship does have eight sides and eight arms hanging off it out there.'

Movement in the hangar caught Pickyrd's eye. Ed picked up on his attention switch and swivelled around to see two Klatt personnel strolling through the lines of fighters. Quickly extinguishing the cabin lights, they ducked down and watched as the two patrolling guards approached.

They stopped and considered the GDA vessel for a moment, then had a little discussion with each other before one of them began approaching, obviously talking into a microphone and gesticulating at Ed and Pickyrd's ship.

'Ah, shit,' said Ed, as he reached for the engine start controls. 'I think our decision has been made for us.'

'Wait,' said Pickyrd, grabbing Ed's hand before he could hit anything. 'We could take them with us. They'd be a mine of information about this thing.'

Ed didn't waste any time, knowing that was a good call.

'I'll play dead,' he said. 'You let them in and hide.'

Pickyrd dropped down on the floor and scuttled across to the airlock. He drew and checked his weapon was on stun before reaching up and opening the outer door. He shrank back, concealing himself in the shadows of the rear cabin, and waited. Ed slid into the pilot's seat, slumped over the control console and concealed his pistol down his right side.

They could hear voices behind the inner door after a moment or two.

'Come on, come on, take the bait,' whispered Ed to himself.

It didn't take long for inquisitiveness to do its work, as the porthole window in the inner door darkened with a face and shortly after came the whine of the door making its way into the ceiling.

Ed watched through partially closed eyes as the first guard stared at him and entered cautiously, closely followed by the more nervous second. Both had weapons drawn, but weren't very experienced, as they had them pointed at the floor.

Pickyrd waited until the second guard was fully inside the cockpit before giving him the good news. The guard grunted and slumped into the back of his colleague, who was caught with his pistol facing the wrong way. He swivelled as fast as he could with an unconscious body trying to knock him over, but with Ed whipping his pistol up he now had two weapons pointing at him and he soon joined his partner in the land of unconsciousness.

'I'll deal with these two,' said Pickyrd, disarming their two guests. 'You get us out of here.'

Ed dropped his pistol on the floor, sat back up and reached to hit the airlock close icon. He was distracted by a loud thump from outside and all the lit icons in front of him went dark.

'Oh, shit,' he said, turning to see a familiar face smiling at him through the airlock doors.

Pickyrd, hearing Ed's exclamation, began to turn, but

was unconscious on top of one of the guards before he got half way around.

'You really are a right pain in the arse, aren't you, Virr?' was the last thing Ed heard as the Skirmat Eagle stood in the doorway firing for a second time.

57

THE STARSHIP GABRIEL, USKRRE, IN THE ALPHA CENTAURI SYSTEM

RAYL WASN'T KIDDING about the traffic above Uskrre as Andy brought the *Cartella* quickly back into space. He had to be careful as some of the bigger ships, thinking the nuclear detonation had been an attack from space, were firing randomly, searching for a cloaked warship.

Phil had retreated the *Gabriel* thirty light seconds away, giving him ample time to dodge anything nasty coming in their direction. Even though the *Gabriel*'s shields were incredibly robust and had the latest anti-flare technology when hit, an eagle-eyed gunner could witness his shot vanishing suddenly, giving away the ship's location.

Having returned the *Cartella* to the port hangar, Andy, Rayl and Bache hurried up to the bridge to discover everything had gone quiet again.

Although there was still a lot of movement from the fleet, the random firing seemed, at least for the moment, to have ceased, as had the stream of freighters to and from the surface.

'What made them stop?' Andy asked, sliding onto his couch under the dominating holomap.

'I believe they reviewed footage of the event and have come to the conclusion it was in fact an accident,' said Phil.

'We only meant to take out two or three on the landing area,' said Bache. 'I don't know yet if this was an unexpected bonus or not.'

'How many of the fleet on the ground are still serviceable?' asked Xutan from the side of the room.

'Difficult to tell,' said Phil. 'The dust cloud needs to settle a bit first, but from initial scans, I don't think it will be many.'

'That's gotta be a good thing isn't it?' asked Rayl, looking up to gauge everyone's reactions.

'Yes and no,' said Bache. 'So long as they don't change their plans now and do something totally unexpected.'

A *ping* sounded from the holomap as a new red ship designator appeared in system and began approaching Uskrre.

'Who's that, Cleo?' Andy asked. 'Why's it not designated?'

'Ship of undetermined origin,' she replied. 'It's big and not in the GDA database.'

'Can we get a close-up?'

The red dot grew rapidly into a huge blue and grey-striped octagonal vessel.

'What the fuck is that?' said Andy. 'Anyone seen one of those before?'

The bridge remained silent for a moment, before Groxl cleared his throat.

'Erm, a couple of years ago a Spleeta ship designer approached us with the blueprint for an octagonal warship. I seem to remember it being somewhat similar to that.'

'What are all those arms sticking out of it for?' asked Rayl.

'I think it was some sort of revolutionary beam weapon that utilised mirrors or something,' he answered.

'When was it commissioned?' Bache asked.

'That's just it,' said Groxl. 'It wasn't. Deemed vastly too expensive and a weapon of unproven design. He lost his job and shortly afterwards disappeared.'

'It looks as though someone with a lot of cash took him seriously,' said Andy. 'Can you tell us anything more about it, Cleo?'

'Not really,' she said. 'It's very well shielded, so apart from being five kilometres in length and a kilometre at its widest point, that's all I have at the moment.'

The mystery ship slowed savagely as it approached Uskrre and settled into a high orbit.

'The wind's picked up down on the surface,' said Rayl, transferring the holomap view from the mystery ship to the site of the earlier nuclear detonation.

As they watched, it became clear the destruction was close to total. Nothing remained of any buildings and ships, at or near the epicentre. A few upturned hulls could be made out on the fringes, but nothing remained that was anywhere near operational.

'Well, that's that then,' said Andy. 'No more battle fleet

for them. What they've got in space now is all they're gonna get.'

'How many have you knobbled so far, Cleo?' asked Phil.

'Just over half,' she said.

'How many are left operational?' asked Bache.

'Four hundred and eleven, well, twelve if you count the new arrival,' she said.

'Better than three thousand,' said Bache.

'Still a lot if we're on our own,' said Phil, looking nervous. 'That new ship worries me too.'

'It didn't seem to have any weapons nacelles hanging off it,' said Pol.

'They were hidden,' said Groxl. 'At least, on the original design they were. He tried to sell it as a dual-purpose ship, one minute a full-on planet-killing battle cruiser and the next as we see it now, a non-threatening diplomatic vessel.'

'Diplomatic?' scoffed Bache. 'Not a word I'd ever associate with your clan.'

'I agree,' said Groxl, seemingly unoffended. 'That's why he was ridiculed and the design ignored.'

'Can you remember anything else about it?' asked Bache. 'It's that bit you said about planet-killing that worries me.'

'And me,' said Phil.

'Me too,' said Pol, all of them turning to face Groxl.

He gave them a Klatt's best impression of a shrug.

'It was a while ago,' he said, staring intently at the floor. 'All I can remember is the eight arms with shaped mirrors were important.'

'What about its capabilities?' asked Andy.

Another shrug.

'Something to do with abrupt climate change, I think. Anyway, the council decided if it couldn't seriously engage other ships, it was a waste of time and wasn't of interest.'

'There's something going on,' said Rayl, interrupting them and pointing at the holomap.

The fleet of Klatt ships were streaming out away from the planet and forming up behind and around the octaship, which itself was slowly turning on its axis.

'What the fuck are they up to?' said Andy. 'They better not be off to Earth – we're not ready.'

'They're not leaving,' said Bache. 'It's like they're forming a shield around the newcomer.'

'Have we been detected?' Phil asked, his eyes nervously flicking from person to person.

'No,' said Cleo, appearing in the centre of the bridge, dressed today in her nineteen-sixties biker chick outfit again, head to toe black leather, with big zips and tassels down the arms. 'I would've felt it if we'd been discovered. That new octagonal ship, however, is powering up for something and it's not for a jump.'

They all looked back at the holomap and the hundreds of ships crowding in around the bigger ship that had now fully turned its back on Uskrre.

'Shit,' said Bache. 'I have a feeling they're going to test the weapon against the planet.'

'You might be right,' said Rayl. 'I've got some strange power fluctuations on that ship. Wow, its shields have just dropped, as has environmental.'

As they watched, the giant ship seemed to light up from within. Its central hull area began to glow, light appeared to pulse down the blue hull stripes, travelling down the eight arms before a concentrated blinding white light beam flashed out from each of the tips. They glistened as they ran down the outside of the vessel before being concentrated through some sort of lens inside the eight smaller arms at the very rear of the ship. The intense narrower beams then converged about two kilometres behind the ship, immediately becoming one huge fluorescent purple shaft of light that flashed down into the upper atmosphere, blinding everyone and lighting up the bridge with its intensity.

At first, nothing seemed to change, then the beam ceased, casting the *Gabriel*'s bridge back into its normal operating low-light gloominess. Where the beam had struck, a dark stain was left that grew and spread alarmingly quickly.

'What is—?' said Pol.

Before she could continue, Cleo appeared again and interrupted her.

'Ed's here,' she said.

'What?' said Andy.

'Be more specific,' said Bache. 'Where – and is he alive?'

'He's unconscious but alive on that ship.'

Pol emitted a squeak, closely followed by a sob.

'We have to get to him,' she cried, her voice cracking.

'How's the silly bugger still alive and then get on that thing?' said Andy, putting his head in his hands. 'He's so bloody irresponsible.'

'Whereabouts on that ship exactly?' asked Bache, addressing Cleo.

'The shields are back online now,' she said. 'But in the brief period they were down, he seemed to be situated somewhere near the bow of the ship.'

'We need to formulate a plan to get him off,' said Xutan. 'We have the marines from the *28*, remember.'

'I haven't exactly told you everything,' said Cleo.

Everyone on the bridge went quiet and stared at her.

'I'm already on the ship.'

'I thought the shields were impregnable,' said Bache.

'They are,' she said. 'In the seconds they were down, I transported myself into their systems.'

'But the shields are back up,' Andy said.

'Yeah, but I'm still over there acting independently and doing what I can.'

Bache and Andy's eyes met.

'Can you shut the thing down?' Andy asked.

'I'd like to think so,' she said, sounding a little irresolute.

'But?' said Bache, picking up on her hesitance.

'I'd only got eighty-four percent of me across by the time the shields went back up.'

'Is that enough?' asked Andy.

'I'm sure it'll be fine,' she said, with a half smile.

'You're a computer,' said Bache. 'You'll have the exact odds.'

She adopted a pinched expression.

'Well?' said Andy.

'Eighty-four percent sure,' she said, hopefully.

'I thought you'd say that,' said Bache, rolling his eyes. 'Well, I suppose we'll find out soon enough.'

'Look at the planet, guys,' said Rayl.

They all turned back to the holomap to witness the dark area had continued to spread, now obscuring at least half of the surface. Hundreds of lightning flashes pulsed irregularly across the dark region as it continued to swirl and develop.

'The surface temperature has dropped by twenty-two and a half degrees already under that thing,' said Rayl.

'That'll probably create an instantaneous and permanent cooling of the planet,' said Phil.

Xutan turned to stare at Groxl.

'Perfect for the Klatt though,' he said, accusingly.

'For Spleeta, yes,' said Groxl, returning the glare. 'But not the Grondalle.'

58

OCTASHIP, ORBITING USKRRE, ALPHA CENTAURI SYSTEM

THE FIRST THING she sensed was the lack of light. She was convinced her eyes were open, but the complete blackness confused her. She knew she was there for an important reason and time was short. Exactly what that reason was eluded her. It was there, she could feel it, almost touch it, but somewhere, somehow, a small connection was missing.

'I am Cleo,' she blurted in frustration, remembering her name.

The lights flickered on, taking her by surprise, until she realised they were voice activated and she was alone. A store room had illuminated around her. Shelves stocked with engineering equipment from floor to ceiling surrounded the corner she was sitting in. Looking down she discovered she was wearing some sort of uniform; one she didn't recognise. It was a little grubby, with what looked like old oil stains that wouldn't quite wash out. A badge on each shoulder displayed a wrench of some kind, which brought back to her she was supposed to be masquerading as an engineer. Clapping her hands and stamping her feet, she checked the quality of the holo-emitters on this vessel. No glitches were apparent in her three-dimensional materialisation, which pleased her.

She stood, rummaged along the shelves, picked up a tool box that wasn't too heavy and made for the door at the far end. It was locked, so she thought her way around the mechanism until it clicked. Suddenly realising she didn't have any idea of what she was meant to do, or where she was supposed to go, she hesitated.

I downloaded myself onto this ship for a specific reason, she thought to herself. *I just wish I could remember what it was.*

The door opened suddenly, pushing her back into the room. A young engineer almost jumped out of his skin when he saw her, although what he saw was an older senior male Klatt engineer.

'Sorry, sir,' he mumbled. 'Didn't know anyone was in here.'

The use of the title "sir" indicates I'm senior to him, she thought. *He seems quite nervous.*

'Then pay a bit more attention in future,' she snapped back and strode purposefully past the cowering junior engineer. Attempting to look as though she knew where she was going, she turned right down a dimly lit corridor that opened out further down into a much larger and more brightly lit area.

She glanced left and right as she passed through, recognising some of the machinery as power supplies to the massive antigrav motors hulking at the far end of the room, which she was rapidly approaching. Thankfully, they weren't in operation, as the noise would've been ear-splitting and she didn't have any ear defenders. She smiled at the thought, realising she could just adjust her hearing parameters to compensate if the situation arose.

The doorway at the far end of the cavernous room slid to one side as she approached. Passing quickly through, she stopped in her tracks as she found herself on a narrow bridge above a huge drop. Looking down, she could also see the void below curved around the inside of the hull. She could see two massive blue-coloured beam emitters pointing outwards towards closed octagonal sliding doors. She looked up to find another two of the same curving away above.

There must be eight of these if they encircle the ship, she thought.

After crossing the five-hundred-metre bridge as fast as she could walk, another door swished open at the far end of the chamber and she was glad to be away from the frightening drop. Thankfully, the corridor she now found herself in could have been in any ship, being four metres wide and three high, with white walls and lighting panels glowing in the ceiling. She felt a little more secure.

An airlock on the right-hand side caught her attention, and peeking through the small porthole revealed what she thought was a hangar on the other side. Thinking the inner door open, she checked through the outer door before opening that one too. She had been right – row upon row of small unrecognisable fighters filled the vast hangar stretching away hundreds of metres to a shimmering atmosphere shield at the far end.

Shrugging and turning to leave, she stopped abruptly.

A small black shuttle sitting in one of the service bays at the back of the hangar to her left caught her eye.

That's a GDA shuttle, she thought. *What's that doing here?*

She approached to find both the airlock doors open, two GDA-issue laser pistols set to heavy stun lying on the cockpit floor, together with two helmets and two *28* identification wristbands that had been cut off. Scanning them, she found the first belonged to the *28*'s Captain Nicodemus Pickyrd and the second was registered to— She sat down heavily on the navigator's seat, reading the second name over and over. Captain Edward Virr.

Is he the reason I'm here? she thought. *A rescue mission?*

Realising that made the most sense, she found she had to completely reboot the ship's systems to prep for a quick departure, then programmed a random embedded jump into clear space and picked up one of the laser weapons and hid it in her tool box.

This time the shuttle's airlock was closed and code locked so no one could alter anything before departure. Picking up her tool box, she made her way back to the airlock and once through, turned right and scanned ahead for Ed's DOVI.

She was cross with herself for not trying that before, as she found him straight away nearer the front of the ship in a detention wing.

'Ship has everything except a fucking taxi rank,' she said, beginning the long walk towards the bow. 'I'm coming, Ed. Just hang on.'

OCTASHIP, ORBITING USKRRE, ALPHA CENTAURI SYSTEM

THE HEADACHE WAS the first thing Ed acknowledged as he emerged from the fog of oblivion. Luckily the armoured suit had taken the heat out of the heavy stun shot, but being of Klatt design it merely transferred the load of the charged bolt around the whole body, in reality, only saving him from a localised burn mark. His ribs throbbed every time he took a deep breath too.

Opening one eye cautiously, he took in his surroundings. A small cell of some kind. Grey painted walls, with a backlit ceiling, far too bright in his opinion. What looked on first glance like a bundle of rags in the corner was in fact Pickyrd, lying just as he had been dumped, with his tied hands sticking up at an awkward angle.

'Captain,' he croaked, nudging Pickyrd with his foot.

'Shiity fuuckk,' was his mumbled reply, which Ed considered summed up the moment exactly.

Slowly opening both eyes, Ed sat up and stretched as best he could.

Pickyrd eventually did the same thing, only even

slower. With his hair plastered down over one eye, he reminded Ed of a new wave singer on the cover of one of his dad's dodgy old eighties albums. Pickyrd noticed his disparaging glance.

'You're no beauty contestant yourself, Virr,' he wheezed, wincing as he ran his eyes around the cell. 'Where the hell are we now? And why are we still alive?'

'He doesn't have permission to bundle us out an airlock,' said Ed. 'Whoever's calling the shots wants us alive for some reason or other.'

Movement outside the cell caught their attention, the squeak of boots on polished floors. A range of toned beeps sounded before the door swung open.

'Morning, you pains in the arse – sleep well?' asked the Skirmat Eagle, grinning like a Cheshire cat. 'Saved the presidential suite specially for you,' he added, running his eyes appreciably around the cell. 'Luckily, because of operational radio silence, I have been unable to converse with my employer, which means I don't have permission to send you on a cold walk just yet, but I'm sure it'll happen quite soon. In the meantime, enjoy the resort's facilities and galaxy-renowned cuisine, I'll be—'

A shout and thump from outside the cell interrupted him. He turned to see a pair of legs prone on the floor outside the cell and another of his personal guards fly backwards past the door, followed by a thump then a crash.

'Oh dear – having staffing problems?' said Ed. 'New ship and all that, takes a while to get the right team together.'

The Skirmat sneered and stepped back towards the door, drawing his personal weapon as he went.

'Sergeant, what's going on?' he called.

Before he got a reply, a male Klatt face peered around the door frame.

'Hello,' he said, smiling. 'Engineering department to sort out your electrical fault. Did you know there are people sleeping on the floor out here?'

The Skirmat pointed his laser pistol at the engineer's face.

'Who the fuck are you?'

'Games,' he said, stepping into the doorway, completely ignoring the weapon in his face and inspecting the interior of the cell.

'Games who?'

'Game's up,' said the engineer, morphing into Cleo, a weapon in her hand too, pointing at his head.

The Skirmat fired. Cleo disappeared, reappearing just to the left of where she'd been before. The bolt, thudding into the wall on the opposite side of the corridor, started a small fire.

'Oops,' said Cleo. 'You've scratched your new ship.'

He curled his lip, moved his aim across and fired again. The same thing happened the other way round this time. He growled and tried again and again, with the same result. The corridor wall was now mostly gone and the fire had become a little more serious.

'Are you bored yet?' she said. 'Cuz I am.'

He flew back across the cell doubled up as Cleo lowered her aim and fired into his crotch.

'Fuck me,' said Pickyrd, pulling his legs in tight and covering his crotch with his hands.

Ed laughed and struggled into a standing position, holding his hands out to Cleo so she could untie them.

'Hi, beautiful,' he said, accepting a hug once he was free. 'I take it the ship is nearby?'

'Well, I hope so,' she replied, looking a little sheepish.

'You're not sure?'

'Well, that's just the thing,' she said. 'When I arrived, I didn't have any memory of why or what I was here for.'

'Excuse me,' said Pickyrd, picking himself up and eyeing and pointing at Cleo apprehensively. 'Just who the hell is she?'

'Sorry, Captain,' Ed said. 'May I introduce Cleo, our sentient ship's computer.'

Cleo stepped forward, a serrated eight-inch knife appearing in her hand. Pickyrd's eyes widened and he instinctively stepped back, his shoulders immediately hitting the rear cell wall. She smiled at his reaction and pointed at his hands still tied in front of him.

'Oh,' he said, his relief palpable as he offered them up to have the plastic ties cut. 'Is he dead?' he asked, eyeing the Skirmat lying awkwardly at his feet.

She shook her head.

'I am unable to take a life,' she said, cutting Pickyrd's bonds and kicking the Skirmat in the side of the head. 'Doesn't mean I can't dish out a little discomfort to the occasional arrogant fuck head,' she added.

'What caused you to have a memory lapse?' Ed asked, peering out the door to make sure they were alone.

'This ship has excellent shielding, it must have come back online before my transfer was complete,' she said.

'The shielding was offline?' Pickyrd asked, his anxious gaze meeting Ed's equally concerned look.

'The weapon must have been fired,' said Ed, glancing back at Cleo. 'Do we know what at?'

Cleo shrugged.

'No idea,' she said. 'I only found out you were here when I found your bracelets on the shuttle and started searching for you. Everything else is a blank.'

'The shuttle is okay?' he asked.

'It was fine when I left it. I rebooted it and programmed an embedded jump into neutral space, so if you gentlemen would like to follow me, I'd like to fully execute this daring rescue. At least I hope that's what this was supposed to be.'

Dragging all the unconscious bodies into the cell and locking it, they armed themselves from the collection of weapons lying on the corridor floor and followed Cleo as she made her way aft, quickly retracing her footsteps before the bellowing fire alarms brought unwanted attention.

60

THE STARSHIP GABRIEL, NEAR USKRRE, ALPHA CENTAURI SYSTEM

'ANY CONTACT WITH YOURSELF YET, CLEO?' Andy asked, as he exited the tube lift and slid onto his control couch.

'Nothing yet, but I'm quietly confident,' she replied. 'Even eighty-four percent of me would be quite resourceful.'

'Getting a few unusual movements in the fleet though,' said Phil, who'd manned the bridge while everyone got some rest.

'What d'you mean?' said Andy, gazing up at the holomap.

'For the last hour or so they've been gathering in little clusters,' he said. 'A couple of the big cruisers, three or four destroyers, a few corvettes with support ships and a bundle of fighters.'

'Cleo, can you call Bache up here?' Andy said. 'I want him to see this.'

Bache arrived on the bridge a few minutes later and grimaced as soon as he saw the forming groups.

'Attack echelons, I'm afraid,' he said. 'If the Klatt are

anything, they're predictable. It's their classic form of space warfare. Lots of smaller groups coming at you from all directions. They'll be ready to deploy very shortly.'

Andy nodded and exhaled.

'Shit,' he said, under his breath. 'We're not ready and where the fuck is the *28*?'

'I shouldn't stress too much,' said Bache. 'You can prep and make all the plans you like; they usually turn to shit as soon as the shooting starts anyway.'

'Hmm,' Andy grunted. 'I'd still prefer to have at least one to back us up taking on this horde of arseholes. Cleo, can you get all the others up here and plot an embedded jump to Sol?' he asked, the worry evident in his voice. 'It seems our little excursion down to the planet may have wiped out a third of the fleet, but has inadvertently brought the attack date forward.'

He stood and looked at Bache.

'Can you take over the ship?' he asked. 'I'll take out one of the mini-me fighters and wreak some havoc in that. I just wish Ed was here to fly the other one.'

'How about I take out the other one?' said Bache. 'I'm sure Phil can fly this thing without my help, after all he's been doing it for a very long time and with Rayl and Pol on array and weapons, you have everything covered.'

Andy pondered that for a moment as he stepped towards the tube lift.

'Ed's mini-me is personalised to him though,' he said, turning.

'Don't worry about that,' said Bache. 'I was on the design committee and I know the bypass codes.'

'You happy with that, Phil?' Andy asked. 'There'll be a lot of combat.'

Phil looked up. He attempted a half smile and nodded.

'I'll be flying, not operating weapons,' he said brusquely, and looked away again.

Andy knew from previous experience that Phil got a bit prickly when he was nervous. Nodding his consent, he left it at that.

Rayl and Pol arrived together as he turned back to the tube lift.

'What's going on?' Rayl asked, wiping the sleep from her eyes and frowning at Andy.

Before he could open his mouth, Bache stepped in and explained the situation. Andy could see the anguish in his wife's face as she realised they didn't have much choice in what happened next.

She hugged him tighter than he could ever remember being hugged.

'Don't do anything reckless. I love you,' she whispered in his ear, before turning and taking her couch without another word.

Neither Bache or Andy spoke on the way down to the hangar and Andy waited to make sure Bache was able to reprogramme Ed's fighter before he left. He was surprised and pleased to see how quickly Bache was able to enter and have the antigrav motor spinning up. He did the same and opened a communication channel.

'Do we go out and mess with some of them here or wait until they arrive in Sol?' he asked.

'It would be a declaration of war if we attacked them here,' Bache replied. 'They have to take the first shot.'

'Haven't they already done that?'

It went quiet in the other mini-me for a moment.

'There could be arguments for and against that,' Bache said, eventually.

'You've been a politician too long,' said Andy, without any humour. 'Go back to when you were an impulsive warship captain.'

'Who have you been talking to?'

Andy smiled to himself.

'Just an educated guess,' he said. 'Everyone's a little more impetuous in their youth.'

Bache's fighter lifted off the hangar floor and rotated until Andy could see Bache glaring at him through the small armoured front screen.

'Go for the bigger ones first,' Bache said, his ship suddenly turning, zipping across the hangar and through the atmosphere barrier, cloaking as he went.

'Fuck me, I've awoken a monster,' Andy said to himself, as he quickly spun up his antigrav and followed.

By the time he emerged from the *Gabriel*, Bache was away travelling at point three light, directly towards the manoeuvring fleet above Uskrre.

'The groups have started jumping,' called Rayl. 'Do you want us to stay here or follow?'

'You follow,' said Andy. 'We'll cripple as many here as we can and if that big blue fucker turns its arse towards Earth, hit it with everything you've got as soon as it lowers its shields.'

'Okay, stay safe,' she replied, as the *Gabriel*'s position locator disappeared from his awareness.

Andy stared ahead as his tiny ship closed on the Klatt

fleet, silently praying that wasn't the last time he'd hear her voice.

A huge flash up ahead brought him out of his melancholy as he realised Bache had gone in guns blazing and was not holding back. A large Klatt supply ship was listing badly and beginning to tumble end over end. As Andy approached, another blast from within the ship blew it into several pieces that spun outwards, hitting several of the panicking smaller vessels. He overflew that car crash and headed straight for the next group in line. In his surrounding vision, he saw Bache flash down towards a group below.

Selecting one of their medium-sized cruisers, he scanned the vessel and set up a jump inside one of its larger hangars near the stern. From previous experience he knew that was where you generally found more volatile stuff that went bang with more emphasis.

The hangar he materialised inside was chock full of tracked military vehicles, all ready for a land assault. Each one had their rear doors open ready for thousands of troops to embark.

That's an unexpected bonus, he thought, as he sprayed laser fire down inside each line. The vehicles, all stocked with a full complement of munitions, lit up like Sydney Harbour on New Year's Eve and he quickly had to back up as the hangar turned into a firestorm. A second before he jumped away, he let off a kataligo missile straight down towards the back of the hangar – a trick he'd learnt a while back in the Messier Galaxy, where they'd learned that generally behind a hangar was a common place for an armoury.

This didn't seem to have changed, as after jumping away he turned the ship back to witness an almighty detonation. Temporarily blinded, he blinked away the flash etched into his vision. He searched for the group he'd attacked, only to find a few lumps of spinning debris expanding out from the epicentre and a large shower of flame trails dropping into Uskrre's rapidly cooling atmosphere.

'Shit, Andrew, did you use a nuke?' asked Bache.

'No, we don't carry them,' Andy replied. 'That was one of theirs – seemed to do the job though, didn't it?'

'Did it ever – just don't want to be slow jumping out though.'

The rest of the Klatt fleet, spurred on by the suddenness of the attack, didn't hang around, quickly jumping before they lost any more vessels, including the octaship and its surrounding horde of protection.

'Bugger,' said Andy. 'I was hoping to get a crack at the big one.'

'Even with Ed still on it?'

'Just to damage it, so it can't turn Earth into permanent winter.'

'Wasn't that the idea you had with that cruiser?'

'Hmm – time to join the *Gabriel*,' said Andy, quickly changing the subject.

'Indeed,' said Bache. 'See you in Sol.'

In an instant the two tiny but lethal fighters had blinked away.

61

OCTASHIP, ORBITING USKRRE, ALPHA CENTAURI SYSTEM

CLEO NOTICED the giant ship had come alive in the time she'd spent in the detention centre. Ed and Pickyrd hid their weapons inside their suits as Cleo adopted the appearance of a security officer and marched them back through the ship at gunpoint.

This time the corridors were buzzing with activity as the multiple dormitories spilled out hundreds of personnel, all heading to their adjacent hangars.

'Shit,' mumbled Ed. 'We had to pick a hangar at the very back, didn't we?'

'Good for your cardio fitness,' said Cleo, nudging him in the back with a laser pistol.

The lighting in the corridor dimmed and the background hum of the ship changed pitch for a second.

'We're jumping again,' said Ed, as his eyes met Pickyrd's. 'Judging by all this activity, the invasion must be imminent.'

They turned, as Cleo swore behind them. Her hologram was flaring and losing solidity. It quickly stopped, but hadn't gone unnoticed.

A Klatt soldier blocked their way through the next bulkhead doorway, waving his weapon at them menacingly.

'Who are you?' he demanded.

'GDA prisoner transfer,' said Cleo, quick as a flash. 'Captain's orders.'

He looked her up and down with a nonplussed expression, prodding her with his rifle muzzle.

'Why you flicker?' he asked.

'Why did I what?' she replied. 'That was the lights when the ship jumped.'

He stared at her, his stern demeanour not changing.

'I will check for confirmation of this transfer,' he said, pressing a button on his wrist and lighting up a small panel.

Before he could call anyone, Cleo reached over and touched the back of his hand. The soldier convulsed violently and hit the ground like a dropped rock. Continuing to spasm, he quickly began to attract attention.

'Need a medic here,' called Cleo, pointing at the quivering soldier at her feet.

As two passing soldiers bent down to attend to him, they quickly moved on and marched as fast as their legs would go without actually running. When they finally reached the rearmost hangar a few minutes later, Ed peered through the inner airlock door. The outer door was still open after the last pilots had exited a few seconds before. He could see many of them milling around their ships and seemingly preparing to fly.

'Shit,' he mumbled, as he noticed their shuttle getting some unwanted attention.

Three, what could only be engineers judging by their dress, stood by the shuttle's airlock trying to gain entry. Cleo took a look and shrugged.

'Leave this to me,' she said, cycling them through the airlock.

When they emerged into the vast hangar, she marched them smartly towards the shuttle.

'Hey – what d'you think you're doing?' she shouted.

The three engineers turned and stared at them as they approached.

'Get away from that ship, or I'll have the captain lock you in the brig.'

'This vessel isn't in the ship's inventory,' one of them plucked up the courage to say, the other two backing off slightly with expressions of uncertainty.

'It belongs to the Skirmat Eagle,' she said, tapping the correct code into the door's keypad. 'Perhaps you'd like to explain your displeasure to him personally?' she added, as the door whined up and the steps descended.

The engineer's eyes widened at the mention of the Skirmat and much to his colleagues' relief he chose wisely and backed away to join them.

Cleo kept up the ruse and prodded them through the airlock with her rifle. Ed could see the gobby engineer still wasn't convinced and stood having a heated discussion with the other two, his arms flailing about, generally in their direction as he spoke.

Just as Cleo turned to close the doors, the engineer

appeared again, a determined expression on his face, and blocked the door from closing.

'I'm not happy about this,' he said. 'I'm the hangar director and I say what flies and when in here.'

'Are you sure you don't want to reconsider?' Cleo asked, rolling her eyes at Ed as the engineer glanced around the cockpit.

'No, I don't,' he said, snapping his gaze back to her. 'I just want to confirm with the bridge that you're authorised to remove these prisoners and utilise this vessel.'

'Oh, that's a shame,' she said, hitting the door close button.

He had two choices. He picked the wrong one and stepped inside the shuttle as both doors came down and sealed with a hiss.

'Now you belong to us,' she said, morphing back into the real Cleo.

The engineer's eyes widened as shouting and tapping could be heard from outside the airlock. Cleo nodded at the pilot's seat and glanced at Pickyrd.

'I trust you know what to do with that chair?' she asked.

'Absolutely,' he said, the plastic restraints on his wrists miraculously dropping to the floor as he slid into the front seat.

'What the hell is going on?' said the engineer, the earlier arrogance all but gone.

'You're a prisoner of the GDA navy,' said Cleo. 'That's what's going on.'

He made a grab for the airlock controls, only to find

his arms set in concrete as he slowly lifted off the floor and hung in mid-air.

'Woah,' he yelped, wriggling about, which only succeeded in turning him to face the bulkhead. 'Fuck,' he said, wriggling around again to face the cockpit once more. 'You won't be able to fly through the barrier,' he said, sneering. 'It's coded to our ships only.'

He shut up then and hung there, a smug expression replacing the sneer.

'We didn't fly in here earlier, idiot,' said Ed, nodding at Pickyrd that it was time to leave.

The antigravs began playing their tune and the banging on the airlock immediately ceased. Pickyrd lifted the shuttle, retracted the struts and floated into the middle of the hangar. Ed could see a lot of confused pilots eying them from inside their fighters as they prepped them for flight.

'No,' said the engineer, the penny finally dropping. 'You can't jump out of here – it'll damage a load of my fighters.'

'The more the better,' said Pickyrd, shrugging his shoulders as he cloaked and touched the jump icon.

They reappeared in a random area of clear space half a light year from the octaship. Checking the holomap, instantly resetting above their heads, Pickyrd turned to Ed with a perplexed expression.

'What the fuck are we doing out here?'

THE STARSHIP GABRIEL, MATERIALISING NEAR EARTH, SOL SYSTEM

‘WHAT THE FUCK?’ Rayl blurted.

ANDY'S MINI-ME, MATERIALISING IN THE SOL SYSTEM

'WHAT THE FUCK?' said Andy.

'They're not here,' said Bache. 'Scan further afield, they've gotta be here somewhere.'

'We've got nothing either,' said Cleo, from the *Gabriel*. 'And I've scanned out further than Alpha Centauri.'

'Shit,' said Andy. 'Where've the bastards gone?'

'They could have an assemblage point somewhere,' said Bache. 'Where perhaps other ships are joining them, or we've been fed a red herring right from the start.'

'What – you mean it might not be Earth at all?' stated Rayl, glaring across the *Gabriel*'s bridge to where Groxl was sitting.

'It's no good staring at me,' Groxl carped. 'I'm as much in the dark with what's going on as the rest of you. That fleet was originally intended to occupy Gaia, or Earth as you know it. If it's being utilised to annex somewhere else, then it's news to me.'

'Can you think of any other planets your ruling body

has expressed an interest in over the last few years?' asked Xutan.

'D'you want a list?' he said, impatiently.

'That'd be nice,' snapped Rayl, her expression stern.

Groxl visibly recoiled, his face a mixture of surprise and indignation. Clearly not accustomed to being questioned quite so abruptly, especially by a female.

'Oh,' was all he could initially muster. He scanned the expectant faces around the bridge and realised an answer was required. 'Erm, well.' He seemed almost embarrassed and wrung his hands as he looked down at the floor. 'To be honest…'

'That'd be a first for a Klatt,' said Xutan, crossing his arms and giving Groxl an indignant glower.

Groxl exhaled and pursed his lips before continuing.

'Almost every inhabitable planet has been assessed over time,' he said, shrugging.

Bache and Andy arrived back on the bridge, having landed their fighters back in the hangar.

'Think, Groxl,' said Bache, grasping the way the conversation had been going. 'There must have been somewhere that's had more than its fair share of attention in the recent past?'

'There was Krix'ir a few years ago,' he said.

'That's just a bloody dust bowl,' said Andy. 'I've been there.'

'Too dry and hot for any of the clans, even Spleeta,' said Bache. 'Think again.'

Groxl continued staring at the floor.

'There was a ship designated to do a study on Gannon a couple of years ago,' he said, finally looking up again.

'What?' blurted Phil, suddenly gaining everyone's attention.

'Not a planet I'm familiar with,' said Bache, looking between Groxl and Phil.

Phil stared at Groxl and, realising the Klatt wasn't going to answer the question, he spoke instead.

'Gannon is the ancient name for Paradeisos, before the nuclear war forced the survivors to seek refuge underground.'

'Is that right, Cleo?' Andy asked, looking up.

'It is,' she said. 'The Theos changed the name one thousand, six hundred and forty-two years ago, when they began the long cleaning up of the surface and building the protected domed cities.'

'Fuck,' shouted Phil, his face going pale.

The bridge went quiet for a moment, partly as a result of Phil swearing, something he very rarely did.

'Surely not, Groxl?' said Bache. 'Those people have only just begun emerging from thousands of years underground. They finally get their planet back and you actually planned to take it from them?'

'Don't you put that on me,' said Groxl, raising his voice. 'I freely admit to kidnapping Virr so he could stand trial for the loss of my ship. That's it. None of the rest of this has any connection to me. Although, now I realise why the information of Virr's whereabouts strangely came into my possession.'

'It can't be Paradeisos,' said Andy. 'If I remember rightly, a ship was stationed there to oversee and encourage the gradual emergence of the population from below.'

'Oh dear,' said Xutan, with a grimace.

'I think I know what you're going to say,' said Bache. 'That ship was recalled recently, wasn't it?'

Xutan nodded slowly.

'I chaired the committee that made the decision to recall the ship. In my defence, its remit was as good as completed,' he said. 'Had we any idea the Klatt had ambitions for the planet we wouldn't have recalled the vessel and would most likely have sent another two.'

'Can we shut up with the conjecture and just go there?' said Phil, clearly getting agitated.

Andy nodded and pointed at Phil.

'The man's right,' he said. 'Set a course and get us there as fast as possible.'

Phil had the *Gabriel* flashing across their region of the Milky Way, heading directly towards the Aspro system and his home planet of Paradeisos. Choosing to jump illegally outside system space, he avoided having to register each jump and saved a lot of time. The risk of a collision was possible, but infinitesimally small and he reasoned the need far outweighed the hazard. If the GDA noticed and decided to fine him, then so be it.

He re-called everyone to the bridge before the final short jump, choosing to materialise on the very fringe of the system, close to its outer belt.

As he quickly brought the ship into the vicinity of one of the larger rocky satellites to make detection almost impossible, Rayl immediately spread the array wide and, as the results of the system scan were gradually revealed on the holomap, a collective gasp echoed around the room.

The invasion fleet was indeed here. The attack echelons had spread wide and in the short time they'd been here, had already attacked any and all vessels within the system's space.

Debris and the wreckage of several dozen private and commercial ships littered the region as the fleet moved in on the planet.

Rayl panned in on one of the larger vessels, split open from stem to stern and slowly tumbling end over end.

'The murdering fuckers,' shouted Andy, as it became apparent a large percentage of the debris spewing from the wreck were bodies, some of them children. 'That was an unarmed passenger liner.'

Andy's eyes met Bache's and they both stood and made for the tube lift.

'Come back to me,' said Rayl, only lifting her gaze from the control icons for a moment.

Andy knew, any more than that could cost lives. He nodded, blew her a kiss and joined Bache in the lift.

For the second time that day, they shot out of the hangar in their tiny but lethal fighters and engaged the Klatt fleet.

64

GDA SHUTTLE, NON-SYSTEM SPACE

'WHERE ARE THE FLEET?' asked Ed, quickly sliding into the navigator's seat and scanning the holomap above his head.

'Various locations around the Aspro system and they seem – oh shit!' muttered Pickyrd. 'They're attacking unarmed civilian ships and heading for Paradeisos.'

'Bastards,' snapped Ed, turning, scowling and pointing at the Klatt engineer. 'You'll be made to pay for this outrage,' he added.

'You and whose navy?' the engineer sneered. 'The GDA navy's on the other side of the galaxy. You going to destroy a battle fleet with an unarmed shuttle?'

'So, invading Earth was just a ruse then?' said Pickyrd, not even bothering to look at the man.

'Earth?' questioned the engineer. 'Where's that? Paradeisos has always been our new home, once we've cooled it down a bit.'

Just at that moment one of the Klatt support ships and a destroyer in one of the outlying groups exploded. Ed noticed the look of surprise on the engineer's face. Then their attention was caught by fire suddenly erupting from a hangar of a Klatt cruiser that had earlier lasered a civilian passenger liner in half. A secondary explosion blew the side out of the ship and it began corkscrewing, then colliding with and badly damaging two other ships in its echelon.

'That's Andy in one of the fighters,' said Ed. 'It has to be, that's his signature move. The *Gabriel* must be here somewhere.'

He looked over at Cleo, who smiled and nodded.

'Jump here and head on this course,' she said, pointing at Pickyrd.

A green line appeared on the holomap, heading straight towards Paradeisos.

'I've had a conversation with myself and the *Gabriel* will meet us there.'

'Oh, so you've got one ship against two thousand,' the engineer chuckled. His mirth gradually tailing off as over half the fleet instantaneously and bizarrely seemed to lose all power.

His smile vanished completely as hundreds of the attacking fleet began tumbling and spinning in the direction they were travelling in. Many, because of their close proximity to each other in their attack echelons, collided and ricocheted off each other, causing untold damage.

'Ed, are you there?' came Phil's voice, echoing around the small cockpit.

'Shit,' said Ed, glancing up. 'Am I glad to hear your voice. Is everyone else okay?'

'We are.'

He heard Rayl shout in the background.

'I'm here too,' said Pol.

Ed jerked back in his seat. Although he recognised her voice and from just those three words he knew she was in a bit of an emotional state, somehow he discerned the voice was different in some way – softer, more feminine perhaps.

'Hello, Pol,' he said, adding a smile to his voice. 'I'm so sorry, did you have to go through your rebirth alone?'

'I'm fine,' she said. 'Don't you worry about that. We saw the news feeds; you had your own problems at the time.'

'Hmm, you saw that?' he mumbled, remembering his blood-soaked clothes. 'Is Andy out in the mini-me?'

'He is,' said Phil. 'With Bache in the other one.'

'Oh – I thought they were personalised?'

'They are – but you know Bache.'

Ten minutes later they met up with the *Gabriel*. Phil turned the vessel side-on away from the Klatt fleet and momentarily opened the starboard hangar door. Pickyrd, quite familiar with cloaking technology, took the shuttle straight inside. Ed still thought it gave the impression of entering another dimension.

'Are you able to deal with him?' said Ed, glancing over

his shoulder at Cleo and jabbing his thumb at the Klatt engineer.

'Don't you worry,' she said. 'I'll just kick him out the nearest airlock.'

The engineer's eyes widened.

'You can't do that,' he whined. 'It's against GDA regulations.'

'You're not GDA.'

'But you said you are.'

Cleo looked at Ed with a quizzical expression.

'Did I?' she asked.

'I don't remember that,' he said, shrugging. 'And anyway, who'd notice in the middle of a battle?'

The engineer began wriggling again, his face white as a sheet.

'You murdering bastards,' the Klatt spluttered. 'No wonder you're always at war.'

'Is that what they tell you?' said Cleo. 'The most bloodthirsty and aggressive race in the galaxy, who spend most of their time killing each other and on the cusp of committing genocide of an entire race, accuse us of being the warmongers!'

The shuttle clunked down on the hangar floor. Pickyrd shut everything down and opened both airlock doors. As Ed stood to follow Pickyrd out of the ship, he stopped and glanced back.

'Stick him to the hangar wall or something, Cleo,' he said. 'Perhaps play him the history of the GDA video or something.'

'He'll just think it's propaganda,' said Pickyrd.

Ed smiled and turned back, immediately stopping in

his tracks as a tall leggy brunette sprinted past Pickyrd and slammed into him, hugging him so tightly he could hardly breathe.

Pickyrd stared and tilted his head to one side, a slightly bemused expression on his face.

'Do your crew always greet you like this?' he asked. 'If so, then I've been doing it wrong all these years.'

'We really thought you were dead,' she squeaked.

Ed, who'd been a little confused for a moment, suddenly cottoned on.

'Pol, is that you?' he said, pulling back and trying to get a look at her. He could also see the confusion on Pickyrd's face, at why he wasn't recognising a member of his own crew. 'You look amazing,' he managed to get out before Rayl called from the bridge.

'If you two have quite finished, we do have a war on up here,' she said, a little cantankerously.

'Sorry,' said Ed, raising his palm in the air, as Pol wiped tears from her eyes and, holding his hand, began leading him past a damaged military ship and towards the hangar door.

The three of them arrived on the crowded bridge to find a very busy holomap. Pol reluctantly released Ed's hand and slid into her couch. Both Rayl and Phil opened their eyes just long enough to nod at Ed and then resume their stations. He got a scowl from Groxl and a smile from Xutan, the others sitting around the back wall he didn't recognise, but he presumed, as they were wearing military uniforms, they were from the damaged ship down in the hangar.

'Good to see you're safe,' said Xutan.

'Likewise,' said Ed, slipping into his couch and assessing the state of play around Paradeisos. 'Why are all those Klatt ships dead but seemingly undamaged?' he asked.

'That's my doing,' said Cleo, her voice echoing around the bridge. 'I blew them up a little bit.'

'Riiight,' he said slowly, realising she wasn't kidding. 'And where's that big blue bastard?'

'Here,' said Rayl, as a cluster of ships telescoped up into focus. 'They're protecting it well; it loses its shields when it fires that climate-changing thing. The boys are trying to get us a shot at it just before it fires.'

'You're relying on one shot?'

'There's only three of us against hundreds,' she said, opening her eyes again and nodding at Pickyrd. 'Unless the Captain here can call in his cruiser in the next few minutes, it's all we've got.'

'Oh shit,' said Phil, carefully manoeuvring the *Gabriel* though a clutch of dead tumbling and spinning vessels. 'The octaship's turning around.'

'I thought it had to be in orbit before it fired,' said Pol. 'Perhaps not.'

As she spoke, hundreds of fighters began pouring out of the hangars dotted down the length of each of the huge ship's eight sides.

'Oh bollocks,' said Rayl. 'More bloody ships – that's just all we need!'

Ed looked at the planet for a moment.

'Has anyone tried to contact the planet?' he asked, turning to scan the faces in the room.

A bunch of blank faces was his reply. As his gaze lingered on Pol for a second, she smiled across at him and his heart missed a beat.

'Those fighters are surrounding the octaship,' shouted Phil, snapping Ed back to reality.

'Pol,' he said. 'Can you open a channel to the surface, calling either President Klai or Prota? Bounce the signal around a bit to disguise the source.'

A few moments later a blurred hologram appeared in the centre of the bridge. A white-bearded man in a grey robe stood phasing in and out of focus.

'Edward…that you? …the hell…going on...? Why… attacked? …are they?'

'Prota, it's the Klatt and they want your planet. Get the cities' defensive domes back up and defend with everything you have. Do not let them get a foothold on the surface.'

'Domes…coming…line. Not able…life…kill.'

Ed glanced at Phil and raised his eyebrows.

'I think he's saying the domes are coming online but an Exy Theo can't condone any killing,' Phil said, grimacing.

'Does he not realise…?'

'Naturally born Theos can fight back,' said Rayl, interrupting Ed.

'Is Klai there?' Ed called.

'President…underground…days.'

'The fighters have joined all their shields together,' said Pol. 'They're replacing the big ship's shielding. It must be about to fire.'

'We can't let this happen,' shrieked Phil. 'It'll put the planet into an ice age for thousands of years.'

Ed suddenly sat up straighter on his couch.

'Jump us between the ship and the planet, then maximise the shields between us,' he said. 'Hurry.'

As Phil got busy tapping icons, everyone else on the bridge stared at Ed.

'Can this ship's shields take that beam?' said Xutan, asking the question everyone was thinking.

'Can anyone think of anything else?' Ed replied, as the *Gabriel* jumped in ten kilometres directly behind the octaship.

Everyone in the room knew from that reply what that meant and sat back against their seats. Zero gravity handles popped out of the walls, floor and ceiling, which did nothing to allay people's fears.

'Good luck, everyone,' said Ed, as the octaship's shields dropped and it began glowing from within.

The eight pure-white flames of light flashed out of the octaship's arms, hitting the lenses at the rear of the ship. The beams arrowed out behind the ship and inwards, colliding and becoming one huge purple-tinged column of light, plunging towards the surface. That was the last thing anyone on the *Gabriel* witnessed. They were immediately blinded, felt the ship shudder beneath them, and a cacophony of alarms shrieked their displeasure before everything went black.

65

ANDY'S MINI-ME, ABOVE PARADEISOS, ASPRO
SYSTEM

'WHAT THE FUCK JUST HAPPENED?' Andy asked. 'The ship fired and the beam didn't get to the planet. Did it malfunction?'

'No – look at that!' said Bache. 'It's a cruiser.'

An enormous matt black vessel had jumped in between the octaship and the planet. Its cloaking had become intermittent and as it fazed in and out of vision, fires could be seen in the vicinity of where the giant beam had impacted its hull.

'That's the *28*,' called Andy. 'It blocked the beam and fired back on the octaship.'

'It's been damaged too,' said Bache.

The octaship, however, was having issues of its own. It had taken many direct hits from the *28*'s huge cannons. Three of its eight arms were spinning away, completely severed by the ferocity and close range of the *28*'s lasers. Debris and fluids could be seen hosing from the stumps, and there were several other wide gashes along the vessel's many sides.

'We need to help defend the *28*,' said Bache.

No sooner had he spoken than hundreds of fighters similar to their own poured out of the *28*, cloaking as they exited, and began engaging the Klatt fleet.

'Delay that and pull back quickly,' said Bache. 'They're on a different frequency and we run the risk of a collision while we're cloaked.'

'Rayl, we're coming back inside,' said Andy. 'Where can we rendezvous?'

No reply came.

'Cleo, Phil, are you there?' he called, checking his transmitter was actually working.

Again, no reply.

'Where are they,' said Bache, quickly backing away from the melee of trouble erupting in the heart of the fleet.

'They must be having issues too, otherwise they'd—'

Andy stopped as a loud female voice interrupted him.

'Unknown GDA fighters above Paradeisos, this is Lieutenant Den'rok, *28* defence command, please identify yourselves?'

'Hello, *28* defence command, this is Commander Bache Loftt and Captain Andrew Faux from the starship *Gabriel*,' said Bache. 'If you send us the engagement cloak frequency, we can provide some assistance.'

'Commander Loftt, wow, it's an honour, sir,' the lieutenant replied, reverently. 'ECF is inbound, sir.'

'Thank you, Lieutenant, and give my regards to the captain.'

'I would if we knew where he was, sir,' she replied almost apologetically. 'We were kinda hoping he was with you; the last time we saw him he was in a shuttle with Captain Virr. Is he not on the *Gabriel*?'

'I'd give you an answer if we could find it,' said Bache. 'You're not the only one with misplaced personnel.'

'Understood, sir. I only have Klatt vessels showing red on my array and no unidentified debris,' she said. 'I'm sure they're out there somewhere, sir.'

'Have you got those fires contained?'

'Yes, sir,' she replied. 'The beam penetrated our shields for nine hundredths of a second and struck the hull between decks twenty-nine and forty-three. Fire suppression is activated and bulkhead doors are secure.'

'Casualties?'

'No information as yet, sir.'

'I'm starting to get really pissed with this shit,' grizzled Andy. 'Nothing's been straightforward since the bloody start. It's one step forwards and three back all the time. People and ships disappearing and reappearing, fleets of ships going here, there and everywhere, assassinations, potential invasions, disappearing captains, it's doing my head in. Someone, somewhere, is responsible for this fiasco and if you ask me they need a fucking hard kick up the arse.'

'Oh, I think it'll be a little more severe than that when they're caught,' said Bache. 'In the meantime, can you assist me in saving my friend's cruiser from getting overwhelmed and finding the *Gabriel*?'

'Yeah, sorry, I needed to get that out – let's go.'

Now they had the same frequency as the other GDA

fighters, their ships' computers were able to assist in ensuring there were no blue on blue cloaked collisions.

The *28*'s shields, although weakened, were easily able to shake off any attacks from the swarms of Klatt fighters and the huge vessel's defence gunners were having a field day. The larger Klatt warships, however, tasted blood after witnessing the damage inflicted to the GDA cruiser by the octaship and moved in closer to bring their bigger weapons to bear.

What they hadn't envisioned was Andy quickly showing some of the other GDA fighter pilots his trick of jumping inside the enemy's shields or even into the larger hangars and attacking them from the inside.

Over the next half an hour, the Klatt fleet threw everything it had at the wounded *28*, taking catastrophic losses in so doing. The space around Paradeisos became littered with broken ships and debris, and over time, more and more succumbed to the planet's gravity well and provided a fiery backdrop to the battle above.

Many of the Klatt landing ships made use of this as cover and disappeared down to the surface, hidden amongst the confusion of fire trails.

'Do we go after them?' Andy asked.

'Let them go,' said Bache. 'Klai will have to deal with them. Do you have any missiles left?'

'None,' said Andy. 'Where the hell is the *Gabriel*? We need to rearm.'

66

THE STARSHIP GABRIEL, ABOVE PARADEISOS, ASPRO SYSTEM

'IS EVERYONE OKAY?' Ed called, his eyes gradually adjusting to the faint red glow of his floating display.

'Well, we're still here,' said Rayl, from somewhere in the gloom. 'Holomap is rebooting.'

'That beam overloaded just about every system,' said Pol. 'Our shields barely slowed it down.'

'Do we have any shielding now?' Phil asked.

'Is the ship still cloaked?' asked Ed.

'Slow down, guys,' said Rayl, looking up at where the holomap was slowly swirling back into some form of normality. 'I'm hoping to have some answers when this thing sorts itself out.'

'Cleo, are you there?' Ed asked.

No reply came.

They all watched as the display returned but seemed to be missing areas of detail on one side.

'Why's it done that?' Pol asked.

'The array must have been compromised on that side

by the beam,' said Phil. 'It's only showing what's on our port side.'

'Shit,' said Rayl. 'I'm starting to get hull breach warnings on the starboard side too.'

'We need to regain control and address the slow spin too,' said Ed, the worry evident in his face as Paradeisos gradually turned in and out of view. 'We don't want to be dropping in there without power.'

'What's that?' Pol exclaimed, pointing at a huge black slab phasing in and out of vision.

'Wow,' said Pickyrd. 'That's the *28* and it's damaged too.'

'It jumped in front of the beam just after us,' said Phil. 'Probably saved our arses.'

'Lucky it didn't jump onto us,' said Rayl, rolling her eyes. 'Is anything coming back to the helm yet, Phil?'

'I've got nothing,' he said. 'No Alma drive, no jump drive, one of the port side antigravs is responding though.'

'Shit, is that it?' said Ed, looking up at the planet turning through the holomap's view and visibly getting closer with every rotation. 'Can you get us down safely on only one?'

Phil shook his head slowly.

'It'd be a very heavy landing,' he said, gloomily. 'Well, when I say landing, perhaps I should have prefixed it with crash. But, it's not that I'm most concerned about.'

He pointed up at the holomap image, which was slowly rotating – after hitting a lump of space junk, a gradual tumble had developed too.

'Without the attitude thrusters to position the ship

correctly for re-entry, we wouldn't make it to the surface anyway.'

'Can't you use your tractor beam and utilise the inertia of some of that other junk falling near us?' Groxl asked. 'That's what I'd try.'

'That's offline too,' said Rayl.

Rayl suddenly sat up straighter and stared at Phil.

'Which hangar is the *Cartella* in?' she asked.

'Port, why?' said Phil.

'Doesn't that have a tractor beam?'

'Shit, yes it does.'

Rayl jumped out of her seat and made for the stairway hatch down to the hangar decks.

'Hang on,' said Ed. 'It should be me who does that.'

'Let me know when I've got you in the right position,' she said over her shoulder, completely ignoring Ed.

'Belly first, bow slightly up,' shouted Phil, as she disappeared through the hatch. 'And use it to help slow me down too.'

'How are you going to talk to her if communications are down?' Pol asked.

'She'll figure it out,' said Phil. 'She's a smart girl.'

'Do we need to strap in or something?' asked Xutan, searching around his seat and finding nothing resembling a safety harness.

'No,' said Ed, firmly. 'I want you all in the lifeboats and ready to go on my command. If I give it, do not hesitate.'

'What about you?' Pol said.

'The captain stays with the ship and I'll just get it down as best I can.'

'You can't do that, Edward,' said Pol, tears forming in her eyes.

'Yes I fucking can,' he said, forcibly. 'Now get in the lifeboats.'

Pol sat back in her seat. She'd never heard Ed get angry and certainly hadn't heard him use that language at her before.

Ed looked up and pointed at the two lifeboat hatches on either side of the bridge. Their entrances had been bathed in green light since he'd activated the weightless handles.

Groxl, Xutan, Phil, Pickyrd and the group of GDA marines split themselves into two equal groups and climbed into the lifeboats. Pol, on the other hand, had stood and loitered next to the nearest lifeboat and helped Xutan, who was last, climb inside. When they were all settled, she looked across at Ed, who was busy at his station. She hit the door close button, ripped off the safety cover and punched the launch toggle.

Ed looked up, puzzled, when he heard the explosive bolts firing and the lifeboat burst its way up the launch tunnel and away from the ship. Pol was already sprinting across to the other one.

'No, Pol, don't—'

Before he could get the words out she'd sealed the second lifeboat and launched that one too, then proceeded to stroll back to her seat and glare across at him.

'I will not allow you to do this alone,' she said as the ship shuddered under them. 'You're family.'

'There's two more lifeboats next to the cabins, you know,' he said.

'You going to tie me up and carry me there?' she asked sarcastically, raising her eyebrows.

The ship shook again and they both caught a glimpse of the *Cartella* on the holomap as the spin and tumble decreased and finally stabilised as the smaller ship's tractor beam grappled with the bulk of the *Gabriel*.

'Well, that seems to be working,' she said cheerily, giving Ed a smug grin.

'Wonderful,' grunted Ed. 'Now all we've got to do is get rid of the Mach 30 we're currently realising.'

They both heard the single antigrav drive spin up and add its melodic shriek to the creaks and bangs echoing around the damaged ship, as its influence began to bite into the planet's natural gravity.

They watched Rayl pull around behind and felt the drag as she used the tractor and the *Cartella*'s own anti-gravs to aid in scrubbing off the *Gabriel*'s huge velocity.

'Where should we aim for?' asked Pol, showing the planet's surface in front and below on the holomap.

'Close to a city,' said Ed. 'At least if we survive the landing, we'll have rescuers nearby.'

It was all ocean below at present, but one of the larger landmasses was east of them.

'That's the Canlain Coast over there,' he said. 'I remember from last time I was here. There's a city about a thousand kilometres inland, I'll aim for that.'

He dropped the struts and opened all of the operational weapons bays as wind brakes to aid in slowing them. He initially worried about damaging them at this speed, but realised that was moot, as they weren't going to be landing gently on them today. He remembered watching his dad's videos of Earth shuttle pilots making huge sweeping turns fifty years ago to scrub off speed and thinking how skilful they were to come in from space at seventeen and a half thousand miles per hour and land a thirty-tonne glider.

Without any warning the ship suddenly turned and swept back further so the stern was almost pointing straight down.

'Shit,' shouted Ed. 'I've lost contro—'

He opened his eyes to find Cleo standing in the centre of the bridge with her arms straight out from her sides.

'Lie on the floor with your feet against the front bulk-head,' she shouted. 'Quickly.'

Ed and Pol didn't argue and did as they were told.

'I'm having to divert power from the artificial gravity to bring in the other port antigrav,' she said. 'This might be a bit rough for the two of you.'

'How did you get back?' Ed asked.

'Pickyrd's ship in the hangar.'

'But that was in the starboard hangar.'

'Don't I know,' she said. 'Little bit messy.'

'And you're a Cleo missing some files.'

'Perhaps you'd like to shut up and let Ms Retarded save your fucking life.'

67

THE 28, ABOVE PARADEISOS, ASPRO SYSTEM

'MAKES PRETTY DECENT COFFEE,' said Andy, sniffing his mug, as they watched the *28*'s autoloader rearm their fighters.

In the absence of the *Gabriel*, they'd been given permission to rearm in one of the *28*'s many hangars and found themselves waiting in the pilots' briefing room on the side of the hangar.

'Course it does,' said Bache. 'Wouldn't expect anyone to go on a two-year voyage with shit supplies. A mutiny with forty-seven thousand crew could get confusing.'

A junior officer entered the room, looked around and hurried over when he saw them.

'Sorry to disturb you, Commander,' he said, a little out of breath. 'One of our array operators recorded this a few minutes ago down in the planet's atmosphere.'

He handed Bache a tablet and Andy leaned in to look.

'A small vessel was using its tractor beam to stabilise a larger damaged ship as it entered the atmosphere, sir.'

'And this might be of interest because?' Bache asked.

'The smaller ship is registered on Earth, sir.'

'What?' said Andy, squinting at the hazy images.

'It's the *Gabriel*,' said Bache. 'It was damaged somehow and they used the *Cartella*'s tractor to ensure it didn't tumble and burn up.'

'Bloody hell, it can't have had any drives online,' said Andy.

The officer pointed at the tablet again.

'Two lifeboats are launched at about a hundred thousand metres,' he said.

'Where did they land?' Bache asked.

'We don't know, sir,' he said. 'We're travelling against the spin and they were over the horizon before landing.'

Andy and Bache's eyes met.

'I can't think how the *Gabriel*'s going to come back from this one, I'm afraid,' said Bache.

'Fuck,' said Andy. 'I hope everyone got off and – oh, no…'

'Oh, no, what?' Bache asked.

'One of my bikes was in the hangar.'

Bache rolled his eyes and turned back to the lieutenant.

The junior officer realised Bache was waiting for someone to say something sensible and he pointed at one of the latest fully armed marine carriers parked at the back of the hangar.

'The First Officer said you could take that personnel carrier over there, sir,' he said.

'Very generous of him,' said Bache, eyeing the officer suspiciously.

'We detected Captain Pickyrd's locator chip on one of the lifeboats, sir,' he said, looking a little sheepish. 'The

First Officer thought as we're a little busy at the moment and you're his friend…'

Bache smiled.

'If you're sure you don't want us helping out here anymore?' he said, nodding at the hangar exit.

'We seem to be out of danger here now, sir,' he said. 'Some of the surviving Klatt ships have been jumping away.'

'Come on, Andrew,' said Bache, striding out towards the carrier. 'Let's go pick up their captain and the *Gabriel*'s crew.'

———

The personnel carrier was a monster compared to their little fighters. With lasers and missile pods hanging off every square metre and shielding that could shrug off a supernova, they felt reasonably secure popping out into the middle of a war zone.

Bache piloted and made sure the carrier was cloaked as they followed a bunch of debris into the upper atmosphere and headed for the coordinates where the lifeboats were most likely to have grounded. Sparks cascaded past the front screen as Bache presented the shielded underbelly at the thickening atmosphere.

'We should be picking up the distress beacons by now, surely,' said Andy, as the firework display slowly dissipated.

'They'll have turned them off,' said Bache. 'There's a lot of Klatt activity down here. They wouldn't want to attract them.'

'Ah, of course, yes,' said Andy. 'Then again, the Theos had been fighting an underground guerrilla war here for many millennia, so I don't imagine the Klatt ground forces are getting it all their own way.'

Even as he spoke, columns of smoke could be seen on the horizon.

'Oh, dear – one of those could be the *Gabriel*,' he said, dejectedly.

'It's the Klatt landing ships getting a polite hello from the Theos,' said Bache, as they quickly got closer.

He wasn't worried about the sonic boom the ship was creating, as the forces on the ground seemed to be making plenty of noise of their own.

The wrecks of three crumpled Klatt landing ships sat engulfed in flames, while four others had made it down and were attempting to discharge their troops while under heavy fire from a nearby hilltop.

'This wasn't what they planned, I bet,' said Bache. 'They've lost their air support.'

'And more than half their forces are sitting on dead ships up there, thanks to Cleo,' said Andy, jabbing his thumb at the ceiling.

In the distance they could see the defensive dome over one of Paradeisos's cities, glistening in the sunshine.

'That would have been their target,' said Bache, pointing, as they overflew the battle. 'They won't have been expecting to do this in such warm weather either.'

'I've got something big on the ground near that city too,' said Andy.

Bache headed straight towards it and descended to a thousand metres. As they approached, a long trail of destruction led across the valley floor where something had come in fast and gouged a trench through the scrub and trees.

'It's the *Gabriel*,' shouted Andy. 'Oh, shit, what a mess, and that's the *Cartella* parked next to it.'

The *Gabriel* sat at the end of the trench, its landing struts completely gone and the underside of the hull badly gouged and scored. It was leaning over on what was left of its starboard side, thin trails of steam and smoke emanating from exposed pipe work along the remains of the melted hull.

'That was a controlled crash landing,' said Bache. 'I was expecting just a hole in the ground.'

'About bloody time,' boomed a familiar voice in Andy's ear.

'Knew it was you,' replied Andy, also using his DOVI. 'Can recognise your parking anywhere.'

'Actually, it was Cleo that saved the ship,' he said. 'If it had been me, there'd be just a hole in the ground.'

Andy glanced at Bache and smirked.

'Are you and Cleo okay then?' he asked.

'We're okay. She's a bit pissed off with the state of her ship, but otherwise all right,' said Ed.

'Who was in the *Cartella*?' he asked.

'Hello, husband,' said Rayl, joining the conversation.

'Oh, hi,' he said, a smile evident in his tone. 'I thought you were on one of the lifeboats.'

'I used the *Cartella*'s tractor to help slow the *Gabriel*.'

'That was a good plan,' said Andy. 'Tell Cleo to do what she can until we get back to recover the ship.'

'I can hear you, you know,' Cleo moaned. 'I don't

think there's much I can do without a fully equipped ship-yard. I screwed up big time.'

'You saved us and the *Gabriel*,' said Ed. 'I'll have you both back in showroom condition if it takes every penny I own.'

'Did he see where the lifeboats landed?' Ed heard Bache ask in the background.

'No, we didn't,' Ed replied. 'I kinda hoped you might've. Doesn't your array show where they are?'

'There's so much shit falling out of the sky, I've got thousands of potential sites,' said Andy.

'I take it they've switched off their locators then?' Pol asked.

'Pol?' exclaimed Andy. 'You're there too. I presumed you'd be on one of the lifeboats.'

'She was supposed to be,' grumbled Ed.

'Ah, right,' said Andy, knowing from Ed's tone he ought to drop that subject. 'Can you find an operational airlock and we'll pick you up?' he said instead.

Pol and Ed found their way down to a port airlock. Opening it manually, they found, because of the ship's tilt, the door was several metres above the ground. Bache lowered the rear ramp of the carrier and with directions from Andy, brought the ship close enough so they could hop across.

The two friends grinned at each other and all three hugged, before climbing up to the cockpit where they were able to pat Bache on the back too.

Rayl lifted the *Cartella* up and joined them.

'Okay,' said Ed. 'We need to find the others before the

Klatt do. I'm sure they'd love to capture the captain of that ship if they knew he was down here.'

'This is the area the lifeboats were heading to,' said Bache, taking the carrier back up to a thousand metres. 'I'm sure we can – oh…'

The other three turned to see what had surprised their pilot.

'You might want to hear this,' he said, switching the ship's communications through to the cockpit speakers.

'…ward Virr, this is Proedros Klai, can you hear me? I know you're out there somewhere, please respond.'

68

GDA TROOP CARRIER, PARADEISOS, ASPRO SYSTEM

BACHE HIT a couple of icons on the ship's control panel and nodded at Ed.

'Mr President,' said Ed. 'I'm here and we're very pleased to hear your voice.'

'Oh, thank the ancients,' he replied. 'We witnessed your ship crashing heavily and feared the worst.'

'Crashing?' said Andy, in the background. 'That was one of his better landings.'

'Ah, I see Mr Faux and his weird sense of humour is present too,' said Klai, with a smile in his voice.

'Yes, he's here,' said Ed, in a disappointed tone. 'We need to find the rest of my crew though; they came down in the lifeboats.'

'I might be able to help you there,' said Klai.

'Hi, Ed,' said Phil. 'We're all safe under the dome in the city. Guests of the president.'

'Well, thank heavens for that,' said Andy, the relief evident on hearing Phil's voice. 'Finally, something's gone right for a fucking change.'

'How did you get inside the dome?' Ed asked.

'The lifeboats brought us straight to the closest city and of course with the *Gabriel* being a Theo vessel, they also transmitted the correct frequency to pass through the shield. We landed in a park next to a hospital. How organised is that?'

'Amazing,' said Ed. 'Is Captain Pickyrd with you?'

'I am,' said Pickyrd. 'I take it my ship sent you to pick me up considering you're in one of my carriers?'

'I think your first officer misses you,' said Bache.

'Ah, he's more than capable, Commander,' said Pickyrd. 'I taught him everything you know.'

'I'm including your two ships into the city's database,' said Klai, interrupting. 'Fly straight through the shield and release the controls. The system will land you here.'

After the reunion, which took place in a restaurant opposite the hospital, Pickyrd loaded his detachment of marines and President Xutan onto the carrier and left to return to the *28*. Everyone else remained to aid in the recovery of the *Gabriel*.

Xutan waved from the cockpit window as the carrier, piloted by one of the marines, lifted, turned and headed up towards the shield.

Ed watched as it climbed and wondered how long it was going to take to repair the *Gabriel* this time. The damage was extensive.

At least it's on its home planet, a planet it saved from a never-ending ice age, he thought, as he turned and walked back.

'Why have they stopped?' Rayl asked, still watching the carrier.

Ed squinted back up again and raised his hand to shield his eyes. The GDA ship had indeed stopped climbing and sat motionless at about five hundred metres.

'What are they doing?' said Andy.

By now, everyone had stopped walking back to the nearby buildings and looked up to see the carrier now descending again at a rapid rate.

Klai ran towards them, gesticulating wildly.

'Ah, shit – what now?' said Ed. 'Just when you think things are calming down.'

'Get under cover,' shouted Klai. 'There's a problem with the cruiser.'

They began to run as the carrier thumped down heavily on the grass behind them, its struts burying themselves in the soft ground. Its rear ramp slammed open as everyone inside also ran for the buildings. Two of the marines half carried Xutan, as his running days were well behind him.

'What the hell?' said Ed, slowing so Pickyrd could catch him up.

'It's the *28*,' Pickyrd said. 'It must have suffered more damage than they thought. The core is overloading, they've set a remote jump into clear space and are abandoning ship.'

'What about all the fail-safes?' said Bache, overhearing.

'Non-functional,' Pickyrd said, panting as he ran.

'Sabotage,' shouted Bache, as they entered the building

and followed Klai's direction straight into an elevator. 'My father was on the design team of the Katadromikos. The possibility of a core overload is millions to one. All the fail-safes cannot be defective all at the same time.'

'Well, it's happened, impossible or not,' said Pickyrd. 'My concern is to get everyone off and the ship away from this planet.'

He stepped back from the elevator.

'You're safer underground in one of the shelters,' said Klai, his finger hovering over the descend button.

'I'm not hiding underground when my crew are in danger,' he said, turning and heading back towards the door.

Bache stuck his hand across the threshold and prevented the doors from closing.

'He has a point,' he said, stepping back out, closely followed by the entire crew of the *Gabriel* and the marines.

It took them two days to gather all the *28*'s crew. Hundreds of lifeboats had to be accounted for, helped by dozens of ships evacuated from the cruiser's hangars.

The cruiser itself had jumped away, outside of the system, before detonation, as planned. Quite how the ship had been sabotaged was a mystery. None of the Klatt prisoners taken either on the planet or from the remaining dead and damaged ships had any idea, or so they said.

All remaining spaceworthy Klatt vessels had jumped away to destinations unknown when the writing was on the wall. The forces that had made it to the surface, considerably fewer than planned, were either destroyed or captured. The Theos had utilised their labyrinth of underground tunnels to surround the Klatt ground forces and in less than a week, had completely neutralised the threat planet-wide.

Finally, the slow-turning wheels of the GDA woke up to what had really been going on. The fleet sent to Klatt space at last returned, late to the party, but welcome all the same. The recriminations ran on and on in the GDA council chamber, with two more ambassadors not admitting guilt but resigning all the same, and then disappearing in unusual circumstances.

Four cruisers arrived above Paradeisos, two to recover the *28*'s crew while the other two got busy recovering the personnel from the dead and damaged Klatt ships. The agreement with the still Grondalle Klatt government was for the return of the mostly Spleeta crews who, knowing the history of the Grondalle, would suffer a dismal fate.

The ships, however, were not to be returned and either destroyed if they were too badly damaged or stripped of their weapons and converted into freighters and sold to privateers, the funds going towards the clean-up of hundreds of wrecks on the surface of Paradeisos and the space above.

Ed sat in the *Cartella*'s airlock, his legs dangling as he leaned against the door frame. He stared out at the wreck of the *Gabriel*, a ladder stretching up to the gaping airlock high on its side, and exhaled a sigh. He'd just returned from inside the ship, gathering his things. Some of the others were still aboard doing the same.

He looked up as the sound of antigravs approaching broke the silence and melancholy of the moment. A small Theo shuttle settled in a cloud of dust a hundred metres away. Ed recognised Prota, the first-born and leader of the artificially created Theos, as he stepped down from the airlock. He watched him grimace at the wreck, before turning and approaching the *Cartella*.

'I'm so sorry,' said Ed, as Prota got within earshot. 'We will fund its rebuild.'

Prota stopped at the foot of the stairs and glanced over his shoulder at the *Gabriel* again.

'I believe that was one of the most altruistic and brave acts the galaxy has ever seen,' he said, turning back and staring at Ed. 'Throwing yourself and your ship in front of that beam to save our home was extraordinary.'

'I didn't think much about it at the time,' said Ed, shrugging. 'It just seemed the only option left.'

'You can play it down all you like,' Prota said, shaking his head. 'It seems for the second time, the people of this planet owe you their lives.'

'They don't owe us anything,' said Ed. 'It was you that gifted us the ship in the first place.'

'Yes,' he said, smiling for the first time. 'Which is why I've got something to show you.'

Prota nodded at the shuttle he'd arrived in.

'Come with me,' he said and before Ed could argue, he strode off.

Ed sighed again, jumped down from the airlock and ran to catch up with the bearded old man.

Prota flew the shuttle himself and took Ed across the city, approaching and landing next to an enormous building near the city's space port. He led Ed across the apron and into the building through a small innocuous door similar to many others down the length of the gargantuan structure.

It was pitch dark inside and Ed watched Prota as he touched a switch panel on the wall just inside the small door. There was a *clunk, clunk, clunk* as dozens of huge floodlights illuminated the inside of the stadium-sized building.

Ed squinted as his eyes adjusted to the whiteness of the lighting and then he gasped as the object that took up the majority of the inside of the building came into focus.

'A ship,' said Ed, eying a matt black monster with yellow leading edges that towered above him.

'Oh, yes,' said Prota. 'A ship like no other. This is, at this moment in time, the most advanced space craft ever built. We were constructing it as an example of Theo technology and ship building prowess, with an eye to marketing them to the GDA and other interested parties. But in light of what just happened, the President, the government and I agree there really shouldn't be navies with unknown agendas out there with ships as powerful as this.'

'So, you've cancelled the project?' Ed asked.

'We have.'

Ed gazed up at the monster squatting on twelve huge struts, each the size of the shuttle they'd just arrived in. He counted twelve of the biggest laser cannons he'd ever seen, six down each side. Countless missile pods hanging beneath, two twenty-metre asteri beams, four multi-barrelled rail guns and the list went on.

Prota removed a small control box from his robe and pressed a button. All the projecting weaponry around the entire ship folded away almost silently. Leaving the now sleek vessel, which Ed thought resembled a stealth plane his father had had a poster of on the garage wall when he was a kid.

'It's like a Blackbird,' he said, getting a blank look in return. 'A giant one on steroids.'

He turned to Prota and raised his eyebrows.

'How big is it?'

'Six hundred metres in length, a hundred and fifty wide, and three hangars. Four massive arrays and those engines are forty-three percent more efficient and quicker than the *Gabriel*'s.'

'It's a shame you've cancelled the project,' he said, dejectedly. 'I would've ordered one.'

'That's just it,' said Prota. 'You don't have to. This one – the only one there'll ever be – is yours.'

'What?'

Ed felt the hardness of the hangar floor as his legs gave way.

'Oops,' said Prota, offering his hand to help Ed back up. 'Ups-a-daisy.'

Something resembling the *Gabriel*'s tube lift materialised on the floor under the ship and Prota pulled a still rather shocked Ed into the glowing column of light.

In the blink of an eye, it whisked them up the twenty

metres and into the vessel, opening into a kind of vestibule that Ed was surprised to see was lined with what looked to be very similar to the dark oak panelling he had in his house.

'This one, you will see, is a little less white and a little more homely,' said Prota, running his finger down the polished wood walls and nodding in satisfaction.

'Good afternoon, Edward,' said Cleo, appearing in her favourite royal splendour.

'Woah, Cleo,' exclaimed Ed. 'How long have you been here? I just spoke to you on the old ship.'

'I was sworn to secrecy,' she said, winking at Prota. 'D'you like the new *Gabriel*? You won't believe what this ship can do. Come, let me show you around.'

EPILOGUE
THE GEORGE INN, SOMERSET, EARTH, SOL SYSTEM

ED WATCHED the open fire crackling and occasionally spitting a spark onto the open hearth of the residents' bar of The George, a seven hundred-year-old coaching inn in a small, pretty village in deepest Somerset. Pol was sat opposite, smiling at him, and his heart glowed as brightly as the fire.

He still couldn't believe how utterly beautiful she had become, or accept she could possibly be so in love with him. They'd both decided on their return that the house in Cambridgeshire would be sold. Neither of them felt safe there anymore, and they had chosen this hotel as their base while they looked around the West Country for somewhere new.

They'd just returned from Florida, after overseeing the return of the old *Gabriel* from Paradeisos. It had been decided to repair the antigravs and jump drive, just to get it back, but leave it damaged exactly as it was after the crash landing. It made a more exciting exhibit and, judging by the fact the tour bookings were full for the next three years, it had been the correct decision.

Phil, with his love of living on a ship, was over the moon with the new *Gabriel*. Ed had commissioned several pieces of art, pictures for the walls and a lot of period furniture, to enhance the ship's period feel and comforts. He was spending the days organising this and most of his spare time in the ship's atrium, sitting under one of the many trees, reading his favourite Earth fiction genre of crime thrillers.

A draught gusted around Ed's ankles and he peered over his shoulder to see who'd been uncivil enough to open the door and let the cold air in.

He raised his arm and waved as he recognised Bache peering in, looking a little lost.

'Ah, there you are,' said Bache, drawing up a chair and joining them. 'Hope you don't mind me butting in and I'm sorry it's taken so long for me to get back.'

'Shit hit the fan?' Ed asked.

'To put it mildly,' he said, sitting back in the armchair and sighing. 'I think the repercussions of this are going to go on forever. D'you know, there was even a complaint about you having the new *Gabriel*.'

'Who the hell would moan about that?' he asked.

'The Klatt government.'

'Grondalle?'

'Of course.'

'Typical,' said Ed, rolling his eyes. 'What about Groxl?'

'Disappeared.'

'And his son?'

'Murdered on Dasos along with Ganelaine,' said Bache, rubbing his chin in thought. 'The octaship disappeared too. Hasn't been seen since.'

'How's Pickyrd getting on?'

'Suspended and under house arrest until the investigation is complete.'

'Oh, crap,' said Ed. 'As if the bloke hasn't been through enough.'

'Ah – he'll be fine,' said Bache, nodding. 'He's got Xutan and myself in his corner. He'll get his command back once the lawyers and politicians have finished pissing about.'

Pol chuckled at Bache's turn of phrase.

'Did you find out who was bank-rolling the whole affair?' Ed asked.

'That's the reason I'm here. It was a bit of a shock to everyone.'

Ed sat forward, listening intently. Finally, the moment had come when he was to find out who was to blame for his and Pol's abduction all those weeks ago.

'What I'm about to tell you is classified at the highest level,' he said. 'And partly the reason why Pickyrd is being kept out of the scene.'

Bache checked around them to ensure no one was in earshot.

'You remember Salft Engineering, the ship builders with construction satellites at Jagnorite and Sidero?'

Ed nodded.

'Absolutely,' he said. 'They were a huge concern.

Pickyrd and I visited both. We met that bloody Skirmat Eagle at both too.'

'Okay. I need to fill you in on a bit of GDA history first,' said Bache, rubbing his chin again and staring intently into the fire.

'Almost forty years ago I had a part to play in uncovering a conspiracy involving a long-running mining and engineering company owned by the Flasts, an unscrupulous husband and wife team who'd stop at nothing, including genocide, to further their influence, power and company profits. The husband, seventy-eight year old Laraccorz Flast, was killed, but his wife Ystolion Flast disappeared with a considerable portion of the family wealth and was never heard from again.'

'How old must she be now?' Pol asked. 'Unless she was considerably younger.'

'Well, that's where it gets interesting,' said Bache, glancing at Pol. 'She wasn't younger at all; she was actually a year older.'

'So, all this was organised and bank-rolled by a vengeful wife of nearly a hundred and twenty years old?' said Ed, sitting back in his chair and doing a bit of mental arithmetic.

Bache smirked.

'Pickyrd said you might remember the two top levels at the Sidero platform were the owner's accommodation.'

'Yes – although we didn't actually go up there.'

'Okay, well, we've been there now and very plush it was too. That's where Ystolion has been hiding all these years. You see, Salft Engineering is an anagram of Flast Engineering.'

'No one realised or recognised her for all that time?' asked Pol.

'She was a recluse and her private yacht could dock directly to her apartment. But that's not the best of it. In a secret chamber they found hidden behind one of the bedrooms was a Theo auto nurse.'

Bache sat back this time as Ed's eyes widened.

'I asked Prota if they'd ever sold any – he said no, but one had been stolen in a raid nearly thirty years ago.'

'Oh, fuck,' said Ed. 'So, she's kept herself alive all these years with a stolen auto nurse.'

'Not only that,' Bache said. 'She's turned the clock well back and made herself a young girl again. Similar to Phil on your ship.'

'Have you got a picture of her or is she going to be able to disappear again?'

Bache smiled and reached inside his jacket and retrieved a tablet.

'The auto nurse still had the programming in its memory.'

He flicked on the tablet and turned the screen so Ed could see the picture of a young girl. His mouth dropped open as soon as he saw the face.

'Oh, fucking hell,' Ed stammered. 'What the hell did we do?'

Pol stared at Ed questioningly.

'Who is she?' she said, pulling the tablet over so she could see the image.

Ed turned to look at her, his face white as a sheet.

'Pickyrd and I supposedly rescued her from a hangar on the Sidero station,' he said. 'She was injured by a ship jumping away from the hangar she was in. She told us she was a junior engineer by the name of Scylla. Pickyrd gave her sanctuary on the *28*.'

'Thank you,' said Bache. 'We just needed to have Pickyrd's testimony confirmed.'

'So, she was amongst the *28*'s crew down on Paradeisos?' Ed asked.

'No, she wasn't,' said Bache. 'We've checked the camera footage from all the lifeboats. She didn't get off the *28*.'

'Well, she's definitely dead now then,' said Pol.

Bache grimaced and glanced back at the fire.

'She's not, is she?' asked Ed.

'To be honest, we don't know,' Bache admitted. 'An explosion certainly happened where the ship was programmed to materialise. But whether it was the *28*, or a loaded drone as Pickyrd had done in Klatt space, we really can't be sure.'

'So, you're saying there could be a psychopathic teenager with an axe to grind, in possession of one of the galaxy's most powerful battle cruisers?'

Bache winced and puffed out his cheeks.

'Don't ever say that anywhere near the council,' he said.

'Why, don't they know?'

'Yes, but we've got the shutdown codes for the ship.'

Ed studied Bache's face.

'You don't, do you?'

'First thing she would have changed.'

They all turned as someone approached them.

'Room for one more?' said a voice they all knew.

'Linda,' exclaimed Ed, standing and enveloping her in his arms. 'I had no idea you were around.'

'I had to come and see that you were okay,' she said, glancing over Ed's shoulder. 'Hi, Bache and hello, pretty stranger.'

Ed chuckled and turned so Linda could face Pol.

'No stranger,' said Ed. 'It's Pol and she's just joined us in the rebirth club.'

'Hi, Linda,' said Pol, also standing and giving her a hug.

'Well, look at you,' she said, holding Pol back at arm's length and studying her closely. 'Did you have anything to do with this?' she added, glaring at Ed and nodding at Pol.

'Nope, it was all Cleo's work.'

'Hey,' said Pol. 'Make me sound like a robot, why don't you?'

'Sorry, Pol,' she said, hugging her again. 'But you are like Ed's perfect girl.'

Bache laughed as Linda dragged him out of his seat and hugged him too.

'If you're here it must mean there's a job for the *Gabriel*,' she said.

Bache frowned.

'Not necessarily,' he stammered, his eyes meeting Ed's involuntarily.

'But you do – don't you?' said Ed, in a slow and suspicious manner.

'In this new upgraded *Gabriel* I've heard all about,' said Linda, excitedly.

'Well, err, yes…'

'The council would like us to sort out their dirty laundry again,' said Ed, interrupting Bache.

'Not exactly the council this time,' said Bache, sitting back down and folding his hands in his lap. 'This one is a private charter from President Xutan, myself and Captain Pickyrd.'

'Find the *28*?' Ed asked.

'Yes,' said Bache, his face turning serious. 'And destroy it.'

'With her in it?'

'Preferably.'

'Hmm,' grunted Ed, slumping back down on his chair. 'Where the hell would we even start?'

'Well – we might have a little lead on that,' Bache admitted, twiddling his thumbs.

The other three remained silent and just stared at him. He took the cue and spoke again.

'Just after the *28* was supposedly destroyed, we believe something big and cloaked went through the Pyli galactic gateway.'

'Where to?' Linda asked, before anyone else posed the question.

'The Medusa Merger,' he said. 'It's a pair of merging galaxies one hundred and thirty million light years away.'

'We'll be having a bit of a break first?' said Ed. 'And I'll expect my hangars to be sufficiently well stocked with useful kit,' he added, giving Bache an expectant stare.

'Xutan has given me a blank cheque,' he said.

'Are you coming?' Pol asked.

'Not this time,' said Bache. 'I want to, for personal reasons, but I have a lot of fires to put out here first.'

'I will,' said Linda. 'I've discovered retirement's not very exciting.'

'Good, excellent, right,' said Ed, taking a sip of his cognac. 'Better let the others know.'

FROM THE AUTHOR

Dear Reader,

First of all, I wanted to say a huge thank you for choosing to read *The Acheron Fold*. I sincerely hope you enjoyed Ed and his crew's fifth adventure into space.

If you did enjoy it, it'd be fantastic if you could write a review. It doesn't have to be long, just a few words, but it is the best way for me to help new readers discover my writing for the first time.

If you'd like to stay up to date with my new releases, as well as exclusive competitions and giveaways, you're welcome to join my Reader Group at my website (below). I will never share your email address, and you can unsubscribe at any time. You can also contact me via Facebook, Twitter, or by email. I love hearing from readers – I read every message and will try to personally reply to every one.

Thanks again for your support.

Best wishes,
  Nick Adams
  www.nickadamsbooks.com

www.ingramcontent.com/pod-product-compliance
Lightning Source LLC
Chambersburg PA
CBHW011924190726
48285CB00011BA/2779